T0363191

COWBOY By Heart

STELLA BAGWELL REBECCA WINTERS TANYA MICHAELS

MILLS & BOON

CONTENTS

The Texan Tries Again

Stella Bagwell

After writing more than eighty books for Harlequin, **Stella Bagwell** still finds it exciting to create new stories and bring her characters to life. She loves all things Western and has been married to her own real cowboy for forty-four years. Living on the south Texas coast, she also enjoys being outdoors and helping her husband care for the horses, cats and dog that call their small ranch home. The couple has one son, who teaches high school mathematics and is also an athletic director. Stella loves hearing from readers. They can contact her at stellabagwell@gmail.com.

Books by Stella Bagwell

Harlequin Special Edition

Men of the West

Her Kind of Doctor
The Arizona Lawman
Her Man on Three Rivers Ranch
A Ranger for Christmas
His Texas Runaway
Home to Blue Stallion Ranch
The Rancher's Best Gift

The Fortunes of Texas: Rambling Rose

Fortune's Texas Surprise

The Fortunes of Texas: The Lost Fortunes

Guarding His Fortune

Montana Mavericks: The Lonelyhearts Ranch

The Little Maverick Matchmaker

Visit the Author Profile page
at millsandboon.com.au for more titles.

Dear Reader,

Welcome back to Yavapai County, Arizona! Spring has arrived and Three Rivers Ranch is hopping with activity. Calves and foals are being born every day, hay meadows are growing, cowboys are moving the herds to greener pastures and the Hollisters are welcoming a new foreman to keep everything in order.

Widower Taggart O'Brien has arrived on Three Rivers with only one thing in mind—doing his job and doing it well. He certainly isn't looking for love. That is, until he meets Emily-Ann Broadmoor, the one and only waitress at Conchita's coffee shop. The talkative redhead is unlike any woman he's known and though he tries to squash his attraction for her, he soon finds himself yearning for coffee and pastries.

In spite of catching Camille Hollister's bridal bouquet at her friend's Christmas wedding, Emily-Ann seriously doubts she'll ever find a man to marry. Men didn't fall in love with her—they simply wanted a fun date before they moved on. She thinks Taggart is no different from the other guys who'd let her down. Yet the more time she spends with the man, the more her heart wants to believe the bridal bouquet might actually bring her true love.

I hope you enjoy reading Taggart and Emily-Ann's love story as much as I enjoyed writing it!

God bless the trails you ride,

Stella Bagwell

To my beloved editor, Gail Chasan.
This one is for you!

Chapter One

"If I hear anyone mention that damned bridal bouquet one more time I'm going to scream," Emily-Ann Broadmoor muttered. "Catching the flowers at *your* wedding is not going to get *me* a husband. The whole idea is a silly old wives' tale. So why do you keep harping on the subject?"

Unaffected by her friend's annoyed outburst, Camille Waggoner chuckled and used her toe to push the wooden glider into a rocking motion.

From their comfortable seat beneath a large, old cottonwood, Emily-Ann could see a portion of the Hollister family, along with many friends and ranch hands, beginning to gather beneath the roof that covered the wide patio behind the Three Rivers Ranch house. Tonight, Maureen Hollister, the matriarch of the family, was throwing a barbecue for two reasons. For the first time in more than two years, Camille, the prodigal daughter, was back for a short visit. And second, the massive ranch was welcoming a new foreman.

"I'm not harping," Camille said, "and you don't think the folklore is nonsense. That's why you're afraid. That's why you don't want me, or anyone else, suggesting that your time as a single woman is coming to an end."

Emily-Ann stared at her best friend since elementary school, until the absurdity of Camille's prediction caused her to burst out laughing.

"Camille, pregnancy has done something to your brain. You're losing touch with reality."

Smiling smugly, Camille pressed her left hand to her growing belly and Emily-Ann didn't miss the diamond wedding ring sparkling on her finger. Camille Hollister had become Matthew Waggoner's wife nearly four months ago in a beautiful little Christmas ceremony down on Red Bluff, the Hollisters' second Arizona ranch.

Since then, Emily-Ann had never seen her friend so happy. And why not? After being the foreman at Three Rivers Ranch for many years, Matthew was now manager of Red Bluff, along with being one of the sexiest men to ever step foot in Yavapai County and beyond. Plus, he was madly in love with Camille. How could any woman be so lucky?

Certainly not herself, Emily-Ann thought drearily. She considered herself fortunate if she got a wink from the old man behind the meat counter at Wendell's Groceries.

"My thinking has never been clearer," Camille spoke concisely, then reached over and gave Emily-Ann's hand an affectionate pat. "I'm so glad you could make the party tonight. The two of us haven't had a chance to spend time together. Not since my wedding and that was such a hectic occasion with so many people around us that we hardly had a chance to talk."

"We've talked on the phone several times since your wedding."

Camille frowned. "Not the same. When we have a conversation I want to see you."

"You should've told me," Emily-Ann said dryly. "The next time I call we'll do FaceTime."

Camille chuckled. "That's not the same, either. So what have you been doing with yourself since the wedding? Other than running Conchita's?"

Conchita's was a little coffee and pastry shop located on a

quiet street in Wickenburg. Since Emily-Ann was the only employee, other than the owner who prepared the pastries, the job kept her very busy six days a week. The salary she made was never going to do more than pay her rent and other living expenses, but she loved the job.

"I don't have time to do much," Emily-Ann reasoned.

"You're still doing online college classes, aren't you?"

Emily-Ann shrugged. "Yes. Just a few more hours and I'll get my degree. But sometimes I wonder why I chose such a field to get into. I'll probably make a miserable nurse. Taking care of a sick cat isn't like tending an ailing human."

"I happen to think you'll make a wonderful nurse. When your mother's health started to fail, you were always so good with her."

"I had to do what I could. We couldn't afford a real nurse to take care of Mom," Emily-Ann replied, not wanting to think about that especially hard time in her life.

"Well, there's always a demand for nurses." Camille smiled encouragingly. "You should be able to get a job right in Wickenburg."

"Making coffee for my friends would be far less stressful," Emily-Ann said frankly. "But Mom had a dream for me and I don't want to disappoint her."

Camille slanted her a meaningful glance. "Just like I didn't want to disappoint Dad about getting a college degree. Now your mom and my dad are both gone. But let's not dwell on that sad stuff tonight. It's party time." With a cheerful smile, Camille reached over and hooked her arm through Emily-Ann's. "And it looks like Jazelle has just arrived with a cart to restock the bar. Let's go get something to drink."

The two women walked across the backyard to join the group of people mingling on the patio. There were far more guests than Emily-Ann had expected and she was glad she'd taken extra care with her appearance this evening. Even though her mustard-colored blouse and dark green skirt weren't anything fancy they flattered her curvy figure and she'd taken the time to braid a top portion of her hair and pin it to one side. She'd never be beautiful like Camille or her sister, Vivian, but for tonight she felt as though she looked decent.

"Emily-Ann! I didn't know you had arrived!"

At the sound of the female voice, Emily-Ann turned to see Maureen Hollister hurrying toward her. The lovely woman in her midsixties gathered her up in a tight hug.

"I'm so glad you could come tonight and be with Camille," she said happily. "My two little gingers. It's just like old times seeing you girls together."

"Except that now we don't have our matching bangs and Groovy Girls dolls," Emily-Ann joked.

Maureen laughed. "Too bad you grew out of those days. But I have the dolls packed away in a trunk of toys. Someday you two might want to give them to your daughters."

"Uh—in about three months or so, if Camille has a girl, she'll need hers," Emily-Ann told her. "But you might as well keep mine packed away in mothballs."

Maureen wagged a finger at her. "You're forgetting, honey. You caught Camille's wedding bouquet. Your time is coming!"

Laughing, Camille rolled her eyes toward Emily-Ann. "Don't scream."

Confused by her daughter's remark, Maureen frowned. "Scream? Why would she want to do something like that?"

"Nothing important," Emily-Ann answered, then quickly steered the conversation in a different direction. "Thank you for inviting me tonight, Maureen. I can't wait to eat some of Reeva's barbecue. Is there anything I can do to help in the kitchen?"

"Not a thing. I want you and Camille to stay out of the kitchen. Katherine and Vivian are helping with the food and Isabelle and Roslyn, bless their hearts, have volunteered to keep all the little ones upstairs and occupied. So everything is under control, I think." She looked at Camille. "I need to get back to the kitchen. Be sure and introduce Emily-Ann to the folks she hasn't met."

Maureen hurried away just as a group of men sauntered over to the bar, where Jazelle, the Hollisters' housekeeper, was mixing drinks. Spotting them, Camille grabbed Emily-Ann's arm and tugged her in the direction of the men.

"Come on, I want you to say hi to my brothers."

Emily-Ann had never been a bashful person and she loved meeting people, which was the main reason she loved her job at the coffee shop. But for some reason tonight, she felt hesitant about joining the group of men to say hello.

"I honestly don't think they want to waste their time with me, Camille," Emily-Ann suggested. "Let's just get a drink and go back to the glider."

Camille frowned at her. "Since when have you turned into a wallflower? Now quit being ridiculous and come on."

Camille tugged her forward and Emily-Ann had no choice but to follow her friend over to the group of men, all of whom were dressed casually in jeans and boots and various shades and styles of cowboy hats.

"Hi, guys," Camille greeted. "I thought you all might want to say hello to Emily-Ann."

Holt, the middle sibling of the Hollister clan, stepped forward with a wide grin. "I want to do more than say hi. I want a hug from Little Red."

Laughing at the nickname Holt had given her years ago, Emily-Ann hugged the tall, good-looking cowboy, who'd often been considered the wild playboy of the bunch. Now the horseman was settled down with a wife and new baby son.

"Hello, Holt." Stepping back from his affectionate hug, she smiled at him. "How does it feel to be a new father?"

The twinkle in his eyes was the same sort of joy Emily-Ann saw on Camille's face. Yes, the Hollister siblings were all happily married with children and babies now. The reality left Emily-Ann feeling as though she was standing on the porch in the cold rain, while everyone inside the house was cheery and warm and together.

"Having a son is just incredible," Holt responded to her question. "Even if I have to get up in the night to change diapers."

"Hah!" Blake, the eldest of the Hollister brothers and manager of Three Rivers Ranch, reacted with a short laugh. "I think I'll ask Isabelle just how many diapers you've changed in the wee hours of the morning."

"Not nearly as many as me," Chandler, the veterinarian of the group, boasted.

Chuckling, Joseph, the deputy and youngest Hollister, gouged an elbow in Chandler's ribs. "That's what you think, brother. Blake has us all beat. He has twins."

"Thank you, Joe," Blake said with an appreciative grin.

Camille pulled a playful face at her brothers. "I didn't bring Emily-Ann over here to listen to you four boast about your diaper changing. You're supposed to be saying hello to her."

"Hello, Emily-Ann!" they all said in loud unison.

Emily-Ann could feel a blush stinging her cheeks. It was true she'd known the wealthy Hollister family for years, but since Camille had moved away, she'd not been here to the ranch for any reason and she felt a little awkward about showing up tonight. In spite of Camille being a dear friend, that didn't put Emily-Ann on their social calendar.

Just as that self-deprecating thought went through her mind, Blake stepped forward and gathered her up in a hug. "I see you at Conchita's fairly often, but it's nice to have you here on the ranch. Jazelle is mixing drinks. Tell me what you'd like and I'll get it."

"Not yet," Camille told him, her gaze searching the ever-growing crowd. "I thought Matthew and Tag might be over here with you guys. Where—oh, I see them coming now."

Grabbing her by the upper arm, Camille tugged her forward and Emily-Ann followed, albeit reluctantly. She was fairly acquainted with Matthew, Camille's husband, but the tall cowboy with him was a total stranger to her. A wide-brimmed cowboy hat, the color of dark coffee, shaded a tanned face with roughly honed features. His eyes were hooded beneath a pair of dark brows, while his chin jutted forward just enough to give him a dash of arrogance. Or it could be the way he was looking at her, as though she was a geek, or worse, that made him seem arrogant. Either way, Emily-Ann would've been happy to avoid the man entirely. But she couldn't escape the tight hold Camille had on her arm. Not without making a scene.

"So you two finally made it to the party?" Camille teased, directing the question mostly to her husband.

Matthew's grin was a bit guilty. "Sorry, honey, I've been showing Tag some of the more important things down at the ranch yard."

"Uh-huh," she said with a perceptive smile, "like the saddles and tack and training arena and cow barn and—"

Matthew stopped her with a laugh. "We didn't get that far," he said, then inclined his head toward Emily-Ann. "Nice to see you again, Emily-Ann. Glad you could make it to the party."

"Thank you, Matthew," Emily-Ann replied, while trying not to pay extra notice to the tall, hard-looking cowboy standing next to him. From this distance, she could see his eyes were warm brown and his hair a mixture of rust and chocolate. "It's wonderful having you and Camille back at Three Rivers. Even if it's just for a short while."

She felt Camille's hand urging her to take a step toward the foreman, and though she wanted to glower at her friend, Emily-Ann purposely kept a smile fixed upon her face.

"Tag, I'd like for you to meet Emily-Ann Broadmoor, my best friend since childhood," Camille introduced. "And Emily-Ann, this is Taggart O'Brien. He's going to be Three Rivers's new foreman."

The man's lips curved into a semblance of a polite smile and Emily-Ann found her gaze transfixed on his mouth. The lower lip was full and plush, while the top was thin and tilted upward just enough to show a glimpse of white teeth.

Extending his hand to her, he said, "Hello, Ms. Broadmoor. It's a pleasure to meet you."

A strange roaring in her ears very nearly drowned out the sound of his voice and, in spite of feeling as though she'd suddenly fallen into some sort of trance, she managed to place her hand in his.

"Thank you," she told him, while her swirling senses recognized the hard-calloused skin of his palm and the warmth of his fingers curling around hers. "Nice meeting you, too, Mr. O'Brien."

With an impatient roll of her eyes, Camille interjected, "Oh, this just won't do at all. Surely you two can use your first names. We're all family around here."

"I'm fine with it," Taggart said. "If Ms. Broadmoor doesn't mind."

"First of all, Emily-Ann is a Miss, not a Ms.," Camille corrected him, then turned a clever smile on Emily-Ann. "And she doesn't mind. Do you?"

For the life of her, she couldn't figure out why Camille was making such a big to-do out of this introduction. It wasn't like she'd be seeing the man after tonight. And from the stoic look on his face, he was totally bored by this whole meeting anyway.

Well, that was okay with her, Emily-Ann decided. She wasn't exactly thrilled about exchanging hellos with this hard-looking cowboy, either. With that thought in mind, she pulled her shoulders back and tried to forget she'd always been the poor little girl who lived on the shabby side of town.

"I don't mind," she answered, then forced her gaze back to Taggart O'Brien. "Everyone calls me Emily-Ann."

The faint smile on his lips twisted to a wider slant. "Well, everyone calls me Tag, or a few other things I shouldn't repeat."

He released her hand and Emily-Ann resisted the urge to wipe her sizzling palm against the side of her skirt.

"Tag is from West Texas," Matthew informed her. "This is his first trip to Arizona and definitely his last. The Hollisters will see to that. He's going to be a permanent fixture around here."

"Welcome to Arizona, Tag," Emily-Ann said with genuine sincerity. "I hope you like it here—in spite of the heat."

His brown eyes were roaming her face as though she had two noses or something equally strange. The sensation was definitely unsettling, she thought, almost as much as the unadorned ring finger on his left hand. Surely this sexy-looking rancher was married. From the looks of him he had to be somewhere in his thirties. Plenty old enough to have a wife and kids stashed away somewhere.

He said, "I'm used to hot weather. And from everything I've seen since I arrived, I think I'm going to like it here just fine. The Hollisters are great and the area is beautiful."

"Yes, the Hollisters are the best," Emily-Ann murmured, then purposely turned her gaze on Camille. "Uh—don't you think it's time we go get that drink?"

"Sure! I can't have anything alcoholic, but Jazelle will mix up something tasty for me." She looped her arm through Emily-Ann's, then cast a pointed look at her husband. "Would you men care to join us? It shouldn't be long before they start bringing out the food."

Smiling just for her, Matthew wrapped his hand around his wife's free arm. "I don't know about Tag, but I'd love to."

TAGGART HATED PARTIES, even when they were being held partly in his honor, such as this one. He'd never been good at mixing and mingling with people and being single made everything more awkward when he was introduced to the unwed women in the group. He didn't have a wife to help him escape unwanted company, or to give him a reason to excuse himself.

Yet in this case, he wasn't looking around for an escape route. Emily-Ann Broadmoor didn't appear to be one of those boring cookie-cutter young women who spent hours trying to improve their appearance and five minutes or less educating themselves on things that actually mattered.

She wasn't batting her long lashes at him or slanting him a coy look. She wasn't grabbing his arm and hanging on as though she'd suddenly lost the strength to stand on her own two feet. No, this woman was refreshingly different, he thought. She might even be one he'd like to get to know as a friend. There couldn't be any harm in that, he assured himself.

"I'm more than ready for a drink and dinner." Purposely stepping up to the pretty redhead's side, he offered her his arm. "What about you, Emily-Ann?"

For a moment he thought she was going to ignore him or simply walk away, but then she smiled and wrapped an arm through his.

"Thank you, Tag."

The four of them moved slowly through the crowd toward the bar area where the four Hollister brothers were sipping cocktails and chatting with a few of the ranch hands. It was a sight that Taggart would've never seen on the Flying W back in Texas. Once the Armstrong family had taken over, the hands were never invited to mix with the employers, unless it was to take orders.

Hoping to shake away the unpleasant thoughts, he glanced down at Emily-Ann. She wasn't exactly a beautiful woman, but she was very pretty in a unique sort of way. Her square face had a wide plush mouth, high cheekbones and a sprinkling of pale freckles across the bridge of her upturned nose. Long brown lashes shaded eyes that were emerald green. Or, at least, that had been his first impression of their color. Until she'd turned her head and the light had hit them from a different angle. Then her eyes had taken on the color of a spring leaf that hadn't yet ripened in the sun.

"Do you come out here to the ranch often?" he asked her as they followed Matthew and Camille through a group of milling guests.

"When Camille lived here I visited the ranch quite often. Now I don't have much reason to drive out here. Most of the family stops by the coffee shop where I work, so I see them regularly."

Ahead of them, Matthew and Camille paused to acknowledge a small group of old acquaintances. While Taggart and Emily-Ann stood waiting, he turned his gaze back to the redhead. And suddenly he wished the gentleman in him had never offered his arm to this woman. The casual touch of her hand was causing hot sparks to shoot all the way up to his shoulder, making it difficult to concentrate.

Doing his damnedest to ignore the unexpected reaction, he tried to focus on her last remarks. "You work as a waitress?" he asked.

"I guess you could call me a waitress," she told him. "The coffee shop is small and I run it by myself. The owner does the pastry baking, then leaves everything else up to me."

"I'd never be able to do your job," he told her. "I'd end up eating all the profits."

The smile on her face drew him like a warm fire on a frigid night and he silently cursed himself for being so responsive to her. He was in no position to be feeling such things toward any woman.

A week had hardly passed since he'd arrived here on the ranch. Boxes of his belongings were still stacked in the modest house where Matthew had lived during his tenure as the ranch's foreman. What with getting to know the Hollister family and learning his way around the ranch, he'd hardly had a chance to draw a good breath, much less unpack. He didn't have time for a woman. And even if he did, he wasn't in the market for marriage or even a serious affair. Furthermore, he never would be.

Her rich voice suddenly broke into his dire thoughts. "Once you have one of Conchita's pastries you're hooked. I try not to eat them, but it's a fight. Now Holt's wife, Isabelle, is a different matter. She comes in and eats a pile of brownies or whatever she wants and never gains an ounce. It isn't fair. Little Carter hasn't turned a month old yet and Isabelle already looks great. Must be all that horseback riding she does."

Taggart could've told Emily-Ann, she had no cause to worry about her figure. It was nice. Hell, it was more than nice, he thought. She was curvy in all the right places and he had no doubt she'd feel soft in his arms. Just the way a woman ought to feel.

The unsettling thought forced him to clear his throat. "Do you ride horses?" he asked.

She nodded. "When Camille and I were much younger we rode all over the ranch," she answered, then went on in a pensive voice, "Because she was my friend I got the chance to do things that I couldn't have done otherwise. But now, working and taking classes doesn't leave me much leisure time. And with Camille living at Red Bluff things have changed. But then you already know that. I mean, you're here because Matthew runs Red Bluff ranch now."

"Yes, that's why I'm here. To try to fill his boots," he said wryly. "It's not going to be an easy job."

She smiled at him. "If Blake and Maureen believe you can do the job, then I'm positive you can."

He was thinking how the confidence in her voice made him feel just a bit taller when Matthew and Camille turned back to them.

"Sorry about that," Matthew said. "Everyone wants to talk. You'd think I'd been gone for five years instead of five months."

Camille slanted a loving glance at her husband. "Shows how well you're thought of around here."

The first time Taggart had met Matthew and Camille, he'd not missed the affection that naturally flowed back and forth between the newlyweds. It was obvious they were deeply in love and though he was happy for them, seeing them together was a constant reminder of all that he'd lost. All that he'd never have.

"My wife is trying her best to give me the big head," Matthew said with a chuckle, then gently nudged Camille onward.

The four of them moseyed on through the crowd until they reached the long bar constructed of native rock and topped with rough cedar boards. Behind the rustic counter, Jazelle, a young blond-haired woman was pouring a hefty amount of tequila into a tall pitcher of margarita mix.

"Oh, I'll take one of those, Jazelle," Emily-Ann spoke up.

"Same for me," Taggart added his request.

Jazelle poured the concoction over two iced glasses and handed them over, while Camille continued to study the large assortment of refreshments lined up on the counter.

"I can't make up my mind," she said after a moment.

After giving his wife an indulgent smile, Matthew said to Jazelle, "I know what I want. Just give me plain ole coffee."

Camille groaned. "That's too hot. I want something sweet and cold."

"We know Camille can't have alcohol so just give her tomato juice," Emily-Ann joked. "Or water."

Pulling a face at Emily-Ann, Camille said, "Don't listen to her, Jazelle. She doesn't know about cravings. She's never been pregnant."

"No. I haven't been pregnant," Emily-Ann replied. "And I'm beginning to think I'll never be."

"Oh, come on, Emily-Ann," Jazelle teased, "I wouldn't be saying anything like that. You caught Camille's wedding bouquet. You know what that means."

Somewhat puzzled by the whole exchange between the women, Taggart watched a dark blush steal across Emily-Ann's cheeks. The added color made her face even prettier, he decided.

"All right, that does it!" Emily-Ann muttered. "As soon as I down this margarita, I'm going home and tearing that damned bouquet into shreds and throwing it in the trash can."

Instead of getting angry at her friend's ominous threat, Camille burst out laughing. "Sorry, Emily-Ann, but you're not going anywhere—except to the dinner with your friends. Tag, just grab her arm if she tries to leave."

Taggart had no way of knowing what exactly the women were arguing about, other than it had something to do with a wedding bouquet. The word had seemed to set off a mild explosion in Emily-Ann. And why had she said that about never being pregnant? Was there a reason she couldn't have, or didn't want, children? Maybe she was one of those women who decided motherhood is not for her. But Taggart seriously doubted that. Her body moved with a sensuality that said she was made to make love to a man.

"I'm not sure I should try that," Taggart said. "She's a redhead. She might slap me."

Camille laughed again, while Emily-Ann gazed over the rim of her frosted glass at him.

"I'm sorry, Tag," she said, then smiled impishly. "I'm not really bad-tempered. Until I get around my old friend."

He was about to tell her that he wasn't thinking she was bad-tempered when Blake suddenly appeared at his side and clamped a friendly hand on his shoulder.

"Sorry to interrupt, Tag, but there's a group of men from the cattlemen's association who are anxious to meet you."

"Sure," he said, but as he walked away with the ranch manager, he wondered if he'd get a chance to talk with Emily-Ann again before the night was over. And wondered, too, why he'd want to.

Chapter Two

Damn it all, Taggart O'Brien had already ruined her evening, Emily-Ann silently cursed. She'd been looking forward to seeing the Hollisters and spending time with Camille. Now she couldn't focus on anything, except the tall Texan with warm brown eyes and slow, melting smile.

Absently pushing a pile of brisket and potato salad around her plate, she lowered her lashes and glanced at the object of her thoughts. He was sitting across the portable table and three chairs down from hers. Since everyone had sat down to eat, Matthew and the Hollister brothers had consumed Taggart's attention, but that hadn't lessened the impact of his presence.

Before the party had started this evening, Camille had told Emily-Ann how the whole family had nothing but praise for the man. At the time, Emily-Ann hadn't taken much note of her friend's chatter about the newly hired foreman. After all, she'd never be crossing paths with the man. But now that she'd stood close to him, looked into his brown eyes and felt the hard warmth of his arm beneath her hand, her thoughts were spinning with questions about him.

Her reaction to him was worse than foolhardy, Emily-Ann thought ruefully. All she had to do was glance at him to know he could have his pick of women. And for all she knew, he might have a special one tucked away somewhere. Most likely back in Texas where he'd migrated from. Yet those assumptions did little to stop the race of her pulse when she looked in his direction. Nor did they stop her from wondering if she might have the opportunity to speak with him again before the party ended and she headed home to Wickenburg.

"Are you angry with me?"

Camille's question had Emily-Ann turning a look of surprise on her friend. "Why, no," she said. "Why would you think that?"

"You've not said more than ten words since we sat down. And instead of eating, you've been using your food to build a dam across your plate."

Shaking her head, Emily-Ann said, "There's nothing wrong. I guess the margarita ruined my appetite."

Camille hardly looked convinced. "Look, I'm sorry I teased you so about the bouquet. As far as I'm concerned, you can toss it in the garbage. I won't say another word about it."

Feeling more than a little ashamed of herself, Emily-Ann smiled at her. "Don't be silly. I'm not angry at you. And I'm not about to throw the bouquet away. Why should I? It's probably the closest thing I'll ever have to bridal flowers."

"Well, if I hurt your feelings—"

Emily-Ann let out a good-natured groan. "You're being ridiculous now. You could never hurt my feelings. So tease all you want."

"So if it's not me, then what is it?" Camille persisted. "In all our years as friends I've never seen you this quiet."

Emily-Ann shrugged. "Sorry. I guess I've been thinking a lot tonight. Seeing your family and how much things have changed in the past few years. In some ways it makes me a little melancholy."

Camille reached over and squeezed Emily-Ann's hand. "But we're all so happy now," she said. "Even Mother is really smiling again."

Yes, Emily-Ann had noticed how cheerful Maureen seemed

tonight. She'd also observed how Gil Hollister, brother to Maureen's late husband, Joel, was never very far from the woman's side. Emily-Ann had met the man a long time ago, during one of his brief visits to the ranch, but over the past years, she'd not seen or heard much about him. Other than the fact that he worked as a detective on the Phoenix police force. Then a few months ago, at Camille's wedding, word began to spread that after thirty years of service, the man had retired and was moving back to Yavapai County.

"I am glad about that," Emily-Ann said. "There for a while it was like the real Maureen had gone into hiding."

Camille nodded and Emily-Ann watched her friend's eyes travel down the table to where Maureen and Gil were sitting side by side. In many ways, the man in his sixties reminded Emily-Ann of Joel, Camille's late father. Although Gil's hair was graying somewhat, the dark sections that remained were the same color that Joel's had been and he also possessed the same strong, stocky build as his brother.

"I think Uncle Gil is making a big difference in her life," Camille said thoughtfully.

Emily-Ann searched her friend's face. "Are you and your brothers okay with that? I mean, I know how much you all adored your father. Maybe you're thinking your uncle is trying to move in and take his place."

Camille released a heartfelt sigh. "Daddy was ten feet tall to all of us. No one could ever replace him. But as far as I'm concerned I don't want Mother pining her life away for someone who can never come back. I can't say for sure how each of my brothers feel, but I do know they want Mother's life to be full and happy."

Several years ago, Joel's body had been discovered out on the range not far from the ranch yard. His boot was still hung in the stirrup and he'd obviously been dragged for miles before the horse he'd been riding had finally come to a halt. The family and anyone who'd ever known Joel Hollister had been devastated by his untimely death.

Emily-Ann had hurt for the loss her friend had endured. Even so, she knew that Camille had been blessed for having a father for nineteen years. Emily-Ann had never had one. Not a real father, anyway.

"Yes, I'm sure your brothers feel that way," Emily-Ann said thoughtfully. "And your uncle seems like a genuine kind of guy."

"I think so, too," Camille replied, then smiling she pointed to the food on Emily-Ann's plate. "Eat. Before you turn that stuff into a pile of hash."

IT WASN'T UNTIL hours later, after most of the guests had gone, that Taggart slipped away from the handful of people left on the patio and walked around to the side of the house where a view of the ranch yard could be seen in the distance.

Leaning his shoulder against the large trunk of a cottonwood tree, he gazed out at the numerous barns and sheds and endless maze of connecting corrals. Before he'd ever thought about leaving West Texas and the Flying W behind, he'd heard of Three Rivers Ranch. It had a reputation for prestigious horses and crossbred cattle that could thrive under the harshest conditions. Taggart had expected the livestock to be top-notch. What he hadn't expected was the sheer vastness of the property. Even by Texas standards it was massive and rough and beautiful.

"Did you decide you needed a little peace and quiet?"

The female voice startled him and he glanced around to see Emily-Ann stepping out of the deep shadows. He'd not known anyone was around and he wondered if she'd been watching him. The idea sent a shaft of heat slithering down his backbone.

"Something like that," he answered, then asked, "What about you?"

She joined him beneath the tree. "I've been upstairs to see the kids and the babies. Billy, Chandler's baby, is teething now and yelling up a storm. He makes that coyote out there in the hills sound wimpy."

Taggart chuckled. "Doc will be proud to hear his new son has stronger vocal cords than a coyote."

She didn't make a reply and Taggart glanced over to see she was gazing thoughtfully out at the ranch yard. In many ways, she seemed at home here on Three Rivers, but in other ways, he sensed that she felt apart from the Hollisters and their friends. Although, he couldn't imagine why that would be. They all treated her like a family member.

Because she was my friend I got the chance to do things that I couldn't have done otherwise.

Her remark about Camille had struck Taggart and left him wondering what she'd meant by it exactly. That the Hollisters being rich made them different from her? Well, that was hardly a surprise. The Hollisters' wealth superseded most everyone in the area, including him.

"Is this place anything like the ranch where you worked before?" she asked.

Her question brought him out of his reverie and as he continued to rest his weight against the tree trunk, he allowed his gaze to linger on her face and hair. At the moment, it was splotched with moonlight and he couldn't help but wonder what it would be like to kiss the silvery spots upon her skin.

"The Flying W was big, but not this big. There weren't any mountains on it, but there were lots of what we Texans call cuts and breaks. It's where the years of rain and wind create deep gorges and cut banks into the ground."

"What about trees? Did you have many of those?"

"Some blue cedar and cottonwood. But they were few and far between and the wind usually kept most of the leaves stripped off the cottonwoods. That's the way it is up near the panhandle. But there was plenty of cholla cactus and it's real pretty when it blooms."

"Sounds desolate," she commented.

"I suppose it is—in a way. But it was home to me."

He could feel those green eyes of hers studying his face and though they were partially covered by shadows, he knew they were full of questions. Many of which he didn't feel comfortable answering. Not now. Maybe after this place began to feel like home to him, he'd want to talk about his life back in Texas.

He said, "Now you're thinking if I felt that way, why did I ever leave. Right?"

"It did cross my mind," she admitted. "But you don't have to tell me. That's your business. Not mine."

She was exactly right. And he should feel glad that she respected his privacy. Yet a part of him was disappointed that she wasn't interested enough to pry at him. Had moving to Arizona turned him into a wishy-washy fool, he suddenly wondered? Or was this sexy redhead the reason his thought process had gone haywire?

"The Williamsons, the people who owned the Flying W, were great to work for. I started as a day hand there when I was twenty-two. Three years later I'd worked my way up to foreman."

"Sounds like Matthew. He was very young when he first started working here on Three Rivers."

"Matthew has been blessed and he knows it. The Hollisters will always be here. They'll always hold the reins. He's never had to worry that a syndicate or some other owner would come in and start changing the way the ranch should be run."

"And that's what happened at the Flying W?" she asked.

Nodding, he tried not to feel bitter. His old job was behind him now and the problems there would continue to go on without him.

"The Williamsons built the ranch years ago and owned it, up until a year ago," he explained. "But then Mr. Williamson, who's in his mideighties, suffered a mild stroke. He recovered nicely, but his daughter didn't waste time in persuading him to sell the property. She convinced him that the ranch was the reason for his stroke."

"Was it?" Emily-Ann asked.

The choked sound he made was intended to be a laugh, but it held no humor. "That was a joke. She was the reason the old man carried around a load of stress. She'd been married and divorced twice and the cost of her mistakes had pretty much bankrupted her parents. So he sold to a family from Georgia. The Armstrongs know nothing about the West or raising cattle. Nor do they want to learn. So you can pretty much figure out the problems that caused for me and all the hands."

"Were you the only one who left the ranch's employment? Or did the other hands feel like you and leave, too?"

"All the original crew of men who worked the Flying W have left and gone on to different jobs now. I was one of the last holdouts. I guess I was foolishly hoping that something would change. That Mr. Williamson would find a way to buy the ranch back. But it never happened."

She looked at him. "I'm going to assume that the daughter was an only child. There were no other children to help with the ranch or the finances?"

Taggart shook his head. He'd been the closest thing to a son to Walt Williamson. But Emily-Ann didn't need to know that. Nor did she need to know that the daughter had always been bad-mouthing Taggart because he refused to warm up to her sexual propositions.

"Unfortunately, Joanna was the only child the couple had. Things might have been different if there'd been another grown son or daughter or around the ranch."

She moved a step closer and Taggart caught the gentle scent of flowers and desert wind on her hair. The fragrance was alluring and unique, just like her.

"Well, I don't know about the other men you worked with on the Flying W and whether they've moved on to better things. But you certainly have. You're going to love working for the

Hollisters. They're fair and honest and they care for their cattle and horses the same way their forefathers did a hundred and fifty years ago."

The sight of her upturned face grabbed something inside of him and to save himself from doing or saying something idiotic, he forced his gaze back on the ranch yard.

"Yes. I've learned this place has a long, colorful history," he said. "I feel honored to be a part of it now."

She smiled. "I'm guessing your family probably wasn't keen on you moving away to another state."

As always when he thought of his parents, a part of him shuttered down. It had been so long since all of his family had been together and even then, his father had never really put his wife and children before himself. His mother had worked hard to put meals on the table and made sure that Taggart and his little sister were clean and cared for. She'd been the rock that had held them all together.

"My mother has been dead for a long time and my father, such as he is, only comes around when he wants something. I do have a younger sister, Tallulah. We're close."

"Does she live in Texas?"

"Yes, in a little town close to the New Mexico line." He looked back at her. "What about you? Do your parents or siblings live around here?"

She looked away from him and for a moment Taggart thought she was going to totally ignore his question and then she finally spoke in a small voice.

"My mother passed away a few years ago," she said. "And my father was—never in my life. I don't have any siblings. I wish I did. I think things would've been a lot better if I'd had a brother or sister. But it didn't turn out that way."

It was easy to tell from the strained sound of her voice that it was difficult for her to talk about her family, or lack of one. Taggart could have told her that he understood, that he, too, had come from a broken home. But he'd already told this woman much more than he should have. In fact, he couldn't believe he'd told her all those things about the Flying W or his parents. It wasn't like him to divulge such personal things about himself to anyone.

Down toward the ranch yard, he could hear a few penned calves bawling and farther on a stallion called to his mares. The familiar sounds were comforting to Taggart, but apparently Emily-Ann hadn't taken notice of them. She was focusing on the lonesome wail of a coyote far off on a ridge of mountains west of the ranch house.

"When I was a young girl I used to be afraid when I heard a coyote," she said wryly. "I was a town girl and didn't know much about the outdoors. Camille told me that coyotes are very family oriented and that when they mate it's for life. I never did really believe her. She's such a romantic I figured she made it up. Because the whole thing sounded so dreamy and tender."

He grunted while wishing a part of him could still feel loving and tender. But there were no soft spots left in his heart, no room for a romantic dream to dwell and grow.

"I can assure you that Camille told you right. Coyotes do mate for life. So do mourning doves—until one of the pair dies."

Until one dies. Yes, Taggart had mated for life, he thought. Only that life hadn't lasted long.

"Oh," she said, then laughed softly, "I've learned something tonight. Mainly that I should believe Camille when she tells me something."

He pushed away from the tree trunk. This wasn't good, he thought. Standing out here in the shadows with a voluptuous redhead that smelled like an angel and looked like a seductress.

"I should get back to the patio," he said. "Most of the guests are leaving and the Hollisters are probably wondering where I've gotten off to."

"Time I was going, too. The drive back to my house takes about thirty minutes and I have to open Conchita's early in the morning." Smiling at him, she offered him her hand. "I've enjoyed talking with you, Tag. And I wish you the best with your new job. Maybe one of these days you'll get the urge for a pastry and some coffee and drop by Conchita's. It's open every day but Sunday."

His fingers tightened around hers and before he knew what he was doing he was tugging her forward until the front of her body was very nearly touching his.

She looked up at him and Taggart's gaze took in her wide green eyes and parted lips. She was clearly surprised by his action, but not nearly as stunned as he was feeling.

"Tag, what—"

"I couldn't let you walk off," he said. "Not until I told you how much I've enjoyed these few minutes with you."

Her breasts rose and fell as she drew in a deep breath, then quickly exhaled. "If you really got to know me, you wouldn't be saying that."

Her hand felt so soft and warm that all he could think of was pulling her closer, letting his hands roam her back and his lips explore hers.

"Why?"

He watched her teeth bite into her bottom lip. "Because I'm not your kind of woman."

That was far from what he was expecting her to say. "I wonder how you came to that conclusion. You don't know me—yet."

Her nostrils flared and he could see a vein at the base of her throat throbbing at a rapid pace. It was obvious he was making her nervous, but she was doing a hell of a lot more to him than that. Just holding her hand, feeling the heat of her body radiating toward his was enough to stir a flame deep inside him.

Her lips twisted with wry resignation. "Let's just say I know my limitations. And you're on the other side of the boundary. But it would be nice to be your friend, Tag. I'd like that."

Maybe she'd like things that way, Taggart thought, but he wouldn't. At some point from the moment he'd met her a few hours ago, until now, his mind had tossed away the idea of wanting to be her friend and changed to wanting to get to know every inch of her. The idea was shocking and scary, but it was there in his head anyway and he couldn't get it out.

"That's not the way I see things, Emily-Ann. I'm seeing you in my arms—like this."

Confusion flashed in her eyes, then she opened her mouth to speak, but he didn't wait to hear her reply. Instead, he bent his head and placed his lips over hers.

Soft, sweet and velvety smooth. Her lips were all that and more. And for a long, long moment Taggart lost himself in the pleasure of kissing her.

It wasn't until his arms slipped around her waist and he felt her hands fluttering helplessly against his chest that he realized he had to end the contact. Otherwise his senses were going to forget where he was, and why a kiss was all he dare take from this woman.

Forcing his head up, he drew in a ragged breath and watched her eyelids flutter open. He saw surprise flickering in the green depths and something else he couldn't quite identify. Was that longing, or regret, or a mixture of the two?

It doesn't matter, Tag. You can't get caught up in what this woman is thinking or feeling!

The voice in his head made him want to curse out loud. Instead, he did his best to smile and act as though her kiss hadn't shaken him all the way to the soles of his boots.

"You go around locking lips with women you've only known a few hours?" she asked.

The husky note in her voice was such a sexy sound it made him want to pull her back into his arms and kiss her all over again.

"Uh—no. I don't normally—kiss any woman." His throat felt raspy and he tried to swallow the sensation away as he lifted his hat from his head and swiped a hand through his hair. "Must be something about the moonlight."

An incredulous look appeared in her eyes and then she let

out a cynical snort. "Aww, shucks ma'am, I just couldn't help myself," she said in an exaggerated drawl. "Am I going to hear that next?"

"No. And you're way off on the accent. I'm not from South Texas. I'm from West Texas."

Her nostrils flared. "There's a difference?"

"A huge one."

Something flashed in her eyes and then her gaze dropped to the middle of his chest. "Sorry. I shouldn't have been so flippant," she mumbled. "But you have the wrong idea about me."

Long brown lashes were veiling her eyes, yet he could see enough of her lips to know they were trembling. Damn it, he'd never intended to insult her.

"No. I got the wrong idea about myself," he said flatly. "I'm sorry. And you're right. I shouldn't have been kissing you. Instead, I should've been asking you to be my friend."

Her gaze lifted to his and Taggart felt punched by the mistrust he spotted in her eyes. What kind of man did she think he was? One that held little regard for women? Oh Lord, he'd made a mess of things.

"If you truly mean that," she said, "then I'd like to be your friend, Tag."

Friend. Yes, he definitely needed friends in this new life he was making for himself here in Arizona. But did he need a friend like Emily-Ann? She made his stomach flutter and his mind turn to dreams he'd given up long ago. If he wasn't careful she could play havoc with his peace of mind.

But for the past ten years he'd managed to keep his heart tucked safely behind an impenetrable wall. There was no reason for him to think Emily-Ann could ever breach it.

"I do truly mean it," he told her, then smiled and reached for her hand. "Let me walk you to the patio, my new friend."

She smiled back at him and as they strolled side by side through the shadows, she didn't pull her hand away from his. And Taggart couldn't summon the inner strength to let go of her.

Chapter Three

Human anatomy. Learning the subject was far more difficult than Emily-Ann had expected and she wondered for the umpteenth time why she'd ever believed she could acquire a nursing degree. A person needed a high intelligence and laser focus to make it through chemistry, physiology, microbiology and all the other terrifying classes that ended in *y*. Emily-Ann possessed neither of those attributes. Especially the focus part.

Ever since she'd gone to the Hollister party a little over a week ago, she'd been going around in a goofy daze and trying, without much success, to shake Taggart O'Brien from her mind. She still couldn't figure out why the man had taken the time to have a conversation with her, much less kiss her.

When she'd walked upon him in the darkness, she'd not intended to strike up a conversation with the man, much less get tangled up in his arms. She'd simply planned to acknowledge his presence with a few words, then move on. But that plan had quickly gone awry and now, days later, her mind was jammed with thoughts and questions about the man.

Forget the long, tall Texan, Emily-Ann. He's more than trouble. He's a walking heartache. That phony explanation of why he'd kissed you was pathetic. You know exactly what that little embrace had been about. He was just testing the waters, try-

ing to see if you'd be willing to go to bed with him. That's all any man wants from you, sweetie. A tumble between the sheets and a goodbye kiss.

The taunting voice in her head caused her to close the textbook with a loud snap and a long sigh. She was wasting time trying to concentrate on her studies, she decided. And anyway, the clock on the wall said it was a quarter to three. It was time to start shutting the coffee shop up for the evening.

Sliding off one of the wooden chairs provided for the customers, she walked behind the tall glass display case that served as a counter and stuffed the textbook into a duffel bag she'd stored on a shelf against the wall.

Up until an hour ago, she'd seen a steady stream of customers all day. Now there were only a few pastries left on the red plastic trays inside the display case. Conchita would definitely be pleased with the sales, she thought, as she began to load the leftovers into white paper sacks.

She was halfway through the task when the bells fastened over the door facing jingled, announcing that someone had entered the shop. It never failed, she thought, as she finished placing a baked donut covered with nuts into a sack. The minute she started to put everything away, someone wanted to come in for coffee or pastries, or both.

Glancing through the front glass of the display case, she could see the customer was a man wearing blue jeans and worn brown boots covered with dust. Other than the Hollisters, she didn't get too many cowboys in the place, especially at this time of day.

"I'm closing, but you're welcome to get a takeout order." She pulled her head from the case and raised up to find herself looking straight into Taggart O'Brien's face.

A slow smile creased his cheeks. "Hello, Emily-Ann. Looks like I picked a bad time to come in."

Anytime would be a bad time for her peace of mind, she

thought. Especially when just looking at him set her heart thumping like a rocket about to shoot into space.

She nervously swiped the tip of her tongue over her lips. "No problem. I'm just dealing with the pastries that were left over from this morning. Whatever doesn't sell I drop off at the local nursing homes. The residents love getting them."

"That's a nice gesture," he said.

She shrugged one shoulder while wondering why he'd showed up today. For a day or two after the Hollister party, she'd thought, even hoped, that he'd come by to say hello. But after more than a week passed, she'd given up and decided he'd forgotten all about her.

"I like seeing the smiles on the old people's faces whenever I walk in," she told him.

"I'm smiling. I hope you're liking mine," he said in a teasing voice.

As he walked up to the glass counter, Emily-Ann's gaze traveled over his face and she realized his image was even more striking than the one she remembered at the party. Seeing him in the light of day, his complexion was a much darker brown and so was his hair. The arrogant chin was more like a concrete abutment, but that feature was definitely softened by the faint dimples bracketing his lips.

Had she actually kissed that mouth? The mere idea caused a shiver to slide down her spine.

"It's nice to see you again, Tag," she said, while hoping her voice sounded casual to his ear. "You're a long distance from Three Rivers. What brings you to town?"

"I got a hankering for pastries."

It felt like his gaze was swarming all over her and she wondered what he was thinking. That she looked rather plain in her brown shirt and faded blue jeans?

As her fingers fiddled with the long red braid lying across her shoulder, she assured herself that it didn't matter if her makeup had disappeared hours ago. She didn't want to impress this man. She wanted to forget him. Well, sort of.

"I don't know about the bunkhouse cook, but I know that Reeva, the Hollisters' cook, keeps all kinds of sweets made for the family. I'm sure she'd be happy to serve you some of them—whenever you get a hankering."

He chuckled. "Well, I did have to make a trip to the saddle shop. So I'm treating myself now. That is, if I'm not too late to get something."

Emily-Ann couldn't help it. She was so happy to see him, she couldn't act cool if she tried.

Smiling, she said, "It's not too late at all. What would you like?"

He gazed at the baked goods that were left in the display cabinet. "Hmm. I'm partial to chocolate so give me a brownie and what is that round thing that's covered in chocolate?" he asked. "It looks good, too."

"That's a Bismarck. It's like a donut covered in chocolate icing and the center is filled with custard."

"I'll take that, too. But if you've already drained the coffee-pot, I'll just drink water."

"No problem. I can make a single cup for you. Want to have a seat?" She gestured to the little square table where she'd been sitting only minutes before he'd arrived. "Or you might like to sit outside. The weather has been beautiful today."

"I'd rather eat outside—if you can join me," he said.

"I'd love to," she told him. "Like I said, I was closing up anyway."

While she gathered the pastries he wanted and made the coffee, he meandered around the small room, studying the old local memorabilia that adorned the walls, particularly photos of Wickenburg in its early, gold rush days.

"This is interesting," he said. "I like history. It makes us who we are, don't you think?"

"Yes," she agreed. "In more ways than most people imagine."

With the coffee done, she carried the cup and a small tray holding the pastries out to him.

"If you want anything in your coffee, it's all over there." She pointed to a small table containing all sorts of creamers, milk, sugar and sweeteners.

"No thanks. I like it black." He took the goodies from her, then asked, "Aren't you going to have something with me? At least some coffee. I hate to eat without you having something, too."

She groaned, while thinking the temptation of spending time with him was far stronger than the call of her sweet tooth. "Well, since I didn't eat lunch I suppose I could have a brownie," she said. "Just give me a minute and I'll make another cup of coffee."

Once she had her food and drink, the two of them walked outside to where a group of three small wrought iron tables and chairs were grouped beneath the lacy shade of two mesquite trees.

At a table nearest to the stone walkway leading up to the building, he pulled out one of the chairs and helped her into it. Once he was comfortably seated across from her, she asked, "So how has your new job been going?"

One corner of his lips curved upward. "It's been going well, I think. I've not had any complaints from Blake and Maureen yet. They have far more confidence in me than I do in myself. And they seem to understand I need time to learn the ranch— and the men."

She thoughtfully sipped her coffee. "Have the guys all accepted you as their new boss?"

"That's my biggest concern. Because if I don't have their respect I'm going to have problems. And since they all thought Matthew could walk on water that makes him a tough act to follow. But I'm trying. And so far they've all seemed fairly receptive of me. I don't know for sure, but I expect that's because Blake probably laid down the law to them before I ever arrived."

She pinched off a bite of brownie. "You're selling yourself short, Tag. The Hollisters don't have stupid men working for them. They can see you know your business."

The full-fledged smile he shot her caused her breath to momentarily hang in her throat. How could a man who looked like this still be single? It didn't seem possible.

He's single, you ninny, because he wants to be that way. He's thirty-two. He's had plenty of time to marry if he'd wanted to.

Mentally shaking herself, she sipped more coffee, while across from her, he ate the brownie in four bites then started on the Bismarck.

"Can you see that I know my business?" he asked with a soft chuckle.

Her cheeks suddenly felt hot. "Uh—well, I've not seen you in action. And I don't exactly know the things that a ranch foreman does, but you look like you'd be very comfortable on a horse—with a rope in your hand. This town is full of cowboys and after a while it's easy to tell which ones are genuine and who's trying to play the part."

Amusement crinkled the corners of his eyes. "I'm relieved to hear I look genuine."

As Emily-Ann nibbled her way through the chocolate dessert, she couldn't help but wonder if he'd thought about their kiss. Probably not the way she'd thought about it. Not the way she'd obsessed over the taste of his lips, the scent of his hair and skin, and the hardness of his body. Hopefully in a few more days the memories would dim. But for now they were as fresh as though it had just happened.

"The other night at the party, did I hear you mention that you were taking some sort of classes?"

Surprised that he'd remembered, she said, "Yes. I'm taking online classes to become an RN."

"A nurse. That's an ambitious choice. So I guess that means you don't always plan to work here at the coffee shop."

She glanced over her shoulder at the small square building

with slab pine siding and a tiny covered porch, then turned her gaze back to him. "I love working here. But it pays just enough for me to get by. And my mother had a dream for me to be a nurse."

"What about your own dreams?"

She'd not expected that kind of question from him. In fact, Camille and Maureen were the only two people who'd ever asked her about her private wants and wishes.

"A minute ago you mentioned ambition, but I've never really had much of that, Tag. If it wasn't for me making a promise to my mother before she died, I doubt I'd be pushing myself to get a nursing degree. I'd probably be content to just sell coffee and donuts and keep living in the same little house that I grew up in."

"Nothing wrong with that if you're happy. Money, and the things it can buy, doesn't necessarily equal happiness. I know. I saw it firsthand with the Armstrong family. Cold and bitter. The whole bunch of them."

"Well, I don't want to become a nurse just to make a better salary. And deep down, I'm not doing it just to follow my mother's dream. I've thought about it long and hard and even though I'm not exactly ambitious, I'm drawn to the idea of helping people. You see, Mom was in bad health for a couple of years before she passed away. I saw how much it meant for her to have the right care."

"If it means anything I think you have the nature for nursing, Emily-Ann. And since you're studying to be a nurse, do you have any suggestions to treat a horse bite?"

She frowned. "You've been bitten by a horse?"

He put down his coffee cup and pushed up the sleeve of his pale blue shirt. As Emily-Ann caught a glimpse of the wounds on his forearm, she took hold of his hand and pulled it across the table toward her.

"This is serious, Tag." She studied the crescent-shaped tears that appeared to go deep into the flesh of his forearm. The gashes were an angry red with dried blood crusted around the edges. "You need a tetanus shot and possibly some stitches. How did that happen?"

"I was playing with one of Holt's young stallions and made the mistake of turning my back on him. He nabbed me on the arm to let me know he wanted the game to keep going. I'm going to stop by Doc's animal clinic on the way home. He'll take care of it."

She rolled her eyes. "We do have regular doctors here in town. No need for you to go to a veterinarian."

Chuckling, he pulled his hand back and refastened the cuff at his wrist. "I'll feel more comfortable with Doc treating me. Regular doctors make me nervous."

"What about nurses?" she asked pointedly.

One corner of his mouth cocked upward. "Nurses unsettle me, too. Especially when she has a syringe and needle in her hand."

She showed him her empty palms. "I can't give you a tetanus shot. But I could clean those wounds for you," she offered. "I keep antiseptic and things like that in the coffee shop. Just in case I cut or burn myself."

"Thanks for the offer, but I'd rather just sit here and drink my coffee." He gazed around the shaded dining area, then across the street to where a fat saguaro shaded a small building that housed an insurance agency. "This is quiet. No bawling cows or nickering horses. Not that I don't like those sounds, but sometimes a man wants to just listen to the wind. And a woman's voice."

She cleared her throat and his gaze swung back to her. Emily-Ann was surprised to see the humor had disappeared from his face. In fact, if she didn't know better, he looked lonely, almost lost. Which hardly made sense. This man had everything going for him. He'd just landed a prestigious job as foreman of Three Rivers Ranch. Why should he be feeling anything but ecstatic? Unless he was missing some woman back in Texas, she thought.

"You forgot the coyotes," she said in an attempt to lighten

the moment. "None of those howling around here. Although, they do show up in town once in a while."

He smiled and she was relieved to see his good humor returning. The other night at the party she'd been drawn to his easy, laid-back nature. It was a nice change from the guys she'd dated in the past who'd been so busy trying to play the cool, tough man that they'd rarely smiled. And even when they had, it had looked so phony she'd had to bite her tongue to keep from laughing.

"No. Can't forget them." He took the last bite of Bismarck, then wadded up the empty wax paper.

As Emily-Ann watched him tilt the foam cup to his lips, she realized she didn't want him to leave. Spending time with him made her feel different, almost special. She realized that was foolish. Especially since she'd believed her past mistakes with men had taught her some valuable lessons.

"So has anything exciting been going on at Three Rivers since the party?" she asked, then before he could answer, added, "I guess everything about the place must feel exciting and new to you."

"It does," he agreed. "Matthew has been trying to show me the different sections of the ranch and how they're used throughout the year. The majority of the land has to be explored on horseback. So we've been spending lots of time in the saddle."

"Camille implied that she and Matthew would be staying for a few more weeks. Maybe until the end of the month. I hope they do. Once they go back to Red Bluff I'll only get to see her occasionally."

"Matthew tells me that Camille owns and operates a little diner down there. I think he said the town was called Dragoon. Is that right?"

Emily-Ann nodded. "Yes. It's a tiny desert town. Not much is there, but the diner is located on the edge of a main highway that runs from Wilcox to Benson. So she has lots of travelers who stop in to eat."

"Hmm. Just between me and you, I'm surprised that Camille runs a diner." He shrugged. "Not that anything is wrong with running a diner. It's just that she's a Hollister. There's no need for her to work at such a strenuous job."

"You're right about no need. But her being a Hollister explains everything. In spite of their wealth, or maybe because of it, they all have a fierce ambition. Camille couldn't sit around and twiddle her thumbs any more than her brothers or sister, Vivian, could. Besides, she loves to cook and she's darned good at it. If you ever make a trip down to Red Bluff, you'll see what I mean."

"I plan to go for a visit later on in the year," he said. "Just to see how Matthew is putting that Hollister property to use."

"You know, Camille was a bone of contention for a while with her family. When she moved down to Red Bluff and refused to come back here, her brothers threw a fit, so to speak. And Maureen wasn't happy about it either," Emily-Ann told him. "But that's all been smoothed over now that she and Matthew have married and are going to have a baby soon. Funny how things can look so bleak for a while and then everything suddenly turns to sunshine again. Sort of gives a person hope. You know what I mean?"

Smiling faintly, he put down his cup and leaned back in the chair. "I know exactly what you mean. And everybody needs hope."

He was right. Everybody needed hope. But no one had ever clung to it as much as Emily-Ann's mother. She'd always looked forward and believed that the men in her life were actually going to come through with all their promises. In the end, Emily-Ann had ended up having no contact with her biological father and her stepfather had been little more than a stranger who'd come and gone as he pleased.

"Well, I need to be going," he said after a moment. "Doc is expecting me and I promised Matthew I'd be back to the ranch in time to go with him to check on some calves."

All sorts of words she wanted to say rushed to her tongue. But none of them were appropriate or proper. Besides, she didn't want him to get the idea that she was gushing over him.

She gestured to his injured arm. "Promise me that you'll have Doc treat that bite wound. It could become seriously infected if you don't take care of it."

"I promise as soon as I leave here, I'm going straight to his clinic," he told her.

"Well, I'm glad you came by, Tag. Now that you know where the coffee shop is you might get a hankering to drop by for another pastry—sometime."

He looked across the table at her. "I expect I will. But before I go I have something else on my mind—to ask you."

That serious look had returned to his face and she wasn't sure what to make of him. Nor did she understand what had caused her heart to suddenly leap into a ridiculous tap dance. "Oh. What's that?"

"Would you be willing to have dinner with me? I can't tonight. But I think I'll be free tomorrow night—if you are."

Free? He couldn't possibly know just how long ago a man of any caliber had looked in her direction, much less asked her on a date.

"Uh—I'm not busy, if that's what you mean. But I—"

"But what?"

She frowned, unwilling to believe that this cowboy wanted to spend time with her. "Are you—would this be like a date?"

"I guess you could call it that. Why?"

She felt her jaw drop and she realized she was probably staring at him like she'd lost her senses.

"Well, you—uh, you said we were going to be friends."

"That's right. Friends can eat dinner together, can't they?"

She was growing more flustered by the second. "Yes. But friends don't go on dates."

A slow smile spread his lips and she found herself staring at his white teeth. What would it feel like to push her tongue past their rough edges? To taste his inner mouth and press her body so close to his that not even a hair could be wedged between them?

Oh Lord, she was already losing control, she thought desperately, and they'd not gone any farther than the front yard of the coffee shop.

He reached across the table and clasped his hand around hers. The contact caused her heart to thump even harder.

He said, "After we go on a date we might decide we want to be more than friends."

"No!"

His brows arched in question and before he could make any sort of reply, she tried to explain, "I mean—you don't know who I am, Tag."

"Why don't I? Your name is Emily-Ann Broadmoor. You work at this little coffee shop and you're studying to be a nurse. You've always lived in Wickenburg and you're not married or attached. Right?"

The sigh she released was rough and shaky. "Yes. But you don't understand. I'm not a girl that someone like you would want to date."

He appeared unaffected by her admission. "Why not?"

Annoyed with herself and with him, she pressed her lips together and shook her head. "Look, Tag, I know you're a smart guy, so don't insult my intelligence by playing dumb. There are social ladders, you know. And I'm on the bottom rung. Got it now?"

"No. I don't have it. You can't be a friend of the Hollisters and be on the bottom rung. That just isn't possible."

"The Hollisters see everyone as equal. And when two little girls become friends in elementary school—they don't care about such things. They just want to be together. And because of Camille, the Hollisters have always included me. It's not that way with everyone around here. And please don't ask me why. It's something I don't want to get into. Not now."

She rose from her chair and gathered the remnants of her snack from the tabletop. "I need to go back in and finish closing up," she told him.

He rose and, with his trash in hand, followed her into the building. After the door had shut behind them, he asked, "Would you like to know what I'm really thinking?"

Walking behind the counter, she began to sack up the last of the pastries. "Sure. Go ahead," she told him.

He tossed his trash into a nearby basket, then pulled out his wallet and placed several bills on the glass countertop.

"I think you're talking a lot of nonsense. If you're afraid to go out with me just come out and say it. That would be much better than you giving me all this double-talk about you not being good enough—or whatever it is you're trying to say."

She closed the doors on the back of the case and placed the last of the sacked pastries on a cabinet top that ran along the back wall of the room. Behind her, she could hear Taggart's boots shuffle restlessly against the tiled floor.

He was obviously waiting on her reply. But what could she say without lying? She was afraid to go out with him. Afraid she'd do something foolish like fall head over heels for him.

Turning, she walked over to where he was standing. "Okay. You're right. I am a little afraid to go out with you, Tag. I—you see, I haven't wanted to date anyone for a long time. It never turns out good for me. And to be honest, I like you too much to ruin things between us."

He shook his head. "Having dinner together isn't going to ruin anything."

Before she could stop it, a cynical laugh rushed past her lips. "That's what you think."

He grinned a charming little grin at her. "I promise I'll be a perfect gentleman."

She laughed again, only this time it was a sound of amusement. "I believe you."

"So does that mean you'll go?"

It was stupid for her to keep hesitating, she thought, when every cell in her body was screaming at her to accept his invitation.

"Yes, I'll go. I just don't understand why you're asking me. If you'll look around town you'll see there are all sorts of women who are much prettier than me."

"Maybe I want more than pretty," he said, then smiling smugly, he tapped a finger on the bills he'd placed on the countertop. "Here's the money for my things. I'll see you tomorrow night. About seven. Is that time okay with you?"

"Sure."

She scratched down her address on an order pad and handed the small square to him. "That's where I live. And I put my cell number below. Just in case you change your mind and need to call me."

He slipped the paper into the pocket on his Western shirt. "No chance I'll change my mind," he said, then tipping the brim of his hat at her, he left the shop.

After the door had closed, Emily-Ann let out a long breath and sank weakly onto the wooden stool sitting next to the cabinets.

This morning as she'd driven to work, she'd pretty much convinced herself that Taggart had put her out of his mind. Now she was going on a date with him. It was a bit unbelievable to Emily-Ann. And what was Camille going to think about it?

She wasn't going to tell her, Emily-Ann thought. Not yet. If she did, her friend would immediately start harping about that damned bridal bouquet again. No, she'd wait until the date was over and Taggart came up with a reason not to see her again. Then she'd have proof that she needed more than a bridal bouquet to find a man to love her.

Chapter Four

Taggart hadn't realized just how many things he'd accumulated until he started unpacking the boxes he'd brought with him from Texas. Dishes, bedding and bath linens, clothing, boots and toiletries. Each evening before he'd gone to bed, he'd tried to unpack at least one box and put the items where they belonged.

This evening Matthew had insisted they wrap up work early so he could finish getting his house in order. Now, as he stacked coffee cups and cereal bowls in one of the kitchen cabinets, he was interrupted by a knock on the front door.

Forgetting the task for the moment, he went out to the living room to answer the door.

"Blake, come in," he said, surprised to find the ranch manager standing on the wide wooden porch.

"I can just stay a minute. Mom and I are about to leave for Prescott to a cattle buyer's convention."

Taggart pushed the door wide and gestured for Blake to enter the house. "I was in the kitchen trying to put away the last of the dishes. This moving thing is a pain."

"I'd be happy to send Jazelle over here to help you. That is, if Katherine and Roslyn can make do without her. These days she's turned into more of a nanny than a housekeeper," he added with a chuckle. "Poor girl. Mom has decided she needs to hire someone to help her and I agree."

"Thanks for the offer, but I have most of the necessary things put where they belong. Come on back to the kitchen," Taggart told him. "We can talk while I finish with the dishes."

"Fine. This won't take long," Blake said, while following him through the living room. "Actually, I stopped by because I have something to give you."

Inside the kitchen, Taggart gestured toward a long white farm table with matching chairs. "Pull up a chair. I have a bit of coffee left in the carafe if you'd like a cup."

"Thanks. But I'm fine." He reached inside his Western-cut jacket and pulled out a long envelope, then handed it to Taggart.

"What is this?" Taggart asked curiously.

"A check."

Taggart paused and looked in stunned fascination at the ranch manager. "What for? Are you terminating my job already?"

The question produced a long, loud laugh from Blake. "Not hardly. We couldn't be happier that we have you here. The check is a little bonus. Just to show how much we appreciate you. We understand it's been costly for you to move out here. Especially with you bringing horses and tack, besides your household goods and personal things. We want to help cover the expense."

"I don't expect that, Blake. And it's totally unnecessary." He opened the envelope and the amount of the check he pulled out very nearly floored him. "No! No way can I accept this. I didn't spend a fraction of this on moving cost."

Blake laughed again. "Don't argue. Just trust me. You'll earn it all back before the first month is out."

Shaking his head, Taggart said, "I don't know what to say. This is far beyond generous, Blake."

The ranch manager swatted a dismissive hand through the air. "No need for you to say anything about the check. But I would like to know how you're settling in. Not with the house, I can see things here are taking shape. I'm talking about the ranch and the men. You and Matthew have been so busy, I've not had a chance to talk with either one of you."

Taggart studied the eldest Hollister brother, while thinking how differently he was being treated here at Three Rivers compared to the last year he'd spent on the Flying W. No matter how hard he'd worked, the Armstrongs had never been satisfied. They'd demanded more from him and all the hands, all the while insisting they had to cut their wages or go under. Which the whole crew had known was utter nonsense. It had been a hellish situation and one that Taggart was glad to have behind him. "Everything is going good, Blake. Thank you for asking."

Blake gave his shoulder an affectionate slap. "That's what we want. But if you do have any problems of any kind I want you to feel comfortable about coming to me. Or Mom. She stays in the thick of things and knows more about this ranch than I'll ever learn in my lifetime. But you've probably already figured that out for yourself."

"Matthew told me what an incredible woman his mother-in-law is and I'm beginning to see he wasn't exaggerating. Today Maureen helped drag calves to the branding fire and I'm being honest, she outworked most of the men," Taggart replied.

"That's Mom," Blake said with a grin, then turned to go. "And speaking of Mom, she's probably waiting on me. I'll see you tomorrow."

"Uh, Blake, if you have another minute I would like to ask you something."

At the back door of the kitchen, Blake paused to look at him. "Okay. Shoot."

Feeling a bit foolish, he cleared his throat, then asked, "How well do you know Emily-Ann?"

If the question surprised Blake he didn't show it. In fact, he chuckled. "I thought you were going to ask me something about roundup."

"I'm not worried about roundup," Taggart told him.

Blake looked even more amused. "But Emily-Ann does worry you?"

"Not exactly worries me," Taggart tried to explain. "More like she confuses the heck out of me."

"I didn't realize you were interested in her."

Taggart could feel his cheeks growing warm. He never discussed women with anyone. Since he'd lost Becca, he'd never really thought that much about any particular female. But since he'd met Emily-Ann something had happened to him. He couldn't seem to get his mind off the curvy redhead or that kiss they shared the night of the party.

"I'm taking her out to dinner tonight," Taggart admitted, then with a helpless shake of his head, added, "To be honest, Blake, she came damned close to turning down my invitation. Which is her right, of course. I hardly expect just any and every woman to go out with me. But she—well, it's like she mistrusts me or something."

Blake grinned. "You must've done something right. She's agreed to go out with you. But as far as giving you advice about women, I'm not the right man for that job. You need to talk to Holt. He's the charmer of the family."

Taggart swiped a hand through his dark rumpled hair. "Go ahead and laugh, Blake. I realize I sound like I'm twenty years old instead of thirty-two. It's just that she puzzles me. She seems to have a low opinion of herself and I can't figure why. I thought you might clue me in about her."

Blake's grin quickly vanished. "I don't know that much about Emily-Ann's personal life, Tag. Except that it hasn't always been easy. She's had to deal with plenty of heartaches and hardships. But she's a good person and very hardworking. We all love her."

"Hmm. It's odd that you say that. She has the notion that you Hollisters just tolerate her because she's Camille's friend."

Blake muttered a curse. "That's not true at all," he said, then after a thoughtful moment added, "but I can see where she might see things that way. Feeling accepted doesn't always come easy for some people. Especially when they've been raised up hard. I figure Emily-Ann needs to move on from the stigma of her past. But that's a hard thing to do, too."

Taggart frowned. "What about her past?"

Blake shook his head. "That's something she'll have to tell you."

Blake let himself out and as the door shut behind him, Taggart thoughtfully picked up the check from the countertop.

The bonus was nearly half of the year's salary he'd made on the Flying W. The Hollisters' generosity was hard to believe, much less accept. He wasn't worth this kind of money.

Let's just say I know my limitations. And you're on the other side of the boundary.

Emily-Ann's words suddenly pushed their way into Taggart's thoughts and he wondered if her lack of money made her think there was a wall separating them. Or did her reluctance have something to do with a man? One that she'd loved and lost?

Taggart intended to find the answers to his questions.

WITH A CRITICAL eye, Emily-Ann studied herself in the dresser mirror. Throughout the day, she'd promised herself she wasn't going to fret over her appearance tonight. She'd told herself she wasn't going to agonize over what to wear or how to do her hair. Glamming herself up for Taggart would be foolish and futile. She couldn't turn a dandelion into a lovely rose.

Yet, in spite of all the self-lecturing, she'd taken pains to pick out a dress that flattered her complexion. And she'd done her hair three different times to get it to drape perfectly against her temple.

And why not, she asked herself. Futile or not, any normal girl would want to look her best when she went on a date with a man. Especially a man like Taggart.

Turning away from the mirror, she reached for the thin yellow cardigan lying across the foot of the bed. Even though it was April, and the days were hot, the nights cooled enough for a jacket. And since Taggart hadn't given her any hint as to where they might be eating, she had no idea if she'd be spending any time outdoors.

With the sweater thrown over one arm and her handbag in tow, she left the bedroom and walked out to the living room to wait for Taggart to arrive. As she took a seat on the couch, she wondered what he would think about her house.

What can he think, Emily-Ann? It's the same little bungalow your mother lived in when you were born. You've never gotten beyond its walls. Except for a few little road trips, you've never ventured outside Wickenburg. You have a small, modest life. Before the night is over he's going to see all of that for himself.

Emily-Ann was fighting against the disheartening voice in her head when she heard the sound of a vehicle pull up in the short driveway in front of the house.

She was struck with the urge to jump up and go meet him on the front porch, but she quickly told herself that she needed to behave in a dignified manner. He didn't need to see that she was chomping at the bit to welcome him. Besides, he needed to get a good look at the inside of her house. Just so he'd see the huge gap in their living conditions.

After a short moment, a knock sounded on the door and Emily-Ann tried to gather her composure as she went to answer it. But as soon as she pulled back the door and saw him standing across the threshold, everything inside her began to tremble.

"Hi, Emily-Ann."

"Good evening, Tag. Please come in." She pushed the door wider, then waited while he stepped past her and into the house before she shut it behind them.

"I don't suppose you had trouble finding the place," she said as he came to a stop in the middle of the small room. "Wickenburg isn't very large."

"No problem," he told her. "GPS wasn't going to let me make a wrong turn."

"Would you like to sit for a minute?" she asked gesturing toward an armchair. "Or are you ready to go?"

"Since we have plenty of time I'll sit a minute," he said.

Emily-Ann watched him sink into the armchair, then remove his Stetson and place it on his knee. She'd expected him to want to leave. Most men did once they saw her house. Not that it was cluttered or nasty. But the old furniture had seen better days and the flooring needed to be replaced.

"If you'd like something to drink I can make coffee," she offered. "Or I have soda."

"Thanks," he said, "but I'm fine."

Feeling more nervous than she could ever remember being, she sat down on the couch directly opposite of where he was sitting. As she smoothed her skirt over her knees, she could feel his gaze sliding over her and to know he was looking at her was enough to light a fire in her cheeks.

"So how—"

"I thought—"

They both spoke at the same time and then laughed.

"Sorry," Taggart told her. "You go first."

"I was only going to ask you how things are going on the ranch," she said, while thinking how terribly sexy he looked tonight. He was wearing a deep blue shirt with black diamond-shaped snaps down the front and on the cuffs. A bolo tie with a slide fashioned from black onyx hung loosely below the collar of his shirt. He looked dressed up without being too fancy. In fact, he looked exactly right.

"They're going great. Better every day, in fact."

"That's nice. I'm glad for you. And the Hollisters," she added. "Before you came, Blake and Maureen were very concerned about losing Matthew."

"Well, they haven't exactly lost him. He's just working a different property now."

"Yes. But this ranch in Yavapai County is the biggest one," she reasoned.

"I'm reminded of that every day I pull up in the ranch yard and see all the hands coming out of the bunkhouse. Back on the Flying W I maybe had to deal with a third of the amount of men that I do here. For the first day or two after I arrived, I felt daunted by the sheer size of everything."

"But now you're growing accustomed to it, I'm guessing."

"More and more every day," he replied, then glanced around the small room. "You have a homey little place here, Emily-Ann. I like it."

"You're being overly nice, Tag. And it isn't necessary. I'm sure you see plenty of things that need repairing or replaced. I do what I can, whenever I can."

He frowned at her. "I'm not being overly nice. This room feels lived-in and I'm sure the rest of the house does, too. And that's a nice feeling. It's something you can't fake."

"Well, the house is very old. I think it was built in the 1940s and had several different owners until my mother moved into it in 1990. I was born a few months later. Some of my friends often tell me I should move into an apartment building. That it would be more modern and I wouldn't have to worry about the upkeep. Which is true. But I wouldn't feel comfortable. Here I have a little yard and my neighbors aren't right on top of me."

He smiled. "I think you should tell your friends to mind their own business."

She let out a long breath. Maybe Taggart truly was different, she thought. Maybe he didn't care that her closet wasn't full of fancy clothes or her house needed repairs. Maybe he actually wanted to be with her just because she was Emily-Ann and no other reason.

Laughing softly, she said, "That's not a bad idea. Do you have everything moved into your house now?"

He chuckled. "Everything is inside the house, but that's about all I can say. I still have things piled here and there in boxes. But I'm a typical bachelor, Emily-Ann, I don't care if my bed is made or I have to dig my clothes out of a box. I have more important things to think about. But I like the house. It even has a little fireplace and a small patio out back."

"That's nice. Actually, I've never been inside the house," she admitted. "Camille and I used to ride horses by the place. But, of course, that was years before she and Matthew got together so we never stopped or anything. In fact, right after he went to work for Three Rivers Ranch, he was married to someone else. But his wife was—I'll just come out and say it—she was awful. You see, she was hollow on the inside. No substance at all. When she flew the coop I don't think anyone was surprised. Not even him."

By the time she stopped speaking she realized he was eyeing her closely. Embarrassed heat suddenly poured into her cheeks. "Oh my, I'm sorry, Tag. I'm running off at the mouth and sounding like the town gossip. But I—didn't mean it that way. It's just that I wanted you to know that—well, I think I should just shut up before I make myself look even worse."

Shaking his head, he smiled faintly. "You don't sound like a gossip—you were just telling me about the past. And actually I'm thinking how fortunate Matthew was to have a second chance at happiness."

Relieved that he understood, she nodded. "Yes, if only everyone could be that fortunate."

Suddenly restless, she rose to her feet and draped the light sweater over her bare shoulders. "If you're ready to go, I am," she told him.

"Sure." He rose from the chair and levered the hat back onto his head. "I've not said anything yet, but you look extra beautiful tonight, Emily-Ann."

Beautiful. The only time she ever heard that word and her name coupled together was when her mother spoke them. To hear Taggart call her beautiful filled her with pleasure. It also made her very wary.

She'd made the mistake of believing a man's pretty words before. She couldn't make those same missteps with Taggart. And yet with all of her heart she wanted to believe he was sincere.

"Thank you. Since you didn't say where we'd be going I hope my dress is suitable."

He stepped closer as he eyed the off-the-shoulder dress made of red calico printed with tiny yellow flowers. A matching belt cinched in the waist, while the tiered hem fluttered against her calves.

"The dress is perfect," he murmured. "I like it."

Oh my. His voice reminded her of cool water trickling over rough stones. And he smelled like a real man. One with strong hands, broad strong shoulders and a constitution to match.

"I'm glad," she said huskily, then clearing her throat, she purposely stepped away from him and retrieved her purse from an end table. "I'm ready."

As soon as the last words came out of her mouth, she very nearly laughed. She was far from ready to deal with the feelings that Taggart was creating inside her. But she wasn't going to shy away from him. For once in her life, she was going to believe, if just for one night, that she was good enough to have this man's respect.

JOSE'S, THE RESTAURANT Taggart had chosen, was located on the edge of town, where the empty desert stretched toward a far range of jagged mountains. The building was a rambling, hacienda type with stucco walls painted a pale turquoise and a red tiled roof. A deep porch ran the width of the front and was shaded with a roof supported by arched columns. Potted plants hung from the center of each arch, while an enormous bougainvillea covered with yellow-gold blossoms grew far past the roof. At the opposite end of the porch, a single saguaro with three arms stood against the darkening sky.

As Taggart and Emily-Ann walked across the graveled parking area to the building, he said, "I'm sure you've probably eaten here dozens of times. But Doc tells me the place has great food."

"To be honest, Tag, I'm rarely ever out this way. I usually just fix myself something at home. Or if I do decide to treat myself, I grab something close in town. This is very nice. And it's lovely here, don't you think?"

He looked down at her, while thinking nothing could look as lovely as she did at this moment with the twilight falling on her soft features and the smile on her face directed solely at him. He'd never known a woman as guileless as Emily-Ann and when he was with her, he forgot most everything. Even his vow to never let himself care for another woman.

"If the food is as good as the outside looks, then I think we're in for a treat," he told her.

Inside the restaurant, a hostess ushered them to a table covered with an orange-and-white checked tablecloth. In the center a fat brown candle flickered in the faint breeze wafting down from the blades of a ceiling fan. Beyond the small table, a long window exposed a view of the desert, while the sounds of a Spanish guitar played softly in the background.

Taggart helped Emily-Ann into one of the cushioned chairs, then took a seat for himself. All the while it struck him that he could've driven for miles and not found a more romantic spot than this. He'd not exactly planned this type of dinner, but now that they were here, and he saw the enchanted expression on Emily-Ann's face, he was glad.

As soon as the waiter arrived, Taggart ordered wine for each of them, then picked up the menu and began to study the long list of dishes offered.

"I should've asked if you like Mexican food," he said. "But I see they serve typical American food, also."

"Oh, I love Mexican food," she exclaimed. "It's my favorite. What about you?"

"Well, where I come from we had what you call Tex-Mex food. It's a little different from the Mexican food served here in Arizona, but it's just as good. I like it all," he admitted.

"Do you eat in the bunkhouse with the men?" she asked. "Or do you cook for yourself?"

"I do both. Depending on what I have planned in the mornings or if I'm tied up late with work in the evenings. The cook in the bunkhouse is a gruff old guy. But he makes fairly good biscuits and beans and steak. Blake eats in the bunkhouse, too, on certain days. I think he enjoys being a regular cowboy."

Emily-Ann nodded. "Blake went to college to get a degree in ranch management thinking one day when his dad grew old and retired he'd take over the job of manager. No one could've dreamed that Joel was going to die so young and that Blake would have to step into his father's position. Katherine, his wife, says that the job weighs on him at times, but he'll do whatever he has to do to keep the ranch thriving."

The waiter arrived with their drinks and after they'd given him their choices from the menu, Taggart took a long sip of the dry, fruity wine.

"Do you know Katherine well?" he asked, picking up on their conversation where they'd left off.

She nodded. "Yes. She comes by the coffee shop on the days that she's working at the school. She's secretary for Penny—the school principal."

"She and Blake seem like the perfect match."

"Perfect," she agreed. "Their twins are adorable. And their older son Nick is such a nice kid. Blake was the second of the Hollister men to get married. Joe, the deputy, was the first. I know you met him at the party."

Taggart had especially liked the youngest Hollister brother. "Yes, I did. He seemed like a quiet guy, but when his mother started talking about ranching, he really opened up. I got the impression that he does quite a bit of ranch work when he's off duty. By the way, he introduced me to Sam, foreman of the Bar X."

Emily-Ann gave him a huge smile. "Ahh, Sam. He's adorable."

"I've heard that women find him charming." He slanted her a wry smile. "I see that includes you, too."

Laughing softly, she drew the wineglass to her lips. "What can I say? His face looks like a piece of cracked and crinkled leather. He's as thin as a rail and his legs are just a little bowed. But there's something about that old man that—I don't know what it is. But women feel drawn to him. I think it's mostly that soft look in his blue eyes when he looks at us. Like he cherishes all females."

"Well, he's certainly snagged a nice one. Isabelle's mother rarely left Sam's side the night of the party. I hear they're going to get married."

Emily-Ann sighed and Taggart could see the starry expression in her eyes. She was clearly a romantic. But he'd come to that conclusion the first time he'd met her. So why had he brought her to dinner? Why was he here drinking wine with her and watching candlelight flicker golden fingers upon her bare shoulders?

Because you've lost your mind, Taggart. You've forgotten how it felt when you watched Becca being lowered into the ground. Because you can't remember what it was like to have every dream and hope you've ever carried in your heart crushed into bits of ashes.

No, damn it! He silently cursed at himself as he fought to block out the voice in his head. He hadn't forgotten anything. But he was determined not to allow the past to haunt him tonight. He was tired of remembering. Tired of living in the past and trying to hold on to a memory that only brought him pain.

"Honestly, I was shocked when I heard the news about Gabby and Sam," Emily-Ann replied. "I mean, yes, Sam is a charmer. And I have no doubt he'd treat a wife like a queen. But Gabby is so opposite from him. Besides the fact that she's probably twenty years younger and very attractive, she's a city person— an artist. Sam spends his days on the back of a horse."

Amused, he grunted. "What do you think I do?"

"The same thing. But I figure you're—" pausing, she made a palms-up gesture "—more of a well-rounded man than Sam."

"Hah! Don't kid yourself. I got the impression that Sam has already forgotten more than I'll ever know about anything. And sometimes it's that stark difference in people that make them attracted to each other." He leveled a smile at her. "But that's enough about those folks. What about you, Emily-Ann? How many hearts around here have you broken?"

Above the rim of the wineglass, her eyes made a slow study of his face. "Seriously? You have the idea that I've broken a heart?" Laughing cynically, she lowered the glass back to the table, but her fingers continued to grip the stem. "That's funny, Tag."

"Why?"

Frustration tightened her features. "Because—I'm not a girl who men fall in love with. That's why."

He frowned at her. "That's nonsense."

"I'm sorry," she said. "But it's true."

"You'll never convince me."

As he watched her lips curve into a wan smile he tried to imagine another man kissing her mouth, feeling her warm breath on his face, tasting the smooth skin of her cheek. But the image refused to form in his mind. Not because she was undesirable; everything about her was alluring. No, it was impossible to imagine her with another man because he was already thinking of her in possessive terms. As his and his alone.

The faint smile on her face suddenly vanished and she let out a short, mocking laugh before turning her gaze to the window. "Oh yes, you'll be convinced. You'll soon learn that I talk too much, that I'm irritating and sometimes even ditzy. I'm a bit plump for most men's taste and my mouth is too wide. My eyes are too big and I couldn't grow a long fingernail if I tried."

He could see she was deadly serious, but Taggart couldn't help himself, he had to laugh. "Oh, Emily-Ann, do you realize how ridiculous all of that sounds?"

Her gaze returned to his face and the cynicism Taggart spotted in her green eyes took him by surprise.

"Yes, I can admit that most of it is trivial stuff," she said sullenly. "But that doesn't change the fact that I'm Emily-Ann Broadmoor. Everyone knows my father was the real estate tycoon's son. The one who believed he was too high-class to marry the poor girl he'd gotten pregnant. Too important to be a father to the child she bore, or to ever acknowledge he had a daughter. And I'm no different than my mother, Tag. I'm the girl the guys want to take to bed, but never fall in love with!"

By the time she spoke the last few words her voice was wobbling and her face had turned to the color of paste. The dark pain in her eyes was like a knife in his chest and he desperately wanted to round the table and take her into his arms. He wanted to tell her in so many ways how very precious she was to him. But that would be the same as saying he was falling for her. He wasn't ready for that. And from the sound of things, she wasn't either.

"Emily-Ann, I—"

His words were suddenly interrupted as she jumped to her feet and blinked at the tears filling her eyes. "I'm sorry, Tag. I—you'll have to excuse me."

She hurried away from the table and for a moment Taggart thought she might run from the restaurant completely. Relief rushed through him when he saw her turn in the direction of an alcove where the restrooms were located. Clearly, she was seeking a private space to collect herself. He could only hope she wouldn't allow this little episode to ruin their evening.

Sighing heavily, he reached for his wineglass and emptied it with one long swallow. Her emotional revelation had shaken him. Not because they were in a public place. And certainly not because he'd learned she'd been born out of wedlock. Nowadays no one looked down on a woman for being a single mother. Most of the time it was because she'd chosen to parent the child alone rather than enter into a marriage that wouldn't work. No, the part about her lack of a father hadn't meant that much to Taggart. Hell, for the majority of Taggart's childhood his father had been absent and now that he'd grown into adulthood he saw the man even less.

No, the part of Emily-Ann's admission that had cut Taggart so deeply was the last part. The part about being used instead of loved. Is that how she viewed most men? Did she put him in that same category? The idea sickened him.

Where do you come off being so righteous, Taggart O'Brien? Isn't that exactly what you've been thinking about Emily-Ann? You don't want love or marriage. But when you look at her, you definitely imagine having sex with her. You're no better than the rest. If you had any gumption about you at all you'd take her home and never see her again. And maybe, eventually, she'll meet a real man who'll give her real love.

Sighing heavily, he wiped a hand over his face, then stared out the window at the darkening desert. He'd asked Emily-Ann to have dinner with him tonight because in spite of the great job he'd just landed at Three Rivers, and the money it was bringing to him, he wanted more than that. She made him feel alive again. She made him feel like a man.

He couldn't give her up now. But how did he think he could hold on to her when the very thing she wanted from a man he no longer had? His heart was buried back in Texas.

Chapter Five

By the time Emily-Ann returned to the table, she had pulled her emotions together, but that didn't stop her from feeling like a complete fool. And when Taggart rose to his feet and promptly reached for her hand, she wanted to burst into tears all over again.

"I'm so sorry, Tag," she said lowly. "I hope I didn't embarrass you."

He smiled at her and the warm light in his brown eyes was more comforting to her than he could possibly know.

"What's embarrassing about your date going to the ladies' room? Everything is fine. I've ordered more wine and the waiter said our food should be arriving any minute."

He pulled out her chair and helped her into it as though nothing had happened. Emily-Ann couldn't possibly guess what he was actually thinking, but he was certainly making it easy to face him after the emotional debacle she'd pulled.

After he'd settled back into his own chair, she looked across the table at him. "Thank you, Tag. And I promise there won't be any more hysterics tonight."

"Forget it." He leveled an empathetic look at her. "To be honest, I'm glad you told me everything that you did. I understand you a little better now. There for a while I thought you didn't like me all that much."

She laughed and her reaction put a happy smile on his face. *Thank God*, she thought. Before she returned to the table, she was afraid he'd probably clamp a hand around her arm and lead her straight outside to his truck. And she wouldn't have blamed him. No man wanted to deal with an overwrought woman on their first date.

"I like you, Tag—a whole lot. And that outburst I had, it had nothing to do with you," she said, then promptly shook her head. "Well, that's not true. It had everything to do with you. Because I kept thinking I was ashamed for you to know about my life—my family. I thought you wouldn't want to be with me."

He reached across the table and squeezed her fingers. "I'm sorry that you ever thought such a thing. None of it makes any difference, Emily-Ann. I mean, I hate that your mother had her problems. But you know what I see when I look at you?"

She tightened her fingers around his. "No. Tell me."

"I see that your mother did a good job of raising her daughter."

She felt a part of her heart melting and she blinked her eyes as more tears threatened to appear. "That's the nicest thing anyone has ever said to me, Tag," she murmured. "I'll never forget it."

He started to reply, but the waiter suddenly arrived with their dinner, putting an end to the intimate moment. Still, Emily-Ann didn't mind the timing of the interruption. The night had just begun and she'd already stored away a lot of memories with this special man.

WHEN EMILY-ANN AND Taggart left Jose's, the night had cooled drastically and she draped the sweater she'd carried with her around her bare shoulders and buttoned the top button to hold it in place.

Taggart understood she needed protection from the cold, but throughout their meal, he'd loved the sight of her bare shoulders. She had that creamy complexion that most redheads possessed and the freckles that dotted the bridge of her nose and cheekbones also speckled her shoulders. Several times during dinner, he'd caught himself fantasizing about kissing all those tiny brown dots and wondering if they were on other parts of her body.

But the fantasy of making love to Emily-Ann was not something he could act upon. The last thing he wanted was for her to think that this time he was spending with her was a prelude to sex. Still, none of that stopped him from resting his hand against the small of her back as they walked slowly to his truck. And to his relief, she didn't move away.

"It's still early. Would you like to take a drive out on the desert?" he asked, as he helped her into the passenger seat.

"I'd love to," she answered. "There's some interesting scenery to the west. But you're the driver, you choose."

"West it is."

After he'd settled himself behind the steering wheel, Taggart drove away from the parking lot and turned onto a street that would eventually lead them to a main highway.

"I've not been in this direction yet," he said once the city of Wickenburg began to appear in the rearview mirror. "I've mostly just driven the highway between town and Three Rivers."

"It's pretty in any direction," she commented, then asked. "Have you ever been to Prescott or Phoenix?"

"No. But sooner or later, I'm sure I'll be going for one reason or another. Actually, Maureen and Blake were going to Prescott tonight for some sort of cattle buyer gathering."

"And they didn't ask you to go with them?"

He grinned. "No, thank goodness. I think they're taking pity on me because we've been so busy. And spring roundup is about to start. That keeps everyone tied down for a week or more."

"I'm glad you didn't have to go to the meeting."

He said, "I'm glad, too. But I feel a little guilty. The Hollisters gave me a huge bonus check today. It was a total surprise. To be honest, the amount of it blew me away."

"You don't think you deserved it?" she asked.

"Not yet." He grunted with wry disbelief. "Heck, I'm not worth that kind of money."

"I don't think you've quite yet absorbed the huge job you've taken on. But the Hollisters do and they clearly appreciate you and trust that you're going to do things right."

"Yeah, I suppose. But I felt very undeserving." He glanced over to see she was studying him with an earnest expression. The idea that she was interested in his job and that she cared enough to discuss it with him not only surprised him, it drew him to her in a way he'd not expected.

"That's the way I felt when you asked me out to dinner," she said. "Very humbled."

"Oh, Emily-Ann. I don't ever want you to feel that way. Not about me or anything else."

From the corner of his eye, he could see she was smiling at him.

"I don't ever want you to feel that way, either," she said. "So we're even."

After traveling several more miles westward on the lonely strip of asphalt, a large picnic area appeared on the right side of the highway. Three concrete tables and a trash receptacle were positioned among two tall saguaros and several Joshua trees. At the moment there didn't appear to be anyone around. In fact, there wasn't any kind of light suggesting civilization was anywhere nearby.

"Let's stop and stretch our legs," he suggested.

"Sounds nice."

He parked the truck to one side of the graveled area and helped Emily-Ann down from the truck. The night had grown even colder than when they'd left Jose's and she quickly pushed her arms into the sweater.

"If it's too chilly for you we can get back inside the truck," he suggested.

"Not at all. It feels good."

Anchoring a hand on the side of her waist, he guided her forward past the tables and over to one of the Joshua trees. To the north of them a ridge of mountains jutted upward toward the starlit sky.

"This is beautiful," he said.

She asked, "I know you said Three Rivers's property looks different than the Flying W where you used to work. But what about this area? Does it look anything like your old stomping ground in Texas?"

"No. The only thing similar is the vast openness."

"Did it snow there?"

"Yes. Sometimes we even had blizzards. That's when ranching is especially hard work."

She looked up at him. "It rarely ever snows here. But that's okay. I'm a terrible driver on slick roads."

Icy fear suddenly lodged in his throat and he outwardly shivered as he tried to swallow away the sensation.

"Tag? Are you okay?"

He wiped a hand over his face. "Yeah, sure. I was just thinking that you should always be careful when you're driving. I lost someone I cared about to a car accident. I don't want anything to happen to you."

"Oh."

As her gaze continued to slip over his face, he could see all sorts of questions in her eyes and Taggart prayed that she wouldn't quiz him. Someday he would tell her everything. But not tonight. Not when he was beginning to feel a change coming over him. A change that he desperately needed.

"Then I promise I'll be extra careful from now on," she said, then with a cheerful smile, changed the subject completely. "See that area to the north? Where the mountains are in the far, far distance?"

He followed the line of her pointed finger. "Yes."

"That's where lots of gold was found in the Congress Mine back in 1884. A town by the same name boomed there for many,

many years. But hardly anything is there now. And Constellation, another nearby mining town, is more or less a ghost town. Maybe you'd like to see them sometime? That is, if you like that sort of history. To me it's fascinating to think of all that sudden wealth and how it affected people back in those days when there was very little law and not much civilization."

"I'm sure there were a few men who were murdered for their gold," he said thoughtfully, then glanced down at her. "I would like to see the area sometime if you'd be willing to show me around."

"I'd like that," she said, then laughed. "Actually, one of the women who works at Chandler's clinic lives at Congress. And in her spare times she likes to pan for nuggets. Maybe we could hike up one of the canyons and try it. A good-sized nugget nowadays would buy new flooring for my living room."

He laughed. "That's a practical thought. But only one nugget would be enough?"

"I'm not greedy. Acquiring wealth never really was that important to me. Except…"

When her words trailed away, he looked down to see she was gazing wistfully out at the dark desert.

"Except what?"

"Oh, there were many times when my mother was alive that I wished I could have given her things and made her life easier. I did what I could, but I wish I could've done more." She turned her gaze up to his face. "Do you ever feel like that about your mother?"

He tried not to let the emptiness inside him show on his face. His mother had been the only real anchor he'd ever had in his life. When he'd lost her, it was like he'd drifted out in a big rough ocean with no way to swim back to shore.

"I used to. Before she died." His sigh could barely slip past the achy lump in his throat. "When Blake gave me the bonus check today, I couldn't help but think about her. She would've been amazed and proud. I wanted to change things for the better in her life, too. But her heart gave out before I had the chance."

She reached for his hand and, as the warmth of her fingers tightened around his, a sweet sort of contentment poured through him. The sensation was like nothing he'd ever felt and he wondered if he would ever experience it again. Or was this night something out of the ordinary and tomorrow all the magical feelings would vanish with the light of day?

"At first I didn't think the two of us had much in common," she said softly. "But I'm beginning to see that isn't entirely true."

With his hand still entwined with hers, he turned so that he was facing her. "We do have things in common and the best one is that we like each other's company. Don't we?"

She let out a long breath as her fingers tightened ever so slightly on his. "Yes, we do."

His free hand lifted and he touched the hair that framed part of her forehead. "You're a special woman, Emily-Ann. I want you to always remember that. Promise me that you will."

Starlight illuminated her face enough for him to see her lashes flutter and then her gaze latched on to his. The contact caused his stomach to clench.

"I promise," she whispered.

He allowed his fingers to drop to her cheek and as the tips moved ever so slightly against her petal-soft skin, he knew the rest of her would feel just as incredibly smooth.

"Emily-Ann," he said softly, "would you mind if I kissed you?"

Her gaze continued to cling to his and what he saw there caused his heart to hammer. She wanted him. Maybe just as much as he wanted her.

"I'd be disappointed if you didn't."

He drew in a sharp breath and then before he could change his mind or analyze the wisdom of his actions, he bent his head and softly placed his lips over hers.

She tasted just as good as she had the night of the party, yet somehow he managed to keep his passion tempered through-out the short kiss. Not for anything did he want her to get the idea that he had sex and only sex on his mind.

"That was nice," he murmured as he nuzzled her cheek with the tip of his nose. "Very nice."

Her tongue came out to nervously moisten her bottom lip. "Yes, it was. But I think we—uh, should head home now. I have an early morning scheduled and I'm sure you do, too."

In other words she wasn't going to give him, or herself, a chance to let a second kiss carry them away.

Well, that was good, Taggart thought. That was exactly how it needed to be. Until he was sure that she trusted him. More-over, that he could trust himself.

"You're right. We should be getting back to your place. I have to meet Matthew at the cattle barn at five thirty in the morning."

His hand still on hers, he gently turned her in the direction of the truck. As they walked slowly back to the vehicle, he was acutely aware of her hip brushing against the side of his leg and the flowery scent of her hair drifting up to his nostrils. Over the years, he'd forgotten all the little things that made a woman enticing. Having Emily-Ann so close was a reminder of all that he'd been missing as a man and he wondered how long he'd be able to keep his desire reined in and his common sense intact.

WHEN TAGGART ENTERED the cattle barn early the next morn-ing, Matthew hadn't yet arrived. But he found Chandler busy wrapping up a C-section on a young cow. Since the two ranch hands that were trying to assist him were inexperienced with the process, they were both relieved to see Taggart.

"Boy, are we glad to see you, Tag," Jerry, the taller of the two men told him. "Me and Flip are trying to take care of this little guy, but we've never done this before."

While Chandler continued to stitch the cow's uterus back to-gether, Taggart squatted over the newborn calf that was lying on a special bed to keep it warm. The mucus had already been cleaned from his nose and the rest of his body dried of afterbirth.

"He isn't struggling to breathe and you have him dry and warm. Looks like you've done things right so far," he told the two men.

"Yeah, but Doc says we'll have to see that he gets his mama's milk in the next couple of hours. That ain't gonna be easy," Flip said.

"Easy or not, the calf needs his mother's colostrum," Taggart told the men. "If the mother doesn't want to nurse we'll have to change her mind."

He turned back to Chandler, who'd already moved on to stitching the incision in the cow's flank.

"How is she, Doc?" Taggart asked.

Not bothering to look up, Chandler continued to stitch. "She'll be fine. And the calf doesn't appear to be too stressed. Hopefully, he'll stand within the hour."

Taggart glanced over at the black calf. "He looks big."

"Hell yes, he's far too big for this girl to give birth the normal way. I've been telling Blake the bull he has on this bunch of heifers is too large. I hope you can convince him to do something about it."

"He wants big healthy calves," Jerry spoke up in Blake's defense.

Chandler frowned at the ranch hand. "What good is that going to do if the mamas die trying to give birth to them?"

"I'll talk to him about it," Taggart assured Chandler. "But I'm not sure I'm the right person to convince him."

Chandler muttered a curse as he tied off the suture and poured antiseptic over the incision. "You're the foreman, Tag. It's your job to give him advice about the cattle."

"I know, but Blake is—"

"Not some sort of ranching god," Chandler insisted. "He's just the manager. He doesn't know everything."

Taggart heard shuffling feet behind him and looked over his

shoulder to see Jerry and Flip exchanging amused glances. They might think it funny to hear Chandler say Blake didn't know everything. But Taggart hardly found it amusing. He didn't want to get caught in a war of wills between the two brothers.

Taggart said, "I'll talk to him about the bull. If Blake is agreeable to the idea, we could exchange him with the one on the Buzzard Gap range. He's nicely built but a bit smaller."

"Good choice," Chandler said.

With his job finished, the vet gathered his tools and medications, then turned his attention to the calf. Taggart joined him and watched closely as Chandler checked the calf's vitals.

"Thank God his respiration is good." Hanging the stethoscope around his neck, he rose to his full height. "I wish TooTall was here. He's a wizard with calves like this."

"TooTall? Is he a ranch hand I haven't met?" Taggart asked.

"He's Matthew's foreman down on Red Bluff. They're also the best of friends. I don't know if it's because TooTall is Yavapai or what, but he understands livestock and instinctively knows how to care for them. As for this little guy, I'll have to leave him in your hands, Tag. I've got to get to the clinic, pick up Trey and be at the Rafter R Ranch by six thirty. And considering that place is twenty minutes west of Wickenburg, I'm going to be late."

Chandler started out of the barn in a long stride and Taggart called after him, "Don't worry. Doctors are never on time. And put the calf out of your mind. I'll see that he's taken care of."

IT WASN'T UNTIL the end of the day, after Taggart and Matthew had ridden back into the ranch yard, that Tag had a chance to stop by Blake's office.

Since he'd started working at Three Rivers, which had been about three weeks ago, he'd only been in the ranch manager's office a handful of times. He was already learning that his secretary, Flo, a redhead in her late sixties, had a louder bark than she did bite, and that Matthew and Holt were two of her pets.

Now, as Taggart stepped into the outer office where her desk was located at one end of the long room, the secretary peered over the tops of her bifocals at him.

"Hello, Tag. How's it going today?"

He took a moment to walk over to the woman's desk. So far he'd never seen the work space anywhere close to being tidy. Papers and envelopes, manila folders, and all types of pens and pencils were scattered across the desktop, along with several coffee mugs. Among the jumble was an up-to-date computer and monitor, but so far he had yet to see her using it.

"Busy. Very busy," he told her. "What about you?"

"It never lets up. And at this time of the year Holt gives me the task of filling out all the registration papers for the new foals." Tapping a pencil against the desktop, she regarded him with a thoughtful gaze. "Are you enjoying Three Rivers Ranch so far?"

"I am. The Hollisters are good people."

"You got that right," she said, then sighed. "I miss the heck out of Matthew, but he just had to go and get himself married. Good for him, but just terrible for my heart."

She laughed then and Taggart chuckled with her.

"I hope you're not thinking about getting married yet, Tag. I'm beginning to like you and I'd hate to see you go, too."

Him married? Before his mind could scoff away that idea, Emily-Ann was pushing her way into his thoughts. Not that she'd ever been that far away. All day long she'd been lurking at the edges of his mind, making it hard for him to focus.

"Rest easy, Flo. I don't have any kind of plans for matrimony. And even if I did, I wouldn't leave Three Rivers."

He was about to ask her if Blake was still in his office when a door leading into the man's private office opened and Blake stuck his head around the wooden panel.

"Flo, is—" He paused as he spotted Taggart standing in front of the secretary's desk. "Tag! I didn't know you were here. Did you stop by to see me or Flo?"

Taggart grinned at the secretary. "Well, Flo is much prettier than you. But I'm not sure she wants to talk about cows."

Flo batted a dismissive hand at the two men. "You two go talk about cows. I have work to do."

Blake motioned for Taggart to join him and he followed the ranch manager into his private office.

The room was furnished with plush leather furniture and decorated with all sorts of photos taken from different sections of the ranch. Some of them depicted huge herds of horses, while others were images of cattle grazing on desert mountain slopes and along the river's edge.

"Would you like some coffee? It's only two hours old," Blake said with a chuckle. "But I can have Jazelle bring us some fresh."

"Don't bother with that. I'm fine." He started toward one of the wooden chairs in front of Blake's desk, but detoured at the last moment when one particular photo on the wall caught his eye. It was a picture of a very old cabin shrouded by cottonwoods, pines and blooming sagebrush. "This is neat. I'm guessing it must be on the ranch somewhere."

"It's the original Three Rivers Ranch house. That's where my great great grandparents lived when they first arrived in Yavapai County."

Taggart was amazed. All along he'd assumed that the Hollisters had always had wealth. Obviously this photo proved that theory wrong.

"Are you saying the ranch started like this and grew into what it is today? That's incredible, Blake." He turned away from the photo to see Blake was sitting in the executive chair behind his desk. The wan smile on his tired face held a touch of pride.

"I agree. Sometimes I have to stop and remind myself that the ranch wasn't always like this." He shrugged one shoulder. "Actually, I think my great great grandfather came to Arizona planning to find a fortune in gold. But he didn't take to mining and soon figured out he could make money by raising beef to feed all the miners and people who'd flooded in to the area in search of wealth. And as it turned out, he figured right. The gold ran out, but the need for beef still remains."

Taggart sank into one of the chairs and propped his ankles out in front of him. He'd had a long day and it wasn't over yet. But when he listened to Blake talk about his ancestors and the beginning of the ranch, he realized that he'd become a part of something bigger than he could've ever imagined. It was a heady feeling for the little boy who'd once worn hand-me-down clothes and helped his mother stuff rags around the window facings to keep the dust and cold wind from blowing into their house.

"The man obviously had a vision," Taggart remarked.

"Yeah. And sometimes not following the crowd takes courage," Blake said, then lifted a brow in his direction. "But you didn't come by to talk about the history of the Hollisters and Three Rivers. What's on your mind?"

"Bulls. And calves," he said bluntly. "Chandler had to perform another C-section this morning. The fourth one out of that particular head of heifers. I understand that four is a mighty small number when you're dealing with thousands, but the way I see it, each cow and calf is important."

"Damn right each one is important." He swiped a hand over his face. "I haven't had a chance to talk to Chandler today. Is the cow/calf pair okay?"

Taggart nodded. "The cow is in fine shape. The calf is a little weak, but he's coming around. I have Flip and Jerry caring for him."

Blake's brows pulled together in a frown. "And that's two men you could use elsewhere."

"I'm not concerned about being shorthanded."

"Then you're worried that more C-sections are going to be needed." He rose from the chair and walked over to a small table holding a coffee maker and all the fixings. After he poured himself a cup of the black liquid, he carried it over to a long leather couch and sank onto the end cushion. "Last year I took a chance and put Rambler—that's the bull on Juniper Flats—on that particular herd of heifers. Every rancher wants big healthy calves and I was hoping there wouldn't be problems. Looks like I made the wrong choice."

"I wouldn't say you made the wrong choice," Taggart reasoned. "A man has to take chances if he ever expects to get what he wants."

Grimacing, Blake sipped the coffee. "True. But in this case it looks like I need to make another choice."

Taggart shifted uncomfortably on the chair. "I'd like to make a suggestion. That we move the bull that's presently on the Buzzard Gap range to the heifers' pasture. His size would be much more compatible. I think it would cut down on the number of difficult births."

Blake leveled a knowing look at him. "You've been talking to Chandler about this."

"Only this morning when he was finishing up the surgery. But if you're thinking I'm here to be Doc's voice, you're wrong. I'm speaking for the welfare of the heifers and babies."

"Well, I'll tell you, Tag, Mom and I hired you because of your experience and knowledge. We value and welcome your opinion."

While Blake leaned back against the couch and thoughtfully considered the situation, Taggart rubbed a hand against the stubble on his jaw. His face hadn't seen a razor since last night, before he'd picked up Emily-Ann. But he'd never liked shaving and avoided the task as long as he could. If he looked grungy now, he doubted the ranch manager cared.

"All right, Tag, I'm going to go along with your suggestion. Even though part of the breeding season has already taken place, it might save us problems on down the line."

More relieved than he cared to admit, Taggart thanked him and the two men went on to discuss how and when to move the bulls. Once everything was decided, Taggart stood.

"I've taken up enough of your time," Taggart told him, then

glanced at his watch. "You've probably missed dinner with your family."

Blake chuckled. "The twins are always waiting to join me, so their daddy never eats alone," he said. "And speaking of dinners, how did yours go with Emily-Ann last night?"

With everything Blake had to deal with, Taggart hadn't expected Blake to remember about the date with Emily-Ann, much less ask about it.

"It was good. I enjoyed it and I think she did, too."

Blake nodded with approval. "Glad to hear it. She deserves a nice guy like you."

She certainly deserved a nice guy, Taggart silently agreed. But he could hardly put himself in that category. Not when half of his thoughts about Emily-Ann were far from nice. In fact, they were downright naughty.

Clearing his throat, Taggart said, "Emily-Ann deserves the best. But I—I'm not really in the market for anything serious."

Crossing his arms across his chest, he studied Taggart for a long moment. "Dear God, don't tell me you're like Holt used to be."

"How's that?" Taggart asked.

Blake snorted. "Too many women and not enough time. That was Holt's motto—until he met Isabelle. I didn't know a man could be that transformed until I saw it with my own eyes."

Taggart was as far from a womanizer as a man could get. And he sure couldn't picture himself as a husband or daddy. Not now. With a shake of his head, he said, "I don't think I need to be transformed. Not like Holt."

Laughing, Blake shooed him toward the door. "You must be tired. Get on out of here."

Taggart left the office and as he shut the door behind him, he saw Flo still working diligently over a ledger book. Did people still use those things? Apparently, she did.

Not bothering to glance up, Flo said, "I heard laughter. You must have said something really funny to make Blake laugh."

"Just a little something about my love life, Flo."

That brought her head up and as she stared at him with her mouth open, Taggart hurried out of the office.

Chapter Six

"Oh, look at that yellow-print dress! It's adorable!" Camille exclaimed as she and Emily-Ann paused on the sidewalk to peer in the plate glass window of Cactus and Candles Boutique. "You would look great in it!"

Emily-Ann groaned. "I don't have the waistline for that. But you do."

"Don't be silly. You have curves from here to yonder and the belt at the waistline will show them off. Now me, I have no waist at all right now."

"Well, not at the moment," Emily-Ann told her as she eyed Camille's very pregnant belly. "But you'll have one soon. Come on, let's go in and you buy the dress for yourself. It'll look great with a pair of cowboy boots."

Laughing, Camille grabbed her by the hand and the two women went into the little boutique.

An hour later, they came out with Emily-Ann carrying two sacks filled with dresses, shoes and fashion jewelry.

"You shouldn't have bought these things for me," Emily-Ann continued to argue as she loaded the items into the back seat of Camille's truck. "I thought we came out this afternoon to spend time together, not your money."

"Oh, pooh, I didn't spend that much. And if I can't buy

my friend something once in a while, then what good is having money?" Camille said as she slipped behind the steering wheel. "Besides, do you know how often I go shopping for girly things?"

"I doubt very often," Emily-Ann said as she climbed into the passenger seat and fastened her seat belt. "From what you say, you're usually at the diner, or working on the baby's nursery. And what about that sweet little tot you're carrying? There's a children's store on the next block. It has all sorts of clothing and toys and baby furniture. Let's go in there and I'll pick out something for him."

"Whoa, did you say *him*?"

Emily-Ann grinned. "I did. A boy is what I think it's going to be. Why? Do you or Matthew want a girl?"

Smiling, Camille reversed the truck onto the street. "Well, I think a girl would be nice. After all, I have four brothers and only one sister. As for Matthew, it doesn't matter to him. I think he's already got it in his head that we're going to have a dozen babies."

"Uh, that might be kind of hard on you, don't you think?"

Camille laughed. "Well, twelve was kind of an exaggeration on my part. But I know he wants at least two or three children and so do I."

Emily-Ann looked over at her friend. "I can't imagine how you must feel, Camille. To have Matthew love you like he does and to know you're going to have his baby. You must feel like you're floating on a cloud or something."

Spotting the sign of the children's store hanging beneath the awning over the sidewalk, Emily-Ann pointed to an empty parking spot. "There's the store. Pull in here."

Camille parked the truck, but kept the motor and the air-conditioning running as she turned on the seat to look at Emily-Ann. "Before we go in I want to say something about your floating-on-a-cloud idea. Marriage isn't a big party where everything is fun and perfect."

Emily-Ann grimaced. "I might be scatterbrained at times, but I have sense enough to know that nothing in life is perfect. Including people and marriages. God knows I had to watch Mom suffer through years of a worthless husband. But you're very happy, Camille. And you do have a man who loves you."

"You're right on both counts. But that doesn't mean every day is smooth sailing. I'm busy trying to keep the diner a profit, while planning for the baby. And Matthew is working long hours to build up Red Bluff. But," she added with a dreamy grin, "we're doing it all together. And that makes everything worthwhile."

Shaking her head, she said, "If you're trying to give me marriage advice, Camille, you're wasting your time. It's going to take more than your bridal bouquet to find me a good man. It'll take a miracle."

Camille reached over and pressed Emily-Ann's hand between both of hers. "This life I have with Matthew—that's what I want for you, Emmie. To have someone who loves you. Someone you can share the good and bad times with. I know it will happen for you if you just let it."

The image of Taggart's handsome face suddenly floated to the front of Emily-Ann's mind, yet to imagine a man such as him loving her, sharing his life with her seemed impossible.

Three days had passed since he'd taken her to Jose's for dinner and she'd not seen or heard from him even once. But that discouraging fact wasn't enough to get the man's kiss out of her mind. And he had kissed her. Oh yes. The memory of when they'd stood beneath the Joshua tree and he'd pulled her into his arms was still achingly fresh in her mind. But apparently it had been a forgettable moment for him. Otherwise, he would have surely contacted her by now.

Determined not to let Taggart O'Brien ruin this evening with her friend, she purposely put on a cheery face. Not for anything did she want Camille to guess that she was pining foolishly over something she couldn't have.

"I'll try to let it happen. And maybe one day it will. Right now I'm just thrilled for you," she said, then tugged on her hand. "Now come on. Let's go buy the kid something he can have fun with later on."

Camille laughed. "You're saying *he* again. I might as well give up and accept the fact that we're going to have a son. That's what TooTall has been saying all along anyway. And you can't argue with that guy's predictions."

"Oh yes. TooTall is the mystic Yavapai. The one who kept telling Matthew he was going to marry you." She thoughtfully tapped a finger against her chin. "Wonder what kind of prediction he'd make for me?"

"Hmm. Probably that once you become a nurse you're going to fall in love and marry a handsome doctor."

Emily-Ann burst out laughing. "I wouldn't take a doctor if you handed him to me on a silver platter. If he wasn't working, he'd always have his patients on his mind. Just give me a good ole Joe. Preferably, one with a heart."

Rolling her eyes, Camille cut the motor and reached for her handbag. "You know what's wrong with you, Emmie? When it comes to men you're just too picky."

Laughing again, Emily-Ann opened the truck door. "Come on. Let's see if we can find junior a pair of miniature chaps like his daddy wears."

BY THE TIME Taggart left Hollister Animal Clinic and pulled into Emily-Ann's driveway, it was nearing eight thirty. He doubted she would be in bed at such an early hour, but he also realized it was rather late to make an unexpected visit. But three days had passed since their date and he'd waffled about contacting her. If she slammed the door in his face, he couldn't blame her.

A short moment after he knocked on the door, he saw the flutter of a curtain at the window, then the rattle of the doorknob.

"Tag!" she exclaimed, as she pulled the door wide. "Is something wrong at the ranch?"

Bemused, he asked, "You think something has to be wrong for me to drop by and say hello?"

She hesitated for only a second. "Well—uh—no. I'm just surprised to see you, that's all. Please come in."

He stepped into the room and waited for her to deal with the door before he spoke. "I apologize for coming by so late. I did try to call you a couple of times, but the signal on my phone kept failing. I had to bring a mare to Doc's clinic this evening and I just got away from there."

She stood with her hands folded in front of her, surveying him with uncertainty in her eyes. It was obvious she still didn't trust his motives and that frustrated the heck out of him. But maybe she had a right to be suspicious of him, Taggart thought. Especially when he didn't know himself just where his feelings for Emily-Ann were headed.

She said, "You and the Hollisters keep late hours."

"That's part of the job," he said, as he took in the pretty picture she made in a dark red skirt and white blouse. "Were you— er—busy? I don't want to interrupt."

"You're not interrupting. In fact, I was just about to make myself a sandwich. Would you care to join me? Or have you already eaten?"

Relieved that she was inviting him to stay, he took off his hat and raked fingers through his flattened hair. "A sandwich would be great. I haven't eaten since early this morning."

She motioned for him to follow her. "Come with me to the kitchen."

On the way out of the living room, he dropped his hat on an end table, then trailed her through a short hallway that led off in three different directions. A wide door directly in front of them was open and as she entered the brightly lit space, he could see it was an old-fashioned kitchen with knotty pine cabinets and a single white porcelain sink.

A stack of books was piled at one end of the farm table and

she quickly began moving them to the far end of the cabinet counter.

"I've been studying for a test. Human anatomy. The last one I made a B, but I'm afraid this one is going to be much harder," she said, then gestured for him to take a seat. "Make yourself comfortable and I'll get the sandwich makings."

"I can help if you'll tell me what to do," he offered.

"Thanks, but I can manage."

She opened the refrigerator and bent down to the crisper. Taggart couldn't bring himself to look away from the rounded shape of her bottom and the way the fabric of the skirt clung to the tempting curves.

He drew in a deep breath and let it out. "Do you normally eat this late?"

"No," she answered, with her head still half-hidden in the refrigerator. "After I closed the shop this afternoon I went out with Camille on a little shopping venture and she insisted we go for milkshakes. So I'm just now getting a bit hungry."

After piling packages of lunchmeat and cheese onto the cabinet counter, she glanced over her shoulder at him. "What about you? You didn't have time to stop for supper?" she asked.

"No. Everyone on the ranch has been very busy. We're getting ready for spring roundup and that takes all hands and the cook."

"Yes, I've heard Camille talk about those days. She and Vivian used to go help." She gathered more items from the refrigerator and shut the door. As she washed a tomato and a head of lettuce at the sink, she said, "I haven't heard from you since we went to Jose's. I'd pretty much decided you probably didn't want to see me anymore."

"Why would I decide that?" he asked, while feeling like a heel. Not that he owed her any explanations. It wasn't like they were a couple or anything. But it was like Blake had implied, Emily-Ann deserved a nice guy. She deserved to be respected and he wasn't giving her that by ignoring her. Nor was he being a nice guy by leading her along to nowhere.

"Personal reasons," she said frankly. "What else?"

Taggart couldn't bear the distance between them. Not while she was talking as though there was nothing between them except a meal and a bit of conversation. Damn it, he'd kissed her. Had she already forgotten that? Or did she have the idea that a kiss meant nothing to him?

How could she possibly figure out what you're thinking? About kissing or anything else, Taggart? She doesn't know who you really are. You haven't told her about Becca or the baby, or any of the things that are still twisting your vision of the future.

Heaving out a heavy breath, he walked over to where she stood. "Well, I could say I've been working overtime and I wouldn't be lying. But that doesn't mean I couldn't have pulled out my phone and sent you a text."

Her gaze locked on the task of slicing the tomato onto a plate, she said, "That notion did cross my mind. But you've mentioned before that you don't like phones. And anyway, it's all okay, Tag. You don't owe me explanations or anything. It's not like we'd planned to see each other again."

Her casual attitude stung him. Which was really stupid. That's the way he wanted things to be with Emily-Ann. Simple and easy with no ties or promises. So why did he want to grab her and hold on? So he could be hurt all over again? And possibly hurt her, too?

Shoving away that dismal thought, he said, "I didn't call or send a message because I've been telling myself that the best thing I could ever do for you is to never see you again. I mean—as in a date."

She dropped the knife and turned to face him. "Why? Because you thought about all those things I told you about my mother? About the irresponsible bastard who fathered me?"

Frowning, he gently placed his hands on her shoulders. "No! You're not even close. The doubts are inside of me, Emily-Ann. I think you ought to know that when it comes to women—well, several years ago some things happened in my life that changed everything for me. Now, I honestly don't think I could ever be a husband to any woman. And I don't believe I'm supposed to be a father. So you see, if we started dating and getting close... it...wouldn't be fair or right for you."

Her eyes darkened as she continued to stare at him. "Then why did you ask me out in the first place? Why in hell did you kiss me?"

His fingers tightened on her shoulders and it suddenly struck him that trying to be a nice guy was the toughest challenge he'd ever faced. "Because I like you. Because I was lonely and wanted company. Your company. And why do you think I kissed you? You're damned desirable, Emily-Ann. And I'm not made of steel."

"Here's a revelation for you. I'm not made of steel either," she muttered.

Groaning, he said, "Now you're angry with me."

A resigned look came over her face and then she turned away from him and walked to the end of the cabinets. As she pulled out plates and glasses, she said, "No. I'm not angry with you, Tag. In fact, I want to thank you for being honest and not leading me down a dead-end street. That's more than I've ever gotten from other men. It's just that the other night—when we were together—I honestly began to think you might be different. I was wrong. But that's okay, too. I've been a fool before. Many times."

She looked at him and smiled, but the expression didn't reach her eyes. Actually, everything about it said she was looking at the biggest disappointment she'd ever seen in the shape of a man. Until this moment Taggart didn't know it was possible to feel lower than a heel, but he did. He was now on the level of a snake.

"But that doesn't mean we can't still be friends," she told him, then held up a hand as he took a step toward her. "But no kissing. No romance. No ideas that we're going to be a couple. Ever."

He felt sick inside. He felt like he'd been hammered and

nailed and tossed aside like a horseshoe that couldn't bend to a shape that would fit.

"That's—uh—fine with me, Emily-Ann. We can be friends and not hurt each other."

"Right. I'm good at being a friend. Not so good at being a lover."

Lover. His lover. Dear Lord, he had to be the biggest hypocrite walking the earth. He was standing here trying to pretend that he wasn't aching to take her to bed right this minute. But having sex with her wouldn't work. No. Not now or ever.

He tried to smile, but the best he could do was twist his lips to a lopsided slant. "Now that we have all that settled, let's have that sandwich. What do you say?"

She didn't smile back at him. Nor did she bother looking him in the eye. Instead, she quickly turned back to the cabinet. "I say the sandwiches are coming right up. And I've changed my mind, you can help by getting ice for the glasses and putting the plates on the table."

Well, that was that, he thought. She knew where he stood and he understood how she felt about it. Problem solved. All he needed to do now was to figure out how to get rid of the empty feeling in the middle of his chest.

With a silent sigh, he rose to his feet and joined her at the cabinet.

IT WAS SILLY of her to feel deflated, Emily-Ann thought, as she choked down the last bite of ham-and-cheese sandwich. From the very first, she'd known that she didn't have the slightest chance of having any kind of meaningful relationship with Taggart. Even after their evening at Jose's and that kiss on the desert, she'd continually told herself not to set her dreams on the man. She wasn't his kind of woman. And heaven knew he wasn't her kind of man.

And yet, her heart was heavy with disappointment. Maybe if Taggart had been the first man to tell her he wasn't the marrying kind, she could shrug the whole thing off. But now she had to add him to a long list of guys who'd been too commitment shy to give her a serious thought. It was something that had happened to her over and over. And in spite of Camille's optimism that Emily-Ann would find true love someday, she was beginning to accept the fact it wasn't meant for her. Just as it hadn't been meant for her mother.

Rising from her seat at the table, she went over to the cabinet and began filling a coffee maker with grounds and water. "If I'd known you were going to drop by I could've had something better than sandwiches for you. But I do have a few fried apple pies—if you'd like one for dessert."

"No. I've already eaten two sandwiches and most of your potato chips. I don't want to eat up all your groceries," he said.

Shaking her head, she opened a flat plastic container and placed three of the small pies onto a paper plate. "I can't eat them all. Besides, you bought my dinner the other night. So we're even on the groceries. Sort of. You got the short end of the stick."

He smiled at her. "I don't think so."

Grabbing two mugs from the cabinet, she filled them with coffee and carried them and the plate of pies over to the table.

"Did you make these?" he asked as she placed one of the pies onto his plate.

She chuckled. "No. Don't worry. Conchita made these for the shop. Fried pies are something she doesn't do on a daily basis. Just whenever she gets the urge. I'm not that good of a cook. I can do simple things like spaghetti or pork chops and mashed potatoes. I do try brownies once in a while, but they usually turn out like rubber. Conchita tells me I'm cooking them too long. Easy for her to say. She's cooked for fifty years."

"Mmm. The pie is delicious," he said. "And so is the coffee."

She gave him a wry smile. "At least I'm good at that."

He consumed the pie and she motioned for him to take another. "They're small. And I don't want to be tempted. So please eat all of them."

While he continued to eat, she asked, "Was the mare you brought into the clinic injured or something? I hope she's going to be okay."

"She doesn't have any kind of injury. Holt wanted a few tests done on her that Doc could only perform at the clinic. She lost her first foal, so he wants to make sure everything is well with her before he breeds her again."

"It was nice of you to haul her to the clinic for him. I'm sure Holt wants to spend as much time as he can with Isabelle and baby Carter."

Taggart sipped his coffee. "I'm not so sure Holt was going straight home. He wanted to use the extra time to have a talk with Blake. I think the brothers are trying to figure out the situation with Gil and their mother."

Emily-Ann shrugged. "What's to figure out? Gil has moved back and he wants to spend time with Maureen. That's the way I see it."

"Yes, but he's moved into the ranch house with the rest of the family."

"Makes sense to me, too," Emily-Ann said. "The house is huge. Even with Blake and Chandler living there with their families, there's still plenty of room."

Nodding, he said, "On the surface it should be that simple. The way I see it, if Maureen wants to be close to her late husband's brother, then that's her business. Not Blake's or Holt's or anyone else's. But from what Doc has conveyed to me, the brothers are still trying to solve the mystery of Joel's death."

"Don't you mean murder?" she asked grimly, then shook her head. "I realize the family doesn't come out and say those words in front of just any and everybody. But Camille and I have discussed it. And Isabelle has also talked to me about the situation. She says Holt is haunted over the circumstances of his father's death. Camille says the same thing about Matthew."

Nodding soberly, he said, "Losing a loved one is bad all around. But I figure the not knowing makes it even harder for the Hollisters, Gil included. After all, the man lost his brother. Being a detective for thirty years makes Blake and his brothers wonder if he's really come back to Three Rivers to do some investigating of his own, or if he's only interested in their mother."

"Maybe he's interested in both," Emily-Ann reasoned. "I didn't talk to the man that much the night of the party, but he seems very sincere. I only wish—"

He arched an inquisitive brow at her. "What do you wish?"

She looked away from him and sighed. "Only that my mother could've had a man like him in her life."

"Did your mother ever marry?" he asked.

Glancing back at him, she nodded. "Yes, once. Gorman Smith was a salesman from California. Somehow he ended up here in Wickenburg—that was about the time I turned a year old. Back then I think he sold tires or cars. Later on, he turned to selling insurance policies. But never had much money to show for it."

"Where is he now?"

"I have no idea and I'll be happy to keep it that way. As a stepfather, he wasn't abusive or anything. He was just mostly absent, if you know what I mean. The neighbor next door was more of a father to me than Gorman ever was." She clutched her coffee cup and tried to keep her emotions in check. "Iris thought he could do no wrong and when he talked about all of his big dreams, she honestly believed he was going to achieve them. She was always telling me that someday Gorman was going to make our lives much better."

"Did your mother love the man?"

Emily-Ann stared into her coffee cup. "That's the saddest part about it. She loved him with all her heart."

"I don't see that as sad, Emily-Ann. Loving the man must have made her happy, otherwise she would've kicked him out."

Lifting her gaze to his, she said, "Mom didn't know any better. She was gullible and softhearted and Gorman used that to his advantage. A week hadn't passed after her death when he packed up and lit out."

His eyes narrowed as he studied her face. "Were you grown then?"

"I was eighteen and had just graduated high school. So I suppose I qualified as an adult. I tell you one thing, I was better off with him gone than I would've been with him sitting around drinking beer and bragging about his next moneymaking scheme."

"I'm sorry, Emily-Ann," he said quietly. "I wish it had been different for you and your mother. But you're still very young. You can make your life what you want it to be."

No, Emily-Ann thought. It was impossible to make a man love her if he didn't want to. But then that kind of self-pitying attitude was not going to get her anywhere. In fact, she needed to be smart enough to see that she didn't need a man in her life to make her happy. She didn't need babies like the Hollister families were having right and left. After all, she was going to be a nurse. The profession would provide all the caring and nurturing she needed to feel fulfilled.

"You're so right. And I want to be a nurse. Anything else, I'll leave up to fate."

Rising from her seat, she began to clear the remains of their light supper from the tabletop.

Taggart rose, too, and carried his empty plate and cup over to the sink. "Fate isn't always kind, Emily-Ann."

"Neither are some people."

"I suppose you're talking about me now," he said.

She twisted open the hot water knob and dropped the stopper into the sink. As it filled, she glanced over to see a frown on his face. Both his expression and remark surprised her.

"Why no. I don't think you're unkind at all, Tag."

"Well, I feel very unkind and very phony." His frown was more like a look of anguish as he stepped toward her. "I'm a hypocrite, a liar and a coward to boot. A while ago when I told you I didn't want us to be anything more than friends I was lying. Hell, even as I was speaking the words, I wanted to make love to you."

Make love or have sex. She didn't know which one he meant and her mind was spinning at such a rapid speed she couldn't begin to absorb everything he'd just said. But she had managed to latch on to one key word. *Want*. He wanted her.

"If that's the way you honestly feel, then why did you lie to me?"

Groaning, he wrapped his hands over her shoulders. "I was trying to be a gentleman and do the right thing. Blake says you deserve a nice guy and he's right. You deserve a good man and everything he can give you. But I—" He paused and shook his head with defeat. "These past few minutes I've come to realize that I'm too selfish to give you up to some other man. I want to be the guy who holds you, kisses you—makes love to you."

By the time the last of his huskily spoken words had passed his lips, he was drawing her into the tight circle of his arms and Emily-Ann's heart began to thump so hard and fast she felt light-headed.

Her breathing turned to shallow sips as she dared to flatten her hands against his chest and slide them slowly and surely up to his shoulders. "I lied, too, Taggart. I don't want to be just your friend. I want to be everything to you."

Desire flashed in his brown eyes before his head dropped and his face hovered so close to hers that she could see the pores in his skin, the tiny lines marking his lips.

"Everything," he murmured. "Yes. That's what I want, too."

His soft breath caressed her cheeks and lips and she closed her eyes against the onslaught of sensations rippling over her skin.

She whispered his name but that was all she could manage to say before his lips settled perfectly over hers.

The contact was instant combustion and as his mouth created a firestorm upon her lips, flames spread throughout her body, scorching every spot, every cell it touched.

Beyond the incredible heat washing through her, she was aware of the hard band of his arms tightening around her, drawing her ever closer to the hard wall of his body. Yet it was his kiss that continued to monopolize her senses.

She wanted more. And as his tongue prodded at the opening between her teeth, she realized he felt the same. She opened her mouth to welcome him inside and he immediately began a slow search of the ribbed roof and sharp edges of her teeth. The erotic exploration was more than enough to set off an ache deep between her thighs and, with a needy groan, she wrapped her arms around him and allowed herself to become lost in the total domination of his kiss.

Somehow, her swirling senses managed to register the loud thump of her heartbeat, the humming of the refrigerator and the faint tick of the clock hanging on the wall near the table. Outside the window, the branches of an ash tree scraped against the glass. Strange that she could be aware of all these things and yet not know how much time had marched by since he'd taken her into his arms.

She didn't have a clue as to whether the embrace had gone on for short seconds or several long minutes. Nor did she recognize how the kiss had grown into something far deeper, until his hands latched on to the sides of her hips and pulled them tightly against his. The bulge of his erection straining against his jeans was evidence that he wanted her as much as she wanted him.

She was wrapping her arms around his neck and trying to press herself even closer when he suddenly tore his mouth from hers and stepped back. The unexpected break was so abrupt, Emily-Ann very nearly staggered backward and into the wall of cabinets.

Darting a confused glance at him, she could see he was breathing hard and staring at her with dark, narrowed eyes.

"Tag, what's wrong?" Fearing he was about to bolt from the

kitchen, she latched a hand over his forearm. "If you try to tell me that you don't want me, I'll know you're lying. Because you do. Just as much as I want you."

A look of torment came over his face and then he rested his forehead against hers. Emily-Ann couldn't resist slipping her arms around his waist.

"I'm sorry, Emily-Ann. I realize I probably look like an ass to you—or something far worse. But this isn't how I want things for us. I want our time together to be right—special. Not acted out on a hurried whim."

Our time together. The words rolled around in her head, but she dared not take them to heart.

"And how are you going to feel tomorrow, or the next day?" she asked. "Are you going to change your mind again about me—us?"

As she waited for him to answer, she could only think how she didn't want to let him go. She wanted to lead him to her bedroom, shut the door and not let him out until the morning sun was shining through the window.

A wry smile touched his lips. "It wouldn't make any difference if I did. I can't stay away from you. Tonight proves it."

God only knew how very much she wanted to believe him, but so far he'd not done much to help her build any kind of trust.

The doubts circling her thoughts must have shown on her face because he frowned and shook his head.

"You don't believe me," he said.

A sudden feeling of hopelessness washed over her and it cooled the last remnants of the hot desire she'd felt only moments ago. "It's hard to trust you, Tag, when one minute you're hot and the next you're cold. You tell me you want to stay away from me and then you tell me you lied."

She slowly turned away from him and walked over to the table where the last of the leftovers of their meal remained. As she plucked up the bread and a basket of potato chips, he came up behind her and slipped his arms around her waist. His warm body lightly touched hers and she did her best to keep the traitorous stirring in her body far away from the region of her heart.

"Emily-Ann, I don't want to be like the other men who've let you down. I'm trying to be honest," he said, his voice muffled by her hair. "But we've not known each other all that long and it would be wrong of me to start making promises that I can't keep."

Some things happened in my life that changed everything for me.

What could have happened? If it was affecting him that much, why didn't he want to share it with her? She wanted to question him, to demand that he explain. But something told her that now was the wrong time to try to peel away the curtain where he'd hidden his past. Besides, if he ever did truly start to care for her, she wouldn't have to push him to share those things inside him. He'd tell her all on his own.

I know it will happen for you if you just let it.

Camille's advice joined Emily-Ann's tumbling thoughts and suddenly she realized what her dear friend had been trying to tell her. If she ever expected to find love, she was going to have to open her heart and take a chance.

Smiling softly, she turned and looked up at him. "I understand, Tag. Really."

Surprise widened his eyes. "You do?"

Nodding, she reached up and smoothed a finger over the day-old whiskers on his face. "I do. Because I—I'm a little mixed-up. Part of me wants you with a vengeance, while the other part wants to run until I put miles and miles between us."

His sigh was a sound of relief. "That sort of describes what's been going on with me." His hands wrapped gently over her shoulders. "We can figure this out, Emily-Ann. We just need time—together."

"I like the sound of that," she told him.

He bent his head and placed a soft, swift kiss on her lips. "It's not polite to eat and run. But it's getting late and I have a long drive back to Three Rivers." Lifting a hand, he traced fingertips along her cheekbone. "And if I continue to stay I might not be able to leave."

With a clever smile, she looped her arm through his. "And I might not let you leave. So I'll walk you to the door."

Out in the living room, he let himself out and Emily-Ann stood in the open doorway and watched as he crossed the small porch.

When he reached the bottom of the steps, he turned and lifted a hand in farewell. "I'll call you soon," he promised.

She laughed softly. "This from a man who dislikes phones?"

"If it gives me a chance to hear your voice I can deal with it for a few minutes." He shot her a smile, then disappeared into the shadows shrouding the driveway. After a moment, his truck fired to life and then he was driving away.

Emily-Ann watched until she could no longer see his taillights in the distance, then walked thoughtfully through the house until she reached the kitchen. And as she finished cleaning up the remnants of their meal, she prayed that Taggart wasn't going to make a mess of her heart.

Chapter Seven

With his back propped against a desert willow, Taggart stared into the low flames of the campfire and listened to the distant sound of a ranch hand singing along to the rhythmic twangs of a guitar. The last calf had been turned loose at the branding fire two hours ago. The horses had been fed, watered and confined in a simple rope corral the cowboys had erected next to the wall of a rock bluff. The long day's work had finally ended.

The cowboy's song trailed away, but plenty of sounds remained to fill the silence of the night. A hoot owl joined the crackle of the flames, while in the far distance coyotes yipped and howled.

I've heard that coyotes mate for life.

Even when Emily-Ann had been talking about the wild animals, he'd caught a dreamy, romantic note in her voice. She wanted to think and believe that there was such a thing as true love that lasted forever. But he figured her past held her back from truly believing she'd ever be a part of such a union. Just like his past was throwing up a thick wall every time he tried to picture a long-term future with her.

There were some people that weren't ever meant to live a happily-ever-after, he decided, as he closed his eyes and rubbed fingertips against the weary lids. He didn't know if Emily-Ann was one of those misfortunate few, but he definitely figured he was. Why else would Becca and the baby have been taken away from him so cruelly and suddenly?

He'd been sitting there for several long minutes, his thoughts drifting, when a familiar voice sounded nearby.

"Tag, are you asleep?"

Roused by the question, Taggart opened his eyes to see Chandler standing a few feet away. Since the veterinarian hadn't worked roundup today, he was surprised that the man had driven several miles from the ranch house to join them here at camp tonight.

"I wasn't asleep. Just resting my eyes. I think the hot sun has burned holes in both of them." Taggart slowly pushed himself away from the tree. "What are you doing here? Blake told me you had a heavy day scheduled at the clinic."

"I had a hell of a whopper day at the clinic," he told him. "But it all went well. I came out tonight because Holt and Blake wanted to talk. While Mom isn't here," he added pointedly.

Since they'd started the roundup five days ago, this was the first and only night that Maureen hadn't remained in camp. This evening a couple of hours before dark, she'd ridden back to the ranch to deal with some paperwork that Flo couldn't put off any longer.

"Is anything wrong?" Taggart asked.

Chandler grimaced. "Nothing is wrong. We just rather her not know that her sons are putting their heads together—behind her back, that is."

"I'm sorry. I don't understand. I thought Maureen knew everything about the ranch."

"She does. But this isn't about the ranch. It's about Dad."

"Oh." Taggart reached for his hat lying near his thigh and levered it back onto his head. As he rose from his seat on the ground, he asked, "Is there something you need for me to do?"

"Yes, there is. We want you to join us. We all figure that

you're a part of this family now and it wouldn't be good if you didn't know and understand what's going on."

Glancing around, Taggart noticed that sometime during his drowsy musings, the last of the men had slipped away from the fire to hit their waiting bedrolls.

"Damn, Doc, I'm just the foreman. I don't have any right to sit in on a family meeting."

Chandler frowned at him. "If you had known Dad you would've loved him and he would've felt the same about you. And don't ever let any of us hear you say you're *just* the foreman. That's not the way we are here on Three Rivers. We're family."

Seeing that Chandler was completely sincere, Taggart felt humbled. "All right. Since you put it that way, I'd be honored to sit in."

At the opposite end of the night camp, a chuck wagon and a large tent sat near a huge mesquite tree. A paint horse was tied to a nearby picket line and Taggart recognized it as the late Joel Hollister's personal horse. The one he'd been on when he'd met his death.

"That's Major Bob. How did he get here?" Taggart questioned him about the horse, while thinking Chandler had surely driven one of the four-wheel drive vehicles from the ranch yard.

"I rode him over. Major Bob loves spring roundup and since he's getting a bit of age on him, we don't want to use him hard every day. I'm going to leave him for Mom to ride tomorrow and I'll ride one of the extra mounts back to the ranch tonight. That will make her and Major Bob happy."

And one of the first things Taggart had learned since he'd arrived at Three Rivers Ranch was that one of the main priorities of the Hollister brothers was making their mother happy.

Chandler motioned for Taggart to follow him into the tent and once they were inside, he saw that Blake, Holt and Joseph were sitting in folding chairs along the east wall of the tent, while opposite from them, Gil had taken a seat on the edge of a sleeping cot.

"You guys look like you're getting ready for a poker game where gambling isn't allowed," Chandler attempted to joke as he handed Taggart a folding chair.

"I wish," Joseph said with a grunt, then glanced at Taggart. "Welcome, Tag, glad you're here."

While Taggart gave the youngest Hollister a grateful nod, Chandler said, "None of you need bother telling Tag to keep his mouth shut about this. He already understands Mom isn't to know."

"Good," Holt said, then shot a meaningful glance at his uncle. "Then we all agree that what's said here stays among us?"

The older man leaned forward and rested his elbows on his knees. Just from looking at him, Taggart doubted any man in this tent would want to tangle with him physically, or for that matter, try to match wits with the man. He had a tough, sharp image that reminded Taggart of a drill sergeant he used to know back in Texas.

"Maureen isn't going to hear anything from me that might cause her sadness or worry," Gil said. "You men can rest assured of that."

Holt nodded, then gestured to Joseph. "You're the head investigator, Joe, so you need to be the one to do the talking."

"Don't you think you should key Tag in on the main points?" Chandler spoke up. "He's walked into the middle of this thing without knowing much."

"Right," Joseph said, then glanced at Blake. "You fill him in on what we know and I'll get the evidence."

As soon as the word was spoken, Taggart saw Gil's brows shoot up with sudden interest, but he didn't interrupt with questions. Instead he waited patiently while Blake recounted all they knew about their father's death. Including the horrific way they'd found him hanging from the stirrup of the saddle.

Once Blake finished, Holt said, "You see, Tag, ever since Dad died, we brothers have searched and dug to find the truth of what happened. At first Mother was all for it. And then all of a sudden, she made a complete turn around and ordered us to leave it alone. She didn't want to hear about it or think about it. Basically, she wanted to put the tragedy behind her."

"She has her reasons for that," Gil spoke up.

All five men turned stunned looks on the retired detective.

Blake was the first to speak. "You know what those reasons are?"

"I do," Gil answered. "But I want to see this evidence you have before I say anything."

Taggart got the impression that Holt wanted to press the man for answers, but then he shrugged and said, "Show him, Joe."

The deputy reached behind his chair and retrieved a small cedar box. The sort that women used to store jewelry or other personal trinkets.

"It's not much, Uncle Gil. But it's more than nothing. We've all been thinking that since you've come home to Three Rivers, you'd be willing to help us find Dad's killer. You do think Dad was murdered, don't you?"

Grim-faced, the man said, "I've never thought anything else. None of it made sense. He was too good of a horseman to lose his seat in the saddle. And there was no sensible explanation as to why he rode off by himself that day. The ranch was extremely busy and the way I remember it, he was scheduled to meet with a cattle buyer that afternoon."

"That's right," Joseph agreed, then opened the box and handed it to Gil. "We found the spur rowel first. We know it belonged on Dad's spurs because it's unique and very expensive. Mom gave them to him as a special gift."

Gil placed the rusty rowel in the palm of his hand and studied it as though the piece of metal could give him the answers they all needed. After a moment he returned the rowel to the box and pulled out two tiny pieces of tattered fabric. Taggart could see that it had once been blue plaid, but sun and outdoor elements had faded it.

"That was the shirt Dad was wearing that day," Chandler said, his voice hoarse with emotion.

Joseph explained they'd found the items in two different arroyos on the far side of the ranch property, not far from water well pump number nine.

"But that's not all," Holt said, then turned a questioning look on Joseph. "I thought we agreed we were going to show him the rest?"

"We are," Blake muttered.

"Yeah, the rest." Grim-faced, Joseph fished a piece of paper from his shirt pocket. "I found this not long ago when I was going through Ray's private notes about Dad's case."

"Ray?" Gil questioned. "You mean the late Sheriff Maddox?"

Joseph nodded and Taggart quickly tried to remember where he'd heard that name. But before it could come to his mind, Blake provided the answer.

"In case you don't know, Tag, Ray Maddox was also an old family friend of ours, who happened to be the sheriff of Yavapai County for many years. He was also Tessa's father."

Taggart looked at Joseph, who was holding on to the square of paper as though it was a snake that could strike any moment.

"So your father-in-law was the late Sheriff Maddox," Taggart said thoughtfully. "Did he inspire you to become a lawman?"

"Partly. He and Uncle Gil inspired me. And I actually worked under Ray for a short time before he became so sick he had to retire. He eventually passed away from a lung disease. That was before Tessa and I married. And before anyone knew he was actually Tessa's father. But that's a long story in itself."

"Yeah," Holt interjected. "Long and twisted. And we don't want to be here all night."

Joseph glanced once again at Taggart. "You can hear the sheriff's story later. But to explain this—" He tapped a finger against the paper in his hand. "Tessa and I live on the Bar X. The ranch was an inheritance from her father and we live in the same house where he always lived. Over time we've discovered lots of notes and papers he left behind. Many of them about Dad's case."

"And this one?" Gil asked. "I'm assuming it has some sort of clue."

Joseph said, "Ray seemed to think it important enough to put in his files. But it was something he never shared with our family before he died. We've concluded that he probably kept it to himself for Mother's sake. And we sure as hell don't want her finding out about it. Not unless it proves pertinent. If that's the case, we won't have a choice. We'll have to tell her and our sisters."

He handed the paper to Gil and as the man quickly scanned the notes, Taggart noticed all four of the Hollister brothers were watching intently for his reaction.

Finally Gil looked up and Taggart could see something like wry acceptance on his face.

"This is—" He muttered a curse, then let out a chuckle that wasn't anything close to an expression of humor. "It's obviously going to come as a surprise to you guys, but Maureen already knows about the woman at the stockyards in Phoenix. She talked to me about it months ago."

Stunned silence followed the man's revelation and Taggart watched the four brothers exchange bewildered glances.

Blake was the first to speak. "Mother knows? How? None of us have breathed a word about it."

Gil said, "She was going through some of Joel's old business correspondence and happened to run into a small day planner with notes about meetings he had scheduled. Several entries were things like—see her during the sale. And—she'll be waiting outside. From the dates posted next to the notes, they're close to the time that Joel died."

Incredulous, all four brothers stared at him as they tried to digest this news.

Eventually, Blake said, "She hasn't said a word to us about it. Why?"

"Yeah, why?" Holt demanded. "Why did she tell you and not us?"

Instead of taking offense at Holt's accusing tone, Gil shook his head and quietly explained, "She didn't want any of her children to get the idea that their father might've been an adulterer. That's why she's been so preoccupied for the past months. She's been worried you guys might uncover the fact that Joel had been associating with a woman before he died. That's why she kept ordering you all to leave the whole matter alone."

"Oh my God," Joseph murmured.

Chandler looked sick as he pulled off his hat and raked a hand through his hair. "We've been stupid," he said flatly. "Mother is stronger than all of us put together. We should've known she could handle whatever we uncover. Now all this worrying and sneaking about has been wasted time."

"That's hardly the point now," Blake said, then leveled his attention on Gil. "The crux of the matter is does *she* think Dad was an adulterer? Furthermore, do you?"

Gil grimaced. "Do you really have to ask that question, Blake? Neither one of us could ever believe such a thing about Joel. Maureen was everything to him. No. There had to be some other reason for him to be associating with a woman."

His expression calculating, Joseph nodded in agreement. "I have a feeling this woman, whoever she was, might be the key to the whole mystery."

"Exactly, Joe," Gil said. "We need to try to identify and locate her."

"Does that mean you're going to help us?" Holt asked his uncle. "Joe's a damned good deputy, but I figure all of our heads put together is better than one."

Joseph shot Holt an appreciative grin. "Thanks, Holt, for the compliment. But you're right. We need to work together on this."

With that decided, the men began to offer suggestions on how to go about identifying the mystery woman. Taggart was content to sit back and take it all in. But as soon as there was a lull in the conversation he decided to speak up.

"I'm just a listener here," Taggart said. "But I do have a question. Are you going to let your sisters in on this information? And are you going to tell your mother that you guys have been aware of *the woman* for the past few months?"

"Those are good questions, Tag," Blake said, then looked to his brothers for answers. "What about it, guys? Should we tell our sisters?"

Joe was the first to answer. "I vote no. Not until we figure out whether any of this information is relevant."

"I agree," Chandler said. "Camille is pregnant and running her diner. She doesn't need the extra worry. And Vivian already has enough stress with baby twins and a teenager, plus her job as a ranger. And we know how both of them adored Dad. They considered him a saint."

"He wasn't a saint, but close to it," Gil said. "And I think all of you are not giving your sisters enough credit. They would never consider the idea that Joel had a mistress or anything close to it."

"Probably not," Holt agreed. "But the whole issue about *the woman* would worry them. Just like it nags at us guys. Who was she? And why was Dad seeing her? I vote no. If we learn more, then we can let Viv and Camille in on it."

"I vote no, also," Blake said firmly, then glanced at his uncle. "What about Mother, do we tell her?"

"I think it might save some awkward feelings if I explain the situation to her," Gil said. "She thinks she's protecting all of you by trying to sweep the issue under the rug. She needs to understand that finding the truth will be better for the whole family."

Taggart wholly agreed with the man. Nothing good could ever come from hiding things. Ever since he'd left Emily-Ann's house, five nights ago, he'd begun to realize that more and more.

Until he explained about Becca and the baby, Emily-Ann would never be able to understand his reluctance to get involved in a serious relationship. If he ever expected to have a life that included her, he would have to find the courage to confess what losing them had done to him. Yet the scarred part of his heart kept asking why bother to pour out all those bad memories. Doing such a thing wouldn't take away his fear of loving and losing a second time.

Love. He'd seen the emotion here tonight with the Hollister men. Love was guiding the decisions they made concerning their family. Love caused them to put the feelings of others first, rather than their own. And as Taggart had listened to them, he'd begun to wonder if he'd ever truly loved anyone.

He'd believed Becca was his true love and when she'd told him that she was pregnant, he'd wanted the child just as much as he'd wanted her. At that time, he'd been twenty-two and considered himself old enough and man enough to deal with the responsibility of a family. But now as he looked back on their brief marriage, he wondered if he'd been more infatuated with the idea of proving to himself he was a better man than his father, rather than truly loving Becca.

So what were these feelings that were pushing him toward Emily-Ann? he wondered. He'd been trying to convince himself they were nothing but lust. He'd not made love to a woman in a long time. So long that he didn't even want to think about it. And yet, something told him that going to bed with Emily-Ann wasn't going to satisfy the hunger she'd built in him.

"Want to go have a cup of coffee, Tag? I think the pot is still hanging over the campfire."

Chandler's voice pulled Taggart out of his deep musings and he looked up to see Chandler standing in front of him. Directly behind him, the other men were filing out of the open flap of the tent.

Quickly rising from the chair, he said, "Sorry. I—was doing some thinking. I didn't realize the meeting had ended. I think I need that coffee in the worst kind of way."

Smiling, Chandler gave his shoulder a friendly pat. "I'm the one who should be apologizing. You just got started as foreman and you've had to jump straight into spring roundup. You have a lot on your mind and I've made matters worse by dragging you into this family issue about Dad."

"No. Don't apologize," Taggart told him. "I'm glad I was here and glad that I know what's going on with your father's investigation. I just wish I could help in some way. If Joe ever wants me to ride with him to look for more evidence, I'd be happy to."

"I'm sure he'll take you up on the offer," Chandler told him. "Now let's go have the last of the coffee before it turns to black mud."

EMILY-ANN LAUGHED AS she watched the baby boy cuddled in Isabelle's arms take a tiny taste of sugary frosting from his mother's finger.

"Look at that puckered expression on his face," Emily-Ann exclaimed. "He thinks it's awful."

Laughing with her, Isabelle glanced down at her son. "Just give him a year or two and then he'll change his mind about the taste of sugar—unfortunately. I never knew a man who didn't have a sweet tooth. I'm sure little Carter will have one, too."

The two women and baby were sitting outside the coffee shop at one of the wrought iron tables. Late afternoon sun was flickering through the limbs of the mesquite tree, while a breeze helped to cool the flimsy shade. When Isabelle and the baby had shown up, Emily-Ann had been on the verge of closing shop, but she'd gladly put the task on pause in order to visit with her friend.

"I'm so glad you had a chance to come by," Emily-Ann told her.

Isabelle offered the baby his pacifier. "I know I'm keeping you from closing up, but I wanted to stop and chat with you for a few minutes."

"I'm glad you did. I rarely get to see you and Carter. He's

growing so fast. And he looks just like Holt. But I'm sure you hear that all the time."

The pretty blonde grinned as she shifted the baby's weight against her arm. "All the time. But that's okay. His daddy is a handsome devil."

Both women laughed at that and then Emily-Ann sighed as she continued to study the baby's sweet face. "Gosh, it doesn't seem like it's been that long ago when you first met Holt. You came by here hopping mad because he wouldn't give you the time of day."

Chuckling, Isabelle rolled her eyes. "You kept telling me Holt was a dreamy hunk. I thought you were crazy. He was so infuriating I wanted to slap his face."

"Now look. You two are happily married and you have little Carter Edmond."

"I have to admit you were right, Emily-Ann. Holt has made me so happy."

Emily-Ann smiled gently at her friend. "You know, you're the first and only woman who's ever asked me to be their maid of honor. You can't imagine how special that made me feel."

Isabelle reached across the table and squeezed Emily-Ann's hand. "I moved here to Arizona not knowing a single soul and you were so kind to me. You were the first person to befriend me and I'll never forget that."

Emily-Ann waved a dismissive hand through the air. "Being your friend was and is my pleasure."

After a long sip of iced coffee, Isabelle asked, "Have you seen Camille lately?"

"Last week. With roundup going on, I think she was going to drive up to the reservation and spend a day with Vivian and the kids. Otherwise, I guess she's been hanging close to Three Rivers. Normally she would go out to camp and stay the night, but with the baby coming she says she needs a soft bed to sleep in."

"Amen to that," Isabelle agreed, then added, "Actually, Holt texted me earlier in the day and said that roundup was wrapping up and that everyone would be heading back to the ranch this evening. So our men will finally be home."

That meant Taggart would be home, too. Since roundup started six days ago, he'd actually sent her three text messages. All had been short and simple. More or less to let her know things were going well and that he was thinking of her. But did that mean he would be anxious to see her again? Several days had passed since he'd stopped by her house and they'd wound up having that heated kiss in the kitchen. Considering the fickle way his mind worked, she could only guess how Taggart might be feeling about her now.

Isabelle's expression took a shrewd turn. "I heard in a round-about way that Tag took you out to dinner. How did that go?"

Emily-Ann felt her cheeks turn a hot pink. "How did you hear that? I haven't told anyone about our date. Not even Camille."

"Blake mentioned it to Holt. I think they were surprised, because the foreman is such a quiet kind of guy when he's around them. He never talks about going out or doing much socially. But you know how the old saying goes. It's those quiet ones that are real tigers underneath."

Emily-Ann was suddenly remembering their heated embrace. At that moment she wouldn't have hesitated to make love to him. And since then, she'd thought of little else. "I don't think he's actually the dating sort. He more or less told me that he asked me out because he was lonely."

"Aww. That's awful. Uh—not that he asked you for a date, but that he was lonely. It's terrible to feel that way. I remember how it felt after my divorce and I moved here to Yavapai County. I lived out there on Blue Stallion Ranch all alone, with no one to talk to but the horses and the wind. And then Ollie and Sol came. Those two old men were a lifesaver."

Not wanting to dwell on the idea of Taggart being lonely, Emily-Ann changed the subject. "How are Ollie and Sol, by the way? Remind me before you leave and I'll sack up some leftover pastries for them."

"Thanks. Both men are doing great. They'll love getting the pastries."

"And your mother? She didn't want to come to town with you today?"

Isabelle let out a wry laugh. "Are you joking? And be away from Sam for that long? Mom met him over at the Bar X early this morning and they've been out riding horses all day. She's going to be too stiff to walk tomorrow."

"So are they planning a wedding yet?"

The baby began to squirm and fuss. Isabelle placed him against her shoulder and gently patted his back. "Oh yes. At first they insisted they both wanted a quiet simple ceremony. But I think they're realizing that won't work. How do you do quiet and simple with all the Hollister family and Sam's countless friends? Not to mention Mother's longtime friends from San Diego. I told her they should elope to Vegas. Sam loves whiskey and cards. He ought to enjoy it."

Emily-Ann was laughing in agreement when she heard the cell phone in the pocket of her skirt announce an incoming message.

"Excuse me, Isabelle. I'd better check this," she said as she retrieved the phone. "I'm expecting to hear from Conchita. She wasn't feeling well this morning and I've been half-afraid she's going to have to miss cooking pastries for tomorrow."

Emily-Ann quickly opened her message box and then promptly felt her jaw drop.

Isabelle quickly questioned, "What is it? Is something wrong?"

"No. Uh—it's not Conchita. The message is from Tag. He wants to know if I want to come over for supper. He'll cook for me."

A wicked twinkle appeared in Isabelle's brown eyes. "That's a long drive out to Tag's place. Do you think it would be worth it?"

Emily-Ann's short laugh sounded like a breathless schoolgirl and she realized she was reacting idiotically. "Well—yes. But I—" Pausing, she released a long sigh. "To be honest, Isabelle, I don't know if seeing Tag will end up meaning anything."

Frowning, Isabelle asked, "Why? The whole Hollister family has been raving about him. He must be a good man. And if he's interested in you—that's a beginning. Or maybe you're not attracted to the man."

Emily-Ann groaned. "I might get a little daffy at times, but I'm not completely crazy. Have you looked at him?" she asked, then shook her head. "No. Probably not. Because the only man you see is Holt. But Tag is—a hot hunk. How do you think I could not be attracted to him?"

"By the hesitant tone I hear in your voice," Isabelle reasoned. "Something about the man worries you."

Biting down on her bottom lip, Emily-Ann turned her gaze to the nearby street. "I'm afraid he's going to end up being like all the rest, Isabelle. The kind that just can't do commitment."

Isabelle snorted. "Don't you think it's a bit too early to be pinning that sort of label on the man? Just think about all the concerns I had about Holt. Everyone in Yavapai County knew he was a womanizer—even me. But I took a chance that he could change and would change. It takes some courage, Emily-Ann, but you might find that Tag just might be worth the risk."

She thoughtfully studied her friend. "I can't imagine how brave you had to be to marry Holt Hollister."

Her smile full of love, Isabelle turned her head and pressed a soft kiss to baby Carter's cheek. "Right. And who knows, someday Tag might give you a little guy like this."

A baby? It wasn't difficult to see herself making love to Taggart. But after that, everything about her future went gray. The only thing she could see was how her mother must have felt when she'd been abandoned by her lover, and her family, because she was pregnant. It wasn't that Emily-Ann would ever be afraid to raise a child on her own. Anything her mother could do, she was positive she could do. But no way did she want a child to ever feel as shunned by its father as Emily-Ann had felt all these years.

"You're just like Camille," Emily-Ann said teasingly, "always trying to find me a husband."

"Well, you did catch Camille's bridal bouquet. That's definitely a sign of things to come."

Emily-Ann let out a loud groan. "Oh, not you, too."

Isabelle looked confused. "What's wrong? What did I say?"

"Nothing. I'll just say that the next time I touch a bridal bouquet, it'll have to be my own. Otherwise, I'm not going near it!"

A comical look on her face, Isabelle said, "Okay, if you say so. Right now I've got to get home. I've been training three young colts and two fillies. And I've not yet ridden the girls today. I need to get home and do that before daylight goes and Holt gets home."

Holding the baby in one arm, Isabelle started to gather up the trash on the table with her free hand, but Emily-Ann quickly brushed her aside.

"Forget that," she told her. "I'll clean up here."

"Thanks."

Isabelle shouldered her purse and Emily-Ann plucked up Carter's diaper bag and accompanied her friend to the truck she was driving.

After Isabelle and the baby were safely strapped in for the trip back to Blue Stallion Ranch, she stuck her head out the open window of the vehicle. "Call me in a few days and let know how supper with Tag goes."

Emily-Ann frowned at her. "I didn't say I was going."

Isabelle let out a calculating laugh. "Who are you trying to fool? You and I both know that you're going."

Her friend drove away and without giving it another thought, Emily-Ann pulled the phone from her pocket and tapped out a message to Taggart.

I'll be there by six thirty.

Before she walked back to the table where she and Isabelle had been sitting, her phone dinged with his reply.

Great. I'll see you then.

Chapter Eight

After six days of riding through thorny chaparral, wrestling calves and spending his nights on the ground in a sleeping bag, Taggart should have felt too tired to do anything except collapse on the bed and stay there. But the idea of seeing Emily-Ann again was enough to energize him.

For the past two hours, he'd been rushing around the house straightening the rooms as best as he could, showering and changing into a respectable pair of jeans and shirt, then cooking what he thought would be a halfway presentable meal for Emily-Ann.

After chopping salad and baking potatoes, he was about to throw steaks into an iron skillet when he heard her knock on the front door.

Setting the cuts of beef aside, he made his way through the house until he reached the front door. When he swung it wide, she was standing on the edge of the porch, petting one of Chandler's cur dogs.

"I see you've met King," Taggart said, while he took in the sight of her smooth red hair hanging to her waist and the pink-and-white flowered dress clinging to her curves. She looked luscious and as pretty as sunshine on a Sunday morning.

Smiling, she continued to stroke the dog's head. "He's beautiful. Is he yours?"

He stepped out of the doorway and walked over to her. "No. He's one of Doc's many dogs. King likes me, so when I left the ranch yard this evening, he decided to follow. Halfway here, I felt sorry for the guy and stopped and let him ride in the truck the rest of the way."

She straightened away from the dog and Taggart leaned forward to press a kiss on her cheek. Her skin was soft and smelled like a gentle rain on a meadow of wildflowers. It was all he could do not to gather her into his arms and taste her lips.

"Hello," he murmured as he forced his head to lift away from hers.

Her gaze darted shyly up to his and the warmth he saw in the green depths made everything about being with her feel good and right.

"Hello, Tag."

"I'm glad you're here," he said.

The corners of her lips lifted ever so slightly. "I'm glad I'm here, too."

She gestured to the dog. "I take it that Chandler doesn't mind King having a second home."

"Not at all. Doc knows I'll bring him back home in the morning." He pushed the door wide and gestured for her to come in. "After I sent the invitation for supper, I worried you might not want to make the long drive out here at night."

They entered the living room where she paused to take a slow survey of the leather furniture, dark green drapes and a large braided rug. To Taggart the room looked fine, but from a woman's perspective it probably looked stark.

She said, "It doesn't bother me to drive at night. I know the road well and there's hardly ever any traffic out this way. Especially after you turn onto Three Rivers' property."

"Hopefully, you'll think my cooking is worth it," he said with a smile. "But before we head to the kitchen, I should warn you not to expect much. With me being gone on roundup this past week, I've not had time to restock my cupboards."

"I can eat anything. Even soggy oatmeal."

"I promise it won't taste that bad. And I do have a nice surprise." He walked over and took her by the arm. "Come on and I'll show you."

"Your house is nice," she said as he guided her to the kitchen. "I like the arched doorways and the floors are real wood. Did you put the polished gleam on them?"

He laughed. "Are you kidding? If I sweep once a week that would be a miracle. This house isn't large by most standards, but it's the biggest one I've ever lived in. I'm about to decide I'm going to have to hire a cleaning lady to keep it looking livable."

"Hmm. That would be a big help. I suppose Jazelle doesn't have time to do it for you. She's already stretched pretty thin helping Reeva in the kitchen and Roslyn and Katherine with the babies. And then she has Raine, her own little boy to take care of whenever she goes home. He's about five now, I think."

"I saw Raine a few days ago. Nick, Blake's teenaged son, brought the boy down to the ranch yard to see the cows and horses. He's a cute little fellow. By the way, I've never asked anyone, but does Jazelle have a husband?"

"No. She's never been married." She cast him a sly look. "Jazelle is very pretty—you've obviously noticed."

He slanted her an impish grin. "She's pretty, but she's not you. And I was wondering because of the little boy. That day I saw him at the cattle barn I got the feeling he didn't have a daddy."

"That's very perceptive of you."

He tried not to grimace. "I'm experienced with the subject of missing fathers."

"Well, so am I," she said, then promptly changed the subject. "Now what is this surprise you have?"

They entered the kitchen and he led her over to the cabinet counter where the pie Reeva had given him was wrapped in aluminum foil.

"Bless her sweet heart, Reeva sent word for me to come to the big house—that she had something for me. She got the idea that I deserved a pie for wrapping up my first roundup here on Three Rivers. I told her I was going to share it with you."

"That was thoughtful." She sneaked a peek under the edge of the foil. "Oh, it's pecan!"

"One of my favorites," he said.

She chuckled. "One?"

"I have many."

She looked at him and in that moment, Taggart realized how much he'd missed her these past few days and how very much he wanted her now.

Wrapping his hands around her upper arms, he looked into her eyes and suddenly without warning, a soft, mushy feeling spread throughout his chest.

Damn. What was the matter with him? How could this woman make him feel happy and vulnerable at the same time? It didn't make sense. But he'd heard there was no logic to being in love. Could that be what was happening to him? Whatever the reason for this strange upheaval inside him, he didn't want to think it was love. That was for other people.

"Is something wrong?" she asked. "You're looking at me like I have a smudge on my nose or something."

He released the long breath he hadn't realize he'd been holding until now. "Sorry. I guess I've been staring. It's just that you look so beautiful tonight I—can't help myself."

An impish smile wrinkled her nose. "Are you feeding me cheese as an appetizer?"

"If I am it's not the fake processed kind. It's the real deal."

He tried to smile back at her and lighten the moment, but the emotions swirling through him wouldn't allow him to do anything other than place a kiss on her forehead.

When his lips continued to linger against her skin, both her hands reached out and anchored a hold on the front of his shirt.

"I probably shouldn't be so obvious, but I've missed you, Tag."

His insides began to quiver with longing and he drew in another deep breath and blew it out. "I'd like to kiss you and show you how much I've missed you. But I'm afraid if I did, we might never get to eat."

Laughing softly, she purposely stepped away from him and moved down the cabinets until she reached a large gas range with a built-in grill on top. "You're cooking steaks," she said, observing the two pieces of meat soaking in a bowl of dark-colored marinade.

"I'm guessing you would probably prefer chicken, but steak was the only thing left in the freezer."

"I love steak. But I do have a question. Why cook them in a skillet when you have this great indoor grill that most people would give their eye teeth for?"

Joining her at the stove, he switched on the blaze beneath the black skillet.

"Because the iron gives it a flavor I like," he explained. "But I can grill yours if you'd rather have it cooked that way."

"Oh, no. I'm anxious to taste the difference."

"Coming right up." He tossed a chunk of butter into the skillet and gathered up the bowl containing the cuts of meat.

Next to him, Emily-Ann asked, "Can I do something to help?"

The best thing she could do to help him, Taggart thought, would be to tell him to forget about the supper and make love to her. But his mind was taking rapid leaps into uncertain territory. Emily-Ann might be thinking about food and nothing more.

Jerking his thoughts back to the present, he gestured to a row of cabinets to the right of them. "You might start with setting the table and icing some glasses. Unless you want to drink wine or beer."

As she headed to the cabinets, she said, "I'll skip the spirits tonight. You never know when an antelope or deer might walk onto the road. And I did promise I'd drive carefully for you. Remember?"

Hell yes, he remembered. That night he'd come very, very close to telling her about Becca and the car crash that had taken her and the unborn baby, and ended the future he'd planned for their lives together. But just when he'd thought he could get the painful words out to Emily-Ann, a barrier of some sort had lodged in his throat and he'd done well to breathe, much less talk about the incident that continued to shadow the choices he made for himself.

"I do remember," he murmured. "And I'm glad you're being cautious—for my sake and yours."

MORE THAN AN HOUR LATER, after Emily-Ann and Taggart had finished eating the meal and pieces of Reeva's pecan pie, she insisted on helping him put the kitchen back in neat order.

After the last dish was dried and put away, Taggart said, "There's a bit of coffee left. Might be nice to have a cup out on the front porch. Unless you'd prefer to stay inside."

Throughout the meal, Emily-Ann had tried to keep her gaze from constantly straying to Taggart, but she'd mostly failed at the effort. The days they'd been apart had felt like ages to her and everything about him, from his dark wavy hair, to the warm light in his brown eyes and the stubble on his chin, was mesmerizing her. While they'd worked side by side doing the dishes, her fascination for him had only increased and several times she'd had to catch herself from reaching over and touching him.

Sitting outside in the cool night air might be enough to put a brake on her runaway urges, she thought, but she doubted it.

"The porch sounds great," she agreed.

Taggart poured their coffee and with cups in hand, they walked back through the house and onto the front porch. At one end a wide, wooden swing hung from the rafters, while on the opposite end, a group of wicker furniture with tropical-printed cushions invited a person to relax.

"Where would you like to sit?" he asked.

"The wicker looks comfy, but I love to swing. Is that okay with you?"

"I've spent so many hours in the saddle this past week that a wooden swing will feel like I'm sitting on a cloud," he assured her.

With a hand resting against the small of her back, he guided her over to the swing. King, who'd been lying in the shadows, followed them across the porch and waited until they were seated before he flopped down on the floor near Taggart's feet.

"It's a lovely evening," Emily-Ann remarked.

His arm came around the back of her shoulders and a soft sigh slipped past her lips.

"If it's too cool for you I can go in the house and find a jacket," he offered.

Even if she'd been freezing, she wouldn't have wanted him to move. Snuggled next to his side, with the warmth of his thigh pressed against hers and the low, raspy sound of his voice in her ear, she wondered how something that felt so good could possibly last. It couldn't. Not for her. But she wasn't going to allow herself to worry about that tonight.

"I'm fine," she told him. "Besides, who can pay attention to the chill in the air with a view like this?"

Situated at the foot of a ridge of rocky hills, the house was shrouded by several mesquite trees, but the gnarled limbs didn't block the landscape directly in front of them. Beneath the starlit sky, she could see a shadowy vista of wide-open range peppered with tall century plants, Joshua trees and saguaro cactus. To the right, in the far distance, the lights illuminating the Three Rivers Ranch yard glowed like a beacon in the wilderness.

Normally Emily-Ann would have been hypnotized by the beauty, along with the pleasant sounds of the breeze whispering through the mesquites and the call of the night birds. But all those things were just a lovely backdrop to Taggart's presence.

"Blake told me this house was built back in the late 1950s

by his grandfather. Back then, the foreman of Three Rivers had a big family and needed a place to live," Taggart explained. "All I can say is that the Hollisters didn't hold back, this house would've been expensive to build even back then."

While he was talking, his fingers had begun to trace abstract designs against her arm. The light, feathery touch against her skin was creating far more goose bumps than the cool night breeze and it was all she could do to focus on his words.

"When Camille and I were in elementary school, I remember the foreman who lived here was an older man with a wife and five kids. Then about the time we became teenagers, he retired and the family moved away. That's when Matthew took over." She glanced curiously over at him. "Did you have a house of your own when you worked on the Flying W?"

He shook his head. "No. I didn't live directly on the ranch. I had a place of my own not far from the nearest town, which was Canyon. The commute back and forth to the ranch wasn't all that bad. But this—" He paused and gestured to his surroundings. "It's like nothing I've ever dreamed. To be honest, when I sent my résumé to the Hollisters for this job, I didn't think I had a chance in hell of getting it. But I didn't see any harm in trying. Sometimes miracles do happen."

Like her sitting here with a man like him, she thought. She'd never dreamed a man of Taggart's caliber would ever ask her out for dinner, much less cook for her. To be fair, the men she'd dated in her past hadn't been losers. But most of them had still been floundering around, struggling to figure out what they wanted to do with their lives. Some of them hadn't had a clue how to better themselves, while others were working on plans.

Even so, they'd all had one thing in common, having a little fun with her, and then moving on. These past few weeks, she'd been telling herself that Taggart had to be different. He was responsible and settled. He was admired and successful. She just didn't yet know if he'd want to be in her life for the long haul.

She placed her cup on a small table situated close to the arm of the swing, then reached over and covered his hand with hers. "If you hadn't sent in your résumé, I would've probably never met you. Or do you believe in fate and that our paths would've crossed somewhere at some point in our lives?"

The gentle look on his face stirred her heart with feelings so tender they brought a rush of moisture to her eyes. Oh my, what was this man doing to her? She felt like a fallen leaf at the mercy of the desert wind. He was carrying her away, tumbling and swirling, and she could only hope she didn't end up landing at the bottom of a steep arroyo with no way of climbing out.

"I do believe in fate," he answered, his voice pensive. "Sometimes it's good, other times it's bad."

"Yes," she solemnly agreed. "And my mother's fate was mostly bad."

He turned his head and for long moments he studied her face as though he was weighing whether he could trust her. With what, she didn't know.

Finally he said, "You've probably noticed that I don't talk about my mother much. Not because I didn't love her—I loved her very much. But talking about her hurts. A lot. And I'm beginning to think you understand how that feels."

"It's never easy to talk about my mother," she murmured. "And even when I think about her, it puts an ache in my chest. She had a rough life, but I try to put that out of my mind and remember the good times we shared as mother and daughter. That helps."

Nodding, he glanced down at the yellow cur sleeping at his feet. "When I was twenty-three my mother, Carolyn, died of a heart attack. She'd never been in perfect health, but her death was totally out of the blue. Or that's the way it had felt at the time. But after I'd had time to think about everything, I realized it was a miracle she'd lived as long as she did."

This was the first time he'd ever really talked about his family and, as she studied his solemn profile, it was fairly obvious that his young life hadn't been easy. "Your mother had a chronic health problem?"

Her question elicited a cynical snort from him.

"No. Her husband—my father, Buck O'Brien was the chronic problem. To put it plainly, the man was a selfish bully. He did his best to keep her and us kids browbeaten. He made her life pure hell. And me and my sister—we just clung to Mom and tried to stay invisible."

This was the first time she'd ever heard such bitterness in his voice and, though it was an ugly sound, she could understand where it was coming from. She'd had plenty of experience dealing with the negative emotion and knew firsthand that once it took root inside a person, it was hard to push aside.

"Were your parents married when she passed away?" Emily-Ann ventured to ask.

His gaze left King to settle on her face. "Oh, yes. At that time he'd been scrounging around the area between Canyon and Hereford taking on little construction jobs wherever he could find them. He was working as a carpenter during that time, but that was only when he really wanted to work. Mom was the one who paid the bills and kept things afloat for them. Not him. She had a bookkeeping job at the same feeder lot where I worked tending cattle."

Emily-Ann shook her head. "Gorman, my stepfather, was mostly shiftless, too. But in most other ways he was very kind to Mother. So I can sort of understand why she loved him and remained married to him. But if your father was actually mean to your mother, why didn't she divorce him?"

Sighing, he gently trailed his forefinger over the back of her hand and down each of her fingers. "I can't answer that, Emily-Ann. Maybe because the choices she made were something only a woman could understand. Or maybe because I've never been in love like that—where a person is blinded to the other's faults. I often wanted to blame it on the fact that she was insecure. She didn't think she could survive without him. But in truth, she would've made it so much better on her own."

Losing her mother had knocked Emily-Ann flat and it had taken her a long time to pull herself together and move forward. She'd often heard that losing a mother was even harder for a man to deal with. Whether that was true or not, she could tell, just from the pain in his voice, that Taggart had suffered deep grief.

"Your mother didn't want to be on her own, Tag. Just like mine didn't want to be," she reasoned, then asked, "What happened with your father after Carolyn died? You mentioned that you don't see him often, but does he still live in that part of Texas?"

"He comes and goes. My sister and I never really know when he's going to leave or show up. Usually when we see him it's because he wants money."

She stared at him in disbelief. "The man asks his children for money? That would take some gall."

"He's got that in spades," Taggart said, his voice heaped with sarcasm.

She turned her hand over and wrapped her fingers tightly around his. "When I first met you, Tag, I would've never guessed that our lives were similar. We both lost our mothers and we both suffered because of the choices they made in their lives."

"Yes. But there's more to mine, Emily-Ann. I—uh—"

When he faltered, then failed to say anything more, she prompted, "You what?"

His gaze continued to delve deep into hers until she thought he was going to ignore her question completely. And then a long breath rushed out of him and he said, "I've been married."

Stunned, she stared at him while questions darted wildly through her mind. "Married? I suppose that means you're divorced?"

Pressing the toe of his boot against the floor of the porch, he paused the gentle movement of the swing.

"No," he said. "It means I'm a widower."

Her gasp was so loud that King lifted his head and looked at her.

"A widower," she repeated blankly, then shook her head. "You were married and your wife died?"

"No, she didn't just die. She wrecked the car she was driving and it killed her and our unborn child."

His revelation struck her so hard that her stomach made a sickening roll. "Oh. Oh my, Tag. I—don't know what to say."

"You don't have to say anything," he said wryly. "I just—felt like it was time that I told you about Becca and the baby. I thought that—well, you ought to know why I've been shy about getting involved with you."

Several years ago some things happened in my life that changed everything for me.

The words he'd spoken to her that night when he'd come to her house were suddenly skipping through the forefront of her mind. His comment hadn't made complete sense to her then, but it was becoming clear now.

"I'm so sorry," she murmured. "I thought your reluctance was all about me—not meeting your standards."

"That was stupid thinking on your part, Emily-Ann. You meet all my standards and more. I think that's why—when I look at you—when I'm with you like this, I get so scared I can hardly breathe. I tell myself that I can't take another chance with a woman. But then when I'm away from you, I hurt to be back with you."

Agony was wrapped around his every word. It knotted his voice and twisted his rugged features. She wanted to take it all away. She wanted to slip her arms around him and assure him that tragedy wasn't likely to strike twice. But she couldn't move, or think beyond the notion that he'd been in love with another woman. So much so that he'd married her. That the two of them had been expecting a child together.

"I—how long ago did this happen?" she finally managed to ask.

"Ten years ago. I was twenty-one when I first met Becca and turned twenty-two when we got married. She was two months pregnant when we stood before the county judge and exchanged vows. She didn't want to get married then. She wanted to wait until the baby was born. She didn't want folks thinking I'd married her because I had to."

Emily-Ann couldn't stop herself from asking, "Did you?"

"No. I mean, yes, I did feel obligated when I'd learned she was pregnant, but no one was holding a gun to my back. I believed I loved her."

Emily-Ann's brows lifted as she watched his features twist even tighter. "You believed? You weren't sure?"

He groaned. "Back then I thought I was sure about my feelings for her—about getting married and everything that went with that decision. Looking back on it all, I don't know. We were so young. I did care for her deeply and the baby—I was a little scared at becoming responsible for a child, but I wanted it. Wanted it with all my heart. But four months after we married, they were both gone from my life."

Oh God, Emily-Ann thought sickly. How could she ever expect to compete with the ghost of his wife and unborn child? Ten years had passed and he was still tortured over losing them.

"Four months. You'd hardly begun your married life together. You must have felt like your whole world was turned upside down."

"To be honest, I was so numb everyone around me was probably thinking I'd turned into a zombie. And then just about the time I was beginning to wake up and start living again, Mom was struck by the heart attack. All of it together just about wiped me out."

The mere thought of the grief he'd gone through squeezed her heart with pain. "I can only imagine," she murmured.

His eyes softened and then his fingers gently smoothed the

hair at her temple. "It was a bad, bad time," he admitted. "But now—meeting you has made everything different for me. You're the first woman since Becca that I've ever really wanted—or needed."

Wanted. Needed. But not loved.

Even as the thought zipped through her brain, she realized it was wrong of her to think it. She and Taggart hadn't known each other that long. She couldn't expect him to fall instantly in love with her. Actually, she was crazy to think he would ever fall in love with her. But tonight, as he'd talked about his grief and shared things about his life that he probably never shared with others, she'd felt closer to him than she'd ever felt to any man.

"I understand that you're afraid to try again. But you needn't feel alone, Tag. I'm just as afraid as you are. But I—" Feeling more emboldened than she had a right to be, she wrapped her hands over his forearms and pressed her fingers into his warm flesh. "I'm willing to take a chance that you're not purposely setting out to break my heart."

He groaned. "Oh, Emily-Ann, I—that would never be my intention." Reaching up, he gently touched a forefinger to the center of her lips. "You've already had too much pain and hurt in your life. And so have I."

The cold fear around her heart began to melt and spread warmth to every part of her body. And then with her gaze locked on his, she placed a soft butterfly kiss upon his finger.

He whispered her name and then he was drawing her into his arms and lowering his mouth down to hers.

He'd kissed her before and each time the intimate contact had shaken her, but this time was different. This time she felt a connection that was boundless and far too strong to break.

By the time he eventually lifted his head and looked down at her, Emily-Ann was not only breathless, she was totally on fire for him.

"I think it's time we—uh—went in. Don't you?"

Without hesitating, she nodded and he quickly rose to his feet and helped her up from the swing. Then with his hand wrapped tightly around hers, he led her into the house and down a dark hallway until they passed through a door on the left.

"Wait here and I'll turn on a lamp," he said as they stepped just inside the dark room.

Emily-Ann stood where she was and while she waited for him to cross the room and deal with the light, she could feel her heart beating hard and heavy in her chest. Not with the fear of what they were about to do, but the concern that he might find her terribly disappointing. If that happened, she'd most likely never see him again.

If sex is all he wants from you, Emily-Ann, then you don't need him.

A soft light suddenly glowed at the head of a queen-size bed and then Taggart turned and smiled at her. And that was all it took to send the taunting voice, along with every other doubt, flying out of her head.

"Don't look at all the boxes that still need to be unpacked," he said.

Emily-Ann didn't bother glancing around at the room. Her focus was zeroed on him as she walked over and slipped her arms around his waist.

"Who cares about boxes?" she asked, turning her lips up to his.

Growling with need, he bent his head and kissed her. "All I care about is you. And this."

While his lips feasted on hers, his hand reached to the back of her dress and tugged on the zipper until it reached the bottom. Emily-Ann dropped her arms and allowed the fabric to slide over her shoulders and onto the floor. Cool air wafted over her half-naked body, but before it had a chance to chill her skin, he was lifting her off her feet and placing her in the middle of the bed.

Once she was settled, he stepped back and with hungry eyes she watched him remove his clothing. By the time he got down to a pair of black boxers and climbed onto the bed to join her, Emily-Ann knew her fate for tonight was sealed. Even if a thousand horses suddenly stampeded through the bedroom, she couldn't have left his side to save herself.

Chapter Nine

His body already on fire for her, Taggart rolled Emily-Ann into his arms and buried his face in the side of her neck. She smelled sweet and mysterious and the scent acted on his senses as much as the feel of her soft skin beneath his lips.

Making love to Emily-Ann had been in the back of his mind almost from the very first time he'd met her. But he'd not thought it would actually happen tonight. He'd hoped, but not believed.

Now that she was in his arms, her bare skin sliding against his, her sighs whispering across his ear, he was half-afraid he was going to wake up from a beautiful dream and find he was still in a bedroll out on the range.

"Aren't you going to turn out the light?" she asked.

Lifting his head slightly away from hers, he looked down to see her lashes were partially lowered over drowsy green eyes, while her oh-so-soft lips were already swollen from his kisses. She looked utterly fascinating. Especially to a man who only a few weeks ago believed his libido had crawled away to die.

"In a bit. Right now I want to be able to see you—how beautiful you look lying on this old quilt with your red hair spilled everywhere." He slipped his fingers beneath the lacy white straps of her bra and slid them downward until they fell onto her arms and the fleshy mounds of her breasts spilled over the loosened cups of her bra. "And I have a feeling you're going to look even better without these pretty little pieces of lace."

Her breathless little laugh was self-mocking. "There's nothing little about me or my lingerie."

"Everything about you is perfect to me, Emily-Ann. From the freckles on your nose to your rounded bottom."

She chuckled. "You're crazy."

"If I am, then please don't try to fix me. I want to stay this way."

At the middle of her back, he unfastened her bra, then tossed the whole thing aside. The pale pink nipples of her breasts beckoned to him and, cupping his hands around the soft fullness, he bent his head to taste the rosy centers.

In a matter of seconds, she was making mewing sounds deep in her throat, while her body arched up to his. Her wordless plea for relief didn't go unnoticed. He quickly peeled off her panties and tossed them atop her dress on the floor.

When his finger found the intimate folds between her thighs, it was hot and moist and waiting just for him. Watching her face, he slipped inside and reveled at the softness he was touching, the longing he saw gripping her features.

Slowly, he stroked her until her hips were writhing against his hand and his own body was on the verge of exploding.

"Tag, oh Tag. Don't make me wait to have you."

Moving away from her, he stood and pushed off his boxers. His manhood was throbbing to be inside her and yet a part of him was reluctant to make the ultimate connection. Once he entered her, it would be the beginning of the end, and he didn't want that to happen. Not when each second of being with her like this was awakening every cell in his body.

"Is something wrong?" she asked.

Shaking away his thoughts, he pulled open the drawer in the nightstand, then frowned. "No. It's just now dawned on me that I might not have any condoms. I—they're not something—I have much need for."

She must've heard the embarrassment in his voice, because suddenly she was sitting on the side of the bed, reaching for his hand.

"No need to worry. I take the pill. Everything should be fine. Unless you're worried about—other things."

He looked at her while wishing they didn't have to discuss such an awkward subject.

"If you're worried," he said. "I can tell you that I've not had unprotected sex since I was married."

"Well, you shouldn't worry about me. I've *never* had unprotected sex."

The impish smile on her face made all the clumsiness of the moment go away and with a wicked chuckle, he eased her back down on the bed.

"Then we don't have a thing to worry about—except making this our night," he said.

Her eyes sparkling like stars, she reached up and linked her hands at the back of his neck, then drew his mouth down to hers. Taggart kissed her softly over and over until the need to deepen the kiss was as strong as the need to join his body to hers.

As soon as her mouth opened to accept his tongue, his knee parted her thighs and he entered her with one smooth thrust.

A moan vibrated deep in her throat and her hands tightened on his shoulders, but other than that, she went stock-still beneath him.

The reaction caused him to lift his head and he was stunned to see tears slipping from the corners of her eyes and roll into the edge of her hair.

Uncertain, he whispered, "Emily-Ann, do you want to end this now?"

Her hands reached up and gently cradled his face and all he could see in her eyes was a longing so deep and tender that it caused a wave of emotion to flood the center of his chest.

"Oh, Tag, I never want this to end," she murmured. "I want you so much. So much."

He struggled to push his words past the tight cords in his throat, but when they did finally release, relief poured out with them. "And I want you, sweet Emily-Ann. More than you could know."

Lowering his head, he kissed the tears away from each corner of her eyes, then moved his mouth to hers.

The moment their lips connected, she arched her hips up to his, drawing him deeper inside her. Sensations such as he had never experienced shot at him from all directions and wiped his mind of everything but her. Having her, loving her.

Her legs wrapped around his and she instantly began to match his rhythmic thrusts. After that, his mind became a blur as his senses tried to absorb everything at once. The hot smoothness of her skin against his, the womanly scent that swirled around him, the sweetness of her lips and the yielding of her body as she gave everything up to him.

Time became nonexistent for Taggart. All he knew was that he didn't want the euphoria to end. He couldn't allow it to end. But she thwarted his plans when she began to writhe in abandon and her fingers raced frantically across his back, then down to his hips.

When she urged him to quicken the pace, it was more than his brain could stand and the rest of his body had no choice but to surrender. Suddenly and totally, he was blinded by a shower of shooting stars and then he was clutching her tightly to him, crying her name and letting the undulating waves of passion overtake him.

THIS WASN'T THE way it was supposed to be, Taggart thought a few minutes later, as he drew Emily-Ann's warm limp body next to his. He wasn't supposed to be feeling all mushy and enchanted just because he'd had sex with a woman.

Sex. Who was he trying to fool? The union they'd just shared had been far more than physical. It had touched him somewhere deep inside and now all he wanted to do was gather her close and let his heart sing with joyous wonder.

He was in trouble. Deep, deep trouble.

That dire thought was suddenly interrupted as she stirred and nuzzled her nose against the side of his neck. He slipped his arm around her waist and snugged her next to his damp body.

"You never did turn off the lamp."

After the wild, stormy ride the two of them had just taken together, her observation caused him to chuckle.

Resting his cheek against the crown of her head, he said, "I didn't have the time. Besides, I like being able to see you."

Her fingertips created tiny circles across his chest and he wondered why her hands felt so magical whenever and wherever she touched him.

Her voice drowsy, she said, "I dreaded for you to see me without my clothes. But you know what, after a bit I didn't care."

"I think somewhere in that remark you were giving me a compliment."

"I am," she said. "You made me forget my imperfections."

He caught her hand and lifted her fingers to his lips. After he'd kissed each one, he said, "I don't know how you see yourself, Emily-Ann. But I see you as lovely and womanly and everything a man could want."

"I wasn't fishing for compliments. But—" she tilted her head in order to plant a kiss on his jaw "—I'll take them and wrap them up with a bow and put them away in my dresser. I might need them later when I'm looking in the mirror."

Smiling, he rubbed his cheek against the side of her head. "Oh, Emily-Ann, you're so—"

"Silly?"

"No. I was thinking more like precious." He turned her face to his and as he looked into her eyes, fear suddenly niggled the back of his mind.

He was feeling too much, he told himself, and thinking things that he had no business thinking. Getting this close to Emily-

Ann was like asking for trouble. But he wasn't going to dwell on the danger now, not when everything about her made him feel so good.

"Tag, you don't have to say all these nice things to me," she said. "I don't expect that from you."

He inwardly winced. "I never thought you did. But I need to say them. And maybe someday you'll realize I actually mean them."

Doubt shrouded her green eyes and he was amazed at how much he wanted to take the dark shadows away. And stunned even more to realize how much he wanted her to believe in him.

A vulnerable quiver touched her bottom lip. "I want to believe them, Tag. I want to believe everything about this night."

He pushed his fingers into the hair at her temple and stroked the silky strands away from her face.

"I'm glad," he whispered. "Because it's far from over."

The tremble to her lips stopped as the corners tilted upward. "Just so I get to work at Conchita's by six thirty in the morning."

He gave her a wicked grin. "I'll give you enough time to make the drive."

Her provocative laugh had him laughing along with her and with a hand on her waist, he rolled the both of them over, until he was lying on his back and her warm body was draped over his.

And when she lowered her head and covered his mouth with hers, Taggart realized he wanted to believe everything about this night, too.

TWO DAYS LATER, Emily-Ann had closed up the coffee shop and was climbing into her car to drive home when Camille's truck pulled up behind her.

Sticking her head out the window, her friend called out to her, "Not so fast! I just got here!"

Giving her a cheery wave, Emily-Ann left the side of the car and walked over to greet Camille.

"What are you doing in town so late in the evening?" she asked, as Camille climbed down from the truck cab.

"Mother sent me after a few personal items she needed from the drugstore. Personally, I think she sent me on this mission to give me a chance to see you."

"Oh, she thought you needed someone other than relatives for company?"

"Something like that." She glanced over Emily-Ann's shoulder to see she'd already hung the closed sign on the door of the coffee shop. "Were you on your way home? Or were you going somewhere?"

"Home. I have another test to do tomorrow and it deals with chemistry. I've been studying between customers, but I need some uninterrupted time to study if I ever expect to pass." Plus, it was damned hard to keep her mind on chemical equations when all she really wanted to think about was Taggart and how the night at his house had changed everything.

Camille groaned with disappointment. "Don't you have time to go to the Broken Spur for a milkshake?"

Emily-Ann frowned. "No more milkshakes for me—I'm cutting back. And why do you want to go to that old café on the outskirts of town? There's a fast-food place a couple of streets over from here where you can get a milkshake."

Camille's short burst of laughter was a mocking sound. "Are you joking? The Broken Spur might be a little ratty on the inside, but the food is great. Makes me feel right at home like I'm in my own diner. And they make their milkshakes by hand one at a time. With real ice cream."

Chuckling, Emily-Ann affectionately patted Camille's protruding belly. "And the little guy is growing. He deserves the real thing."

"Darned right," Camille agreed. "So what do you say? I won't keep you for more than thirty minutes. I need to get back to the ranch soon anyway. Mom wants this new lipstick I picked up for her. Uncle Gil is taking her out to dinner tonight."

Emily-Ann's looked at her with interest. "Really? Is she calling it a date?"

Camille shrugged. "I don't know what Mom is calling the outing, but I can tell you that she's awfully excited about it."

"Aww, that's so romantic," Emily-Ann replied, then suddenly realized that kind of remark might not go over well with Camille. "Sorry, Camille. I spoke before I thought. You might not want to think of your mother having a romantic evening."

"Don't be silly," she said with a dismissive wave of her hand. "I've already told you that I want Mother to be happy. And if that means having Uncle Gil in her life, then that's okay, too."

"Not all children feel as generous toward their parent as you do."

Camille smiled wistfully. "How could I want to deny her the pleasure of loving someone when I have so much with Matthew?"

"True. And you don't have to worry about Gil being like Gorman, thank God," she said, then called over her shoulder as she started to her car, "Okay. Let me get my purse and we'll go to the Broken Spur. I'll have an ice tea while you enjoy *real* ice cream."

Camille drove the two of them to the far south side of town where the old Broken Spur building sat on the edge of the highway that led to Phoenix. The place was usually full of old cowboys and construction workers and today was no different, Emily-Ann decided, as she and Camille sat in a corner booth, sipping their drinks.

"Camille, I swear, each time I see you it's like your face is glowing. Have you found some sort of miracle moisturizer, or something?"

Camille chuckled. "When a woman gets overloaded with hormones, she not only cries, but she has much nicer skin. This glow will go away once I have little junior or baby princess."

Emily-Ann sighed. For the past few years she'd watched the Hollister women give birth to several babies and each time she'd been very happy for them. And when she'd heard that Camille was expecting Matthew's child, she'd been thrilled for her friend. Yet she'd never really allowed herself to dwell on the idea of having her own children. The notion had never seemed to fit her life. Not without a good man in it. But now, after making love to Taggart, she was imagining herself more and more with a baby.

"Actually, I'd better fess up," Camille went on. "Mother did want the new lipstick for tonight, but she also sent me into town on a nosy, fact-finding mission. And I agreed because I'm really curious, too."

Emily-Ann asked blankly, "Curious about what? I didn't know anything new had been happening around here."

Her expression innocent, Camille stirred the straw through the creamy strawberry milkshake. "According to Isabelle something has been happening. She told Holt that Tag cooked supper for you the other night. And you know Holt, you'd have to duct tape his mouth before he could keep it shut."

Emily-Ann couldn't stop a pink blush from coloring her cheeks. "Well, no need to beat up Holt. It's not like we were trying to be secretive or anything."

Camille's blue eyes were suddenly sparkling with interest and she leaned earnestly across the tabletop toward Emily-Ann. "Good. I want to hear all about it. So does Mother."

Maureen had always been like a second mother to Emily-Ann, but she couldn't remember a time that the woman had actually been interested in her dates.

"Why is she interested? The dinner was—well, just a casual outing."

"Do you want your nose to look like a carrot?" She grimaced. "With fibs like that it's going to."

Emily-Ann shifted uncomfortably on the padded vinyl covering the booth bench. There was no way she could tell her friend that she'd experienced something with Taggart that had been totally magical and life changing for her. She'd not had any idea that having sex with a man could make her feel so wanted and loved and needed. She'd not known that she was capable of feeling that much pleasure or that much emotion. But she had. And two days later she still didn't know where their relationship was headed or what any of it might mean on down the line.

"Okay, I'll admit it was more than special." Shaking her head, she momentarily closed her eyes. "Camille, I never thought—well, can you imagine a man like Taggart cooking supper for me? If it hadn't actually happened it would be downright laughable."

"Why?"

Emily-Ann's eyes flew wide. "Why? Are you kidding? Think about it, Camille. I'm the girl that was fed a sandwich from a convenience store for her twenty-seventh birthday and I had to eat that meal sitting in the car in the parking lot because my date had an aversion to picnic tables. I've never been treated as nicely as Taggart treats me."

A wide smile came over Camille's face and she reached across the table and squeezed Emily-Ann's hand. "That's wonderful."

Emily-Ann let out a heavy breath. "I'm not so sure if it is or not."

"Now who's sounding like they've slipped a cog or two?"

"I realize that sounds crazy. But that's because you don't understand, Camille. When something or someone as good as Taggart comes along in my life I'm fairly certain I'm destined to end up a loser—again. He's not going to want to invest much more time in me. And he especially won't want to invest any true emotion."

"That's an awful thing to say, Emily-Ann. Don't you think you're doing Taggart a discredit by thinking that way?"

Emily-Ann sighed again. "I'm trying to be practical about this, Camille. He—uh—he's already told me he doesn't think he can make a long-term commitment to me—or any woman. You see, he—" Unsure as to whether she should say more, Emily-

Ann paused and glanced down at the tabletop. "Well, let's just say he's not looking for love."

"Don't most men say those things? Matthew tried his best to run from me. But in the end he decided that marrying me was a chance he had to take."

Grimacing, Emily-Ann lifted her tea glass and drew on the straw. "Yes, well, Matthew had good reason to be gun-shy. He'd been through a divorce. And Taggart has good reason to be leery of loving again. He—" Pausing, she shook her head, then seeing Camille was waiting for her to continue, she said, "I'm not sure I should be repeating this. But he didn't ask me to keep it a secret."

"You don't have to tell me anything private about you and Taggart. Not unless you want to," Camille assured her.

The thought of what he'd gone through had continued to revolve through her mind, haunting her with images of his loss and pain.

Pinching the bridge of her nose, she said, "Maybe he's told Blake or someone in your family about this. I don't know. He didn't say. But he was married once—years ago. His wife and unborn child were killed in a car accident."

Camille looked genuinely stricken. "Oh, how completely horrible."

"Yes. And not only that, his mother died three months later. From what he told me, he was very close to her and losing all of them so close together has sort of warped his heart, I guess you'd say."

"No doubt. But time heals. We both know that. And none of that means he's incapable of falling in love again—with you," Camille argued. "After all, what man couldn't fall in love with you?"

The absurdity of Camille's question caused Emily-Ann to laugh outright. "Oh, sure. Men have been knocking down my door for years," she said with sarcastic humor.

"Well, you have one on your doorstep now. A good one.

What do you intend to do about it? Mother happens to believe you and Taggart make a perfect match. Should I tell her that you think so, too?"

Emily-Ann groaned, then looked across the room to where a row of men sat at a worn bar eating pie and drinking coffee. The image reminded her even more of Taggart scarfing up the pecan pie that Reeva had made for him. He'd eaten the dessert with the same enthusiasm he'd made love to her.

Swallowing hard, she turned her gaze back to Camille. "Tell your mother that it's going to take more than a bridal bouquet for Taggart to fall in love with me."

THE HORSES WERE TIRED, prompting Taggart and Matthew to pull them to a slow walk as they traveled the last half mile back to the ranch yard.

"The grass is looking good," Matthew said. "The cows are all settled where they need to be and the branding and vaccinating is all finished. I think it's about time Camille and I head back home to Red Bluff. You have everything under control here."

Taggart let out a cynical grunt, but his reaction had very little to do with being foreman of Three Rivers Ranch. He could truthfully say he felt confident about his job, with or without Matthew here to guide him. But as for his personal life, it was totally out of control.

Even if taking Emily-Ann into his bed had been the most incredible experience he'd ever had, it was still a stupid mistake on his part. He should've known that once he touched her, he'd only want more. He should've known that he couldn't just have sex with her, then walk away. No. She was meant to be made love to and he was very much afraid that's exactly what he'd done. Now his brain, his heart, his very being was consumed with her. And he didn't have a clue as to what he was going to do about it.

"I can't speak for Camille, but I'd be willing to say you'll be glad to get back to your own ranch."

This time it was Matthew who grunted. "For years, if anyone had told me I'd be looking forward to leaving Three Rivers for Red Bluff, I would've considered them crazy. Three Rivers was my very lifeblood. But things change. Most of the time in ways a man never expects."

Taggart understood that only too well. And in his own case, the changes weren't good. "Guess you're talking about your wife now," he said, as he absently flipped the ends of the split reins back and forth across the cantle of the saddle.

"Yeah. Nothing would mean much of anything without her and the coming baby. I'm building Red Bluff for them."

"Must be nice."

"Nice, hell. The feeling it gives me is impossible to describe." He glanced over at Taggart. "And frankly, I never imagined myself being this blessed. Sometimes it's scary because I never had much in the way of family. My mother died when my sister and I were young. After that we were sent to live with an uncle that was a real bastard. Finding the Hollisters and loving Camille is sometimes too good to believe. You understand what I'm trying to say."

"More than you could know, Matthew. My mother died, too, when I was in my midtwenties. And Dad—he's not worth talking about. I don't have a loving wife to share things with, but landing here on Three Rivers is more than I ever expected in my life."

"Yeah. I guess being here does feel pretty good to you."

Making his home on Three Rivers and being with Emily-Ann had changed his life drastically. And those good changes were scary. But he wasn't a timid little calf, afraid to follow his mama to greener pastures, Taggart mentally argued with himself. Sure, he'd suffered through some tragedies, but he'd come out on the other side a bit wiser and hopefully stronger. And a man couldn't go forward if he continually held on to the past.

"It feels damned good, Matthew," he finally replied.

For the next few minutes, the two men rode on down the well-trodden cattle trail in companionable silence until Matthew abruptly pulled his horse to a stop and climbed down from the saddle.

Taggart reined his buckskin next to Matthew's horse. "Anything wrong?" he asked.

"No. I'll be right back."

He walked a few steps off the trail and snapped off a long bough of blooming sage. After he climbed back into the saddle, he looked over at Taggart and grinned.

"Camille loves this stuff. It grows everywhere like annoying weeds, but she thinks it's beautiful and special. Go figure." He held up the branch with silver-green leaves and tiny purple blooms. "This will make her happy."

"You're a smart guy, Matthew."

The other man chuckled as he nudged his horse into a walk. "Not smart enough."

No, Taggart thought, a man could be a genius and still not be able to understand a woman. The tears he'd seen in Emily-Ann's eyes when they'd begun to make love had puzzled him. He'd kept wondering what she could've been thinking to put them there.

She hadn't been thinking, Taggart. She'd been feeling. Those tears had come straight from her heart. But you don't want to face that kind of truth. You don't want to think that Emily-Ann could feel that much for you. That would make everything more complicated and painful when it ended. Right?

Shoving at the nagging voice, Taggart glanced over at Matthew and the bough of sage he'd laid across the front of the saddle seat.

The foreman of Red Bluff was more like him than Taggart could've guessed. He'd not been born into wealth and from what he'd just said, his growing-up years had been far from easy. And along the way, he'd lost loved ones. Yet he'd found the courage to give his heart to a woman, to marry her and plan a future.

Could he be that brave? Taggart asked himself. Or was he going to keep on hiding his heart and hoping that Emily-Ann couldn't find it?

Chapter Ten

Emily-Ann leaned back from the computer monitor and rubbed her weary eyes. Ever since she'd gotten home from her outing with Camille at the Broken Spur, she'd been sitting at the tiny desk set up in her bedroom. That had been three hours ago. Now her eyes were burning and her shoulders felt like they were permanently locked in one painful position.

She was shutting down the computer and switching off a table lamp when her cell phone dinged with an incoming message.

Seeing it was from Taggart, she quickly grabbed up the phone and scanned the brief note.

Don't eat. I'll be there in thirty minutes.

Her heart tapping a rapid thud against her chest, she lowered the phone and stared unseeingly at the wall in front of her.

Taggart was coming to see her tonight? Only two days had passed since she'd gone to his place for supper. She'd not expected him to want to see her again this soon. What did it mean? That he was actually beginning to care about her? Or he was simply wanting another round of sex?

It was pointless to ask herself those questions. No matter the answers, she couldn't resist the man.

Focusing on the phone in her hand, she tapped a one-word reply.

Okay.

THIRTY MINUTES LATER after pulling on a pair of faded blue jeans and a red peasant blouse, she dabbed on a small amount of makeup and added a pair of silver hoops to her ears before she hurried to the living room to pick up the clutter.

She'd barely had time to carry a couple of dirty cups and a stack of junk mail to the kitchen when she heard Taggart's footsteps on the porch.

When she opened the door, he was standing on the threshold grinning back at her. Dressed in jeans and a blue denim shirt worn through in several places, he was holding a sack in each arm. The scent of fried food wafted toward her.

"Is that chicken I smell?" she asked, as she motioned him into the house.

The grin still on his face, he moved into the living room. "Since we ate beef the other night at my place, I thought you might like a change," he told her.

After dealing with the door, she crossed to where he was standing. "You didn't need to bring food. I would've made something for you," she said, then chuckled. "Uh—but you were probably afraid I'd give you cold cuts again."

"I love cold cuts," he insisted. "I just wanted to treat you."

Seeing him again was causing bubbles of joy to dance around inside of her and she didn't think twice about rising on the tips of her toes and pressing a kiss on his cheek.

"I'm so happy you're here, Tag. And thank you for the treat—whatever it is," she said, then gestured toward the kitchen. "Let's take it to the table."

He started toward the kitchen and Emily-Ann followed along at his side.

"Sorry about the short notice that I was coming," he said. "I hope you didn't have other plans."

"You mean like stare at the walls?" she teased, then shook her head. "No plans. In fact, I just finished studying for the night. I'm all set for my chemistry test."

"I'm glad it's you and not me. I was fairly good with math, but chemistry usually got me confused. Now Doc can rattle off all those different elements and medicines used to treat animals like he's talking about what he likes for breakfast."

"Chandler is a brain, plain and simple," Emily-Ann said.

They entered the kitchen and he placed the large paper sacks on the table. "I stopped by the clinic before I headed over here and Doc removed the stitches from my arm. He also gave me a warning to go with the service," he said.

"Oh, what was the warning?" she asked curiously, while thinking Chandler had probably warned Taggart to stay away from her. Not that the veterinarian was a snob. He was far from it. And he truly was Emily-Ann's friend. But that didn't mean he thought she'd be the right woman for their new foreman.

"That I quit playing with Holt's yearlings," Taggart answered.

Emily-Ann laughed. "Good advice."

His expression suddenly changed from playful to coy as he reached inside one of the sacks and pulled out a bunch of white tulips mixed with some sort of vivid pink flowers she'd never seen before. The bouquet was beautiful and obviously expensive.

"For you," he said gently. "I hope you like tulips."

Clasping the bouquet with both hands, she stared down at the blooms in stunned fascination. "I love tulips. I—"

Her words broke off as the tears clogging her throat made it impossible to speak.

Embarrassed by the overemotional reaction, she turned and hurried over to the sink. With her back turned to Taggart, she placed the flowers on the cabinet counter and attempted to wipe the tears that were suddenly rolling down her cheeks.

When she felt his hand come down on her shoulder, she sniffed and desperately tried to compose herself.

"Sorry, Tag. The way I'm acting you're probably thinking I never received flowers from a man before. And you'd be right. I haven't."

He didn't reply and, when his silence continued, Emily-Ann figured he was feeling worse than awkward. He was probably kicking himself for becoming involved with a woman who'd never so much as merited a bouquet of flowers.

Clearing her throat, she stepped away from the hold he had on her shoulder and walked to the opposite end of the cabinet to look for something to hold the bouquet. After a moment of digging around in a bottom shelf, she pulled out a pitcher made of blue knobby milk glass.

"I'll put the flowers in some water," she told him. "And then I'll set the table so we can eat. We don't want the food to get cold after you went to the trouble and expense of buying it."

She was chattering, but that was the only way she could handle his silence and keep her tears at bay at the same time.

Her attention focused solely on taking care of the bouquet, she filled the pitcher with water and dropped in the flowers. However, that was as far as she got before Taggart's hands were on her upper arms, pulling her around to face him.

"Forget the damned food," he muttered. "Forget about everything, but this."

He didn't give her time to utter any kind of question. Instead, he tugged her into his arms and fastened his mouth roughly over hers.

The contact of their lips was all it took to wipe everything from Emily-Ann's mind. All she could think about was making love to this man, who was quickly becoming everything to her.

Just as her taut nerves began to relax and her body sagged against his, he lifted his head and sucked in a ragged breath. "You don't have a clue as to how much I want you, Emily-Ann."

Her hands gripped the front of his denim shirt as she tilted her head back to look up at him. "But I thought—"

"You're always thinking too much," he interrupted.

Lowering her lashes, she looked up at him with a properly chastised expression. "And talking too much," she said, unable to stop the corners of her mouth from bending upward. "Aren't you going to tack that on, too?"

"No." His smile a little wicked, his hands slipped to the rounded curve of her bottom and pulled her hips forward until they were snug against his. "I have other ways to keep you from talking."

Her arms slipped up around his neck. "I'd like for you to show me those—other ways."

"It'll be my pleasure, sweet Emily-Ann."

Taking him by the hand, she led him through the small house until they reached her bedroom.

"I don't think we need a light this time," she said as she urged him toward the double bed covered in a white chenille bedspread. "The streetlight shines through the slats of the blinds."

"I wouldn't care if we were in the blaring sunlight or the deepest blackest night, I'd want you just as much," he said.

"I'll be honest, Tag, I didn't expect to see you again this soon." Even as she said the words, her hands were reaching for the front of his shirt, pulling the snaps apart. "You've made me happy."

He pushed her hair aside and pressed a track of kisses up the side of her neck and onto her ear. "Mmm. I'll try my best to make you even happier."

Seconds ticked by as he showered kisses upon her face and lips, then down the creamy column of her throat. When his mouth finally reached the cleavage between her breasts, he lifted his head and went to work removing her clothes.

By the time he got down to her bra and panties, her breaths had gone short and rapid, while her heart was pounding, drumming out a rhythm that he and he alone controlled.

"Tag, I don't think you—you're not supposed to be making me feel this good," she whispered hoarsely. "It's decadent. And scary. And addictive."

He groaned. "It's not me that's making this magic. It's us. Together."

With her lingerie off and out of the way, he eased her onto the bed, then quickly shed his own clothing and joined her in the middle of the mattress.

She reached to wrap her arms around him and as his mouth found hers, his hands began a slow foray of her body, pausing at certain parts to tug and tease, until the fire inside her began to burn hotter than an Arizona wildfire. She did her best to reciprocate the pleasure by soothing her fingers over his broad shoulders, down his rib cage and onto his back.

Between them she could feel his hard erection pressing against her belly and the evidence of his desire emboldened her to give everything to him and take exactly what she wanted.

He continued to kiss her over and over and each time the connection grew deeper until she was certain their breaths had braided into one life-giving function. Thinking became non-existent as her senses scattered like a covey of birds flying in every direction. All she knew was that Taggart wanted her and she wanted him with every cell of her being.

And when he finally rolled her onto her back and coupled his body with hers, Emily-Ann felt, for the first time in her life, that she was totally and truly complete.

MUCH LATER, AFTER Taggart had gathered enough energy to open his eyes, he noticed the cover at the foot of the double bed was striped with artificial light streaming through the blinds. Alongside him, Emily-Ann was lying on her back, her breasts rising and falling as she slowly regained her breath.

Across the small room, on the wall directly in front of the bed, a partially raised window allowed the cool night air to drift over them. The breeze carried no scent of sage or juniper. And though he caught the sound of barking dogs and distant traffic, there was no bawling cows, nickering horses or wailing coyotes.

Next to him, Emily-Ann stirred and slipped an arm across his waist.

In a drowsy voice, she asked, "What are you thinking?"

"How different it feels to be in town." Which was true enough, he thought. But he couldn't tell her all the other things that were swirling around in his mind. Like how the simple touch of her hand turned him inside out and how being with her had become a very important part of his life.

"Hmm. Well, you're not a town guy," she remarked, then rose up on one elbow and looked down at his face. "I've been wondering something about you."

A wry grin slanted his lips. "What's that? If I've ever spent time in jail?"

She chuckled. "The possibility never crossed my mind. But I'll bet you'd look good in orange."

He couldn't help but laugh and when his gaze found her sweet face in the semidarkness, he felt everything inside him go soft and gooey.

"What have you been wondering?"

With her free hand, she trailed fingers up and down the length of his arm. "Where you learned about ranching? How you came to be a cowboy?"

He drew in a long breath, then blew it out in a rough sigh. "From my maternal grandfather and my father. When I was a little kid, my sister and I and our parents all lived with Grandad Walt on his ranch near Hereford. So I grew up learning all about being a cowboy and caring for livestock."

Her brows pulled together. "Oh. Didn't you tell me before that your father was a carpenter?"

"That was several years later," he explained. "See, Grandad Walt died suddenly and willed the ranch to his sister. So we all had to move out. When that happened Dad went to work on the Flying W."

She stared at him in wonder. "Your grandfather didn't consider leaving the ranch to his daughter—your mother? Seems like that would've been the logical thing. Especially with your whole family already living there."

Taggart snorted cynically. "Are you kidding? Grandad couldn't stand Dad. He only tolerated his son-in-law because of his daughter. And to be fair, he knew what my father would do with the place if it went to Mom. Dad would've wrung every dollar he could from it, then let it go to ruin. No, Grandad made the right choice."

Frowning, she said, "Wait a minute. Did you say your father went to work on the Flying W? Isn't that—"

"Yeah. The ranch where I worked before I moved to Three Rivers. Doesn't sound right, but it's true. Several years after they fired Dad, I wanted to get away from the monotony of the feedlot job and asked the family with the Flying W to hire me. I was fortunate. The Williamsons didn't hold it against me because of Dad's shiftless attitude. You see, he didn't like taking orders. Nor did he want to do anything that required him to get off his horse—like mending fences, repairing broken windmills, or whatever needed to be done on the ground."

"What a terrible waste—on your father's part, I mean," she said. "Sounds like he had plenty of good opportunities and blew them."

Talking about his father's shortcomings had never been easy for Taggart, but he learned with Emily-Ann he didn't need to sugarcoat the facts. He could be honest and not have to worry about her being judgmental.

He said, "Well, selfish people tend to squander anything that's worthwhile."

"Hmm. Sad, but true." She eased her head onto his shoulder. "I witnessed plenty of squandering in my family, Tag, and I don't want to be guilty of doing it. Especially with you."

Sliding his hand against her back, he threaded his fingers in her long hair. It was still damp from the exertion of their lovemaking and when he lifted the strands to his lips, the scent was a reminder of all the soft and tender things he'd missed these past years.

No. He didn't want to squander this precious time with Emily-Ann, he thought. He wanted to hold on to it—to her—as long as this thing between them continued to hold together.

"You know, we have food waiting for us in the kitchen," he murmured.

"Mmm. And my beautiful flowers, too." She tilted her head just enough to allow her gaze to settle on his face. "Tag, the flowers—I didn't mean to cry. The tears came before I could stop them—because I was so touched that you thought of me in that way. And I was thinking, too, that all through my mother's life, she never received a single flower from a man. She was a good woman. She deserved better—but I could only think that I didn't deserve better than her. Does that make sense to you?"

He tightened his arm across her back and drew her closer to his side.

"Sorry, but it doesn't make sense," he said gently. "You're a good woman, too. And you're not your mother. Just like I'm not like any of those guys who've disappointed you in the past."

She studied his face for long moments and then she asked, "Do you think we could forget about the food for a little while? Right now I need to kiss your lips. I want to make sure they really did say I was a good woman."

Cupping his hand at the back of her head, he drew her face upward until the tip of his nose was brushing hers. "Right now my lips are going to say the food can be reheated."

With a lusty chuckle, she curled her arm around his neck. "I can be, too."

THE MORNING SUN was just beginning to peep over the eastern hills as Taggart watched the cowboys form groups of two and three as they headed in different directions across the ranch yard. The work orders he'd just given the men for the day had all been received with smiles and good-natured jokes.

Since he'd taken over the job of foreman, not one had grumbled or griped about the task he'd assigned them. Taggart liked to think the men were cooperative because they approved of him being their new foreman. Yet he realized they'd all been handpicked by the Hollisters and most of them had been here on Three Rivers Ranch for years. Some even before Taggart had been born. They weren't the type of men to slough off or complain.

The thought caused his mind to drift back to the night he'd taken Emily-Ann the flowers and he'd talked to her about his father and the problems the man had caused his family. Something had happened to him that night. He'd felt a connection to Emily-Ann that was unlike anything he'd ever experienced before. It had filled him with warm contentment and a sense of homecoming. Now, more than two weeks later, he was still trying to figure out exactly what those feelings meant and how he was going to hold on to them—and her.

Walking over to the horse he'd saddled for his personal use today, he tried to put Emily-Ann out of his mind for the moment. He had work to do and she was coming out to the ranch to see him tonight. He'd let himself concentrate on her then.

Hell, he'd do more than concentrate, he thought. Once he had her in his arms, he wouldn't be letting her go until the wee hours of the morning.

And do you honestly believe having sex is all the woman wants from you, Taggart? Could be that she's just like all other women. She might want to be wined and dined and taken somewhere other than to bed. But then, you don't really care about what she wants, do you? You say you don't want to be like the other men she's had in her life, but that's a laugh. You need to take a long look in the mirror and make yourself face the truth.

Doing his best to block out the caustic voice going off in his head, he got busy tightening the cinch strap on the saddle. With that task finished, he was checking the rest of the tack when the cell phone in his pocket pinged with a new message.

Thinking it might be Blake wanting him to stop by the office, he pulled out the phone and was a bit surprised to see a message so early in the morning from his sister, Tallulah.

To give you a heads-up—Dad has been coming around, asking for money. I haven't given him any. But he's making noises about coming out there to see you. Guess he thinks you're rich now. She ended the message with a heart emoji, along with a smiley face.

Hearing from his sister usually gave Taggart a happy lift, but this warning about their father was unsettling. Damn it. The man was a user and Taggart wanted no part of him. And he definitely didn't want the man making his sister miserable or messing up things here on Three Rivers.

"That frown on your face is about as deep as the Grand Canyon. Trouble this morning?"

Maureen's voice pulled Taggart out of his dark thoughts and he turned around to see the Hollister matriarch walking up to him. She was wearing her usual work attire of jeans and boots and an old gray felt hat pulled over her chestnut ponytail. A saddled bay horse followed close behind her right shoulder.

"No. Nothing that can't be fixed." He dropped the phone back into his shirt pocket and looked at her. "The men are just now heading out. Were you planning on joining some of them, or me?"

Smiling, she said, "Given a choice, I'll take you. I don't know what you had planned for this morning, but I thought we might take a long ride."

Questions immediately circled through Taggart's head. Normally Gil showed up with Maureen every morning and the two of them had been going out together to help with the ranching chores. But the man was clearly absent today.

"I can do that," he said. "Did you have a certain place on the ranch in mind?"

"I do. I want to ride over to water pump number nine."

Taggart stared at the woman and hoped the shock he was feeling didn't show on his face. "Maureen, I—are you sure? That's the place—"

Her lips formed a grim line. "Listen, Tag, you don't have to tiptoe around me. My sons think they need to treat me like I'm a marshmallow or something. They're wrong. Do I look soft?"

"Not exactly." On the outside she was an attractive woman, but Taggart had already learned that on the inside she was as tough as nails.

"Hell, I'm not going to fall apart if someone mentions Joel's name. Or says he was most likely murdered. I've lived with the reality of his death for years now."

"Yes, but do you think it's wise for us to ride to that area? Does anyone, other than me, know what you have planned?"

She scowled at him. "No. And I don't intend on telling any of them. I don't want to hear all their arguments and excuses to try to stop me. As far as anyone knows, you and I are going out to check on a herd of cows. That's what I told Reeva when I left the house this morning and that's what we'll tell anyone else if they ask. Got it?"

"Got it," Taggart assured her. "We're checking on cows."

What else could he say? She was the owner of the ranch. He didn't want to go against her wishes. But the more he thought about it, the more he liked the idea that she felt she could trust him. And if he could help her, even if it was just to ease her curiosity about the area where her husband had met his demise, it would be well worth the ride.

She wasted no time swinging herself into the saddle. "I have a canteen of water," she said. "Do you?"

"I have a couple of bottles in my saddlebags."

She rolled her eyes. "You young people. Those things burst at the drop of your hat. Plus they don't keep the water cool like a canteen. I'm going to make a point to buy you one."

Grinning, Taggart finished tightening his cinch. "Yes, ma'am."

Maureen chuckled as he swung his leg over the saddle and reined his horse alongside hers.

She said, "Forgive me, Tag. I'm sounding like a mother. Sometimes I just can't help myself."

"Don't worry. I can get used to it."

For the next two hours they rode in a southerly direction, occasionally alternating the gait of the horses from a walk to a long trot.

With the ranch covering miles in all directions, Taggart still hadn't seen all there was to see of the property. But last week, he'd ridden with Joseph over to water well number nine and he'd not forgotten how to get there. The deputy was always in hopes of finding new evidence and the two of them had searched several dry gulches before they'd finally given up and headed home.

Taggart was wondering if Maureen knew about their recent trip or any of the past trips her sons had made to this area of the ranch. So far during their ride, she'd not mentioned anything about the investigation the men had been making into Joel's death, but that didn't mean she was oblivious to what had been going on.

"I imagine you've been wondering why Gil didn't show up with me today," she said, as the two of them crossed a shallow stream shaded with willows.

"It did cross my mind," Taggart admitted.

"He had to go to Phoenix today on police business. They still ask for his help sometimes on certain cases. But he doesn't plan on making a habit of going down there. He'd rather be here on the ranch."

"He seems to like doing ranch work." And being with you, Taggart could've added.

"Ranching is what he was really meant to do," she said, then glanced over at him. "I think my children and most everyone who knows me has been wondering why I invited Gil to move into the ranch house instead of getting a place of his own."

"I've not heard anyone remarking on the subject," Taggart said honestly.

She let out a short laugh. "I'm sure the subject has been beaten to death by many, but that doesn't really worry me. There are reasons I feel this way. And no. Gil and I aren't having an affair, but we are growing close. Like you and Emily-Ann, maybe?"

Her question caught him by complete surprise. Not that she knew he'd been seeing Emily-Ann, but because she'd openly asked him about it.

Knowing his expression was worse than sheepish, he wiped a hand over his face and tried to give her a genuine smile.

"We have been spending a lot of time together. She's a special woman."

"I've always known it would take a special man to see that about her. I'm glad it's you, Tag."

What would Maureen think if he told her that he'd been doing more than seeing Emily-Ann? That he was having an affair with her? Most likely, she'd be highly disappointed in him. It was obvious that Maureen thought of Emily-Ann as a third daughter and she didn't want her hurt for anyone or any reason.

Not that Taggart planned to hurt her. But he was beginning to ask himself just how far their relationship could go. In spite of how happy she made him, he still couldn't let himself think in terms of forever. He'd already learned that there was no forever. Not for him.

His troubled thoughts must have shown on his face, because Maureen suddenly asked, "What's wrong? You look awfully glum for a man who has a special woman in his life."

Lifting his hat from his head, he swiped a hand through his sweaty hair. "I haven't told anybody but Emily-Ann about this, but I was married a long time ago. She and the baby we were expecting got killed in a car crash."

"I know."

Stunned, he stared at her. He couldn't believe Emily-Ann

had divulged something he'd told her in private. "How did you know?"

The smile she gave him was gentle and reassuring. "You don't think I would allow anyone to come in and take over the foreman job at Three Rivers without learning all about him first, now do you?"

So the Hollisters had done more than read his résumé, Taggart thought. Well, he should have already realized they would do a background check on him. They ran a multimillion-dollar business. They couldn't take chances on hiring someone who might end up being dishonest.

"Oh. Well, you never mentioned anything about it to me," he reasoned.

"There wasn't any point. And I wouldn't be doing it now but I think I've become somewhat of an expert at being a widow and I know the sort of things that are probably still going through your mind—even though it's been a long time since the tragedy."

Sighing, he absently stroked the sorrel's neck. "You can't forget, Maureen. Not entirely."

"Exactly. But you can move beyond it."

Curious now, he looked at her. "Is that what you've done with Gil?"

Before she could answer, he swiftly shook his head. "I'm sorry, Maureen. I'm being too damned nosy. Just forget I asked that."

"No. I'm glad you did ask it. My answer is that I'm trying. And that's what I hope you're doing, too, Tag. With Emily-Ann. Moving forward. Unafraid. I think you both deserve that."

He could've told her he'd been hoping for the same thing. Hoping that one day soon, he would wake up feeling like a confident man. God only knew how much he wanted to be free of the past and to be able to reach out for the things he truly wanted. But moving on took lots of courage and strength and so far he'd not been able to find those things.

Glancing ahead, he noticed they were approaching an arroyo

that was so deep that cattle and horses could only climb in and out at certain places.

"We don't have very far to go to the well pump now, Maureen," Taggart told her. "If you want to turn around and go back, I'll understand."

Shaking her head, she smiled at him. "I just gave you a talk about moving forward, Tag, and that's exactly what we're going to do."

She nudged her spurs into the horse's side and the bay took off into a long trot straight toward the arroyo.

Taggart realized Maureen wasn't going to give him the option of turning around. Like it or not, he had to follow. And he suddenly wondered if this long trip had actually been taken for her sake, or his.

Chapter Eleven

Later that same day, a few short miles before the turnoff to Three Rivers Ranch, Emily-Ann passed the entrance to the Bar X where Tessa and Joseph lived with their young son, Little Joe, and baby daughter, Spring. The youngest of the Hollister brothers, he'd been the first to marry and have children. Now the men were all married with growing families and so were their sisters, Vivian and Camille. One by one, Emily-Ann had watched them find love and happiness, the kind that tied two people together for the duration of their lives. And somewhere between the weddings and showers and christenings, she'd hoped and prayed that the same sort of love and happiness would come to her.

So far it hadn't happened, and though she'd allowed her hopes to rise when she'd first met Taggart, she was beginning to accept the fact that he'd been completely honest when he told her he wasn't looking for anything long-term.

This past month the two of them had spent every possible night they could manage with each other. And when she'd been lying in his arms, he'd never as much as mentioned the word *love*, much less coupled it with the word *future*. The two of them were simply living in the moment. And she had no idea how much longer this thing between them could last.

The reality caused her to push out a heavy sigh, but it was hardly enough to make her put her foot on the brake and turn the car around. No. Being with Taggart was something she couldn't resist. He made her feel beautiful and sexy and worthy. And for now she had to hold on to the hope that one day he might actually fall in love with her.

You ninny. When are you ever going to grow up? A man like Taggart isn't ever going to fall in love with you. The only kind of man you'll ever snag is one that's afraid of his own shadow, poor as a church mouse, or so slovenly you'll have to knock his feet off the furniture. This cowboy is temporary with a capital T.

Hating the nagging voice rattling around in her head, Emily-Ann pushed harder on the accelerator. Taggart was waiting for her and right now that was all that mattered.

TAGGART WAS LATE GETTING HOME. Through the darkness he could see Emily-Ann's car already parked in her usual spot next to a patch of prickly pear. The fact that she was here to greet him lifted some of the fatigue from his shoulders.

By the time he reached the steps to the porch, he spotted her sitting in the wooden swing. King was up in the seat, lying with his head on her lap.

"So much for King being a big, tough working dog," he joked. "It's no wonder he wants to stay here instead of the ranch yard—where he belongs."

Smiling, she stroked the dog's head. "With a name like his, he's supposed to be treated like royalty."

"Hmm. I think I'll change mine to prince." Grinning, he sauntered over to the swing. "Maybe I'll get more kisses that way."

"Hah!"

Easing the dog's head off her lap, she stood, wrapped her arms around Taggart's waist and planted a soft kiss on his lips. "Hello, Prince."

The sweetness of her greeting pushed away the troubling

thoughts that had drifted in and out of his head all day and he gladly kissed her again. Just to make sure they didn't reappear to ruin this night for him.

"Sorry I'm so late. You should have gone on in the house. Have you been here long?"

"Not too long," she answered. "And don't worry, I've already been inside. I brought food."

Curving his arm around her shoulders, he urged her toward the door. Behind them, King lifted his head and whined in protest.

Pausing, Emily-Ann glanced back at the dog. "We could let him inside for a little while, couldn't we?"

"Are you kidding? He's a cur—a working dog. He's not supposed to be in the house. Doc would have a fit."

"I seriously doubt Chandler would throw a fit. Of all the Hollister brothers, he has the softest heart."

"You say that like you're sure."

She beamed a knowing smile at him. "I should be sure. I've known them since I was in third grade."

And that was a heck of a lot longer than Taggart had been acquainted with the Hollisters. Which made it no surprise that Maureen made no bones about wanting Emily-Ann to be happy and treated with respect. Taggart got the impression that Maureen believed his intentions toward Emily-Ann were honorable and he'd not said anything to make her believe otherwise. So now he could label himself a big hypocrite along with being a coward, he thought grimly.

Caving in to Emily-Ann and the dog, he said, "Okay. Come on, King. I guess you can be a house dog for a little while."

The three of them entered the house and Taggart promptly excused himself. "I'd better go wash up before we eat," he told her.

"Take your time. I'll get things ready for our supper."

Short minutes later, when he entered the kitchen, he noticed Emily-Ann had set the table with paper plates. As she filled iced glasses with sweet tea, he sniffed the air with appreciation.

"Mmm. How did you know I'd been craving pizza?"

She placed the pitcher on the table. "You talk in your sleep."

Laughing, he walked over to the table and pulled out her chair. "Since when have I ever been asleep while we're in bed together?"

A pink blush stole over her cheeks and he was amazed that the intimate part of their relationship still had that much effect on her.

"Good point," she said with a chuckle.

After she was seated, he made himself comfortable in the chair angled to her right elbow. Emily-Ann promptly opened the lid on the pizza box and offered it to him.

"You must have had last-minute work to keep you late," she said. "I was beginning to think there was an emergency going on."

He placed two wedges of pizza on his plate, while marveling how the day had ended up pulling every ounce of energy from his body. Which didn't make sense. Most of the day he'd spent in the saddle, riding with Maureen, and the rest had been spent at the ranch yard sorting steers to be shipped to Red Bluff.

"No. Nothing like that. I was just running behind on everything that needed to get done. Maureen and I rode most of the morning and part of the afternoon—checking on cows."

She looked faintly surprised, but not nearly as surprised as Taggart had felt this morning when Maureen had approached him with her wishes.

"Oh. Did Gil go with you? I remember you saying he'd been going out every day, working with Maureen."

"No. Gil had to make a trip to Phoenix today."

She cast him a curious glance as she helped herself to the pizza. "I'll bet Gil has been looking into Joel's death. Did Maureen mention anything about it?"

He'd promised Maureen he wouldn't mention that the two of them had ridden to water pump number nine. And he would keep that promise. But he didn't want to lie to Emily-Ann, either. "Only in passing. She's aware that her sons have been investigating the matter. I get the impression she has her own ideas about Joel's death. I can see that Maureen isn't a vindictive person, but if it was ever revealed that Joel was murdered, she'd damn well want justice served."

"And who could blame her for that? Losing Joel was like sticking a knife in the heart of the family."

Taggart didn't make a reply to that and as long seconds ticked by without her saying more, he was relieved that she'd decided to drop the gloomy subject.

"You look exceptionally pretty tonight. That dress is nice." The green-and-white fabric formed a ruffle that fell just off her creamy shoulders. The top part of her hair was wound into a bun, while the rest hung loose against her back.

"Thanks. Actually it's a gift from Camille. She loves to buy me things even though I tell her not to." She looked at him with sad acceptance. "She tells me that she and Matthew are going to be leaving for Red Bluff next week. It'll probably be ages before I see her again."

"Maybe not. Matthew has TooTall to keep things going while he's away. They'll probably come in for a holiday or special occasion."

The smile she gave him was wan at best. "I hope so. Anyway, I can tell when we talk that she's missing the diner and her friends at Dragoon. Maybe they'll make the trip back up here for Sam and Gabby's wedding. That's going to be a very special occasion. Isabelle tells me they're going to throw a big shindig on the Bar X and invite the whole countryside."

His sigh was heavy. "I'm not surprised. Weddings seem to be important functions around here."

She looked at him as though she wanted to say something, then quickly changed her mind. Was she thinking it was about time she had a wedding of her own?

Don't be stupid, Taggart. Emily-Ann hasn't known you long

enough to fall in love with you, much less decide she wants to be your wife.

Maybe not, Taggart thought, as he fought against the voice inside him. But when she held him, kissed him, he felt as though she was pouring her heart out to him. And he'd been just greedy enough to take it. Or maybe he'd been misinterpreting all those sighs and kisses and words of desire whispered in his ear. A woman could enjoy sex without having her heart involved. Could be she was beginning to think Taggart was a dead-end street and she wanted to travel down a bigger and better avenue. One where she could find a man more than willing to marry her.

Finally she said, "Weddings are very important—to some people."

He didn't know what to say to that and after a moment they both fell silent until she pushed back her plate.

"One piece is all I can eat," she said. "You can save the rest of it for your supper tomorrow night."

He'd never known Emily-Ann to be a finicky eater. "Are you feeling ill?"

"No." She smiled at him as though to prove it. "I'm fine. I just had a very busy day. I had to try to take a test between waiting on customers this morning. It was chaotic. I only hope I passed."

"I had a surprise this morning," he told her. "I got a message from my sister saying that Dad had been bugging her for money. He's threatening to come out here to Arizona."

Her brows lifted. "Threatening? That's a strange word to use in connection with your father."

"Well, if you knew him, you'd understand why I worded it in that way. He causes trouble wherever he goes. And he doesn't ask, he demands. I don't want to have to deal with him, Emily-Ann. And I certainly don't want the Hollisters to meet him."

She reached across the table and smoothed her fingertips over the fresh scar where he'd been bitten by the stallion.

"I wouldn't worry. I'm betting he doesn't have the money

to make the trip out here. But he wants you to think he'll show up so that you'll send money to him. Just to make sure he stays away."

"You're probably right. And I can't be worrying about him now. I just don't want him harassing my sister."

She rose from the table and crossed the room to where the coffee machine sat at the end of the cabinet counter. As she began to gather the makings, she said, "Sounds like she's the one who needs to make the trip out here. A one-way trip."

"I've considered the idea of asking her to move here. But I need to get some things…settled before I do."

After she flipped the switch and the coffee began to brew, she walked back over to the table and rested her hands on the back of his shoulders. "What kind of things settled? Your job is secure. And you have a nice home here. You don't have anything else to settle—unless you're talking about your finances."

It suddenly dawned on Taggart that sometime during the past month they'd quit talking like people who were simply dating and started conversing like a man and wife. He couldn't rationalize how or why that had happened. Except that somewhere along the way he'd made a huge mistake. He'd slowly and surely allowed himself to get too close to Emily-Ann.

"I'm not concerned about that." He tilted his head around so that he could look up at her. "When the coffee finishes, I'd like to go to the living room. I need to talk to you about something."

DEEP DOWN, EMILY-ANN had always known that sooner or later, she'd get the old "we need to talk" from Taggart. Yet she'd thought, or maybe she'd been hoping more than thinking, that she wouldn't hear those final words from him for a long, long while.

And why not? Everything had been going so great between them. If all the passion he'd showered on her this past month had been an act, then he deserved an award for the performance.

But passion wasn't love, she realized. And love was the binder that held two people together. Not a set of sweaty sheets.

Emily-Ann carried a tray with their coffee and a saucer of Reeva's homemade cookies into the living room and after setting it on the coffee table, she eased down next to Taggart.

He looked unusually tired this evening and she wondered if spending most of the day with Maureen had stressed him out. Not that the woman was difficult to get along with. On the contrary, she was a joy to be around. But she and Blake were Taggart's bosses. He might've been feeling like he was under a microscope. *Anyway, what did any of that matter now?* she glumly asked herself.

Getting right to the point, she asked, "So what did you want to talk to me about?"

He reached for one of the coffees and took a long sip before he spoke. "I've been doing a lot of thinking about you and me. We've been spending a great deal of time together—both of us driving back and forth from here to Wickenburg. Which is hardly a short distance."

"I haven't minded." Her palms were so sweaty she had to wipe them on a napkin from the tray before she could pick up her coffee cup.

"I don't feel good about it, Emily-Ann. I worry about you driving in the dark on these lonely dirt roads. It isn't safe."

She didn't know where he was going with this. "I guess you're thinking about your late wife now."

He looked at her with something like surprise and then the expression turned to a glower. "No. I'm not thinking about her. I'm thinking about *you*—being safe."

"Oh. But surely you're not thinking you'll do all the driving to my place."

"No. I'm not. I'm young and healthy, but I don't think I could hold up to that pace and work, too."

Over the rim of her cup, she studied his face and tried to interpret the expressions she saw in his eyes and on his lips.

He looked frustrated and lost and most of all weary. But from what? Was she doing this to him?

"Okay. So I guess this means you want us to slow down. To just see each other once in a while. Is that what you're trying to tell me?"

He looked at her and frowned. "Hell, no. What I'm trying to tell you is that I want you to move in with me."

Emily-Ann had never been so stunned in her life. For the past fifteen minutes she'd resigned herself to the fact that he wanted to end things. Instead, he was asking her to move in!

She must have stared at him far longer than she thought because he finally scooted to the edge of the cushion and squared around to face her.

"Well? You're not saying anything. What do you think?"

"I wasn't expecting this from you." Dazed, she rose and walked across the room to where the main door had been left open to allow the cool night air to sift through an old-fashioned screen door. "If you want me to be completely honest, I don't like it."

Her throat was so thick she was surprised he'd heard the choked words. But he must have because he was suddenly standing directly behind her and so close that she could feel the heat radiating from his body.

"Why don't you like it?"

How could she begin to answer his question when she couldn't even explain the reasons to herself? She only knew that if she moved in with Taggart, she'd be giving up everything she'd ever wanted for herself.

"I—just don't think it's a good idea," she whispered, as the reality of his feelings were suddenly becoming quite clear to her.

His hands came down on her shoulders and for a second the emptiness inside of her wanted to turn and grab hold of him.

"You have something against a man and a woman living together—is that it?"

"No. It's probably the right choice for some people. Just not for me."

Awkward moments of silence began to tick away as she held her breath and waited for his response. Yet even as she clung to the tiniest hope that he'd say something—anything about loving her, she knew deep down that he was never going to have those kinds of feelings for her.

"I thought you liked being with me," he reasoned. "And I definitely want to be with you. I thought us living together here on the ranch was a good solution."

A solution to what? she wanted to ask. His urge to have sex whenever he wanted? Maybe that was enough for him, but not for her.

Her throat aching, she whispered, "Moving in with a guy has never been what I've planned for myself, Tag."

He tightened his hold on her shoulders. "A person can change their plans."

"Yes, and I can see I'm definitely going to have to change mine."

"What does that mean?" he asked.

Summoning up more strength than she ever dreamed she possessed, she turned to face him and then nearly wilted as her gaze met his. Confusion and disappointment swirled in the brown depths of his eyes.

She said, "It means that I think it would be best if we didn't see each other anymore."

He visibly flinched and she realized she'd surprised him. No doubt he'd seen her as too besotted with him to walk away. Well, she *was* besotted with the man, she thought sickly. More than that. She was in love with him. But no way would she ever admit that to him now. No, at least this way she could walk away with some shred of pride in herself.

"Are you serious?"

"Never more so," she said flatly. "You've made your feelings clear, Tag. And frankly, we're not on the same page."

A scowl caused his brows to form one dark line. "Am I supposed to understand that?"

Sighing, she reached up and gently touched her fingers to his dear face. For days after he'd given her the flowers, she gazed at them and allowed herself to believe they might have a real future together as man and wife—the whole family shebang. What a gullible idiot she'd been.

"No. I don't expect you to understand, Tag. And I'm sorry that you feel slighted. It's all my fault, really. When we first met, you made your feelings clear about love and marriage. I should've run from you then. But I didn't. So here we are at a dead end. That's all."

She hadn't thought it was possible for his frown to go any deeper but somehow it did. Taut lines ran from the corners of his mouth and eyes and furrowed his brow. He looked like a man in physical pain, but she knew that wasn't the case. Not over losing her. A man had to love beforehand to experience that kind of loss.

"Love and marriage? Don't you think you're rushing things?"

His disbelief verged on the comical and the reality that he considered love and marriage to her a joke was all it took to have her backing away from him.

"Get this straight, Tag, I'm not asking anything from you. Now or ever! So relax. Go have yourself a good laugh."

She stalked over to the end table where she'd left her handbag when she'd arrived earlier this evening. After shouldering the leather strap, she walked back to the door with King trotting right on her heels.

"This is your way of solving things?" he asked, his voice incredulous.

She struggled to keep her lips from quivering. "There's nothing to solve. I'm glad for the time we spent together, but all good things come to an end. We both know that. But if you ever decide you want a cup of coffee and a pastry, you know how to find Conchita's."

She pushed past him and out the door. In spite of the pain ripping her heart and the tears swimming in her eyes, she put one foot in front of the other until she was down the porch and out to her car.

When she opened the door to climb in, she realized King had followed her and the sight of the whining dog was enough to cause a sob to slip past her lips.

Kneeling down to him, she cradled his face with both hands. "King, you can't come with me. You have to stay here on the ranch and hunt cows in the brush. That's your job. Tag will take care of you and someday—maybe—I'll see you again."

She dropped a kiss on top of the dog's head, then quickly climbed in the car and drove away. It wasn't until she was a quarter mile away from the house that she noticed King was chasing after her.

Blocking the dog and Taggart from her mind, she pressed down on the accelerator and headed the car onto the main road that would take her back to Wickenburg. Where she belonged.

TAGGART STOOD ON the porch and stared into the darkness where Emily-Ann's taillights had disappeared only minutes before.

What in hell had just happened? How could she just leave like that without giving him a chance to explain and reason with her?

Forget the past. Move forward. Hell! That's exactly what he'd been trying to do when he'd asked Emily-Ann to move in with him. But she'd taken the invitation as an insult. Maureen's theory on life was probably good for her, but it hadn't work for Taggart, he thought glumly.

He muttered a curse, then stuck two fingers in his mouth and let out a loud whistle.

"King! Come here, you damned traitor! There's no use chasing after a woman who doesn't want us!"

A couple of long minutes passed before the dog finally emerged from the dark lane and trotted up to the house.

As King approached the porch, Taggart started to give him

a harsh scolding, but that plan was waylaid the minute the dog sat down next to him and let out a pathetic whine.

"Okay, boy," Taggart said, as he bent to pat the dog's head. "You're not in trouble. You'll just have to forget about her. That's what I'm going to do."

He turned and started back into the house and King determinedly trotted behind him. When they reached the screen door, Taggart hesitated for only a moment before he allowed the dog to follow him into the house.

The tray of coffee and cookies that Emily-Ann had carried to the living room were still on the coffee table. He picked it up and carried it to the kitchen where their meal of pizza was still scattered over the table and nearby cabinet counter.

Taggart began to clear away the mess, while wishing he could clear away the agony and confusion he was feeling.

Today, for the first time in years, he'd decided it was time to try to tear down the walls he'd built around his heart. Not just because Maureen had suggested he move on from the past, but because he felt like things between him and Emily-Ann had reached a point where snatching pieces of time here and there to be together was no longer enough. He'd thought having her move in would be the next logical step. Then he'd have plenty of time to get used to the idea of having her in his life for the long haul. He'd have a chance to decide if he really wanted to commit that much of himself to her.

And what the hell was Emily-Ann supposed to do while you sat around trying to make up your mind, Taggart? She deserves more than a trial run from you and you know it. So if that's all you can give her, then you got exactly what you deserve—a swift goodbye.

Damn. Damn. Taggart silently cursed as he tried to shut out the condemning voice in his head. Didn't he have a reason to be cautious? Didn't he have a right to think things through before he handed another woman his heart?

Yes, he did. But that didn't mean he had the right to take

her to bed and expect that to be all she needed or wanted, he thought miserably.

Jamming the leftover pizza back into its box, he shoved it into the refrigerator, then got out his phone and punched his sister's number.

He was sinking into a chair at the table when she finally answered.

"Hi, Tag. How's my sweet brother?"

Sweet? Right now he felt as bitter as a green persimmon. "I'm fine," he lied, while wondering what he could do to get the clenched knot out of his stomach and the pain in his chest to go away. "I'm just calling to check on you."

There was a moment's pause and then she said, "I'm sorry if my text this morning caused you to worry about me. Everything is okay, Tag, really. I can handle Dad."

"Yeah, by tiptoeing around him like a Gila monster."

She sighed and Taggart could easily picture his sister with her dark hair hanging around her shoulders and her brown eyes full of warmth. Tallulah not only resembled their late mother, but she also possessed her soft heart. That was one of the reasons he didn't want her to have to deal with Buck O'Brien. She wasn't emotionally strong enough. Especially now that she and Trent had gotten divorced.

"He's not that bad—yet. But I'm thinking he's gotten into some kind of trouble that he doesn't want me to find out about."

Taggart gripped the phone, while wondering how much more his aching head could handle tonight. "What kind of trouble?" he dared to ask.

"I don't know anything for sure. It's just a hunch that he might be involved with some nasty loan sharks and they're breathing down his neck to be repaid. He seems more desperate than usual."

He groaned out loud. "That's just dandy. What's the old man going to do next, huh?"

"Who knows? Just be glad you're out there in Arizona, far away from the man, Tag."

He'd thought leaving the Flying W, and the demanding new owners, along with his shiftless father, would make his life free of stress and worry. Now he realized how ridiculous that sort of thinking had been. This rip between him and Emily-Ann was like nothing he'd ever endured. But he couldn't let himself think about her now. If he did, he might just break down and spill the whole pitiful mess to his sister.

"That's another reason I'm calling, sis. I've been doing some thinking. About you."

A teasing chuckle sounded in his ear. "Missing me already?"

"Sure I am. You're the only family I have."

There was a moment of silence and then he caught the soft sound of her sigh.

"You're the only family I have, too, Tag."

"That makes what I'm about to propose make even more sense," he told her. "I'd like for you to move out here, Tally."

"To Arizona? And live with you?" She sounded flabbergasted

"Yes, to Arizona. And yes, live with me for a while. Until you get settled and then I figure you'd like to get a place of your own nearby."

"I'd definitely want that. Otherwise, we'd be trying to tear each other's hair out."

"You mean like we did when we were kids?"

"Exactly."

He could hear a smile in her voice, but the sound wasn't enough to lift the corners of his mouth. He felt like every cell in his body was frozen with pain and shock. Would this awful emptiness go away by tomorrow? Or would he have to wait a week or even months before he began to feel like a human being again?

"I'm serious, Tally."

"I understand that you're serious, Tag. But all my friends are here. So is my job at the real estate office. And—"

"You can get a better job here. That damned boss of yours is just using you. He makes bucket loads of money and pays you like you're the janitor instead of a secretary. He's a jerk and you're putting up with it."

A long stretch of silence passed before she finally spoke. "What in the world is wrong with you, brother? You sound like you're ready to coldcock somebody. Has something happened?"

Yes, something has happened, he thought. His whole world had just stopped spinning and no matter how hard he tried, he couldn't see any sort of happiness in his future.

"No," he said sharply. "Everything here is great."

"You could've fooled me. I'm afraid to hear what you'd sound like if something bad really had happened. Just proves to me that I'd rather stay here and be used by Mr. Graves than be growled at by my bearish brother."

Closing his eyes, he raked a hand through his tumbled hair. If Emily-Ann hadn't walked out on him, he would've already had her in bed by now. At this very moment she would've been kissing him, loving him in a way that no woman had ever loved him.

Love. Love. He never wanted to hear the word or have it enter his mind ever again, he thought bitterly. He didn't want to think that he'd just lost his one and only chance to know what real love actually felt like.

"I'm sorry, Tally. It's been a long, stressful day. I didn't mean to sound sharp. You're my favorite sis, you know."

She laughed then. "I'm your *only* sis. Remember?"

"Yeah, I remember. So will you seriously consider my invitation?"

There was another long pause and she finally said, "Yes. I will think deep and hard about it, Tag."

They talked a minute more and then Taggart finally ended the call and left the kitchen. When he entered the living room, he saw King pawing at the screen door.

The sight was like a knife slicing right through him and for the first time in years he was finding it hard to hold his emotions together. "Okay, so you want out. Now that Emily-Ann isn't here you don't like it inside. Well, just go." He opened the screen door and King shot onto the porch and down the steps like the devil was following him. "Go on back to Doc," he called after the yellow cur. "That's where you belong. And don't come back thinking she'll be here. She's gone."

And she won't be coming back.

The heavy weight of that reality settled on Taggart's shoulders as he shut the door and bolted it.

Chapter Twelve

"Emily-Ann, is that you?"

About to step out of the glass foyer and onto the wide side-walk, Emily-Ann turned to see Camille bearing down on her.

Oh Lord, Camille was the last person she'd expected to run into here at the medical clinic. What was she going to tell her? That she had to visit the doctor because she couldn't eat? Couldn't stop crying?

Biting back a helpless groan, she squared her shoulders and waited for Camille to catch up to her.

"Camille, what are you doing here? Are you having a problem with the baby?"

Her friend quickly dismissed the question with a wave of her hand. "We're in fine shape. Matthew wanted me to have an extra checkup before we travel home," she explained, then laughed. "I think he's worried I'll go into labor while he's driving. He'll be pulling a trailer load of steers back with us and he doesn't think he can handle them and me having a baby at the same time."

Emily-Ann tried to laugh, but couldn't summon up anything that resembled a sound of amusement. She'd left the doctor's office in shock and the fog in her brain was still muddling her senses.

Camille peered closely at Emily-Ann. "What are you doing here at the clinic? Have you been sick or just having a yearly checkup?"

"Neither. I—uh, nothing serious. I've just been feeling a bit off, that's all." Deciding it would be pointless to hide the news from her closest friend, she grabbed Camille by the arm and urged her through the sliding glass doors. Once they were outside, she pointed down the sidewalk to a concrete bench shaded by the overhang of the building. "Do you have time to sit a minute?"

"Are you kidding? I'm not going anywhere until you tell me why you look like you've stuck your face in a bowl of flour."

They walked down to the bench and after both of them were comfortably seated, Camille leveled an anxious look at her.

"Okay, out with it," she demanded. "You were lying to me a minute ago. Something is seriously wrong with you."

"Something is wrong all right," Emily-Ann ruefully agreed. "With my head. I'm a stupid woman, Camille. There's no better way to explain the reason I had to visit the doctor."

Camille rolled her eyes. "You can't fix stupid at this clinic, Emily-Ann."

She groaned. "You're right. The doctor can't fix it. But he can certainly diagnose it!"

Camille must've decided that Emily-Ann's health wasn't in dire jeopardy because a perceptive grin suddenly appeared on her face. "Uh-huh. So what have you done? Spent too much money on something you didn't need and now you're getting ulcers worrying about it?"

The sound that burst past Emily-Ann's lips was something between a sob and a hysterical laugh. "How could I do that when I barely have enough to pay bills?"

Camille's expression softened as she reached over and gently rubbed the top of Emily-Ann's hand. "I'm sorry. I'm only teasing. I can see you're upset. Tell me what's going on with your health. Did the doctor give you a prescription?"

Emily-Ann pulled a small square of paper from her purse and thrust it at her friend. "Only this. I can buy them off the shelf."

Camille read the scribbled words, which promptly caused her mouth to fall open and her shocked gaze to fly up to Emily-Ann's face. "Prenatal vitamins! You're pregnant?"

Nodding, Emily-Ann fought at the tears scalding the back of her eyes. "Dr. Revere believes I'm about a month along. I don't know how it happened, Camille."

In spite of Emily-Ann's obvious distress, Camille laughed. "Of course you know how it happened. Every woman does."

Emily-Ann tried to clear the gravelly lump that had formed in her throat. "Well, yes, that part of it I know. I got too close to a long tall Texan! Obviously he was more potent than the pill I'm taking! That's my theory on the matter. The doctor seems to think the pregnancy occurred because I had a cold for a few days and that can sometimes affect the strength of the pill."

Her eyes twinkling with delight, Emily-Ann said, "When you two met at the party, I was fairly certain you and Tag were going to hit it off."

"Hit it off!" Emily-Ann practically shouted. "We've done more than that. We've created a baby!"

Camille's smile spread wider. "This is wonderful, Emily-Ann! Our children will practically be the same age—only a few months difference. They might both turn out to be redheads and grow up to be great friends, like us."

Camille made it sound like Emily-Ann had just been handed the best news a woman could ever receive. And it suddenly dawned on her that her friend was so very right. A child was a blessed gift. Plus, she'd always dreamed of having children. She had to feel happy about the pregnancy, even if it was an unexpected shock.

"That part would be nice," Emily-Ann agreed. "I only wish—oh, Camille, I don't want this baby to grow up without a father. I don't want my child to ever have to know that he or she wasn't important enough to deserve a full-time father."

Frowning, Camille squeezed her hands. "I don't understand. Don't you think Tag will be happy about the baby? I surely do. He has family man written all over him."

"Hah! Not a family with me, Camille." Shaking her head, she pulled a tissue from her handbag and dabbed it at her teary eyes. "I'm sorry. You couldn't know that Tag and I ended things a week ago. I haven't seen or talked with him since I was out at his house. But now—well, I'm going to have to face him with this new development. And I'm not looking forward to it."

Camille was silent for a thoughtful moment and then she said, "I wasn't aware that anything had happened between you two. Tag must not have mentioned it to Matthew or my brothers. But that's hardly a surprise. What little I've been around him, he doesn't do much talking about himself." She turned a questioning look at Emily-Ann. "So what happened? He's found someone else? Or he's tired of dating?"

Emily-Ann glanced around at the people going to and from the medical building to the large parking lot. This wasn't exactly the ideal place to be discussing something so private, but no one seemed to be paying the two women any mind. Most of them were probably dealing with their own troubles, she thought glumly.

She pushed out a heavy breath. "Nothing like that. Tag asked me to move in with him. And I—obviously, I refused."

"Oh. Move in," Camille murmured. "I see."

Bitter gall was spreading from her chest to the back of her throat, practically choking her. "No. I doubt you understand. So go ahead and tell me I'm an idiot for not grabbing what he offered. And maybe I am the biggest one to ever walk the earth—I don't know. But I am sure about one thing—I'm not going to be like my mother. I'm not going to live my life with a man who doesn't love me."

"Oh, Emily-Ann, this is—I don't know what to say. Except that if Tag wanted you to move in with him that certainly doesn't sound like a man who's tired of you. Or that he doesn't want to be involved."

Bending her head, Emily-Ann muttered, "You don't understand, Camille. He wants the convenience. It's nothing about having deep feelings for me. All the time we were together, he didn't say anything about caring for me—really caring. And then last week before I left, I finally got so angry I brought up the words *love* and *marriage*."

"And?"

"He looked like I'd thrown cold water in his face." Lifting her head, she shook it with grim determination. "No. I made the mistake of falling into the same trap my mother did. She believed she'd found love when actually all she'd been was a sex partner."

"Emily-Ann, I'm having a hard time believing that! Tag doesn't come off as that kind to me. How do you think he's going to react when he hears about the baby?"

Emily-Ann lifted her gaze to the cloudless sky. "I'm clueless there. I'm guessing he's not going to be a bit pleased. I imagine he'll be thinking I want to hook him into marriage." Her lips clamped tightly together, she looked at Camille. "Well, he's in for a surprise. I'd rather walk down the aisle with a jackass!"

Camille was clearly disappointed. "Why are you thinking like this?"

"I'll tell you why. All her life, my mother got nothing but crumbs from my biological father and then from the man she finally married. I'm not going to settle for crumbs, Camille."

"Damn it, Emily-Ann, you aren't your mother!"

"That's right. And I don't ever intend to be." Rising to her feet, she grabbed up her handbag. "I need to go. I took the afternoon off work to visit the doctor and now I have online classes scheduled. I can't afford to miss them."

Reaching down, she gave Camille a hand up from the bench.

Once she was on her feet, Camille said, "I think Matthew is planning on leaving for Red Bluff Sunday morning. Hopefully I can see you again before we go." She smacked a kiss on Emily-Ann's cheek. "I love you. Don't worry. You're going to have a baby and that's all that really matters."

Emily-Ann gave her a wobbly smile. "You're right. This little life I'm carrying means everything to me. And I'm not the only woman in the world who can be a good single mom."

"Now, you're talking." She gave Emily-Ann a parting hug. "Chin up. Everything is going to be fine."

Emily-Ann gave her friend a grateful squeeze, then hurried away before she could see the tears in her eyes.

"YOU DON'T HAVE anything planned for tomorrow evening, do you?"

From his seat in the cushy leather armchair, Taggart glanced across Blake's office to where the man sat behind his desk, signing off on purchases for grain and fencing supplies.

After a long workday in the saddle, Taggart had received a brief text from the man asking him to stop by the office to discuss plans for cutting the irrigated hay meadows. If the grass was ready, haying usually began the next month. But so far the two men had talked about everything but the hay. "Not unless you count doing my laundry and fixing myself something to eat."

"I can't help you with the laundry, but forget the cooking. Reeva will take care of that chore. I realize tomorrow night is Saturday night, but Mom has her heart set on you having dinner with us. It's a goodbye thing for Matthew and Camille."

Taggart wasn't decent company for anyone, but to make Maureen happy and to show Matthew his appreciation for all the support the man had given him these past six weeks, he supposed he could fake it and smile his way through the evening.

"I'll be glad to show up. Actually, I need to present Matthew with some kind of award for all the patience he's shown me since I arrived. He not only taught me lots of things about the ranch, but he also made me feel at home. I'm going to miss him."

"We're all going to miss him. And Camille—well, just when we get her back here on the ranch for a little while, she's leaving again." Leaning back in his chair, he linked his hands at the back of his neck and let out a long sigh. "But this time is different. She's happy and in love. And we don't worry about her anymore, because we know Matthew will take good care of her."

Take good care of her. There'd been times when Emily-Ann had been lying next to him that he'd wanted to hold her tight and promise he'd always take care of her, that he'd always be there for her no matter what the future held. But each time the promises had lodged in his throat. Because each time he'd realized no man can stop fate from stepping in and wiping away the things he loved the most.

Love. That awful night Emily-Ann had left his house, he'd vowed to never let the word enter his mind. But these past few days his mind had gone rogue on him. All it seemed to want to think about was love and how he'd lost his chance at having it, holding it and cherishing it.

Shaking away the bitter thoughts, Taggart focused his attention back to the present. "Yes, Matthew is a good man. He'll make a fine father, too."

Blake gathered the stack of papers he'd just signed and placed them on the corner of his desk before he glanced over at Taggart. "You know, you ought to invite Emily-Ann out to have dinner with us. She'll be wanting to see Camille before she leaves."

Blake might as well have thrown a bucket of ice on him, Taggart thought. He was so frozen by the man's suggestion that for a moment he couldn't speak. Finally, he managed to say, "I don't think that's a good idea. Uh—besides, it's your mother's party. It's her place to do the inviting."

And if Emily-Ann was going to be there, he didn't think he could bear it, Taggart thought.

Blake frowned at him. "Why wouldn't it be a good idea? I thought you and Emily-Ann were getting along great."

Too restless to remain in the armchair, Taggart got up and

poured himself a cup of hours-old coffee and added several spoons of sugar. "We were. But things have changed. We're not seeing each other anymore."

A long stretch of silence passed before Blake finally said, "Oh. I'm sorry to hear that. I thought—"

Blake went silent again and Taggart slanted a curious glance in his direction. "You thought what?"

Leveling a shrewd look at him, Blake answered, "That you two might actually be getting serious about each other."

The pain in Taggart's chest was so unbearable he swallowed several gulps of the awful coffee before he could speak. "I don't know why you'd come up with that idea. I'm not a serious kind of guy. Not where women are concerned. Emily-Ann figured that out for herself. And—that's probably all for the best. No ties or broken hearts. You know what I mean."

His expression solemn, Blake continued to study him. "Yeah. I know what you're saying. You've already lost a woman you loved. You don't want to go through it again."

Taggart's eyes narrowed. "You've been talking to your mother."

"No. Why? Have you?"

There was no way Taggart was going to break his promise to Maureen and tell Blake, or anyone for that matter, that the two of them had ridden to water pump number nine. Nor was he going to tell him the personal things they'd talked about.

"Uh—no. I just thought—well, women kind of have an intuition about men—and she might have voiced her thoughts about me to you."

"No. But I read your background check before we ever hired you. I just never mentioned you're a widower because there was no point in bringing the matter up."

Taggart frowned. "But you think there's a point now?"

"I do. Because I hate to see you make a big mistake. One you might regret for the rest of your life."

Taggart swigged down the last of the coffee and tossed the

foam cup into a trash basket next to the small refreshment table. "If you're talking about Emily-Ann, that's over. She wants more than I can give her."

"Guess you're talking about love and marriage now. Well, why shouldn't she want that for herself? Why should she settle for anything less?"

Moving in with a guy has never been what I've planned for myself, Tag.

Emily-Ann's words circled his weary brain, just as they had a thousand times since she'd walked out the door several nights ago. He'd hurt her terribly. He could see that now. But how did he go about trying to repair the damage? Would she even let him try?

With a heavy sigh, Taggart sank back into the armchair and dropped his head into his hands. "There's no use in me trying to act like I'm a cool piece of steel, Blake. I've been miserable without Emily-Ann. I guess—I didn't realize how much she'd come to mean to me until I—until she was gone." Lifting his head, he cast Blake a wry look. "That's the way it is with a fool, isn't it? He never appreciates what he has until he loses it."

Shaking his head, Blake said, "You're not a fool, you're just a little scared like every other man who's ever loved a woman. You've already learned the hard way that standing at the altar and saying your vows doesn't mean you get a guarantee with the marriage license. Regrettably, our mother learned the same thing. You think my brothers and I weren't afraid to take wives and have children? We all wanted to run like chickens. But we all had sense enough to know that living alone and miserable wasn't a good alternative."

Dear God, he'd been alone for a long time and during those empty years he'd believed that was the answer, the alternative to having his heart torn apart. But Emily-Ann had shown him that living behind a guarded wall was not really living at all.

"I just wonder if Emily-Ann might give me a second chance."

Smiling now, Blake picked up the purchase orders, then

switched off the banker's lamp on his desk. "I'll have Mom invite her. In the meantime, you be thinking about what you're going to say to her. Something meaningful and persuasive."

"You mean like I'm a heel and a jerk?"

Blake laughed. "That'll be a start."

Seeing Blake was shutting things down for the night, Taggart rose to his feet. "I thought we were going to discuss the hay meadows?"

He grabbed his Stetson from a hall tree and levered it on his head. "Oh that. We'll go over the hay situation later on."

Taggart shot him a suspicious look. "Damn it, Blake, did you call me in here to talk about Emily-Ann?"

Blake let loose a guilty laugh. "Look, Tag, you might as well get used to us poking into your private life. You're family now and we want everyone in our family to be happy."

Happy? Was there a chance that he could still find happiness with Emily-Ann? He could only hope.

THE NEXT EVENING in the den of the Three Rivers Ranch house, Emily-Ann sat in an armchair with a dessert plate filled with strawberry torte carefully balanced on her knees. Normally she loved the sweet dish, but tonight she'd only managed three bites before her jangled nerves made it nearly impossible to swallow anything past her tight throat.

Camille must have noticed that she was merely pushing the dessert around the plate rather than eating it, because she suddenly spoke up.

"Emily-Ann, would you like for Jazelle to fetch you a different dessert? You've hardly touched the one you have. You might like the pecan pie better."

Emily-Ann glanced over to a leather love seat, where her friend was cuddled comfortably next to her husband's side.

"No!" she blurted out, while thinking she'd never touch another piece of pecan pie as long as she lived. After sharing one with Taggart, it would never taste the same. "I—uh—this is fine. I ate so much for dinner that I really don't have room for dessert."

Maureen walked up on the group just in time to hear Emily-Ann's excuse for her lack of appetite. Now the woman ran a keen gaze over Emily-Ann's face.

"You ate like a bird," Maureen insisted. "And you look peaked, honey. Are you feeling okay?"

She shouldn't have worn this damned yellow dress, Emily-Ann thought. It made her appear even more washed out than she already looked.

"Sure, I'm feeling wonderful." Between bouts of nausea and having every nerve in her body clenched in a viselike grip, she felt just dandy, she thought sickly. "And dinner was delicious. I'm just feeling a little blue at the idea of telling Camille good-bye."

"You can always come visit us," Matthew spoke up. "We'd be glad to have you."

"That's very nice of you, Matthew. Maybe after your baby gets here I can drive down for a visit. But only for a very quick one. You two are going to have your hands full without added company."

"Well, once baby Matthew gets here, she's definitely going to have to put up with her mother and her sister for a few days," Maureen said teasingly. "But we already have it in mind to shoo Camille off to the diner and keep the baby all to ourselves."

"Hah!" Camille laughed. "Baby Matthew. Who says?"

"TooTall," Matthew answered as if that guaranteed the gender of the baby would be male.

While the three of them continued to discuss the baby and TooTall's prediction, Emily-Ann couldn't help but notice how Matthew had his arm around his wife's shoulders and how the man kept darting loving glances at her. How would that feel, she wondered?

The question had her directing a furtive gaze across the room where Taggart, Holt and Chandler were standing near a wet bar, seemingly in deep conversation.

Thankfully at dinner, Maureen had seated Emily-Ann several chairs on down the table from Taggart, which had made it much easier to avoid looking in his direction. And since then, she'd not once allowed her gaze to land on his handsome face. She couldn't bear it. Just being in the same room with him made her feel sick and stupid and humiliated.

So far tonight, she'd avoided facing him head-on, but at some point before the evening ended she was going to have to speak with him about the baby. Was he going to be angry? Was he going to accuse her of using her body to set a snare for him? Even if he didn't react quite that harshly, he was still going to throw some hard questions at her and how was she going to answer them?

Oh God, the mere thought of standing in front of him, telling him he was going to have a child, was enough to cause clammy sweat to pop out on her forehead and the base of her throat.

Certain if she didn't get some fresh air, she was going to throw up in front of everyone, Emily-Ann jumped up from the couch. "Please excuse me," she said, darting a frantic glance at Camille. "I, uh, need to step out for a moment."

As she hurried toward the French doors that led out to the patio, she noticed Camille starting to rise to her feet, but Maureen said something that caused her daughter to immediately sink back down on the love seat.

Thank God, Emily-Ann thought, as much as she loved Camille, her frayed nerves weren't ready for a pep talk or sermon from her dear friend.

She didn't realize just how far she'd walked until she found herself standing by the cottonwood where she'd found Taggart the night of the party. Had she unconsciously sought out the spot, or was fate simply playing cruel tricks on her? It didn't matter, she decided. Nothing mattered now, except the child growing inside her. His child.

She was leaning against the trunk of the tree, allowing the cool air to wash over her when she heard a twig snap behind her.

Thinking Camille had probably come out to check on her, she turned with a weary sigh, then promptly gasped at the sight of Taggart walking out of the shadows.

By the time he reached her side, she'd managed to gather herself enough to speak. "What are you doing out here?"

"I could ask you the same thing."

"Getting some fresh air," she said stiffly, then turned her back to him and gazed blindly out toward the ranch yard in the far distance.

He said, "I guess you came to dinner because of Camille."

The familiar sound of his voice was like shards of glass raining over her. "And you're here because of Matthew."

"Yeah. We both had an obligation to show up for our mutual friends."

She heard him take a step closer and the idea that he might actually touch her sent her shredded nerves into chaos.

"You purposely followed me out here," she said in a strained voice. "Why?"

"I've been trying all evening to find a private moment to speak with you. When I saw you running out of the den, I decided to follow."

Had she actually been running? Lord, everyone in the room must be thinking she'd lost her mind. And they wouldn't be far off from the truth. For the past week and a half she'd done nothing but cry and throw up everything she put in her stomach. She'd reached the point where she hardly knew what she was doing or saying.

"Oh. Well, you've solved my problem. Because I've been wondering how I could talk to you—alone."

"Really? You haven't so much as looked at me tonight. I can't imagine you wanting to talk to me," he said. "You left the house more than a week ago and I've not heard a word from you. That doesn't sound like a woman who wants to talk."

Was it possible for a heart to split down the middle and still keep beating, she wondered? Because hers felt as though it was slowly and surely cracking.

"I've not heard a word from you, either. But then I didn't expect to. You've made your feelings clear and I've accepted that what we had is over."

"Is it?"

Suspicious now, she studied his shadowed face. "I haven't changed my mind about anything, Tag. If that's what you're thinking."

"I don't want you to change your mind," he said flatly.

The pain in her chest was practically wiping out her ability to breathe and she had to turn her back to him as tears began to fill her eyes. "Oh. Well, that's that. So if you don't mind, would you please go back inside and leave me alone? I don't want to—continue this conversation—not tonight."

"Sorry, Emily-Ann, but I'm not going to leave you alone. Not until I say a few things that… I think you ought to hear."

Bending her head, she swallowed hard. "All right. Say them," she whispered.

His hands suddenly settled on her shoulders and all the familiar feelings of his touch poured through her like warm rain.

"I don't know where to start. So I'll just begin by saying I've been a complete jerk—an idiot. And I'm sorry. Terribly sorry."

Hope tried to enter her heart, but she immediately slammed the door on it. His being sorry didn't change the fact he wanted a bed partner rather than a wife.

"What do you have to be sorry about?" she mumbled the question. "Being honest?"

"But I haven't been honest," he admitted, then gently turned her so that she was facing him. "You've turned me into a habitual liar, Emily-Ann. Ever since I met you, I've continued to lie to you and myself. I've been telling myself I didn't love you. That I didn't need you in my life. Not as a wife or the mother

The Texan Tries Again

of my children. But all along I knew I was lying and yet I was too much of a coward to face up to my real feelings."

She shook her head with disbelief. "Are you trying to say that…you love me?"

"Yes. But I'm butchering it up pretty badly, aren't I?"

A sob burst past her lips and then he was pulling her into his arms, holding her so tight that the side of her face was crushed against his chest.

"I'm hearing it, Tag. But I—"

"I know. You don't believe me. But I promise, Emily-Ann, I'll spend the rest of my life showing you just how much I love you. That is, if you'll let me."

Wedging her hands against his chest, she levered herself away enough to see his face. "I don't understand, Tag. You didn't want strings, or love or marriage. Why now?"

"Ask King. He'll tell you how miserable I've been without you. It only took me a couple of days to realize that my job, my home, my life meant nothing if you weren't with me."

The reality that he really did love her was beginning to set in and the joy that was pouring into her heart was healing the broken cracks she'd felt only minutes before. "And the rest of the days we've been apart?"

"I've been trying to figure out how to get you back—wondering if you could possibly forgive me." Reaching up, he stroked a hand over her hair. "I asked you to move in with me because— I was too afraid to ask you to be my wife. But I'm asking you now, Emily-Ann. Will you marry me?"

His declaration of love had been far more than she'd ever expected to hear from him. Now, he was proposing. It was almost more than she could take in. "Marry you!" she finally whispered. "Are you serious?"

He reached into the front pocket of his jeans and pulled out a velvet ring box. "I went to town yesterday and bought this because I knew you'd be here tonight. Ever since I've been praying you'll accept it."

When he flipped open the lid, Emily-Ann sucked in a sharp breath. The engagement ring was a large square-shaped diamond, flanked by two smaller emeralds and set in filigreed gold. It was far beyond anything Emily-Ann had ever dreamed a man might give her.

"Oh my! Oh, Tag, it's so beautiful! But it's too much," she protested. "A girl like me—"

"A girl like you deserves something beautiful," he finished.

Dazed, Emily-Ann watched him pull the ring from its velvet bed, but when he took her hand to push it onto her finger, she promptly shook her head and pulled back.

"I can't accept it, Tag. Not yet. Not until I tell you something you need to know."

Frowning, he dropped the ring into his shirt pocket. "Okay, what? That you don't love me? Well, I don't care. I'll love you enough for both of us."

She touched a hand to her forehead as her mind whirled with everything that had just happened. "I don't know how to tell you this, except to just come right out with it. You're going to be a father."

It was his turn to look flabbergasted. "A father! Are you saying you're pregnant?"

She nodded, still uncertain how the news of the baby was going to affect him. "About a month or so along. I guess it happened when we—uh—first got together. The doctor said my pill lost some of its strength because I had a cold, but that hardly changes the fact now."

He leaned back his head and let out a joyous shout. "A baby! Our baby!"

Smiling ear to ear, he lifted her off her feet and whirled her around until she was laughing breathlessly.

"Are you really pleased, Tag?"

He set her back on her feet, then pulled her into his arms and kissed her for long, long moments. "Pleased? Oh, my darling, I couldn't be any happier."

Fifteen minutes ago, her heart was bursting with pain, now it was overflowing with joy. "I started to tell you when you first walked up. Now I'm so very glad I didn't. I'll always know that you wanted me to be your wife before you learned about the baby. I didn't want you thinking I'd gotten pregnant to snare you."

He pressed his lips to her forehead. "You got pregnant because you gave yourself to me. Because you put your love and trust in me. And I promise you, darling Emily-Ann, that I'll cherish you and our children the rest of my life."

Leaning her head back, she looked at him with starry eyes. "Children? As in plural?"

He chuckled. "You don't think we'll stop with one, do you? We have a long ways to go to catch up with the Hollisters."

Fetching the ring from his pocket, he slipped it onto her finger, then placed a soft, promising kiss upon her lips.

"Let's go tell everyone our happy news," he said.

She reached for his hand and just as they turned to walk back to the house, she began to laugh.

Pausing, Taggart asked, "What now?"

"I caught Camille's bridal bouquet at her and Matthew's wedding and ever since she's been predicting that I'd be getting married soon," Emily-Ann explained. "I'll never hear the end of this. She'll swear that the bouquet brought us together."

Laughing, Taggart tugged her on toward the house. "Come on, I'm going to go thank her for not throwing those flowers to anyone else but you."

Epilogue

On the last Saturday in June, the hot Arizona sun dipped behind a ridge of red, rocky bluff to spread a spectacular sunset of pink and gold over the huge crowd that had gathered at the Bar X to watch Gabby Townsend and Sam Leman exchange their vows of love.

The wedding ceremony was the second one Emily-Ann and Taggart had attended in the past three weeks, the first one being their own. Which had been a simple, yet elegant ceremony the Hollisters had given them at Three Rivers Ranch.

However, this wedding was far different from Emily-Ann and Taggart's. This event could only be described as a whopper of a shindig. People from every corner of Yavapai County and beyond had come to help the newlyweds celebrate. Now that the pastor had introduced the old foreman and the pretty artist as man and wife, the reception was in full swing. Champagne corks were popping in all directions and live music floated across the rapidly cooling air.

Joseph and Tessa had gone all out to help give their devoted foreman a wedding to remember. The backyard had been set up with rows of tables decorated with flowers and loaded with food and drinks of all kinds. Paper lanterns had been strung from tree limbs and crisscrossed the wide parquet dance floor.

Folding chairs, along with bales of hay, were grouped strategically away from the dancing area for those guests who chose to sit rather than stretch their legs to the music.

"This isn't the sort of music I would've expected to hear at a ranch wedding," Taggart said, as he twirled Emily-Ann across the makeshift dance floor.

"Sam and Gabby wanted to dance to standards, so Isabelle searched until she found a band from Phoenix who could play them well. Personally, I love it," she said, her eyes twinkling up at him. "It's very romantic. Especially when I'm dancing with my handsome husband."

Smiling he rubbed his nose against her forehead. "My beautiful wife will always be a romantic. I just feel bad that you didn't have this big of a wedding."

She laughed. "Are you kidding? I didn't want the whole county at our wedding! Besides, we were in a hurry and Maureen and Camille and Isabelle rushed like crazy to get our ceremony pulled off. It was beautiful and I have a stack of photos to prove it."

"I don't need a photo to remember how you looked that day," he whispered near her ear. "You were a heavenly dream in your long ivory dress and tiny flowers pinned in your hair. Come to think of it, you look mighty heavenly right now."

"It's the extra hormones from being pregnant. Camille says it makes us glow," she said with an impish grin, then added with a wistful sigh, "I wish she and Matthew could've been here tonight. They were planning to come, you know. But her doctor advised against it. The baby could come at any time."

"I'm sure they're thinking about everyone." The song came to an end and Taggart led Emily-Ann off the platform. "Let's go have some punch. We'll dance again in a few minutes. I don't want to wear you out."

"Something to drink sounds good," she agreed.

The two of them made their way to one of the quieter tables

set up near a pair of Joshua trees. Once there, Taggart filled two glass cups with punch and handed one of them to Emily-Ann.

As he sipped the fruity drink, his gaze drifted over the heads of the guests to where Gabby and Sam were being monopolized by well-wishers. "The music isn't the only thing that's surprised me this evening," he said. "I wasn't expecting to see Sam in a Western-cut suit. He looks downright dignified."

Emily-Ann nodded. "Very handsome for a man of his age," she agreed. "And the way he looks at Gabby—it's obvious he adores her. And she gazes at Sam—well, like he hung the moon just for her. It's an inspiration seeing them together."

He cast a wry glance at his wife. "Well, there's another couple here tonight that looks to me like they're very much in love."

Moving closer, she slipped an arm around the back of his waist. "You mean us?"

Taggart tightened his hold on her waist while thinking it was indecent to feel this happy. Being married to Emily-Ann and sharing their home together on Three Rivers Ranch was like finding heaven on earth. Now that they had a child on the way, he was eagerly looking forward to being the father he'd always wanted and needed, but never had.

So far, Buck O'Brien hadn't tried to contact him, but the old man continued to make life hard for Tallulah. Taggart and Emily-Ann were both trying to persuade his sister to move here to Arizona. The last time he'd talked to her, he'd gotten the impression she was close to giving in.

"Other than us," he said, then inclined his head toward the far end of the dance floor where Gil was guiding Maureen into a slow two-step.

Emily-Ann's gaze followed Taggart's. "Oh, you're talking about Maureen and Gil. Yes, the more I see them together, the more I'm sure she's completely gone on the man. Which I think is okay with all her children, don't you? I know for sure that Camille doesn't object. But guys are kind of different when it comes to their mothers—they can be possessive."

"You mean since Joel is gone, the guys might need to protect their mother from assertive males?"

"That's close to what I'm trying to say. Not that I think Gil is assertive. Quite the opposite. He's very nice. He even stops by the coffee shop when he's in town and always leaves me a tip."

Since they'd married, Emily-Ann was still working at Conchita's and planned to keep her job until the baby arrived. After that, she was going to take time off to be a mother and finish her nursing degree. At least, that's what she had planned. Taggart couldn't imagine her giving up the coffee shop job completely. Not when she loved it so much. But that was her choice. All he wanted was for her to be happy and to know that he loved her and the baby utterly.

"Gil is a stand-up guy," Taggart said. "I just wish—"

"What?" she prompted.

"Oh, that the mystery around Joel's death could be solved," he said. "I think it would help Maureen put losing him behind her once and for all."

Her eyes full of love and tenderness, she reached up and touched a finger to his cheek. "And what about you, Tag? Have you put your losses behind you?"

The smile he gave her couldn't have been more honest. "All I see, my darling wife, is the future. With you and me and our children."

He had just finished placing a soft kiss on her lips when Chandler strode quickly over to them and from the look on his face, he had good news.

"We just heard from Matthew. Camille has delivered her baby. A boy—Matthew Harrison Waggoner."

"Sounds like he's going to be a junior," Emily-Ann stated.

Chandler shook his head as he jerked out his smartphone and held it out for them to see the tiny baby swaddled in a blue receiving blanket. "Matthew is calling him Harry for Harrison and since that was our maternal great grandfather's name, Camille is happy with it."

"Are she and the baby okay?" Taggart asked.

"Matthew snapped this pic before they carried the baby off to the nursery. He says everyone is great and little Harry has red hair like his mother."

"Oh my!" Emily-Ann exclaimed, then sniffed as joyous tears filled her eyes.

Spotting them, Taggart asked, "Honey, why are you crying at this wonderful news?"

She dabbed a finger beneath both eyes. "Camille wanted our babies to both be gingers—like the two of us. Now if mine doesn't turn out having red hair, she'll be terribly disappointed."

Both men laughed loudly and then Taggart wrapped a reassuring arm around her shoulders and squeezed her close to his side.

"Don't worry, sweetheart, if this baby of ours doesn't turn out to be a ginger, the next one will be."

Chandler winked at Taggart and gave him a playful swat on the arm. "Welcome to the family, Tag."

* * * * *

The Right Cowboy

Rebecca Winters

Dear Reader,

What is a cowboy?

He can be a lot of things besides a rodeo star and a rancher. When you read this first book from my Wind River Cowboys series, *The Right Cowboy*, you'll be amazed at the depth of Cole Hawkins, a homegrown Wyoming heartthrob who's not only the quintessential cowboy, but a hero to die for.

After a lot of years getting my hair done, my hairdresser and I were talking about this and that when she happened to mention she had a brother who was a Wyoming cowboy. As you read this story, you'll see I went to town picking her brain. Though there's no resemblance to her real-life brother, some of the things he's done and accomplished have made their way into my book and I leave it for you to enjoy!

Rebecca Winters

Rebecca Winters, whose family of four children has now swelled to include five beautiful grandchildren, lives in Salt Lake City, Utah, in the land of the Rocky Mountains. Living near canyons and high alpine meadows full of wildflowers, she never runs out of places to explore. They, plus her favorite vacation spots in Europe, often end up as backgrounds for her romance novels, because writing is her passion, along with her family and church.

Rebecca loves to hear from readers. If you wish to email her, please visit her website, cleanromances.net.

Books by Rebecca Winters

Harlequin Western

Sapphire Mountain Cowboys

A Valentine for the Cowboy
Made for the Rancher
Cowboy Doctor
Roping Her Christmas Cowboy

Lone Star Lawmen

The Texas Ranger's Bride
The Texas Ranger's Nanny
The Texas Ranger's Family
Her Texas Ranger Hero

Hitting Rocks Cowboys

In a Cowboy's Arms
A Cowboy's Heart
The New Cowboy
A Montana Cowboy

Visit the Author Profile page
at millsandboon.com.au for more titles.

To my darling hairdresser Alicia, who has become a friend and has kept me looking great. (Great as *I* can look.) The poor thing has had to listen to some of my stories—which she has done with patience—even though she just wanted a simple sentence or two of explanation. *Never ask a writer what she's been working on!* If you want to hear some of her brother's terrific country-and-western music, check out his website: jaredrogerson.com.

Chapter One

Tamsin Rayburn pulled in her parking space in front of Ostler Certified Accounting Firm in Whitebark, Wyoming. She was running late to get back to the ranch. Dean would be picking her up for dinner and she needed to hurry.

With her light chestnut hair swishing against her shoulders, she got out of the car and rushed through the reception area to her office. Her boss would be pleased to know she'd finished auditing the books for Beckstrand Drilling earlier than planned and could start on the Whitebark Hospital audit.

In her haste, she almost ran into Heather Jennings, a co-worker who'd become a close friend over the last two years. It looked like everyone else had gone home. Smiling at her she said, "I've never needed a weekend more. How about you?"

Heather studied her for a moment with an anxious expression. "You don't know, do you?"

She was being very mysterious. "Know what?"

"I've been hoping you would walk in here before I left. Now I'm almost afraid to tell you."

"Heather—what's wrong?"

Her friend drew in a deep breath. "There's only one way to say this. Today I had lunch with Amy Paskett." Amy was a girl Tamsin had known from high school who worked at Paskett's feed store. "It turns out her father waited on Cole Hawkins this morning. Apparently he's back in Whitebark for good."

Tamsin grabbed the edge of her desk while her world whirled for a moment. "Wh-what did you say?" she stammered.

"I knew this would be hard for you to hear."

Cole was home for good? The cowboy who'd left the state nine years ago, riding off with her heart?

The last time she'd seen him was at a distance when he'd come home for his father's funeral six months ago. He'd been driving down the street in a friend's truck, but he hadn't seen her. Once the funeral was over, he'd left again.

Shock didn't begin to describe what she was feeling. "How long has he been here?"

"I don't know. That was all Amy said in passing. I've been waiting to tell you in case you hadn't heard. If you hadn't come, I would have phoned you."

Tamsin looked at Heather, still reeling from the incredible news. "Thank you for being such a good friend." Heather knew some of her past history with Cole, but not all.

"I'm not sure *thanks* is the right word."

"Yes, it is." She gave her a hug. "I'm grateful to have heard it from you first. Now at least I'm prepared should someone else tell me."

"Look—I've got to go, but call me this weekend and we'll talk."

She nodded. "I'll walk out with you."

Tamsin waited while Heather locked up, then she hurried to her car. She was so shaken by what her friend had told her, she trembled all the way to her family's ranch located two miles south of town.

There'd been an article in the *Sublette Gazette* four months ago about the rodeo legend Cole Hawkins being involved with a country singer from Colorado. It didn't surprise Tamsin since he was a talented musician and songwriter himself. Maybe he'd married the woman and had brought her home to settle down.

If he were recently married, how would Tamsin be able to handle it, knowing she'd be seeing them coming and going?

After he'd left Wyoming, she'd worked through her sorrow day and night for several years to earn enough money to put herself through college. Once she'd finished her schooling, she'd spent the last four years throwing herself into her career as a CPA.

At twenty-seven she had dreams of opening up her own agency one day, and she'd been dating Dean Witcom, an amazing man. Their relationship had grown serious. Lately she was excited about where it was headed. He'd be a wonderful, devoted husband just like his brother Lyle who adored her sister.

Yet the mere mention of Cole—let alone that he was home to stay—sent stabbing pain through her as if it were only yesterday he'd said goodbye to her. She couldn't bear it, not when she'd fought with everything in her power to put his memory behind her. If her sister Sally knew about Cole, she'd kept quiet about it.

Once Tamsin reached the ranch house, she felt a guilty pang when she saw that Dean's truck with the Witcom-Dennison Oil Association logo was parked out in front. How could she be thinking about Cole when Dean was here waiting for her? What was wrong with her?

She drove around the back and rushed inside to find her sister. Sally and her husband, Lyle, who also worked at WDOA, were living temporarily at the ranch. They were probably in the living room talking to Dean while he passed the time until Tamsin got home. No one else was in the house. Their parents were on a vacation in Afton to visit extended family.

Dean had told her to get dressed up. Tamsin had the suspicion he'd planned something special. She'd been looking forward to it and had bought a new dress, but there was no way she could enjoy an evening with him tonight and pretend nothing was wrong.

"Sally?" She knocked on their bedroom door in case she was

in there. The family's golden retriever came running up to lick her. "Hey, Duke. Is Sally in there?" She rubbed the dog's head.

Her pregnant younger sister opened the door, finishing pulling a loose-fitting top over her maternity jeans. "Tamsin—" She looked surprised to see her.

"I'm so glad you were in here." Sally was the one person who knew everything about her heartbreak over Cole and had consoled her through the worst of those early days when she'd thought her life had ended.

"What's wrong? You look like you've seen a ghost."

"Not a ghost." She hugged her arms to her waist. "Cole's back."

Her sister's eyes—sky blue like Tamsin's—narrowed in disbelief. "Come on in."

Tamsin stepped past her. Duke rushed in before Sally shut the door behind her. "You actually saw him?" The question revealed that her sister hadn't known anything, either.

"I just came from work. Heather told me he'd been seen at Paskett's feed store this morning. Do you think Lyle knows?"

"No. Otherwise he would have told me and I would have phoned you." She put a hand on Tamsin's arm. "Did you know Dean is here? Lyle's out in the front room with him."

Tamsin nodded. "I saw his truck, but I need time to recover from the shock. Ever since I started seeing your brother-in-law four months ago, I assured him there'd been no other man in my life for a long time. At this point I'm totally involved with him, but Dean's not going to trust me if he finds out the real reason why I'm so upset tonight. I can't believe how this news has affected me."

"I can. Let's face it. You never got over him."

"Yes, I did!" she defended.

"Then why has this news caused you to lose all the color in your face?"

She lowered her head. "You're exaggerating."

"Look in the mirror."

"I'm going to be fine."

"I hope that's true. As far as I'm concerned, Cole Hawkins made the biggest mistake of his life by walking away from you. He was a fool and *never* deserved you. What astounds me is that he still has the power to do this to you after being gone for so long. Don't let him do this to you." Her voice shook.

"You think I want to feel like this? Oh, Sally. What am I going to do? I guess this day had to come and I've made too much over it because—because I always wondered what it would be like to see him again. I just need tonight to put everything into perspective. Can you understand?"

"Of course I do."

"Dean's the man I care about now."

"I know, and he's so crazy about you it's sickening."

"Thanks."

"You know what I mean. Look. Stay in here. I'll go out and tell Dean you've come home with a migraine and will call him later."

"I hate doing this to him, but there's no way I can hide my reaction right now. I'm afraid it will show and ruin the evening he has planned. I'll have to sleep on it. In the morning, everything will be all right. I'll phone him and let him know I'm so sorry."

"Don't worry. I'll be convincing."

Tamsin hugged her sister who was only two years younger. Some people actually thought they were twins. "Thanks, Sally. What would I do without you?"

"I say that about you all the time. If you hadn't been there championing me during my barrel racing days when I couldn't get it together, I don't know how I would have made it. I'll be back in a minute and we'll talk." Duke followed her out the door.

COLE HAWKINS HAD only been asleep five hours Sunday night when the pager on the side table went off at ten after three in the morning. He shot out of bed and put on jeans and a T-shirt. After grabbing his keys, he hurried to the back porch of the ranch house to pull on his turnout gear. His Ford-350 diesel truck was parked nearby for a quick exit in the warm late-June air.

He climbed inside and headed for the fire station in Whitebark, three miles away. The small town of thirteen hundred people was nestled at the base of the Wind River Range of the Rocky Mountains, known as "The Winds" by those who'd been born and raised there like Cole.

Located in the west-central part of the state, the crest of the magnificent range silhouetted under tonight's half-moon ran along the Continental Divide. Gannett Peak rose 13,804 feet, the highest in Wyoming. That image of home had been inscribed in Cole's mind and heart forever, having grounded him during his nine years away.

During the time he'd been at the University of Colorado in Boulder to complete undergraduate and graduate school, he'd also managed to become a firefighter. After working his tail off, he was finally back in Whitebark, ready to get started on his career, *and* do something drastic about his aching heart.

There was only one woman in this world who could fix it. He knew Tamsin didn't want to see him...not ever. But that was too damn bad because when he'd come home for his father's funeral six months ago, he'd heard she wasn't married yet. Now that he was back in Wyoming territory, he planned to stake his claim no matter how long it took.

More determined than he'd ever been in his life, Cole roared into town and drove around the back of the station to park. Grabbing his helmet, he ran through to the bay and climbed in the tender truck.

Wyatt Fielding, an old friend who'd done bull riding with him in high school, was driving. They took off with the blare of the siren and lights flashing. This baby held twenty-five hundred gallons of water; an accident could be disastrous. He grinned at Cole.

"It's so great to have you back after all this time. I couldn't believe it the other day when Chief Powell told us you'd signed on with the department here."

"Only when I'm available. There'll be times when I'm up in the mountains working."

"Understood. I guess you realize you're still a rodeo legend around these parts."

"So were you."

"That's bull and you know it. I was never good enough to go on the circuit."

"Well, those days are over for me, Wyatt. I'm just thankful to be home at last."

"You and I have a lot of catching up to do, but we'll have to do it later. A fire has broken out on the Circle R Ranch. The ladder truck already took off. Captain Durrant is waiting for us."

Circle R... "You don't mean Rayburn's—"

"There's only one Rayburn in Whitebark."

Cole's heart started to thud unmercifully. Tamsin Rayburn, the girl he'd come home for, *if* she was still living there. A fire had broken out on *her* family's ranch? He couldn't believe it. Maybe he was going to see her sooner than he'd planned, but fear seized him that she could be in danger.

While Wyatt took the turnoff for the ranch, Cole's mind relived their history that went back to his senior year in high school when they'd fallen madly in love. But circumstances beyond his control had separated them. She'd stopped returning his letters and phone calls. She'd even changed her phone number.

When he did visit his father periodically during those years, he knew she wanted nothing to do with him. Until he was home for good, he couldn't do anything about their situation.

Cole had only been back in Wyoming five days. His first responsibility lay with his family's longtime friend and foreman, Sam Speakuna, and his wife, Louise. They were Arapahoes from the Northern Arapahoe reservation who'd come to work for his father early on. Over the years they'd spent part of the time in their apartment on the Hawkins' ranch, and commuted to Lander where they had a home and could be with their family.

All the time Cole had been away, those two had shouldered the full responsibility of the ranch house and the crew of two wranglers who handled their herd of forty head of beef cattle. They were like family to him at this point. Now it was time to discuss their future and the future of the Hawkins' small cattle ranch.

After a meeting with Fire Chief Owen Powell, who'd received Cole's credentials from Colorado, he took him on board immediately. After his father's funeral, Cole had talked to Chief Powell about the possibility of his coming on board when his time in Colorado was over.

The chief was overjoyed at the prospect, telling him Whitebark could never have enough firefighters. Cole knew that was true. It helped to know he would have a place in the department. It wasn't just the extra income, but that sense of belonging he needed to feel after being away so long.

His own father had combined firefighting and ranching. Now that Cole was back, he'd honored his father's wishes to follow in his footsteps and do his part for the community, too. But he'd hardly had a chance to catch his breath before the pager had awakened him tonight.

The Circle R lay outside Whitebark at the other end of town. Cole had been there many times before in the past saying goodnight to Tamsin. He could have found it blindfolded. Tonight he could see flames shooting up in the sky from the barn before they even drove in.

When they arrived, Cole heard quiet pandemonium and horses squealing. A mob of ranch hands had assembled. They were rescuing the animals and leading them toward the paddock in the distance. His eyes searched frantically for Tamsin but saw no sign of her or her parents. Maybe she wasn't even here.

While the guys on the ladder truck were working the hoses, the captain signaled Wyatt to go to the other end of the barn.

As they drove around, Cole whistled. "Somebody left an old wooden work ladder against that window. My gut tells me an arsonist has been at work."

"I think you're right."

The second Wyatt parked the truck, they both jumped out and started pumping water. Their job was to put out any new spots of flames shooting up through the boards. Black smoke was curling out from the seams.

After a few minutes, everything looked under control from their side. They turned off the pump and racked the hoses before driving around to the front of the barn. A couple of the crew were inside looking for hot spots.

Captain Durrant worked as incident commander. He and another fire department official walked over to him and Wyatt. "It's good to have you aboard, Cole."

"I'm glad to be here, sir."

"Call me Jeff. This is Commissioner Rich, head of the arson squad."

The older man nodded to Cole. "Did you see anything that caught your attention around the other side?"

"There's an old work ladder propped by the window. We figured the arsonist used it to either get in, or climb up on the roof and make a hole to whip up the speed and intensity of blaze. Evidently he didn't have time to hide it."

"Good." The commissioner eyed Wyatt. "Do you have anything else to add?"

"Yes. The black smoke indicates an accelerant was used. I couldn't smell it around the side, but I can smell gasoline fumes here." The barn had become an unusable disaster.

"There's been a series of ranch fires that have broken out in Sublette County over the last three months," the older man informed them. "Not all have been the same and we haven't been able to solve the logic of them yet, but every bit of information helps. Thanks for the creditable information. It ties in with the forensics evidence on these other cases that an accelerant was used."

After he walked away to do his own inspection, Cole turned to the captain. "I used to know the people who live here. Where are they?"

"Howard Rayburn and his wife are out of town. Apparently their dog started barking and woke up the other members of the family. They're probably with the horses. I believe their son-in-law, Lyle Witcom, called 911."

Cole reeled. "Did you say son-in-law?"

"Yes. He's married to one of their daughters."

Maybe his information about Tamsin had been wrong. Please God, let it be her younger sister, Sally. The very thought of it being the woman who'd always had a stranglehold on his heart shook him to the core of his being.

Before he lost his grip, he said, "Their horses are going to need a new home until this barn is rebuilt. The barn on my ranch has room for six more horses. I could drive home and bring my rig to transport them."

"I have no idea what arrangements they plan to make, but I'll let them know of your generous offer."

Before Cole could say anything else, another member of the crew called to Jeff, diverting his attention. Cole turned to Wyatt. "While we walk around the barn again to find more hot spots, tell me which Rayburn sister is married. Do you know?"

Wyatt eyed him curiously. "It's Sally. She married Lyle Witcom last year."

With that news Cole was able to breathe again. Everything about this unexpected night had him so tied up in knots he was losing his concentration.

They started another inspection. After twenty minutes they finished examining the exterior of the barn, looking for any evidence that could help identify the arsonist.

"If this guy loves to set fires to watch things burn up for the hell of it, he got careless here."

"Something must have frightened him off," Cole murmured. "If there've been a lot of fires lately, I'm thinking this freak has a definite agenda and that means he needs help to coordinate these raids. I'd be willing to bet he's doing this with a bunch of guys out for some kind of revenge."

Wyatt flashed him a glance. "For what reason?"

"Fire bugs don't need much to go on a rampage. I saw it over in Colorado. The motive in that case had to do with a group trying to intimidate a legislator on the marijuana issue. They were caught and brought up on criminal charges, but not before a lot of damage was done to his property and he spent time in the hospital."

"Incredible." They waved to the guys on the ladder truck who were cleaning up. "Shall we go back to the station?"

"Give me a minute, Wyatt. I'll be right back."

Cole broke into a run as he headed for the corral where he could see some hands gentling the horses. A little closer now, he glimpsed the woman he'd been searching for rubbing her horse's forelock. Her back was toward him. The ponytail looked painfully familiar.

The blood pounded in his ears. "Tamsin?" he called to her.

She turned around, causing his second shock for the night because it was her sister in the last stages of pregnancy who faced him, not Tamsin.

The last time Cole had seen Sally, she'd been sixteen and had just ridden in the local teen rodeo. But her disappointing marks had devastated her and she'd cried against Tamsin's shoulder. Both sisters bore a strong resemblance to each other and had been touchingly devoted.

"Do I know you?"

Whoa. With his five-o'clock shadow and helmet, she obviously didn't recognize him. Or maybe she did and pretended not to. Probably the latter since he knew she had no love for him. He removed his helmet.

Her features tightened as she studied him. "So the rumors

really are true. The great rodeo legend who rode off chasing his dreams is back and working as a firefighter, no less. Who would have thought? If you turn your head, you'll see my sister—she's right over there." Her eyes narrowed. "You just can't help yourself, can you? But if you approach her, you do it at your own peril."

Sally turned back to her horse.

A kick in the gut from a wild mustang couldn't have been more debilitating than her warning. But he shouldn't really be surprised when he knew the girls had been each other's best friend all their lives.

Without saying another word, he looked around and saw Tamsin talking to one of the stockmen while she patted her horse's neck. He walked closer to her, holding the helmet under his arm.

The unremarkable jeans and T-shirt she must have put on when the alarm sounded only emphasized the gorgeous mold of her body and long legs.

First light had already crept across the sky. That pink tone added a tint to her skin and highlighted the shape of the delectable mouth he'd dreamed of kissing and tasting every night.

Her hair hung to her shoulders. He picked out the streaks of gold among the light chestnut sheen no artificial color could improve upon. Once again her natural beauty took his breath.

Maybe she heard his quickly indrawn breath because her eyes suddenly swerved to his. Though she made no motion of any kind, he could sense the stiffening of her body.

"I'm sorry about the fire, Tamsin, but I'm happy to see all your horses are safe. If you need a place to stall them for a while, I have space in my barn and will transport them for you. I've already informed the captain. All you have to do is say the word and I'll be back to load them within the hour."

"Thank you," she said through wooden lips. "We've already had three offers and my brother-in-law is taking care of the arrangements as we speak."

"Tamsin—" He said her name again, but by now another man with brown hair wearing chinos and a polo shirt had come running into the corral and threw possessive arms around her as if she belonged to him. Cole watched her melt against his body. She'd obviously done it before and buried her face against his shoulder.

If this was the kind of peril Sally had been talking about, then Cole got the point. It was more like he'd been run through by Tamsin's twelve-foot lance on the field of battle. He turned away and walked back to the burned barn where Wyatt was waiting for him.

The ladder truck had already started back to town. Cole climbed in the tender truck and they took off. His body felt like it weighed a thousand pounds.

Wyatt flashed him a side glance. "Are you all right?"

"I don't know. Ask me in the morning."

"It already is morning."

So it was.

"Do you want to stop for coffee and doughnuts at Hilda's?"

No, but he knew Wyatt wanted to. "Sure. I could use both. Does this mean you don't have a wife at home who will fix your breakfast when you get there?"

"What woman would that be?"

Cole actually chuckled. "Amen to that. You've just described my life, Wyatt. A half hour ago I was warned that if I approached the woman I was looking for, I had to do it at my own peril. That turned out to be true, unfortunately."

"You're talking about Tamsin. I remember back in high school when you two were so close during our senior year, I couldn't imagine that changing."

"At the time, I couldn't, either. Now we live in separate universes."

"So *that's* why you came back to the truck looking like one of the walking dead."

"Thanks."

"Hey—have you taken a good look at me? We could be brothers. Welcome to the club. We're great at wrangling steers, herding sheep or fighting fires. Give us any task, but get us around a woman and we just don't know how to do it right."

"You said a mouthful."

"I don't mean you, specifically, Cole. I've been a mess for a long time and I don't see that changing anytime soon. There are more guys like us in the department. Take Porter Ewing, who's a recent transfer with the forest service from New York. He swings in when needed. The dude's convinced there's no woman alive who would want him."

Cole laughed out loud despite the pain of seeing Tamsin in that other guy's arms. He'd always liked Wyatt. His sense of humor was a welcome balm to the horrific experience he'd just lived through. Only one thing saved him from oblivion. She wasn't married yet.

Welcome home, Cole.

Chapter Two

While some of the hands stayed with the horses in the paddock, Dean walked Tamsin back to the house with his arm around her shoulders. "Thank God none of you were hurt. When Lyle phoned me, I was terrified that the ranch house might have caught fire, too."

"But it didn't, and I'm fine." She appreciated his trying to comfort her over the loss of the barn. Naturally she was thankful they'd gotten the horses out in time. But he had no clue what a traumatic night this had turned out to be when she saw all six foot two of Cole Hawkins walk toward her.

He was a firefighter? She was incredulous.

Was he out of his mind after the horrific fire in the Winds nine years ago?

Her best friend Mandy had lost her father in that fire. Tamsin had loved her dad. She and Cole had gone to his funeral. Everyone was grief-stricken over the loss. Eleven other firefighters from their county alone had been trapped and killed in the blaze that had brought other firefighters from around the country to fight it.

Maybe she'd been hallucinating.

But no… When she'd opened her eyes again, there he'd been. In cowboy hat and boots or firefighter gear, no man could touch his dark blond masculine beauty. He was an outstanding athlete with a rock-hard body that made him a breed apart. Over the years that he'd been gone and all the dates with other guys, his image had always gotten in the way. Damn, *damn* him.

For him to have stood there now with a quiet authority while he offered his barn for their horses—the first words she'd heard him speak in years, as if there'd been no separation or pain— she'd surprised herself that she could respond to him at all. When Dean came running up to her, she'd clung to him be- cause she'd thought she was going to faint. Thank Heaven he'd attributed her state of mind to the fire while she watched Cole walk away on his powerful legs.

Of course it had been frightening to see flames shooting up from the barn, but they'd soon gotten the horses out and the firefighters had come. The shudders she was experiencing now had their roots in coming face-to-face with Cole, knowing he made his living by walking into danger.

The teenage guy she'd fallen crazy in love with existed no more. In nine years he'd turned into a breathtaking man who'd come home a firefighter. She couldn't comprehend this new image of him. It meant his life could be snuffed out at any mo- ment.

When she and Dean walked in the kitchen, they heard Lyle on the phone making final arrangements for the horses. He'd fixed coffee for them, but one look at Sally's drawn pale face while she drank some bottled water worried Tamsin. Duke stood guard.

"Excuse me for a minute, Dean." She eased herself away from him and put a hand on her sister's shoulder. "Come on, Sally. You need to get back to bed. There's been too much excitement and I'm sure it has raised your blood pressure."

"Okay."

At Sally's six-month checkup, the doctor had said he wanted her to lie down part of every day until she delivered. At that point, their mom had asked her and Lyle to stay at the ranch until the baby was born, where she could be waited on while Lyle was at work. So Sally and Lyle had given up their apartment in town, with plans to move into another one after the baby was born.

Tamsin walked Sally to their bedroom and Duke followed. She waited for her to emerge from the bathroom in her nightgown. Once she got in bed, Tamsin sat down next to her. Duke plopped down at her feet.

"How are you feeling? I have half a mind to call Dr. Ward."

"No, don't do that. I'm fine now. Duke woke us all up in time. He's a hero."

Tamsin smiled down at the dog. "He sure is. I almost had a heart attack when I looked out the window and saw the flames. It sounds like Roy next door will be letting us board our horses at his place until we get the barn rebuilt. We're so lucky."

Her sister stared at her with unswerving intensity. "I agree, but I'm afraid *you're* the one I'm worried about now. You're so pale."

She couldn't pretend with Sally. "I admit I've been a mess since I heard the news Cole was back. But seeing him tonight in firefighter gear gave me another shock."

"Don't you mean seeing him in the *flesh*? That expression took on new meaning for me tonight, too. He's really something. Did I ever tell you I used to have a crush on him?"

Tamsin smiled without mirth. "You and everyone else. What helps me is knowing that he's either married or getting close to marrying that singer I read about in the *Sublette Gazette* a few months ago."

"I saw him talk to you. What did he say?"

She sucked in her breath. "As calm as a hot summer day, he said he'd be happy to board our horses. He even offered to bring his rig over and load them."

Sally gripped her hand. "What did you say back?"

"Don't worry, sister dear. I learned my lesson a long time ago. As Dean was coming toward me, I told Cole that arrangements had already been made. You have no idea the joy I felt to shove the offer in that good-looking face of his before he walked away."

Her sister took another drink of water. "I don't get it. I thought he rode the circuit to make money because he was the hotshot bull rider and wanted the fame. All that pain he caused you when he could have stayed right here and become a fire-fighter... What was the point?"

"To get away from me, of course," Tamsin murmured. Nothing else made sense. The circuit meant being surrounded by women who would idolize him. Why would he stay in White-bark? Tamsin had been such a fool, and what a consummate liar he'd turned out to be!

The letters she'd stopped reading and the phone messages she wouldn't listen to were tokens of his supposed guilt. What a joke! It sickened her. Sally spoke the truth. He could have stayed here to become a firefighter. But no. He had to strive for fame and glory. She'd never have thought he was that type of man back when they were dating.

"I don't want to talk about him. Married to some singing ce-lebrity or not, free to do whatever he wants, he's been out of my life for nine years. Compared to Dean..." She shook her head. "I've got my own life to think about, and I'm furious I've spent one more minute thinking about him. You know?"

"I believe you."

Tamsin smiled sadly at her sister. "No, you don't, but I'm going to prove you wrong."

"Where are you going?"

"To talk to Dean. Try to get some more sleep, Sally. I'll see you later."

"Okay."

Duke stayed by her sister while Tamsin walked through to the kitchen. "Your wife is comfortable now, Lyle. She's going to catch up on some sleep."

"Good." He looked relieved and had made breakfast. She

joined them at the table. "Dean's going to help me load the horses to take over to the Ingram ranch."

"I'm going to help you, too. It'll go a lot faster. Did you phone Dad?"

He nodded. "Sally and I did it together earlier. They're coming home today. We talked about whom to hire to start rebuilding the barn."

"How upset was he?"

"Your father believes it's someone working for the forest service who has a grudge against the government and some of their policies. Your dad has seen this behavior before. A few crazies out there try to take the law into their own hands and start fires. In your father's case, they want him to stop allowing his cattle to graze on forest land even though he has the legal right."

"That's horrible." She looked at Dean. "Do you think Dad's insurance will cover the arson damage completely?"

"I'd have to take a look at the policy."

"When the police catch the man who did this, I hope he goes to prison for the rest of his life!"

On that note, they finished eating. Lyle got up from the table first. "While I go in and check on Sally, will you find the keys to the horse trailer rig? Then we'll start loading the horses."

Tamsin nodded. "They're in Dad's study. I'll get them. Be right back." She hurried through the house and got the keys out of his desk. When she returned to the kitchen, Dean was loading the dishwasher.

"You don't need to be washing our dishes."

He turned his attractive head in her direction. "What if I want to?"

Dean was that kind of guy and so rock solid. She could never find a better man who would always be there for her. Loving him for those qualities, she walked over and gave him a hug.

"You've done enough. Let's go load the horses."

He kissed her thoroughly before they left the house. For the last month he'd wanted to take their relationship to a more intimate level. Tamsin had held back, but for the life of her she couldn't understand why. He was a terrific man and had been so understanding the other night about breaking their date.

Because he and Lyle were brothers, he was over at the ranch a lot. The cozy situation threw the four of them together all the time. She and Dean didn't have enough privacy. Maybe that needed to change. Not for the first time had she thought about getting her own apartment.

What was she waiting for? Seeing Cole again made her realize she'd been living in a deep freeze while he was out having the time of his life. It was time to do something about it.

The more she thought about it, the more she realized she needed her independence. It was long past time Tamsin lived on her own. She'd stayed around her family too long. They'd been there for her after Cole had ridden out of her life, helping her to recover. And she'd gone along allowing it to continue.

She'd saved enough money to get a place of her own. With the horses having to be boarded for at least a couple of months away from the ranch, now would be the time to leave. Her family could wait on Sally.

Once Tamsin was on her own, maybe she would discover just how in love she was with Dean. It was time to find out. After seeing Cole again, all she knew was that she needed perspective to get her head on straight. His arrival in town seemed to have served as a wakeup call, pulling her out of a deep sleep.

All this and more ran through her head while she and Dean helped Lyle load the horses from the paddock and drive them to their new temporary location. Before the day was over, she planned to get online and see what housing rentals were available. The sooner the better.

Two hours later, they'd accomplished their objective. Tamsin did everything in her power to make the horses comfortable in their temporary home, especially her mare Flossie. While she fed her some treats, Dean put his arm around her shoulders.

"You love her the way some people love their children."

She chuckled. "I guess I do."

He turned her around. "Last night I almost lost it when I thought you might have been hurt in that fire. It's all I've been able to think about." With that admission he gave her another long kiss she welcomed.

"I was so thankful you came over when you did!"

"I never want to be separated from you. I wish I didn't have to leave now, but I have an important meeting at work. I'll call you later and we'll get together tonight."

"I'd like that." She meant it. Cole had come home and she'd survived seeing him again. But it was Dean she cared about now and she wanted to show him.

AT EIGHT O'CLOCK Tuesday morning Cole walked into the fire station wearing jeans and one of his long-sleeved denim shirts. He'd been getting ready to go to work on his new job when Chief Powell summoned him to attend an emergency meeting.

When he entered the conference room, he saw a large group of firefighters assembled plus Chief Powell and Commissioner Rich, head of the arson unit. Other men had been called in, too, several of whom wore police uniforms.

Wyatt sat in one corner and signaled to Cole, who joined him in the empty seat next to him. "What's going on with the big confab?"

"I guess we're going to find out."

Another couple of guys walked in the room and found a seat before Chief Powell got to his feet. "Gentlemen? Thanks for coming on such short notice. We've had a serious arson problem here in Sublette County for the past three months. Commissioner Rich, the head of the Arson Task Force, has called a meeting of all of us for help. As I read your names, will you please stand?

"Whitebark Police Chief Holden Granger—

"Director Arnie Blunt of the Wyoming State Fire Services Department—

"Norm Selkirk, head of Sublette County Law Enforcement—

"Orson Perone, regional head of Wyoming forestry that includes fire prevention—

"Thank you, gentlemen. Now I'd like to turn over the meeting to Commissioner Rich."

The sixtyish-looking, sandy-haired man got to his feet. "I've been interviewing the owners of the other ranches who've been hit with fires in the last three months. I've just come from interviewing the owner of the Circle R Ranch, Howard Rayburn, the latest victim in this rash of fires. It happened just two days ago.

"He wasn't home at the time, but he believes he's being targeted for using forest land to let his cattle graze there despite his legal right. Occasionally someone comes out of the woodwork upset over this practice. He's seen it before."

Cole bowed his head. The memory of those few painful moments with Tamsin in the paddock were still too fresh not to be affected by what he was hearing.

"What I'd like is to get an opinion from each of you, especially the crew from this station who fought the fire the other night. Anything you tell us in this meeting could be valuable no matter how insignificant you think it might be.

"Before I call on you one at a time, I'll pass out a map that shows the location of each fire and read the list I've compiled of what we know about them. In all cases, a ranch was targeted."

Once the maps were distributed, he began talking. While Cole listened, he kept studying the areas of Sublette County where the fires had been set and thought he saw a pattern in their locations. His mind kept harkening back to something his mentor had explained in detail during the last year of his graduate studies.

"They were all started in the middle of the night with no witnesses, and an accelerant was used every time," the commissioner explained.

"Eight fires were set inside the fencing that holds the stacked hay bales. None were locked. No lightning was involved.

"The other two were set inside barns where it was estimated that the large fire load of hay inside the barn must have been burning twenty to thirty minutes before it was detected. The electrical wiring and all other potential accidental causes of the fires have been ruled out and no lightning was involved.

"The public outcry is mandating a response to solve these crimes despite the availability of only circumstantial evidence. These fires have now become a priority for the criminal justice system. We're preparing a flier to distribute to every rancher in the county. They need to be alerted to the impending danger to their property and figure out ways to safeguard it.

"We're hoping those warnings will make a difference, but we need to pick the brains of you men who fight these fires every day. Your instincts could help to save lives and millions of dollars. Why don't we go around the back row first and get your opinions? Please state your name and tell us how long you've been with the department."

Cole heard a lot of grudge theories, but nothing specific. When it came to his turn, he got to his feet. "I'm Cole Hawkins. I grew up right here in Whitebark and went to college in Boulder, Colorado. While I was studying, I also trained to become a firefighter with the Boulder Fire Department. I planned to come home to the ranch after graduation and combine my work with firefighting the way my dad did."

He looked at the commissioner. "When you were giving the statistics, I was curious to know if this kind of an outbreak with this same set of circumstances is unique to this year only."

The older man shook his head. "We saw this happen last year to six ranches, but this year's number of outbreaks has increased and summer isn't over."

"Were the fires set at the same time of year last year?"

"Come to think of it, yes, around the end of April and running through August."

"If you had a map of last year's locations of fires, where would they be?"

He stared at Cole. "I'm not sure."

Chief Powell broke in. "I'll get on the computer right now and we'll find out." Within minutes he had the answer. "All of them were near the Winds."

Cole got excited. "Then that cycle fits with the fire locations on the map you just handed out to us. Notice that every ranch targeted this year and last is close to the Bridger Wilderness."

At this point he'd caught everyone's attention.

"There's a war going on between the ranchers hunting the elk coming down from the mountain onto their property, and the ranchers who are against elk hunting."

"Go on," the commissioner urged him.

"Years ago, the elk in the snow country came down to the desert to find food, hay particularly. They ate in the cattle feed grounds where the cattle carried brucellosis disease that caused the cattle to abort. It was transferred to the elk. By the 1930s, calves were dying and humans started getting sick with undulant fever, until pasteurization came along. It's been a battle ever since to eradicate the disease.

"You want a reason for these fires? I believe they've been set to warn the ranchers allowing the hunting. The conservationists want the elk rerouted down to the desert in different migration paths that don't come into contact with the cattle feed lines so the disease won't spread.

"But other ranchers want to bring in the big game hunters who pay a lot of money for the elk hunt. With the hay left out and exposed, the elk are lured to the ranches, thus ensuring plenty of elk for a good hunt. A lot of hay could feed a thousand cattle a day, and the elk, too."

"How do you know so much about this?"

"When I was young, my father used to complain about the brucellosis disease that caused cattle to abort. He hoped that one day it would be eradicated. By the time I went to college, I decided to go into that field and ended up getting my master's to be a brucellosis ecologist.

"I learned that some cattle brought into the States by early European settlers carried this disease. In my role as an ecologist, we're trying to manage the disease and lower it in the elk herds so it's less likely to spill over into cattle."

Orson Perone stood up. "Mr. Hawkins is absolutely right about this. A few years ago there was a small town near the Owl Creek Mountains where the elk had spread disease to a local cattle herd. The fish and game had to depopulate the herd. This caused the ranchers to go bankrupt and the pattern is still the same today. Unfortunately it made for bad relations."

The commissioner looked at Cole. "So it's your contention that there's a group of cattle ranchers sending messages to the ranchers who allow elk hunting to stop luring the elk with hay, and they're resorting to arson to make their point."

Cole nodded. "It makes sense to me considering that all sixteen fires were set in an attempt to destroy the hay as soon as it's harvested."

A collective silence filled the room. The older man smiled at Cole. "Well, aren't we glad you came back home and joined our fire department? I think you're really on to something here."

"I know he is." Holden Granger had gotten to his feet. "I was born and raised in Cody, Wyoming, before I moved here. Our family's ranch suffered a loss of cattle from that disease when I was young. No one ever established a link with the diseased elk that often came to the cattle feed grounds from the Absaroka Mountains."

At this point Chief Powell took over. "Now that we've been educated, we'll explain about the disease in the warning fliers and have them ready by next Monday. By hand or through the mail we'll make certain they're distributed to all the ranchers, urging them to take emergency precautions to ward off the arsonists plaguing parts of Sublette County."

"Excellent," Holden commented. "With this information, I'm going to get together with the county prosecutor. With the cooperation of Norm and Orson, particularly, we can start making lists of ranchers who've never applied for hunting licenses or permits. I'd like to know when and where this group of arsonists meets. That means we'll need a warrant from the judge.

"Setting fires isn't the solution to eradicating the disease. We'll canvas every store that sells accelerants. This is only the beginning." He nodded to Cole. "I'd like to talk to you alone. When you have time, drop by the police station."

"If you want, I'll come now because I'll be leaving for the mountains on my job as soon we're finished and be gone four days."

"Then come with me."

Cole turned to Wyatt. "I'll see you when I get back."

"I plan on it."

Everyone shook Cole's hand before he left with the sheriff. But he was weighed down with worry because Tamsin's father had been targeted and it could happen again before the summer was over. He needed to talk to her and warn her, but he'd have to do that when he got back.

While he was packing his gear to leave for the mountains, he got a text from Patsy Janis.

Call me ASAP. I've got big news.

Cole shook his head. He'd only been home five days and already she couldn't leave him alone. She never gave up. He'd met the good-looking local country singer two years ago in Colorado at a concert in Boulder. He'd grown up on country music, playing the guitar and composing his own songs. Early on he'd made certain to sign up with ASCAP to get his songs copyrighted.

Patsy had a lot of talent and was featured weekends at a local club near the campus with lots of college students and wannabe musicians who got together to jam. It was definitely his kind of place and a great outlet when he'd had a surfeit of studying and needed to get away from it for a little while.

She'd found out he composed music, too, and coaxed him to let her sing some of his songs. Pretty soon, he was accompanying her on his guitar while she sang his tunes for their enthusiastic audience. Everyone wanted to hear more.

Little by little, she encouraged him to do a few recordings at the studio with her just for fun. It wasn't long before they'd recorded two albums.

But he could see where this togetherness was leading when she invited him to her apartment one night after a session. He wasn't into Patsy that way and had to tell her as much. Tamsin had ruined him for other women.

"I hate your honesty, Cole Hawkins," she said with a bitterness in her tone. "So, 'Stranglehold on My Heart' was about her?" He nodded. "In fact all the songs you've written about the woman with the bluebell eyes were about her, right?"

"Yes. I fell in love with her years ago, and never fell out. I'm sorry, Patsy."

"So am I." Her pain sounded real. "You and I make great music together and could earn a lot of money. I could see a future for the two of us on the road."

"That's your dream, but I'm a cowboy at heart. I thought you knew that. I traveled around the country on the circuit, but the truth is, I miss home."

"And the girl you're still hung up on?" He frowned at her persistence. "When are you going to do something about her?"

"Just as soon as I get home next week."

"You're leaving that soon?"

He nodded.

"What if she doesn't feel the same way about you anymore?"

He didn't want to think about that possibility. "That's something I plan to find out."

"Would you hate me if I told you I hope it doesn't work out? You and I could be so good together if you'd give us a chance, Cole. I thought you realized I'm in love with you."

"We both love making music and have that in common, but I never saw it as anything else."

"Not ever?" she questioned.

"I was always in love with Tamsin, but you have to know I didn't mean to hurt you. All along I've been convinced you're on your way to the big time in Nashville and I couldn't be happier for you. You have an amazing talent."

"So you're going to walk out on me without even a hug or kiss goodbye?"

"Of course I'll give you a hug, and I'll be listening to you on the radio. Call me when you want to talk shop. Good luck, Patsy, but you don't need it." He gave her a warm kiss on her cheek and left the apartment. Right now only one person was on his mind. Cole's need to be with Tamsin was consuming him.

Chapter Three

By Friday, Tamsin had found a furnished one-bedroom apartment in town that suited her just fine. She took the day off from work to get settled in. Her parents were great about it when she talked to them. They'd probably wondered why a move like this hadn't happened a long time ago. But she urged them to say nothing to Sally or Lyle.

Her sister had been resting while Tamsin had made half a dozen trips to her car with her things. She would tell her and Lyle she'd found an apartment after she'd settled in. The last person she wanted to know about her plans was Dean. She wanted to get everything done and then surprise him with a homemade dinner once she told him her new address.

When he called to make arrangements for Friday night, she told him she'd be working late and hoped they could have dinner on Saturday night instead. There were still things she had to do to get ready.

Though he'd said that would be fine, she sensed he wasn't happy about having to wait until Saturday. But she'd make it up to him when he realized what she'd done.

At 10:30 p.m., she drove to the all-night grocery store a few blocks away to pick up some batteries for her remotes and some sodas. Then she was going to kick back on the couch and watch an old movie while she hung a few pictures and put books away in the bookcase.

As she was pulling a pack of colas from the refrigerated section, her gaze collided with a pair of brown eyes smoldering beneath a black Stetson.

Her breath caught to see Cole, who'd just reached for a pack of root beer to put in the cart with some other groceries, including a quart of vanilla ice cream.

Root beer floats. One of those treats they'd whipped up on many a weekend their senior year. He still loved them, apparently.

For a moment she was attacked by memories of those times when they couldn't stay out of each other's arms. For a moment she was blinded by the way his body filled out a pair of well-worn jeans and a crew neck brown shirt. Somehow he seemed a little taller in his cowboy boots than she'd remembered. Had he grown another inch?

The other night she'd noticed he wore his dark blond wavy hair a little shorter than he used to. There were more lines around his eyes. His compelling mouth looked a little harder. All in all, he was a gorgeous twenty-seven-year-old man. And she was staring at him, something she'd sworn she would never do if she saw him again. But she'd been caught doing it now.

To see the grown-up version of Cole in firefighter gear or otherwise sent an unwanted thrill of excitement through her body. She couldn't suppress it, no matter how hard she tried.

Tamsin guessed he was a disease she'd caught years ago. It had lived inside her all this time. What haunted her was the possibility that there was no cure. That was why she was making changes in her life. A new place to live with more privacy for her and Dean.

Cole's return to Whitebark was putting her through a refiner's fire. Her greatest fear was that Dean get trapped in it or hurt by it. When he came to her apartment for dinner tomorrow night, she would tell him some things about her relationship with Cole she'd kept private so Dean would understand.

Even if he'd been told a little about her history with Cole through his brother who would've learned it from Sally, Dean needed to hear certain details from Tamsin herself.

For the time being she didn't know where their relationship would end up. But she was hoping that living on her own, she would now have the breathing room to figure out her life. If she ended up with Dean, she wanted it to be with her whole heart and no reservations.

"I'm glad we bumped into each other." Cole's low voice filtered through her turmoil to her brain. "It has saved me from having to find you."

To her horror she almost sighed in relief to see that he didn't wear a ring. Did it mean he wasn't married yet?

"Why would you have to do that?" she asked, trying to fight off the effect he was having on her.

His eyes narrowed between his darker lashes. "To warn you and your family that the arsonists who set fire to your barn will probably set fire to your haystacks before the summer is over."

She frowned. "You honestly think it will happen again?"

He nodded. "I was in a big conference on Tuesday with state officials. We're pretty certain why ranchers like your father have been targeted."

"Why *my* father?"

"He has always allowed hunting on his property in the fall. There's a contingent of ranchers who want to ban the elk hunters, but since they can't stop them legally, they've resorted to arson on the lands where they hunt."

Tamsin still didn't understand. "But Dad isn't the only rancher who allows it."

"That's true. So far in the last two years, sixteen ranches near the Bridger Wilderness that have allowed elk hunting have undergone losses by these arsonists."

"What's wrong with elk hunting?"

"Nothing, as long as the elk aren't transmitting brucellosis disease to the cattle when they both come to feed at the same feeding grounds. The bailed hay on your father's property, both fenced and in the barn, invites the elk to come. In my line of work, we're dedicated to eradicating the disease."

What line of work was he talking about? He was a firefighter!

She blinked. "Isn't that the disease that causes calves to abort?" He nodded. "How do you know so much about it?"

"I received my master's degree in environmental wildlife at the University of Colorado in Boulder. But my technical title is a brucellosis-feed-ground-habitat biologist, and my specific job is to test the elk for the disease. I also work for the fire department here if I'm not up in the mountains tracking elk."

Tamsin was stunned by what he'd just told her. She was having trouble taking it all in. All this time she'd accused him in her heart of going off to be a famous rodeo celebrity.

"These arsonists want the elk to migrate down the mountains away from the ranches. But the lure of the hay makes it impossible. There's a group of men so serious about stopping this, they've been willing to commit crimes like the one on your property in order to make their point."

She put a hand to her throat. "Is this happening all over Wyoming?"

"In parts where a ranch that allows elk hunting is located near a range of mountains. As you've found out firsthand, these men are endangering the lives of people and horses. After we put out the fire, I looked for you to tell you of the danger when I saw Sally. Her being pregnant makes her even more vulnerable in a situation like this and I'm afraid it's not going to stop."

His prediction increased Tamsin's fear, but she fought not to show it. "I had no idea you'd been in college all this time besides becoming a firefighter. How amazing that you know so much about what has been going on around here. How long have you been back in Whitebark?"

Here she was, asking him questions when she'd promised

herself she would never show him the slightest interest. Never again.

"I'd been home five days when I was called out on the fire at your father's ranch."

Only five? "Where did you get your firefighter training?"

"In Boulder while I was in graduate school."

Her eyes widened. "So you did both while you were there."

"Yes. When I left the ranch nine years ago, I was honoring a promise to my father that was ironclad."

"What promise was that?"

"There's a lot you don't know about the reason I had to leave. A reason my father wouldn't let anyone know about. Even on his deathbed he swore me to secrecy."

That revelation only deepened her pain. He didn't give her an explanation then, and wouldn't be giving it to her now. "What about your ranch?"

"It's still here. I'm managing with the help of Sam and Louise. You remember them?"

"Yes." Of course, she did. But how on earth could he handle everything? All this time she'd thought he'd been with that country singer, planning a new life with her. How wrong could she have been? Or maybe not. Already he'd shot her peace of mind to pieces. Before she left the store, she needed one more bit of information.

"An article about you in the *Sublette Gazette* a few months ago indicated you were involved with a country singer. Are you—"

"Patsy Janis you mean?" He cut her off. "We did a few records together. She wanted me to stay in Colorado, make records and marry her. But I told her I wanted to go home. I take it you're involved with the man who threw his arms around you the night of the fire."

Without thinking, she said the first thing to come into her head. "That was Dean Witcom, Sally's brother-in-law."

"And your boyfriend?" After firing the question, he tipped

his cowboy hat. With a rakish smile he said, "Be sure to pass on my warning to your father."

Tamsin smothered a groan as he headed for the front of the store pushing the cart. She waited until he'd checked out before she paid for her groceries. By the time she went out to her car, he'd left. After she got back to the apartment, she was no longer in the mood to watch a movie.

Cole was back and he didn't want anything from her. Why would he when she'd cut him off a long time ago, believing he didn't love her enough to stay in Wyoming?

To think he'd become a firefighter *and* a biologist!

Feeling frustrated and heartsick, she hurried into the bedroom to get her laptop. She set it up on the little kitchen table and began researching brucellosis. That led her to studying about the disease in Wyoming and its history. Never during their time together had he mentioned being interested in biology, let alone fighting fires. He'd been a bull rider for Heaven's sake!

When she'd exhausted every possible avenue of information on the subject, it was three thirty in the morning. She fell into bed physically exhausted from her move, and emotionally spent over a man who'd left her a long time ago.

He'd returned a man she didn't recognize. Tamsin didn't know how long she sobbed before oblivion took over.

Late Saturday morning she awakened to the sound of her phone ringing. She checked the caller ID before answering.

"Hi, Sally."

"Hey—what's going on? Mom just told me you moved to an apartment in town."

Tamsin sat up on the side of the bed. "Yesterday you were sound asleep, so I planned to tell you today."

"This has to do with Cole, but I don't know in what way."

"Why would you say that? I decided I needed more privacy. Getting an apartment will give me a chance to see how I really feel about Dean."

"Does he even know you've moved?"

"No. I'm going to call him this afternoon and tell him my new address. I'm going to make dinner for him."

"I know why you're doing this. It's because of Cole. Admit that if he wants to see you again, he'll be able to come to your apartment and not the house where he'd be sure to run into Dean."

"That's not true, Sally."

"You've been with Cole, haven't you?"

"No! In fact, last night I bumped into him at the grocery store. He has no interest in me anymore. I've moved on and want to concentrate on Dean."

After a silence Sally said, "I'm sorry for him and you."

"Why are you saying that? It's long past time I stopped living in the past. Isn't that what you've always said to me?"

"Yes. Forgive me. You're absolutely right to do what you've done. Being on your own will give you the time you need to see where it's going with Dean without everyone else being around."

"Exactly. Thank you for being so understanding. Now enough about me. How are you?"

"I feel all right."

"You have an appointment with the doctor on Tuesday, right?"

"Yes."

"Please be careful. Only three more weeks and your baby will be here."

"I know. I'm going crazy waiting for it to happen."

"I am, too. I can't wait to be an aunt. Love you, Sally. Call you tomorrow."

Once they'd hung up, Tamsin decided to phone Dean and tell him where she'd moved. Over dinner she would explain her feelings. To her relief, he answered his phone rather than it going to voice mail.

"Hey, honey—I was hoping you'd call."

"I'm sorry I've been MIA until now." She got up from the side of the bed and started pacing. "Yesterday I moved out of the ranch house to an apartment in town, and I've just finished settling in."

There was a long silence. "You *moved*?"

"Yes. I should have done it a long time ago."

"You never mentioned anything about that to me before."

"I know, but it's been on my mind for a long time. The other day I saw the right apartment for me and grabbed it."

"Why didn't you tell me? I would have helped you move."

She knew she'd hurt him. "I would have asked for it, but since this apartment is furnished, all I had to do was bring over my clothes. If you'll come for dinner, I'll explain more." Tamsin told him her new address.

There was another pause before he said, "I'd rather take you out for dinner. I'll be there at seven."

"Then I'll be ready."

"Does Chinese sound good to you?"

"Perfect."

After she hung up, her sister's observation that she'd moved so she could have private time with Cole had struck a deep nerve. It made her question her own motives. Sally had a way of doing that. If Tamsin had made this move because of Cole, it had to have been on a subconscious level. It terrified her that it might be true because that meant she wasn't over Cole and never would be!

"Tamsin—"

She gripped the phone tighter. "Yes?"

"Nothing," he murmured, before hanging up.

Oh, boy. Dean was no fool. He knew something serious had gone on for her to move from the ranch without saying a word to him.

For the rest of the day she did laundry and took a few outfits to the cleaners. When he came to her apartment at seven, she didn't invite him inside. After explaining that she was hungry, they left for the restaurant.

Tamsin knew what she had to say. It could cost her the relationship with Dean, but it was a risk she had to take in order to be fair to him. He was in a no-nonsense mood once they'd started eating their food.

"What's going on? You haven't been yourself since you broke off our date last week. Maybe you did have a migraine, but I get the feeling there was more behind it than that. I'd like to know the real reason for it, Tamsin. There's no point in pretending your feelings toward me haven't changed in some way."

She put down her coffee cup. "I'm so sorry, Dean, and I agree it's time we talked. The truth is my feelings toward you haven't changed." She sighed. "When we started dating, I told you there wasn't another man in my life. As I explained in the beginning, the only guy who ever mattered to me was Cole Hawkins, and he left Whitebark nine years ago.

"I thought we'd get married, but it didn't happen. It almost killed me at the time because I couldn't understand why he left at all if he loved me so much. The fact that he could go away and not ask me to go with him proved I'd misread his feelings and intentions.

"But a few weeks ago Heather told me something that upset me more than I would have imagined. She told me Cole was back in town...for good."

Dean's facial features sobered. "In other words, you still have feelings for him."

She shook her head. "Love has to be fed, Dean. We've been separated nine years and I heard he's been involved with a country singer. With that news I assumed that if he was back for good, it was because he was probably getting married."

He put down his fork. "Have you seen him?"

Her heart thudded hard. "Yes. He was one of the firefighters who showed up at the ranch."

"The bull rider is a firefighter now?" he said with incredulity.

"I couldn't believe it when he walked over to me in the corral and offered to stall our horses at the barn on his ranch."

Dean's mouth tightened. "You never said a word."

"I was in shock."

"Have you seen him since?"

She didn't look away. "We bumped into each other at the grocery store the other night and had a brief conversation. He warned me about the arsonists who are out targeting some of the ranchers. He said my father needs to take precautions so it won't happen to him again."

His eyes narrowed. "Is he engaged?"

"No."

"So what does his being back in town have to do with you suddenly moving out of your parents' home and not telling me until it was a fait accompli?"

"That's a fair question. I wish I knew how to answer it."

"It's obvious you want to be with him again, and need your privacy without me coming around the ranch house all the time." Those were Sally's words exactly.

"I realize it looks that way, Dean, but honestly, I don't know what I'm feeling."

"Has he asked to see you again and pick up where you left off?"

"No!" she cried softly. "Anything but. He saw me clinging to you the night of the fire and made assumptions about us. Dean—I'm trying to figure out what's going on inside me. I wish I knew. I'm telling you this to be totally honest with you. I care for you so much and don't want any secrets between us."

"The truth is you don't love me."

"I do—but—"

"But you're not in love with me the way you were with him. Otherwise we'd be planning our wedding and you would probably have gone to bed with me by now."

She shook her head. "Now that he's back, I just need to deal with my feelings where he's concerned, but I don't want to hurt you in the process. If you can be patient with me while I get answers… You *have* to know I don't want to stop seeing you.

You're too important to me. I refuse to sneak around behind your back."

He put some bills on the table to cover their meal. "I think you know exactly how I feel about you. I love you and want to get married. But when I think it's been nine years and just seeing him again can disrupt your emotions to this degree, it makes me wonder what kind of a chance there is for us. When you've finished your dinner, I'll drive you home."

"Dean—please listen to me. When he left Whitebark nothing was resolved for me. Nothing made sense. But I never thought I'd see him again, let alone get a chance to talk to him again. Now that he's home, I finally have an opportunity to confront him and I need some answers. Can you understand that?"

He pushed himself away from the table and stood up. "Yes, but can you understand that I don't plan to put my life on hold while you make up your mind?"

"Of course I can," she whispered and got to her feet. "I'm trying to straighten out my thoughts. I hope that in being honest with you, you realize how much I care about you."

As she followed him out to the truck, Tamsin feared she'd done too much damage. "Do you wish I hadn't said anything?"

"No," he muttered. "I just wish to hell he'd never come back."

Therein lay the whole problem. A part of Tamsin was still reeling over the fact that he *had* returned.

"Dean—if you and I get married, it'll be because we both love each other with all our hearts and souls."

"But you're not there yet," he bit out.

"Seeing Cole again is like he's come back from the dead. I have to talk to him again and get certain things resolved, but it doesn't mean I want anything to change with you and me. You have to believe me."

"I'm trying."

When they reached her apartment, she opened the truck door and got out. Breaking the silence she said, "I'm so sorry. I hope you know you're the most wonderful man I've ever met. Mom's planning dinner for all of us on Thursday. I want you to come."

She was afraid that her words fell on deaf ears. He refused to look at her before she shut the door and hurried up the steps to her apartment. She could hear his tires squeal as he drove away. The sound haunted her as she reached for her phone and called Sally.

"Tamsin?" her sister answered. "It's only nine o'clock. I thought you were making dinner for Dean."

"He wanted to eat out so we ended up going for Chinese, but he just brought me home. When I told him what has been bothering me and why, he didn't want to talk anymore. I don't blame him for being so upset."

"Neither do I." Sally was always honest. "But you can't help how you feel right now. It's a terrible situation for both of you. I'm glad you told me what's going on so I can tell Lyle."

"Your husband's going to hate me."

"No, he won't. He couldn't, even if he wanted to. He's crazy about you."

"It's a good thing I moved out. Now when Dean comes over, he won't have to face me or be worried about that. How are you feeling?"

"*So* pregnant I'm going insane."

Tamsin couldn't imagine being married, let alone knowing what it would be like to expect a baby. "I love you, Sally. Please take care. I'll call you tomorrow."

"Promise?"

"What do you think? Good night."

ON THURSDAY NIGHT Dean did come to the ranch with Lyle after work, surprising Tamsin. She hurried into the entrance hall to hug him. "I'm so glad you came."

Her mother had made stir-fry. Sally got comfortable on the couch and the six of them, including their father, sat around the TV in the family room and ate. They talked about the arson and went over the plans for the new barn with everyone adding their ideas.

Dean fit in with their family. Every look he gave Tamsin over the course of the evening told her how he felt about her. When he finally said good-night in the front hallway, she saw a new look in his eyes.

"Would it be pushing too much if I asked you out for Saturday night? I've made plans for us."

He was being so careful, and she loved him for it. "You mean the ones I ruined last week because of my migraine? I'm so sorry about that."

"I'm trying to give you time."

"I know you are and I'll look forward to Saturday night."

"Good. Tomorrow night I have to be gone overnight in Riverton, but I'll be back the next day and phone you." His kiss was intense before he left the house.

Tamsin walked back in the living room, finding Sally alone for a minute. "Where is everyone?"

"They're helping Mom with the dishes." She eyed Tamsin with curiosity. "Tonight Dad was trying to feel me out in private and told me in his own way that Dean would make a great addition to the family."

"I've been thinking the same thing. Maybe this apartment has already given me an objective look. He's taking me out for dinner Saturday night."

"Are you sure you want to go?"

She shrugged and said, "He's trying not to push and I have to be willing to meet him halfway."

"That's good, but are you sure?"

Tamsin nodded. "He's a great person. I'd have to be out of my mind to let Cole's existence determine my life."

"I couldn't agree more."

She leaned over and gave her a kiss on the cheek. "You look

tired and should get to bed. I'm going up, too. Love you." Tamsin appreciated it that her sister hadn't brought up Cole's name. It helped Tamsin, who was trying to put the past away for good.

Chapter Four

On Saturday morning Cole swung by the fire station to pick up one of the prepared fliers. They were being mailed out to ranchers, but he wanted to hand deliver one to Howard Rayburn. He'd always liked Tamsin's father and felt the need to warn him in person about this threat.

He also hoped to see Tamsin. Last week he'd left the grocery store without knowing essential things about her life… apart from her involvement with the man who'd pulled her into his arms during the night of the fire. Cole hadn't been able to get that image out of his mind. Tamsin didn't wear a ring, so at least she wasn't engaged yet. He needed to find out more about her relationship with the guy or he wouldn't be able to function.

When he pulled up in front of the Rayburn ranch house, he jumped out of the cab and hurried to the front door, anxious to make contact with her. But once again when the door opened, it was Sally he saw standing there.

She eyed him in surprise. "You're not in your firefighting gear this morning."

"No, but I am here to deliver this flier from the fire department to your father. Is he home?"

"I'm afraid not. He's in town talking to the builder who's going to erect a new barn."

"It can't be soon enough for him, I'm sure. Will you make certain he receives this?" He handed it to her. "All the ranchers in the area will be getting one, warning them that more arson attacks could be coming. He needs to take all the precautions he can."

She frowned. "That's scary news."

"I agree and I'm sorry. The police want these arsonists caught at all costs. Have you been all right since the night of the fire? It must have been frightening for you."

"I'm fine now." He could tell she wanted to slam the door in his face.

"Before I leave, is your sister home?"

"Tamsin doesn't live here anymore." Was that true, or was Sally protecting her? Both sisters had been with the horses during the fire in the middle of the night. "I imagine she's at work by now," Sally added.

"What does she do?"

"She's a CPA."

"Do you mind telling me where?"

"Ostler Certified Public Accounting."

Cole knew the location of that firm. It had been around for a long time. "Thank you, Sally. Sorry to have bothered you. Don't forget to give that flier to your father."

He heard the front door close before he reached his truck. Where was Tamsin living? His frustration grew as he drove back to town and pulled into a vacant parking spot near Ostler Accounting.

He got out of the truck and walked inside to the reception desk where a middle-aged woman was seated.

"May I help you?"

"I'm here to see Ms. Rayburn."

"What's your name? I'll ring her office, but she might not be here."

"Will you tell her it's Cole Hawkins?"

"Very well, Mr. Hawkins. Why don't you take a seat?"

He was too restless to sit, but he walked over to an end table and picked up a business management magazine they put out for clients. Tamsin had been an outstanding student in high school—she could have done anything. He wondered what had made her choose accounting.

While he stood there thinking about the years that had separated them, she came into the reception room wearing a short-sleeved suit in an apple-green color with a white crew neck top. The strappy high-heeled white sandals she had on made her look much taller than her natural five foot six.

He'd never seen her hair swept back that way. She looked classy and professional, and for a moment he was rendered speechless.

"You wanted to see me?"

She'd spoken before he'd even realized it.

Cole put the magazine back on the table and met her halfway, noticing her tiny green enamel earrings. "I stopped by the ranch to leave a flier with your father. Sally answered the door and told me where I could find you."

"You almost missed me. I have an appointment at the hospital in ten minutes."

His breath caught. "Is something wrong?"

"No. I'm going to be working on their books next week and came in to download some materials on my laptop."

Relief swept through him. "I had no idea you were interested in this kind of work."

"I thought the same thing about your line of work. Funny how two high school kids who were crazy about horses and the rodeo ended up. Truth really is stranger than fiction."

His body tautened. "What isn't funny is how two high school kids who were insanely crazy about each other still aren't married. I'd like to take you somewhere so we can talk about that."

"The time for that kind of talk was ages ago."

"Are you engaged to Dean Witcom?"

A little pulse throbbed at the base of her throat. Emotion always did that to her. She was having trouble with his question. He waited so long for her answer, he ran out of the breath he wasn't aware he'd been holding.

"No." That one word made him euphoric. "But let's get something clear. I'll never go anywhere with you unless you promise to make a promise to me."

"What's that?"

"That you break your promise to your father and come clean about the real reason you left the state rather than stay and work things out with me. It's up to you, Cole. You know where to find me."

She wheeled around, but he caught hold of her arm so she couldn't leave, startling her.

"I'd already planned to tell you everything." The long silence had to be broken if he wanted to get on with the rest of his life. "We'll need time to talk. If it's all right with you, I'd like us to get an early start. What's your address? Why don't I come pick you up tomorrow?"

BY SUNDAY MORNING Tamsin was jumping out of her skin, partly with nerves, partly with unbidden excitement, waiting for Cole to come by the apartment complex and pick her up. After her shower, she blow-dried her hair and tied it at the nape with an elastic.

Yesterday, he'd told her to dress for the mountains. If she wanted to hike around a little, they could do that. He'd be bringing everything they'd need.

In the past they'd done a little hiking, but nothing too ambitious since participating in the rodeo had taken up the bulk of their free time. Today he was taking her to a tiny lake he'd named Teardrop, a place she'd never seen. He explained that it was at low elevation in the Wind River Range. They'd be warm and there'd be no snow.

She'd just finished her breakfast when he came to the door and knocked. Tamsin decided not to invite him inside. She was ready in her jeans, hiking boots and pullover sweater with long sleeves. Grabbing a beanie and parka, she walked out to his truck with him. It looked new.

He helped her inside and put her things on the back seat before walking around to climb in behind the wheel. This wasn't a date like they used to have. She'd come with him today for one reason only. Once she heard the true explanation about his going away, then she'd have closure and that would be the end of a life experience she wanted nothing more than to forget.

"If you get hungry, I've packed food and drinks."

"Thank you."

Cole drove them northeast to the Elkhart Park trailhead, fifteen miles from town. They were both quiet while she marveled over the scenery.

Nowhere except a few places on the North American continent would you ever see scenic waterfalls, alpine lakes, massive granite spires, high mountain cirques, glaciers and vast meadows all in one spot like this. The Bridger Wilderness was unique in the world.

He pulled onto a side road that wound around to the little lake he'd talked about. "It does look exactly like a teardrop. What's its real name?"

"I think it's too small to have been given one. Shall we get out and walk down to the edge? I'll bring a thermal blanket."

"What can I carry?"

"Everything's in the truck bed. Have a look and take what you want."

They both got out and walked around to the rear. He lowered the tailgate and levered himself with a dexterity that had made him so exciting to watch when he was bull riding.

Tamsin saw a lot of equipment she didn't recognize. Cole handed her some water bottles. After he'd pulled a couple of loaded plastic bags from a duffel bag, he jumped down with the blanket and closed the gate. She followed him toward the water.

There was no one around to disturb their privacy. Without a

breeze, the stillness of the morning added a magical element, as if they'd arrived in a land out of time. "Did you come here a lot in the past?"

"Only a few times."

Just knowing he came here without her started up that ache in her chest.

He spread the blanket on the ground and lowered the bags to one corner. After taking the bottles from her, he put them next to the bags and sat down, removing his cowboy hat. Once he'd stretched out and rested the side of his head on his hand, she joined him.

His preference for plaid shirts hadn't changed. He wore a blue, green and white button-down tucked into jeans that outlined his hard thighs. Those long legs of his had ridden some of the toughest bulls on the circuit, winning him a lot of money.

She sat down. "Exactly how long were you on the circuit?"

"Three years before I'd made enough to start college and study to become a firefighter."

"I don't understand. Why did it take so long before you enrolled in classes?"

He sent her a piercing glance. "For one thing, I needed to pay for my mother's medical bills."

Tamsin shook her head in bewilderment. "I didn't realize she'd been hospitalized for so long. You never told me the costs had added up to that degree."

"Mother was only hospitalized a few days, Tamsin."

"But if she was so ill, then—"

"My father kept her at home," he broke in on her.

She stared at him. "I thought she died of pneumonia. Did it cost so much?"

Cole sat up and reached for one of the water bottles. After drinking half of one he said, "What I'm going to tell you is something that no one else knows because all the interested parties are dead. I promised my father I'd keep his secret, but now I'm about to break it. Once I tell you, then only four of us will know because Sam and Louise figured it out a long time ago, but they've never said a word."

Her heart started to pound with anxiety. "Know what?"

"She didn't die of pneumonia, though that's what the coroner wrote on the death certificate. He was best friends with the doctor and they kept quiet."

Tamsin got on her knees. "About what? Tell me what you're trying to say."

His jaw hardened. "She died of undulant fever."

Tamsin closed her eyes tightly. After reading about brucellosis on the internet, she knew exactly what it was. It horrified her that something like that had happened to his mother, the woman Tamsin had only met one time.

She recalled it being an infectious disease caused by the bacteria called *Brucella abortus*. It was most often transmitted to humans from drinking raw milk from dairy cows carrying the disease, but pretty rarely these days since the advent of pasteurization. In a human it caused fever that rose and fell, sweats, headaches and generalized weakness. In livestock and wildlife, it caused the animal to abort. The disease could also be spread to other animals or humans by contact with the aborted calf.

"If you don't look too closely, the symptoms mimic the flu," he said, realizing she understood. "My mother had it all, including agonizing back pain."

Tamsin was aghast. "How did she get infected?"

"While she was helping with the birth of a cow in trouble, she wasn't aware of a cut on her forearm. It got exposed to the fluid from the cow infected with brucella."

"Oh Cole, no—" she cried. "Wasn't there a treatment for her?"

"Yes. The doctor strung it out as long as possible, but with the wrong antibiotics. He'd misdiagnosed her illness. He tried many kinds that became terribly expensive, but it didn't matter because she never recovered. Both he and Dad kept up the fiction that her pneumonia was getting worse. The doctor understood what it would mean if word got out there was a sick cow on our ranch and he hadn't realized what was really wrong with her until it was too late. No one was allowed to see her."

"So *that's* why I never got to know her after you introduced me to her."

His eyes glittered with pain. "You have no idea how hard that was for me. I told her all about you, but the doctor warned me to keep everyone away while she was dying."

Tamsin took a struggling breath. "Wasn't there a vaccine that could have made her better?"

"For the livestock, yes. And there is a cure for humans with the right antibiotics.

"But she didn't receive them and my parents were petrified. If the truth had spread, it would have set off panic in a small town like Whitebark where we were surrounded with cattle ranches. Neither of my parents could bear the thought of that. It was a source of embarrassment to Mother."

"How could she possibly have been embarrassed?"

"She felt she must have done something wrong for it to happen to her. That kind of thinking doesn't make sense, but it did to her. She didn't want anyone to know about it. The scrutiny would have been too hard for her to handle."

"Oh, the poor thing. So no one ever found out you had a cow with the disease?"

"Tamsin—we had more than one sick cow."

"What?"

"We lost a lot of calves during the calving season. Dad and Sam transported the aborted calves to the farthest boundary of the ranch and burned them before the other cattle could become exposed. No one knew about it. We thanked God the disease didn't spread to all the cows, but our herd was diminished and Dad lost his source of income."

"That's horrible."

"You're right about that. My parents held their breath while they waited to hear of any other outbreaks, but it appeared our ranch was the only one affected that year. To my knowledge your father never had an infected one on the Circle R."

"Not that I know of, but maybe it had happened to our herd, too, and he kept quiet about it."

"I suppose that's possible."

"If he didn't tell anyone, maybe someone knew and that's why they set fire to our barn."

"No." Cole shook his head. "I can promise that's not the reason."

"How do you know?"

"There's still a lot I have to tell you. You have to understand I was sworn to secrecy about the situation and something else. Dad had no money to bury my mother and was forced to mortgage our ranch to the hilt to pay bills and keep us alive."

"Cole—" She couldn't believe what she was hearing.

"By the time I graduated from high school, there was no money left. He couldn't buy more cows to rebuild our herd and he'd developed heart trouble. It's a miracle that Sam and Louise stayed with him. They were saviors, looking after him while I had to be the one to get out there and make a decent living to save all of us and the ranch."

"So *that's* why you took off like you did!"

"Yes. Dad gave me the truck and the horse trailer. That was all he had left. Before I drove away, he made me promise I'd eventually go to college and work on a cure for that disease so no one else ever had to go through what our family did."

A gasp escaped Tamsin's lips.

"After three years of driving all over the country and winning rodeos, I gave it up, sold my horse and started classes. But I had to find another way to earn money. That prompted me to train to be a firefighter so I could draw a salary that would keep me supported while I finished graduate school.

"Even that wasn't enough, so I began selling some of the music I'd been writing over the years. It didn't bring in much revenue, but it kept me in razors and toothpaste. A year ago I was doing gigs in Boulder on my acoustic guitar on the odd weekends when I wasn't fighting fires. That's where I met Patsy. She was making records and talked me into doing a few, promising it would be lucrative."

Tamsin could hardly see him because her eyes were glazed over with tears. "And was it?"

"It could have been, but that was never my goal. After burying my father, I didn't want to do anything but go home. The minute I graduated, I didn't stay for commencement. Instead I left the rooming house where I lived, loaded up my truck and trailer and returned to get started on the rest of my life."

She turned away from him, unable to handle all the information. Nothing was the way she'd imagined. But the truth brought fresh pain. She didn't know where to go with it.

"Tamsin, it killed me when Dad swore me to secrecy where you were concerned. I couldn't take you with me without asking you to marry me. I had no way to support you at the time. Your parents wanted you to go to college and would never have given us their blessing because you didn't turn eighteen until after I left."

Tamsin knew he was right about that. "At the time, I would have gone with you no matter what if you'd begged me."

"That would have been no life for you. There was only one way I could survive and I had to do it by winning money while I rode the circuit. If you'd gone wi—"

"I know," she cut him off, facing him again. "I couldn't have worked a job and would have been a burden that defeated the whole purpose of your leaving. With hindsight I get it." A tear rolled down her cheek. "I just wish I'd known the truth about your situation."

"If you'd known, it wouldn't have changed anything."

"How can you say that?" she cried. "As far as I was concerned, I believed you didn't love me the way I loved you."

He studied her for an agonizing moment. "After you stopped answering my letters and didn't take my calls, I decided it was better you thought that so you could get on with your life. I knew I wouldn't be back for a long time."

"I think your father was cruel to make you promise to keep it a secret from me. If you have a son one day, do you think you could ask the same thing of him? Walk away from the woman who loves him without telling her the real reason why?"

"Probably not, but nine years ago my father was in desperate straits. I owed my parents everything and had to figure out the best way to help him. If you'd read any of the letters I sent you that first year, you would know I had plans for the two of us once I started college. Though I couldn't tell you the truth of everything, I wrote letter after letter telling you I loved you, and that one day I'd be back."

She averted her eyes. "I read some of them... You asked me to be patient for three years. Once you left the circuit, you hoped I would join you and we would work things out."

"But you didn't write me back."

Anger flared inside her. "That's because I couldn't believe you would leave me. I loved you too much to let you go, but I was forced to and almost died with the pain." She took a quick breath. "So now you're going to tell me that in the end, I didn't love you with enough depth to reassure you I'd wait forever. That's what three years sounded like to me."

He shifted positions. "It sounded like a hundred to me, so I forced myself not to think about it. When I arrived in Boulder to start classes three years later, I wrote you again, but there was no answer. I was terrified I'd lost you, and I knew I was going to lose my father.

"At that point I threw myself into work day and night, praying he wouldn't die before I finished school. When that prayer wasn't answered, I had no more hope for anything that had once been important to me."

Aghast over these revelations, Tamsin got to her feet and walked toward the lake. When she reached the edge, she started sobbing and couldn't stop. It angered her that Cole's father had destroyed their lives so a secret could be kept. She couldn't comprehend it that a father could do that to his only son, no matter how much he'd loved his wife and wanted to protect their reputation.

Mr. Hawkins could have sold the ranch. They could have moved into town and Cole could have gotten a job there so he didn't have to leave. It amazed her that his son had done everything his father had asked him to do. Tamsin never stood a chance.

If she'd left home and had gone to find Cole, he would have told her to go back without telling her why. She could see that now. His determination to carry out his father's every wish had set him on a path she hadn't been able to follow. Now it was too late with a trail of nine years' worth of lost opportunities that would never come again.

Tamsin had come with him today for answers.

You have them now, Tamsin. More closure than you ever wanted.

She wiped the moisture from her cheeks and turned around. He stood behind her, his handsome face a study in anguish.

"How am I supposed to respond now that you've told me the truth, Cole? You have my word that your secret will always be safe with me. Beyond that there's nothing more to say. Now if you don't mind, I don't want to spend the rest of the day with you. I'd rather go back to my apartment."

He stayed right where he was. "There's more I need to tell you."

"What good would it do?" she cried softly. "We've lost nine years!" The honesty poured out of her. "What an emotional waste this has been for both of us."

She walked past him. When she reached the blanket, she picked up the unopened plastic bags and carried them to the truck. He wasn't far behind and put everything in the truck bed while she climbed in the passenger side without help.

Within minutes they reached the main road leading out of

Elkhart Park and headed back to Whitebark. Nothing was ever going to be the same again. Deafening silence accompanied them all the way home.

When Cole pulled into the guest parking of her apartment building, he jumped out to help her. She wanted to get away from him, but he reached in the back for her parka before walking her to the apartment on the second floor.

"You didn't need to walk me to the door."

"Yes, I did. I took this day off from work to be with you. Let's not waste it. If it weren't important, I wouldn't ask."

"What more do you want?"

"We need to talk about the trouble your father could be facing before fall. If you'd invite me in, I'd like to explain."

"I don't understand."

"Please, Tamsin."

No, no, no. Don't let him in.

But he was being insistent. The only thing to do was to let him come in long enough to have his say.

Without comment she opened the door and walked inside the living room, putting her clothes over one of the two chairs. He followed.

"Excuse me for a minute while I freshen up. I'll be right back."

When she returned, she found him in the little kitchen drinking water from the faucet the way he used to. Some habits never went away. Tamsin could have offered him a soda, but decided not to. She didn't want him to think she desired his company any longer than necessary.

"You're welcome to use the bathroom."

He lifted his head. "Thanks."

She waited in the living room on the couch until he came back. He sat down on the chair opposite her, extending his long legs in front of him.

"I told you I was at a meeting at the fire station earlier in the week. The big brass were there. Commissioner Rich, the head of the arson squad, is alarmed by the rash of fires that have been set on ranches in this part of the county since early spring. They follow the same pattern from last year.

"Those of us assembled offered our theories. We're all in agreement that there's a group of ranchers who've been committing arson to stop the elk hunting in the county. Your father is just one of ten ranchers who've been targeted since April."

"Why exactly?"

"Because all of them allow elk hunting. These crazy guys are afraid the elk who come down to eat the hay on your property will bring more brucellosis disease to infect the cattle."

She flashed him a glance. "That's how the cows on your dad's ranch caught the disease."

"Yes. So these arsonists set the hay on fire. In your father's case, they went in the barn and deliberately lit what had been stored in there. They're determined to drive the elk away so they'll migrate down the mountains away from the cattle ranches."

Tamsin shivered. "They're desperate, aren't they?"

"Oh yes, and it's obvious the perpetrators aren't going to stop. That's the commissioner's fear, Tamsin. And mine. They're not worried about casualties. With every fire, lives and livestock are being jeopardized. My heart almost failed me to see you and Sally out in the paddock with the horses, especially when I realized she was pregnant."

"You're right. It's a horrible problem. What can I do to help?"

"Talk to your father. Let him know what's going on so he can speak to the foreman and hands on his property. They need to set up a guard rotation during the night for protection. The police are stepping up to catch these guys and put them behind bars, but in the meantime we're asking for everyone's cooperation."

She eyed him covertly. "Have you been called out every night to deal with these fires?"

"No, but that's because I'm not always here."

"How come?"

"About four to five times a month my work as a biologist takes me up in the mountains. I go for a four-day period at a time. When I come back down, I'm on call while I work on the ranch with Sam and Louise."

How did he manage it all? "What do you do exactly?"

"I've been assigned by the State of Wyoming to work in this mountain range. All winter long I catch elk and put transmitters on them so I can test them for disease. Then, the rest of the year I track the elk and study their movements to learn more about the spread of the disease. I did this on a regular basis my last year in Colorado."

"I don't see how you do that. It must be so hard."

His half smile caused her breath to catch. "Sometimes it's tricky. You have to put a GPS radio collar on the elk and use a portable ultrasound to check for pregnancy. If she's pregnant, she gets another transmitter so I can track where she calves."

She found herself fascinated by everything he was telling her. "How do you know?"

"It's a vaginal implant transmitter. If the elk aborts or calves, this transmitter pops out on the ground and you know something has happened. It's temperature activated and beats twice. I collect the transmitters and send them back to the Wyoming State Veterinary Lab. I'm in luck if I find an aborted calf I can ship off before the coyotes get it. The lab does the testing to detect brucellosis."

"Is it far where you have to go?"

"The trailheads are twenty to fifty miles away."

"But how far up the mountain?"

"This week I rode my new horse up to the eleven-thousand-foot range to escape the mosquitos and camp out. Sometimes I fly over the area and use a handheld directional antenna in my backpack to keep tabs on them when they're out of reach."

"Do you ever have any downtime?"

"Of course. I take my guitar up and write music. Sometimes

I write up proposals for an elk project, in order to apply for a grant to keep the research going. My salary is funded by hunts and angler dollars from license sales."

"You really did honor your father's wishes."

"Not the way he might have envisioned. I don't work in a laboratory to develop a cure for the disease that killed my mother. I can't be shut in. The outdoors is my home, but at least this way I feel I'm doing my part in some small way."

"Do you miss riding in the rodeo?"

"I've been too busy to think about it. I take it you've been so busy as a CPA, you haven't looked back, either."

"You're right about that."

His eyes played over her. "Where did you go to school?"

"In Lander, but like you I worked at several jobs for a long time before I started college. Our family didn't have much money. I had to make my own way and considered myself very lucky when Mr. Ostler eventually took me on with his firm."

"He's the lucky one. You were always as smart as a whip in school." With those words, warmth swept through her. "Do you like working there?"

"Yes. Very much."

"And Dean Witcom. Do you like him?"

Her pulse sped up. "Very much."

"Does he know about our history?"

Tamsin stood up. She'd revealed her deepest feelings about the situation with Cole to Dean and knew he wouldn't be patient much longer unless she could go to him and tell him she loved him from the depths of her soul.

"I've been honest with him about you and the other men in my life." So honest she'd hurt Dean terribly.

"How many others have there been?"

Heat filled her cheeks. "Not that many."

Cole got to his feet. "Does he want to marry you?"

He did, but she didn't want to tell Cole everything. "Yes."

"How long have you known Dean?"

"A year, but we only started dating four months ago. He and Lyle are close."

"If you get married, that would be a nice arrangement. Two brothers and two sisters who love each other. I always wanted a sibling, but it didn't happen."

Cole sounded so reasonable—and for a moment, so lonely—she wanted to die.

"Thank you for the warning. I'll be sure to talk to my father before today is out. He has no idea what you've uncovered and will be grateful for the heads-up."

"I'm the one who should be grateful to you for coming with me today. I wasn't sure you would. Despite what you think, if you want to know the truth, I needed this time to talk to you more than you can imagine."

Why? Tell me—what aren't you saying?

But he didn't answer that question.

In the next breath, Cole left the apartment. After he descended the outside staircase, she watched him stride to his truck from the living room window. When he drove away, it was like déjà vu. He'd taken her heart nine years ago—and just now he'd taken it again.

But this time he'd left her with no promise of phone calls or letters asking her to be patient until they could be together one day. It was too late for them. He knew it and she knew it.

Tamsin had done enough of that to last a dozen lifetimes. She was *so* through with reliving the last nine years of waiting for a future with him that had never come that she hurried into the kitchen for her purse. Once she left the apartment and reached her car, she drove to the ranch at full speed. On her way in the house she ran into her mother who was sweeping the kitchen floor.

"Hi, honey. How's it going at your new apartment?"

"I love it." She kissed her cheek. "Is Dad around?"

"He's outside with the contractor."

"I need to talk to Sally, but when the contractor leaves, I have to talk to you and Dad for a few minutes. It's important."

Her mom got that wishful look in her eyes. "Is this about Dean?"

Sorry, Mom. "No. It's about the fire, but I'll explain later." Not wanting to get into anything else, she hurried down the hall to the bedroom and knocked on the door.

"Come in."

"Sally?" She found her sister lying on the bed reading a book.

She put it down and stared at Tamsin. "Judging by the state you're in, you've been with Cole."

"Yes."

"And?" she prodded.

"It's over. I mean it's really over."

"No, it's not. You can't see your eyes, but I can. I have news for you. It was *never* over."

Tamsin sat in a chair near the bed. "He drove us to the mountains to talk. I finally have answers as to why he left Whitebark without taking me with him."

"Seriously?"

"Their family was in a desperate financial situation. Cole was sworn to secrecy and couldn't tell me anything. He had to go on the rodeo circuit to make money in order to save the ranch and pay the bills. His father was in bad health with a heart condition that was growing worse."

"Oh, Tamsin. That's awful."

Tears stung her eyelids. "I'm still furious that his father forbade Cole to tell me the real reason I couldn't go with him. All these years I've thought he didn't love me."

Sally sat up in bed with effort. "Did he admit he's still in love with you?"

She took a deep breath. "No. And I can tell you right now that I haven't been on his mind, not for years. You wouldn't believe everything he's done since he stopped riding the circuit."

"Is it bad?"

"Not at all. Today I learned that becoming a firefighter was something he did to make money while he went to school."

"School—where?"

Tamsin kneaded her hands. "If you can believe, he got his master's degree in biology at the university in Boulder."

"Biology?"

"Shocking, isn't it? I'm still reeling."

"Why in Heaven's name would he get a degree in that?"

"I was as surprised as you are. He's taken a job working for the State of Wyoming to control brucellosis disease among the elk in the Winds."

"That's so weird, you couldn't make it up."

"My thoughts precisely. Let me explain." For the next few minutes she told her everything she could, only leaving out the personal tragedy that had afflicted Cole's life. She followed up by telling her the reason for the arson and why their father needed to provide safeguards so it wouldn't happen again on their ranch. "I'm going to be talking to Mom and Dad about it later today."

"I can't believe what I'm hearing."

"You're not the only one. But this is such a serious problem, you and Lyle have to help me convince Mom and Dad that you're not safe until these crazy arsonists are caught."

"Good grief." Sally eyed her with an anxious expression. "Okay. Now that you've managed to convince me you're telling the truth, what did you learn about Patsy Janis? Don't tell me you didn't discuss her because I wouldn't believe you."

Sally was way ahead of her. Tamsin sat forward. "I told him I'd seen an article in the paper about the two of them. Before I could ask questions, he cut me off by explaining that she wanted him to stay in Colorado and make records with her, but he told her he wanted to get home. When I asked him if she wanted to get married, he said yes."

"I see. Did you tell him Dean wants to marry you?"

"Yes."

Her sister let out a frustrated sound. "I'm glad you told him. Being dishonest doesn't get anyone anywhere. But the point is, we both know you could never love Dean the way you love Cole."

"You used the wrong tense." She got up from the chair. "I'm not in love with Cole anymore. In fact, I could never love a man who fights fires for a living. You never know if he'll come home from another fire. When I remember what happened to Mandy Epperson's father, I can't imagine how awful that would be. It's no way to live. I refuse to do it."

"Tell that to your heart. Tamsin, do yourself a favor and find out for sure. The next time he wants to be with you, don't hold back no matter how much you hate what he does for a living."

"What do you mean, next time?"

Sally rolled her eyes. "There'll be one. But this time, be open and honest with him about Dean, the way you wished he'd been with you nine years ago about his real reason for leaving. If the two of you are meant to be together forever, then you need to find your way back to each other. Honesty is the first step."

"Cole had the chance to be honest. He said he'd wanted to tell me about his family crisis and admitted he'd needed the chance to explain. Well—he explained, but he said nothing about his personal feelings."

"Did he try to kiss you?"

"Are you kidding? Even when he came into my apartment, he didn't try to make any moves."

"Did you give him the chance to get closer?"

"It wasn't like that." Tamsin averted her eyes. "He didn't look at me like he used to. I told Dean I needed to talk to Cole. But now that I have, there's nothing more to learn."

"So where does that leave you with Dean?"

"I don't know." She half moaned the answer. "I told him that if we get married, it will be because I love him with all my heart and soul."

"Oh, Tamsin. You're in a very bad place."

"You're right. I'm a mess. Maybe I'm not destined to be married. If I continue to be confused, then I need to set Dean free so he can find someone to love who will adore him. I'm thinking I won't ever get married, but that's okay."

"What do you mean by that?"

"On my way over here I decided I'm going to go after more accounts. If I devoted my spare time to picking up some new clients in Lander and Riverton, I could double my income so I can finally branch out on my own. My goal is to own my own business one day and I'm going to make it happen. The sooner the better."

ON LATE THURSDAY afternoon of the following week, Cole came back down from the mountains. After stalling his horse, he phoned Chief Powell to let him know he was back for the next four days. Then he walked in the kitchen to find Louise fixing dinner for her and Sam.

"Good to have you back, Cole. While you were gone, you had a visitor."

His heart thudded unexpectedly. *Tamsin?* She'd been on his mind day and night since he'd left her apartment last Sunday. He hadn't begun to tell her all the things in his heart. If she was in love with Dean, then she wouldn't want to hear any of it.

He walked over to the fridge and pulled out a cola. "Who was it?"

"Patsy Janis."

Frustration caused his hand to squeeze the can so tightly, he was surprised it didn't pop open.

"She's staying at the Whitebark Hotel and said she wouldn't be leaving until she'd heard from you."

The top hotel in the town. Patsy never quit. When he'd ignored her message, she hadn't let that stop her. He took a swig. "How long has she been here?"

"She came to the door the day before yesterday in a rental car."

With some women you could say goodbye and they would get the message. But not Patsy. She'd come to Whitebark knowing he was a firefighter and had asked enough questions to find out his ranch address.

She'd been gutsy from the time she was a talented teenager with a desire to be the best country singer in the business. If she wanted something, she went after it and was determined enough not to tip him off with a phone call.

She might want Cole. He knew part of her did, but she had an agenda, one he wanted nothing to do with because he didn't love her. Her plan that they would be a husband and wife team, singing around the country making records, had been a dream of hers alone.

"Thanks for telling me, Louise. I'm going to take a shower, and then I'll head into town and let her know I got the message."

"Is she someone important to you?"

Louise rarely pried, but if anyone had the right to know things, it was the faithful woman who'd given his father loving care all those years.

"Patsy's a friend in the music world, nothing more. As you know, there's only been one woman for me all these years. I'm working on doing something about that."

A smile broke out on her face, indicating she liked his answer, before he left the kitchen for his bedroom and drained the rest of the can.

She and Sam had known how much he'd loved Tamsin. He knew they'd always liked her, too, back when he used to bring her around. But that had been at another time of life, a time that had come to a painful end and was long since over.

The sophisticated Tamsin of today had emerged a gorgeous, savvy businesswoman who was going to marry Dean Witcom. This was the price he had to pay for those years of silence he was forced to keep because of a promise to his father.

What did you expect, Hawkins? That she'd come running into your arms?

He'd imagined it in his dreams. But he was awake now. Dreams be damned!

After he'd shaved and cleaned up in jeans and a shirt, he took off for town. If he couldn't find Patsy at the hotel, he'd wait for her—unless or until he got a call on his beeper and had to take off.

He parked along the street and walked inside to talk to the man at the front desk. "Would you please ring Ms. Patsy Janis's room? My name is Cole Hawkins."

"Yes, sir."

After a short wait the clerk said, "She's not answering."

"In that case will you leave her a message that she can find me in the bar unless I have to respond to a fire?"

"What's your name again?"

"Cole Hawkins."

The man wrote it down and put it in one of the boxes. Cole headed for the bar and grill to order a meal. He hadn't eaten since coming down the mountain earlier. Now he was hungry and needed food in case he was called out on a fire.

Summer had brought the tourists to the Winds. While Cole ate his meal, he looked around the crowded bar in case he spotted Patsy, but no such luck. She'd been in several magazines lately, touted to be an up-and-coming country star by the media.

She was blonde, sexy and talented—she turned heads, that was for sure. But not his. Tamsin had his heart, pure and simple.

The minute he finished a second cup of coffee, his beeper went off, ending his opportunity to tell Patsy she'd wasted her time coming to Whitebark. Since he presumed she'd flown all this way, he would rather have told her as much in person, though he had zero desire to see her. But now he would have to say it over the phone the next chance he got.

He put some bills on the table and charged out of the hotel to his truck. Within a minute he reached the fire station parking lot and ran through to the locker room to pull on the set of hurry-ups he kept here.

Wyatt had already climbed on the back of the ladder truck when Cole jumped on and the truck took off with the siren blaring. It wasn't long before they arrived on the scene at Kyle Drive. Captain Durrant told them that an evergreen tree had caught fire and ignited the eaves of the house. The fire got into the attic and did significant damage to the roof.

Between the four of them, they doused the flames. Whoever lived there had been out of the house at the time. But the captain found it suspicious that a green, healthy tree had caught fire. It sounded like shades of arson but couldn't be proved until the arson commander investigated further.

While they were outside cleaning up, Cole saw a man drive up in front and get out of a truck with a WDOA logo. He'd seen that truck before in front of the Rayburn ranch house and assumed it belonged to Sally's husband. But of course there were other people employed by the oil company.

Cole and the others did the rest of the cleanup and returned to the station to reload and change their equipment.

"Hey, Hawkins?"

He turned to Steve Perry, one of the other firefighters. "Chief Powell wants to see you in his office."

"Be right there."

On his way, he grabbed some bottled water and had drained half of it by the time he entered the room. But the chief wasn't alone. A man he hadn't seen before sat near his desk. Commander Rich, the captain and the other guys from the ladder truck were also gathered.

"Thanks for coming, Cole. Sit down." He found a seat. "Mr. Hawkins? Everyone else has been introduced. This is Mr. Witcom, production manager at Witcom-Dennison Oil. The captain said that you and the crew put out the fire in the attic at his house. At this point we're certain it was arson and wonder why he might have been targeted."

Cole was dumbfounded. That fire had been started at Tamsin's boyfriend's house? His thoughts flew ahead. If she married Dean, they'd likely be living there. Cole was stunned by the coincidence and got a pit in his stomach that wouldn't go away. First her father's ranch. Now her lover's?

He studied the man who'd held Tamsin in his arms the night of the fire. Cole had to admit the guy would appeal to most women. Judging by the size of his house, he made a substantial income. Cole had never known jealousy before. This was new to him.

"I thought he should hear from all of you about the arson being committed here in the county since April. There might not be a link, but every suspicious fire is worth investigating."

Witcom's blue eyes narrowed as he stared at Cole. With that look, Cole knew in his gut Tamsin had told him about their history. How much of it, he didn't know. No doubt Witcom didn't like the idea that Cole had shown up back in Whitebark after all these years.

Once again everyone gave an opinion of what they thought and saw. Then it came to Cole's turn. "The only observation I could add might not have any relevance."

"Go on," the chief urged.

"The Rayburn ranch was targeted a couple of weeks ago. Mr. Witcom was there at the scene because he and Ms. Rayburn are a couple."

Everyone looked at the man in surprise. Cole hated to be the one to reveal that private kind of news, but this was an official investigation. No doubt Witcom was close to despising him now.

"Maybe they decided to target him in order to send another message. We know these arsonists hope to frighten ranchers like Howard Rayburn to close off their ranches to elk hunters come fall."

The chief nodded. "It could be a possibility. We'll look into it. Thanks, everyone. You're excused."

Cole avoided looking at Witcom and walked through the station with the other guys to change out of his gear. Once he'd put on his jeans and shirt, he walked out the back door and headed for his truck, totally gutted to have laid eyes on the man Tamsin was seeing.

Chapter Five

"Hey, cowboy!"

Cole's head lifted. He knew that sultry female voice. "Patsy?" It shouldn't have surprised him to discover her standing next to his Ford. After what had happened tonight, this was all he needed.

She'd pulled her rental car up next to him. A smile broke out on her face. "I figured I might not see you for some time if I didn't drive over here." She went where angels feared to tread, but she'd made a mistake this time.

"You're probably not aware this is a private parking area."

"Well, it's good to see you, too." She started toward him, but he put his hands on her shoulders and kept her at a distance.

"I don't know why you're here, but this isn't the place for a conversation. I'll drive back to the hotel and wait for you in the bar."

After letting go of her, he got in his truck and backed around. Unfortunately, a couple of the guys reporting for duty had seen them, but there wasn't anything he could do about it and drove out to the street. She wasn't far behind.

He found a spot near the hotel and hurried inside to let her know how he felt about her unwanted presence. Instead of a table, he sat at the bar and ordered coffee. Within minutes she'd joined him.

"It's clear I shouldn't have come to your work."

Cole turned to her. "You shouldn't have come to Whitebark. The last time we were together I told you I wasn't in love with you. I had fun jamming and recording with you, but it never turned into love. I realize those weren't the words you wanted to hear. Now I've come home to my life and am asking you to go back to yours."

The bartender brought him coffee and took her order for a beer. While she drank some, she flashed him a glance. "I didn't know there was this side to you. I think you really mean it."

"You know I do."

"You're so angry, I take it your girlfriend hasn't forgiven you and doesn't want you back. That's what I came to find out. I think I have my answer. Things really aren't going as smoothly as you'd hoped. What do you know…"

He'd had all he could take.

"Patsy—I'm in love with her and I don't want to hurt you. You've got a great career going. We'll always be friends, but you're wasting your time coming here."

"But we made a good team, Cole. This woman you love obviously doesn't want you back. Doesn't it mean anything to you that I want to be the new woman in your life and love you?"

He drew in a breath. "I'm flattered, but it wasn't love for me even though we had fun making music together."

"Wow. She really did a number on you."

"I've been in love with her forever. Goodbye, Patsy."

Cole left the hotel. Before he went back to the ranch, he drove straight to Tamsin's apartment. Her Toyota was in her parking space. He hoped that meant she was home. He needed to see her before she heard from someone else that Patsy had been in town. Some of the guys at the station had seen them together and word got around fast. Too fast.

After pulling up in front of the complex, he got out of his

truck and raced up the stairs to her apartment. Without knowing her cell phone number, he had no other choice but to go there.

He knocked on her door and waited. When she didn't respond, he knocked a little harder. He knew for a fact that she wasn't with Dean right now, but she could have been with him earlier. After the fire that had broken out tonight, Cole could count on Witcom driving over there any minute to tell her he'd come face-to-face with Cole and how he felt about it. But more important, he needed to warn her that the arsonists were so serious they'd targeted Dean.

In case she was nervous to say or do anything this late at night, he called to her. "Tamsin? It's Cole. I know it's late but I have something vital to tell you. If I'd had your number, I would have phoned you first. Tamsin? Can you hear me?"

Seconds later she opened the door looking beautiful and anxious. She'd dressed in jeans and a T-shirt that hugged her curves. "What's wrong? Was there another fire?"

"Yes, but not at your family's ranch."

She put a hand to her mouth in obvious relief. "Come in."

He walked past her, hearing noise from the TV in the background, and waited until she'd shut the door. "Tonight a lodgepole pine next to Dean Witcom's house caught on fire and the flames burned his attic."

A small gasp escaped her lips. "Was he hurt?"

"No. He didn't come home until our crew had put it out and was ready to leave. Chief Powell called a meeting at the station afterward that included Witcom. It's too early in the year for the tree to be dry enough to burst into flame without help. Since there was no lightning tonight, the only way to explain the fire is arson."

A troubled expression broke out on her face.

"We have no proof yet, but are thinking there could be a connection to your father's barn fire since you're his daughter and are involved with Dean. The chief asked for opinions and I had to tell him what I was thinking. But I don't think your boyfriend was too happy about it coming from me of all people."

She sank down on the couch. "So you really believe he was targeted too because I'm Howard Rayburn's daughter?"

"It's a strong possibility. I just wanted you to know so you can tell Witcom to be careful. I don't think he would have liked that advice from me. Have you talked to your father yet?"

"Yes. He's doing everything possible to stay on alert."

"That's good." He shifted his weight. "One more thing before I go. Patsy Janis was waiting for me at the back of the station after tonight's fire. I never thought I'd see her again."

Those blue eyes trapped his. "Why not? You said she wanted to get married."

His jaw hardened. "But I told you I didn't feel that way about her. The truth is marriage takes two willing people who love each other. I told her I'd meet her in the bar at the hotel where she's been staying. A couple of the guys at the station saw her with me. I figured it was only a matter of time before you heard gossip about it.

"We had our little talk at the bar. After I told her I was never in love with her and this had to be goodbye, I walked out without looking back. If she ever comes near me again, she won't be welcome."

Tamsin jumped to her feet. "Why would you think I wouldn't believe you?"

"Because of all the fake news in the magazines and newspapers being printed," he broke in on her. "The truth is, I'm not and never have been involved with Patsy intimately no matter how much she wanted to get married," he informed her. "Ours was a professional relationship. Period."

He headed for the door.

"Wait—"

Cole looked over his shoulder.

"Don't leave yet."

"I'd rather not be here when Witcom shows up. I'm surprised he hasn't come yet." He opened the door.

"If he were going to come over, he'd phone me. I—I need to tell you something first," she stammered.

He stood there with the door still ajar. "What is it?"

She rubbed her hands over womanly hips in a nervous gesture. "For what it's worth, I haven't told Dean I'll marry him."

The blood pounded in Cole's ears. "Are you saying you're not in love with him?"

Tamsin averted her eyes. "I'm saying that I haven't told him I'll marry him yet. He wants to get engaged, but I'm still trying to sort out my feelings."

That was the best news he'd heard since he'd left Whitebark years ago.

"If nothing's set in stone, does that mean you'd be willing to spend some time with me?" His heart thudded while he waited for her answer.

"I don't know if it would be wise."

"Why? I'm home for good. Are *you* planning to leave the state?"

She threw her head back so he could see her eyes. "I have no idea where my career might take me."

Encouraged by those words he said, "Until you do know, how would you like to go to the Arapahoe Pioneer Days Rodeo in Lander with me coming up in a week? Or do you have plans with Witcom for the Fourth of July?"

It appeared his question had caught her off guard. "We haven't talked about it yet," she muttered.

"I'm leaving in the morning to head back to the mountains for my work and will probably be gone for five or six days this time. If you decide you'd like to go to Lander with me, drop by the ranch and tell Louise. She'll let me know after I'm back.

"I was thinking we'd drive there on the fourth and spend it camping overnight in the Setons' backyard. Their daughter, Doris, and son-in-law, Tyler, have invited me. We'd be sleeping in a tent in our sleeping bags. Sam and Louise's fifteen-year-old grandson Jake Sky Tree is riding in the relay. They exchange horses after each lap. It's pretty exciting. Then he's competing in the rodeo and there'll be fireworks afterward. We would drive home the next day.

"If there's no message from you when I get back, then I'll have my answer. Good night, Tamsin. Please be careful and lock your door after I leave."

WHAT WAS IT Sally had told Tamsin?

The next time he wants to be with you, don't hold back.

What do you mean, next time?

There'll be one. But this time, be open and honest with him about Dean, the way you wished he'd been with you nine years ago about his real reason for leaving. If the two of you are meant to be together forever, then you need to find your way back to each other. Honesty is the first step.

Sally had predicted that Cole would approach her again and she'd been right. Tamsin couldn't lie to herself. His invitation had thrilled her to death. But the fear of getting involved with him again scared her out of her mind.

After the years of emptiness while she'd fought her memories, to start that whole thing all over again would be a form of insanity. Of course no one knew what the future held. She wasn't asking for a guarantee, but to spend time again with Cole meant she had to be some kind of fool and hadn't learned that she couldn't go back to their senior year of high school when they'd been crazy in love. It wasn't possible to know that kind of happiness a second time.

By the time she'd turned off the TV and had gone to bed, she was glad Cole had given her time to think about his invitation instead of wanting an answer right away. But before she fell asleep, she knew she wouldn't be going by his ranch. She also knew something else. She didn't love Dean the way he needed to be loved. It truly was over with him.

Maybe a man would eventually come into her life, one who would set her on fire in a brand-new way. Until that day came, she would go ahead with her plan to build her own CPA business.

Thank goodness she'd moved out of the ranch house. Soon her sister would have the baby and they'd move to their own place. After that there'd be little chance of running into Dean when Tamsin went home to see her folks.

With a plan in mind, she left for the office on Friday morning, eager to talk to Heather before she left for Whitebark Hospital to start their audit. Her friend arrived after Tamsin did. She rushed over to her.

"I'm glad I caught you before I had to leave. What are your plans for tomorrow?"

"Nothing special, but I have a date with Silas Ellsworth to go to dinner and a movie."

Tamsin remembered him from high school. "You've been seeing a lot of him lately. Sounds like it could be something serious."

"Maybe." Her friend smiled.

"How would you like to drive to Riverton with me for the day? We'll be back in time for you to meet up with Silas. I want to check out possibilities for some new clients."

"You mean for yourself?" she whispered.

Tamsin nodded. "It wouldn't hurt to try to pick up business, even if it means a move. I don't want to work for someone else forever."

Heather frowned. "But I thought that you and Dean...well, you know..."

"I'm afraid that's over, but I'll tell you about it when I have more time. Give me a call later if you want to go with me."

"I will, I promise."

Tamsin grabbed her briefcase and left for the hospital. But no matter what else she had on her mind, she couldn't stop her glance from straying toward the mountains. They were Cole's world when he wasn't ranching or fighting fires. He was probably halfway up to the area where he'd be searching for elk over the next week.

His ability to be on his own in nature was remarkable to her. He'd always been a fearless cowboy. Now he was up in the remote wilderness of the Winds facing dangers and loving every minute of it.

That ache in her heart would always be there because he was a man who didn't need a woman. He'd proven it over the last nine years. Tamsin wished with every atom in her body that she were a woman who could exist without a man and be happy. If it was possible, she intended to find out.

By midafternoon her cell phone rang. She presumed it was Heather, but when she checked the caller ID, it was her mother. She clicked on.

"Hi, Mom."

"I'm glad you picked up. Guess what? Your sister is in labor and Lyle has driven her to the hospital. Your father and I will be driving there as soon as he comes in."

This was the best news Tamsin could have received. "She's been so good obeying doctor's orders, but it's past time her ordeal was over."

"I agree. Where are you?"

"Would you believe I'm at the hospital doing an audit?"

"What a lucky coincidence!"

"I know. I'll finish up here and go to the maternity floor."

"We'll see you there soon, darling."

As soon as they hung up, Tamsin called Heather to tell her about Sally. "I'm going to have to change my plans about driving to Riverton tomorrow. Will you go with me next Saturday?"

"I can't go then. Our family has plans that weekend and I've invited Silas. Let's do it in two weeks."

"That will be perfect. Talk to you soon," she said.

"Let me know all the fun news about the baby."

"I want to hear about Silas, too."

"Of course."

They hung up.

The audit would take several more days. Since Tamsin couldn't concentrate on debits and expenditures right now, she planned to pick up where she'd left off when she went back to work on Monday. Now that the files were downloaded on her laptop, she packed it in her briefcase and walked through the hall to the bank of elevators.

On her way down to the maternity ward on the third floor, she realized she'd be seeing Dean at some point and wasn't looking forward to it. But it was something she would have to deal with now and in the years to come when there was a reason for both families to be together.

Still, her heart sank when she ran into him as she came out of the elevator. He took one look at her and pulled her aside. "I need to talk to you before we go in to see Sally and Lyle."

Because Cole had come over last night, she knew what Dean was going to tell her about. "Let's go into the waiting room."

They followed the signs that led them around the corner. Several groups of people were sitting in the room on the chairs and getting drinks out of the vending machines.

Dean found them a couple of chairs and they sat down. "Last night someone set fire to my property. The fire department believes it was the same arsonist who set fire to your father's barn."

She nodded. "I heard."

"After the meeting at the fire station, it didn't take Cole Hawkins long to inform you, did it?" he said in a wintry tone. "I saw a truck outside your apartment and figured it was his."

So he *had* come by without phoning her. When she ignored his comment, his lips tightened. "Lyle said Sally doesn't know about it, and we don't want her to know."

"I agree she doesn't need to be worried about anything but having their baby."

He got up so fast it surprised her.

"Wait—" She caught hold of his arm. "I'm so sorry for what happened to you, Dean. I heard the damage was confined to the attic, not the whole house, thank Heaven, but it's still awful. What a shock that must have been!"

"The bigger shock was coming face-to-face with the guy I hate." In a pain-filled voice he said, "Excuse me. My brother needs me right now."

Without giving her a chance to say more, he walked away. She stood up and followed him down the hall to the nursing station where they were given directions to the labor room.

When they walked in, a worried yet excited Lyle reached for his brother. Tamsin hurried over to the hospital bed. "Sally—" Her sister looked drained and exhausted. "I can't believe it. When did the pains start?"

"Last night. But the doctor says the baby won't be born before evening."

"That long? Oh, you poor thing."

"You have no idea." She rolled her eyes in that way of hers. "Mom and Dad will be here soon."

"I know. Did you come with Dean?" she mouthed the words. "No."

Sally closed her eyes. Another contraction had taken over her body.

"You're the bravest woman I know."

Her sister let out a groan.

A few minutes later two sets of parents came into the labor room. Tamsin hugged her parents and left the room before she had to face Dean's parents. She'd only met them once. If they knew what had happened between her and Dean, then they wouldn't be thrilled to have to talk to her until it was absolutely necessary.

Tamsin headed for the waiting room with her briefcase. She would sit out there for the next few hours. Until her little niece was born, she could work on the audit from her laptop. But after a few minutes, she couldn't concentrate. It upset her that all she could think about was what it would be like to be married to Cole and have their baby.

"Tamsin?" She lifted her head, surprised to see Dean standing there. "I'm leaving. I'll come back when the baby's born. You can go in and be with your family now."

"Dean—" she called after him, filled with guilt because she'd hurt him, but he'd disappeared too fast. If she'd gone after him, what would there have been to say? Nothing that would make him feel better. She didn't love him enough to marry him and he knew it.

WEDNESDAY NIGHT OF the following week, Cole returned from the mountains in a rainstorm and headed straight for the shower after taking care of his horses. He was glad to be out of it. When he walked into the kitchen later to make a peanut butter sandwich, he found Louise and Sam enjoying a cup of coffee.

"I thought you two would be taking off for Lander today."

Sam shook his head. "The rain stopped us from going, but it's supposed to clear up before morning. We'll head out then."

"After I take care of a few bills in the morning, I'll drive there later in the day."

They talked about ranching problems for a little while, but it was clear Tamsin hadn't dropped by. He ate his sandwich and swallowed it with a half quart of milk before saying good-night.

Once he'd gotten ready for bed, he put his beeper on the night table, hoping he wouldn't be called out on a fire. He hadn't had a decent night's sleep since leaving Tamsin's apartment. Over the last six days, Cole had hoped she'd thought about everything and wanted to be with him. But his worst fear was realized tonight when Louise hadn't mentioned her name.

The next morning he awakened to a tap on his door.

"Louise?"

"Sorry to bother you. We're just leaving. I would have let you sleep longer, but you have a visitor waiting for you in the living room. It's Tamsin. What shall I tell her?"

He leaped out of bed so fast, he stubbed his toe and let out a moan. "Ask her to wait. I'll be there in a few minutes."

"Okay."

Cole had to be the first man who ever shaved and got dressed in under a minute. He strode through the ranch house to the front room and found the woman he loved studying some small framed photographs of his family on one of the end tables. "What a surprise to see you here."

She turned around to face him, looking stunning in jeans and a tan Western shirt with fringe. "I wasn't sure you would be back until I saw your truck parked at the side of the ranch house." After a slight hesitation she said, "Last week I had no intention of seeing you again."

Why didn't she tell him something he didn't know. "What happened to change your mind?"

"Sally had her baby girl a few days ago."

"That's terrific. Is everyone okay?"

"Yes. Little Kellie took her time being born, but they're both healthy and happy. When I was alone with my sister at the ranch yesterday and she asked me if I'd seen you lately, I told her there'd be no point. She shook her head and said, 'So it's truly over with you two?'

"Without answering her question, I told her I had to go and would talk to her later. As I walked out of the bedroom she called to me. 'Did you know ostriches don't bury their heads in the sand? They're much more likely to face a problem head-on, which makes them wiser than one particular human being I love.'"

A smile broke out on his face. "Your sister is a very intelligent young woman. I take it you've decided to drive to Lander with me and face our situation head-on."

"If the invitation still stands."

He had to tamp down his excitement. "How soon can you be ready to go on an overnight?"

"I'll need to drive back to the apartment and pack a few things, including my sleeping bag. It won't take me long."

Cole checked his watch. "It's ten thirty. I'll be by your place at noon."

"Be sure to bring your guitar and pack some of your recordings. I'd like to hear them."

"With Patsy singing? I don't think so." He wanted no reminder of her. "I only provide backup guitar."

"Her singing won't bother me. I want to hear the songs you composed in the mountains. Will you let me listen to those? Please?"

Her brilliant blue eyes begged him. "I'll see what I can dig up."

"Good."

"We can grab some lunch at a drive-through before we leave town."

"Sounds great. I'll be ready."

He'd been ready for nine years. After walking her out to her car, he hurried inside and rushed around to pack and load the truck. One of his dreams was about to come true.

The bills could wait for a couple of days. Knowing that Sam had given the stockmen their instructions, Cole could leave the ranch with no worries. He left his beeper by the bed, grabbed his guitar and left through the back door to reach his truck. Louise gave him a thumbs-up on the way out.

This trip could be the making of them. *Or the breaking*, a little voice nagged. Cole refused to listen and took off for her apartment. She didn't trust him. Somehow he had to prove that he would never fail her, but that meant she had to stick with him long enough until she knew the truth of his love for her in her heart.

When he reached her place, she was waiting for him outside her door with her cowboy hat and boots on. It reminded him of their rodeo days. He took the steps two at a time to grab her overnight case and sleeping bag. "You don't look a day older than when we were in high school."

"Thanks, but we know that's not true and we can't go back to those days, Cole. I know I don't want to."

The trail to her heart was riddled with obstacles. He would have to proceed with great care from here on out. After putting her things in his truck, they drove to Hilda's for a hamburger. Cole remembered she liked pickles, mustard and a fresh lime-ade. But after what she'd said a few minutes ago, he wasn't going to make any assumptions about the past. Instead he asked her what she wanted.

"A beef taco and a cola."

He ordered his usual triple-stack cheeseburger with ketchup, fries with fry sauce and a frosted root beer and paid for everything. She shot him a glance. "I can see your eating habits haven't changed."

Amused, he said, "I thought you didn't want to be reminded of the past."

She looked away. "My mistake. I'm sorry I was rude to you earlier."

"No offense taken." He drove on to the pickup window for their food, then found a place to park while they ate.

"Has there been any word yet about the arsonists responsible for the fires?"

"Not that I've been told. I know they're working on it. I'll learn more the next time I'm called in. We can be thankful no lives were lost in the last two fires. Did you talk to Witcom about the one at his house?"

"Briefly."

"Do you mind if we discuss him for a minute, Tamsin?"

She finished her cola. "There's nothing to say. Unless he happens to be around family, I won't be seeing him again."

"Because of me."

He heard her take a sharp breath. "Because seeing you again proved to me I was still holding back with Dean. If I'd been in love with him the way I was with you, I'd be engaged by now. Nine years ago I would have done anything to be with you. I was ready to run off with you and defy my parents.

"The truth is, I've never loved Dean with that same intensity, but it took your coming back to Whitebark to make me see what was wrong. So it's better that I've broken it off completely."

Chapter Six

That was what Cole had been waiting to hear. Seeing her in Witcom's arms the night of the fire had practically destroyed him.

"But the timing of the baby and the fire at his house haven't made it easy for us since we've been forced to see each other one way or another," she added.

"That's tough." He didn't tell her that in time it would be easier to see Dean when he came around the family, since he wasn't certain it would be.

She turned to him. "Was it tough dealing with Patsy again?"

"No, because unlike your feelings for Dean, I never felt an attraction to her or thought I might learn to love her. I've only ever been in love with one woman."

He ate his last french fry. "Did you want to get anything else to eat? Otherwise, I'd like to get going."

"Nope, I'm ready."

He started the truck and backed out. Before long they were on the highway headed for Lander. The rain had greened up the mountains below the timberline. He had a sense of well-being as he breathed in the fresh clean air. Cole hadn't felt this alive and invigorated in years. There was only one reason why. She was sitting next to him.

To Tamsin's chagrin it was happening. She could feel it. The old magic that had been in hibernation for nine years had sprung to life once more, suffocating her with feelings and sensations she couldn't suppress. Cole was back. Already he was coloring her world again.

During their two-and-a-half-hour drive, he turned on the radio, but she turned it off and asked if she could listen to some of his recordings.

"I brought one. It's in the glove compartment."

She reached for it. Patsy Janis was featured on the cover in a cowboy hat, holding the microphone. The woman was beautiful and sexy. She found it amazing that he hadn't fallen for her.

Tamsin turned the CD over and studied the list of six titles on the back. Lyrics and music composed by Cole Hawkins.

She gasped softly as she read each one. "Doomed to Love Her." "Her Bluebell Eyes." "Stranglehold on My Heart." "Never a Reply." "Lost to the Winds." "Wind River Lovin'."

Cole—

Years ago he'd told her she had eyes the color of the bluebells growing in the Winds. As she read each title again, she realized it was a history of their relationship. But "Doomed to Love Her" said it all. He'd described her state of mind.

Unable to look at him, she slid the disc into the CD player. Patsy's crooning voice filled the interior of the cab. She was a great singer, but it was Cole's music and words with his guitar accompaniment that made their way inside her soul.

She'd expected his music to have that free, easy, on-the-road kind of feeling. But nothing could be further from the truth as they headed for Lander with the Wind River Mountain Range filling their vision. "Doomed to Love Her" reached right into her soul.

Next came "Her Bluebell Eyes." It was so beautiful and mournful at the same time, the words squeezed her heart.

Their eyes met for a breathless moment before the third song came on.

You know what you do to me,
You know what you do to my heart,
Your stranglehold loving,
Sets our love apart.
You know I'll never be free, babe,
You know I'll never stray.
I'm always here for you,
Until my dying day.

"Cole—" she cried softly.

It seems forever since we held each other tight,
So long since you told me of your love,
So long to smell your fragrance in the night.
So long since our kiss at first light.
You know I'll never be free,
You know I'll never stray,
I'm always here for you, darlin',
Until my dying day.

With those words, Tamsin broke down and quietly sobbed.

"If you ever wanted to know my feelings, you know them now. Those were the words I wrote to you in my letters."

The letters she'd refused to read.

She couldn't talk as the next two songs came on. "Lost to the Winds" and "Never a Reply" almost tore her heart out. But it was when the last song came on that she really lost it.

Remember the day we had to part?
Those broken dreams that stomped on my heart?
Gone were the days of laughter,
Gone were the nights of joy,
The end of Wind River lovin' ripped my soul apart.
Remember the years of longing, of waiting,
Trying to pretend everything was all right?

Remember the mornings you could taste the salt from
your tears?
The dying inside with each passing night?
Too much pain at the day's start?
The end of Wind River lovin' destroyed my heart.

To her surprise, when she finally lifted her head, she discovered he'd turned into a rest stop and had reached for her, pulling her close. His shirt was all wet from her tears. She hadn't been held by him in nine years. Tamsin was so in love with him, she couldn't breathe.

Needing to compose herself, she eased out of his arms and sat back on her side of the truck. The emotions she'd experienced listening to the CD had drained her. He started the truck and they took off once more.

Cole turned on the radio again, but she asked him to turn it off. "Your songs are incredible. You should be out there making more records and performing before a live audience."

"I appreciate the compliment, but that's not my goal in life. I enjoy composing. If one of my songs gets recorded by a great band, that's terrific, but I'm finally where I want to be. That's never going to change. And today I'm with the woman who makes me happy."

Tamsin shook her head. "We haven't made each other happy in years."

"I've had my memories."

So have I.

"Are you ready to make some new ones? We've reached Lander. After we stop by the Setons' and set everything up, it'll be time to hit the Buffalo Barbecue. Then we'll all head over to the arena for the rodeo."

She swallowed hard, trying to find her voice. "I haven't been to a rodeo in ages. Do you wish you were performing?"

"Do you?" he fired back.

"No. For once it will be fun to watch."

"Sounds good to me. I'm getting too old for that kind of fun."

She couldn't imagine him ever being that old.

He drove them to the Setons' home, a charming rambler with a big backyard and patio. Farther on was a barn and corral. But what stood out to Tamsin was the fabulous tan-colored tepee erected on the grass. Someone had decorated it with hand-painted horses and it stood at least sixteen feet high.

She helped Cole carry their gear where they would set up the tent. "Who painted their tepee? It's fantastic!"

"Doris. She's an artist and sells her artwork at the Arapahoe Marketplace in town."

"I'll have to buy something from her."

"You can tell her that yourself. She'll be so happy."

When Tamsin turned, she saw four people walking toward them. She knew Sam and Louise, but not their daughter, Doris, or her husband, Tyler. Cole introduced her to them.

"We're so glad you could come. Our son Jake is so excited. He wants to be a great bull rider like Cole one day. He's over at the arena practicing."

Tamsin smiled at her. "We're looking forward to watching him perform in the rodeo. In fact, we can hardly wait. But now that we're here, I want to know about the artwork you do. I've just moved into an apartment and would love to buy something of yours. Cole tells me you're an artist, and anyone looking at the tepee can see your work is outstanding."

"Thank you. I paint a lot of pottery and wall hangings."

"Well, before we leave town tomorrow, we'll go by the shop."

"Cole said you wanted to camp out, but feel free to come in the house at any time to use the bathroom and fix yourself some food or a drink."

"That sounds terrific. If you don't mind, I'd like to go in right now." She turned to Cole. "I'll be back in a minute to help set up the tent."

His piercing brown eyes played over her, not missing an inch. It sent a rush of desire through her body. "There's no hurry."

Doris showed her inside. Once she was refreshed, she walked down the hall, but paused in front of a deerskin wall hanging. It was obviously something Doris had painted. Tamsin read the words of the quote.

Everything an Indian does is in a circle, and that is because the power of the world always works in circles, and everything tries to be round. The sky is round and I have heard the earth is round like a ball, and so are all the stars. The wind in its greatest power whirls, birds make their nest in circles, for theirs is the same religion as ours. The sun comes forth and goes down again in a circle. The moon does the same and both are round. Our tepees were round like the nests of birds. And they were always set in a circle, the nation's hoop. Even the seasons form a great circle in their changing, and always come back again to where they were.

—Chief Black Elk

Stunned by the last sentence, Tamsin read it a second time. *The seasons always come back again to where they were.*

Was that what she and Cole were doing? Coming back to where they'd begun? Was their love part of the eternal circle? If she'd read this nine years ago after he'd left without her, she would have considered it so much nonsense. But right this minute it made so much sense, it sent chills racing up and down her spine.

"What a beautiful saying and artwork."

"Thank you. We live by it."

Tamsin thanked Doris and hurried outside as if a ghost were chasing her. Cole had been out to this house many times. Had he noticed the wall hanging and read it? Of course he had.

When she reached him, he'd already erected the four-man tent and was chatting with Tyler. She shouldn't have been surprised he'd done it so fast since it was something he did every time he went up in the mountains. She grabbed her sleeping bag and went inside to lay it out.

Cole had put his duffel bag on one side with a couple of lanterns, leaving her plenty of space. But the fact remained that they would be sleeping under the same roof tonight. That was something they'd never done before, but only because Cole had never tried to take advantage of her.

All she had to do was go back outside for her overnight bag, but he brought it in for her, blocking the doorway to the tent with his tall, hard-muscled body.

"When I told you we'd be sleeping outside, I should have offered to set up another tent. It's in the back of the truck. If you're uncomfortable sleeping in here with me tonight, I can do that or I can stay in the tepee."

Tamsin kept thinking about that quote on the wall in the Seton home. Maybe the power that moved the world was working on her. "I'd like to sleep in here with you tonight. It's one of the few things we've never done."

His eyes narrowed on her features. "A new memory to make," he said in a husky voice that caused a fluttering sensation in her chest.

She felt heat rush to her face.

"Shall we go get some dinner before we head to the arena?"

Cole followed her out the door of the tent and walked her to the truck. They drove to the city park where a huge crowd had gathered. The Buffalo Barbecue never disappointed. They filled their plates and sat at a table under the canopy with Sam and his family while they enjoyed the music and entertainment.

Jake joined them, but he monopolized the conversation with Cole, wanting any last-minute tips he could give him. Tamsin loved the camaraderie with their family. Cole had grown up with them. When she thought about the two losses in his life, it touched her that the Setons treated him as one of their own. She had no doubt it filled the hole in his heart so that he hadn't been forced to come back from Colorado to an empty house.

When she tried to put herself in his place, she couldn't. If she'd been gone for years and had to come home to a ranch devoid of her family… She couldn't begin to imagine it. But Sam and Louise had been there for Cole when he'd needed them most. They'd guarded his secret and had taken care of his ailing parents. Without knowing them, she loved them for their goodness.

To Cole's satisfaction, Jake placed fifth in the marathon and second in the teenage bull-riding competition. He gave him a bear hug. "You keep working on it. Next year you'll be number one." Tamsin gave him a hug, too, putting a smile on his face.

The fireworks thrilled everyone far into the night. At ten after twelve, Cole left the park happier than he'd been in years. His thoughts were all over the place by the time he and Tamsin arrived back at the Seton house.

With a three-quarter moon in a sky free of clouds, they saw their way clearly as they walked around to the backyard.

Cole went on ahead to get the lantern from the tent while Tamsin darted inside the house for a minute. When she came back out, he'd lighted it and followed her over to the tepee where she was examining the horse paintings.

"Doris is an amazing artist, Cole. Every horse is a different breed or color. Out here in the moonlight, the tepee looks surreal, like we've gone back in time. I love it. If my parents had one of these when I was young, I would probably have slept in it a lot."

His gaze roved over her face. "We can sleep in it tonight."

"You mean it?" He could tell she was excited by the idea.

"Of course. Let's get our things out of the tent and move in here for the night."

"They won't mind?"

"Tamsin—whenever I drive here, I sleep in it. The tent's a pain to set up."

She chuckled. "So you did all that for me? Why didn't you say so when we first arrived?"

"I didn't know how you'd feel about it."

"After reading the quote on the wall hanging in the house Doris painted, I'll feel honored to sleep in here tonight. With that moon up there, the whole night seems enchanted."

He felt it, too, and walked to the tent to get their gear. She helped him and, before long, they'd entered the tepee large enough to house a family. The floor was laden with gorgeous Arapahoe-designed rugs, and there were several low, rustic divans and log drums that served as end tables. The fire pit in the middle would keep you warm in the winter.

Her eyes followed the line of the poles that rose through the hole at the top. "I had no idea the interior would be so elegant."

Cole nodded. "This tepee is made of elk skin and gives it a richness that canvas never could."

"No wonder you always sleep in here when you come. It's pure luxury."

One of the things he loved about Tamsin was her appreciation for life. She'd shown a graciousness to Sam's family plus a friendliness to Jake that he knew had pleased them.

"While you get ready for bed, I'll say good-night to everyone and then I'll join you." He reached in his duffel bag for a pair of gray sweats and left the tepee. A few minutes later Cole emerged from the house having changed clothes. He was more than excited to spend the night with Tamsin. This was a first for them. It could blow up in his face. But now that he was back home after a nine-year separation, he didn't plan to waste a second with her.

The soft light from the lantern bathed Tamsin in a special glow. She'd already climbed inside her sleeping bag and lay on her side with her head on the pillow.

Cole stretched out his bag a few feet away from her. But after pulling a pillow from the duffel bag, he walked over to her. Once he'd dropped it next to hers, he lay down outside her bag and lowered his mouth to hers, stifling her surprised cry.

At first she tried to wriggle away, but he'd trapped her with his arm around her body, drawing her as close as he could with the bag between them. The taste of her mouth after all his dreams of loving her almost gave him a heart attack.

He drove his hungry kiss deeper and deeper until he heard her satisfying moan. Then there was no more protest as she began to kiss him back in the old familiar way. Cole felt like they were eighteen again, but this was so much better because circumstances had changed. At twenty-seven years of age, they were free to love each other with no more obstacles.

The ecstasy of being able to let go of long suppressed emotions caused him to forget time. Their desire caught fire so he was trembling. "I always wanted to sleep out under the stars with you, but it never happened," he lamented against her lips.

"We were underage, Cole."

"Our age had nothing to do with it and you know it. We couldn't keep our hands off each other. I wanted to make love to you from the moment we met, but the time wasn't right. If I hadn't had parents who needed me desperately, I would have run away with you and lived with you until we could be legally married."

"We're both aware of what went wrong, Cole. I don't want to revisit the pain of the past. Please let's not go there."

"Never again." He tasted salt and realized it came from her tears. "Why did you agree to come here with me?"

He had to wait for her answer. "Sally challenged me to find out if I still loved you. I fought her at first, but when I see the happiness she shares with Lyle and their excitement over the baby, I decided I needed to be certain before I said a final goodbye to you."

"Thank God you did," he whispered against the softness of her neck. "I love you, Tamsin. I always have, and I always will."

He lifted his head and looked down into her eyes. "I only need to know one thing. Do you love me?"

Tamsin searched his brown eyes that burned with desire for her. "You know I love you, Cole, but I don't dare give my heart to you again."

He caressed the side of her face. "How can I prove to you that I'll never do anything to hurt you?"

"You can't." She turned her head to kiss his hand. "It wasn't your fault that you had to leave Whitebark. I know that now, and I know you never loved Patsy. But circumstances beyond our control drove us apart before, and they're doing it again."

A frown marred his striking features. "What are you talking about?"

"Do you remember that terrible forest fire in the Winds the year you and I were dating?"

"Of course. My father provided backup."

"Then you remember that my best friend Mandy lost her firefighter father while he was battling it."

"That was a very sad day. I remember going to the funeral with you."

"Exactly. Eight other firefighters from the county also died after getting trapped. It was so horrific, neither Mandy nor her family ever got over it. Five years ago they moved to California to be near relatives and get away from the pain. I haven't seen her since."

He blinked in confusion. "What are you getting at?"

Tamsin gripped his hand. "I don't want to go through that, Cole. Loving you once was hard enough. But to love you again and be terrified every time you get called out on a fire—" She shook her head. "I couldn't do it."

He sat up, alarmed. "So if I ask you to marry me, you'll turn me down because I fight fires?"

She averted her eyes. "Are you asking me?"

"You *know* I am."

"Then I'd have to say no," she said in a broken voice. "If

we had children someday, I wouldn't want them to have to go through what happened to Mandy and her family."

"That will never be the case," he muttered.

"I'm sure Mandy's father told his wife the same thing. But you can't make a statement like that, Cole," she fought back. "I thought you were a cattle rancher, but you came home from Colorado a biologist committed to working in the mountains at least half of every month. That I could handle. But it isn't enough for you. When you're home, you're fighting fires. I want a man who's home with me every minute he can be."

"Will you marry me if I resign?"

Her breath caught. "No, because in the first place, you're following in your father's footsteps. Everything he's ever asked of you, you've done like an obedient son. Even if you could break a promise to your father, I wouldn't want you to do so for me. I couldn't live with you knowing you'd made that kind of sacrifice. You'd learn to hate me. That's the one thing I could never live with."

Chapter Seven

Tamsin's words had gutted him. Cole got to his feet. "So what you're saying is we're doomed not to have any kind of relationship."

"I guess I am, but I'll always love you."

That wasn't good enough. "I'm going to ask you again. Why did you come to Lander with me?"

"To get my head on straight."

"And now you think you have?" Cole stared down at her. "That's it? In twelve hours everything's clear, cut and dried for you?"

"That's how it felt when you left Whitebark."

"So what you're really doing is paying me back for all those years of pain?"

"No, Cole! I shouldn't have said that. I didn't mean it the way it came out."

"The hell you didn't. When I wrote 'Doomed to Love Her,' I never dreamed I was writing a self-fulfilling prophecy."

In the next instant he reached for his pillow and bag.

"Wait—please don't go!"

"There's nothing you could say that could make me stay. Good night, Tamsin. We'll head for Whitebark in the morning."

He turned out the lantern and left the tepee, but she raced after him. When he reached the tent, he started to zip the screening.

"Don't shut me out!" she cried, and pushed her way inside before he could do it up all the way. The momentum launched her against him and his arms went around her so she didn't fall.

For a moment their bodies were locked together. She clung to him. "We need to talk, Cole."

"We already did that. It didn't work...but since you're here, I plan to kiss you into oblivion." Faster than she could believe, he swept her into his arms and laid her down on top of his sleeping bag. Then he joined her, locking her legs with his so she couldn't move. He plunged his hands into her hair and found her mouth.

"Cole—"

His name was all he heard before he smothered any other sounds and began to devour her. He'd done enough thinking about them for a lifetime. This was the only way to get through to her.

"I love you, Tamsin, but since you've cut us off at every turn, we can at least take advantage of this night. I know you want me, and Heaven knows I want you. I'm too on fire for you to stop now. If this is all we will ever have of each other, then let me make love to you as if tonight was our wedding night. In my heart you've always been my wife."

She made a sound that could have been in protest or something else, but it no longer mattered. He rolled her on top of him, craving this closeness more than he needed air, and kissed every feature of her face.

"Do you have any idea how beautiful you are? I couldn't count all the dreams I've had about you. Don't deny us the pleasure of this night. It's going to have to last us for the rest of our lives."

At first she seemed to be with him all the way. Her hunger matched his as they got caught up in a rapture too marvelous to describe. But suddenly she tore her lips from his and pulled back, placing her hands against his chest.

He groaned. "Don't pull away from me now, sweetheart."

"Cole...we have to stop before we can't. I'm going back to the tepee."

His breath caught and he grasped her arm. "Surely you don't mean that."

She refused to look at him. "I followed you inside here to talk to you and explain everything that's going on inside of me."

"We *are* talking in the most elemental of ways."

"You know what I mean."

His temper flared. "I never thought of you as a tease."

She threw her head back. "If you think that's what I'm doing, then you never knew me. You couldn't possibly understand how terrified I am of losing you in a fire. I've never seen you back down from a challenge. That's what made you such a great bull rider. You've never been afraid of anything in your life."

"That's not true. Every firefighter has to deal with fear. But we compartmentalize it differently."

"I don't know how you do that. When I saw you in your firefighter gear and realized what it meant, I was panicked and horrified. Don't you realize that horror has grown worse over the last few weeks? What if our positions were reversed, and I was the firefighter and you the CPA? How would you feel knowing that every time I went out on a call, disaster could strike and I might not come back in one piece to you and our children?"

He took a deep breath. "I'll admit I'm glad I didn't come home to find out you were a certified member of the fire department. No doubt it would tear me to shreds if I watched you pull on your turnout gear."

She let out a tormented sigh. "Oh, what's the use of going over this? We'll never get anywhere."

"Tamsin? I have an idea for us to meet each other halfway."

"What do you mean?"

"As soon as I came home from Colorado, Chief Powell took me on without question. I feel an obligation to him. At the time I had no idea how you felt about this."

"I realize that," she muttered.

"Over the years I'd had talks with my dad. He impressed upon me at a young age that it was important to be an integral part of the community. That's why he became a firefighter and helped when he could. I never recall my mother being upset by it, but it's possible she felt exactly the way you do."

"You never got frightened when your dad went on a call?"

"I was hardly aware of it. He was a rancher first, and later on he had to slow down. When I look back, I can see how lucky we were that he never had a serious injury that made a deep impression on me. If he did, he never said anything about it."

"I don't understand what you're getting at."

"When we get back to town, I'll have a talk with Chief Powell and tell him the truth. Once he hears that I want to get married, but being a firefighter is getting in the way of our plans, I'll make him a proposal."

"What kind?"

At least she was listening. "That I stay on until the arsonists are caught. Every man in the department is needed. Once the culprits have been identified and arrested, then I'll leave the department. We're hoping this menace will be shut down by next month. Can you give me that much time to work things out?"

"No." She half moaned the word.

"I see." He rolled away from her. "Since you couldn't have made that any clearer, I wish you'd go back to the tepee now."

The next thing he knew she'd draped herself over his back, and pressed her cheek next to his. "I didn't mean that I couldn't give you the time you needed before you quit. I was saying no to the idea of you giving up your job permanently for me. It isn't right."

"Look, Tamsin. This isn't a matter of right or wrong. I'm willing to compromise in order to marry you, yet I can see it's still asking too much of you."

"That's not true!" She moved around so she lay face-to-face with him. Her hand crept into his hair. "If you can give it up after the arsonists are caught, then I'll do my part to make our marriage work. My salary at Ostler's will cover what salary you give up and I'll help with the ranching. I love you too much to lose you, Cole."

He raised up on his elbow, having been elevated from the depths to the heights so fast, he was out of breath. "You're not going to change your mind?"

She pressed a hungry kiss to his mouth. "I wouldn't do that to you."

"In that case, don't move." He sprang to his feet and lit a lantern.

"What are you doing?"

He smiled. "Wait and see. Close your eyes."

"Cole—"

"Just trust me."

"I do," she said emotionally.

What a glorious sight she was in navy blue sweats with her disheveled hair gleaming like chestnuts and her lips swollen from his kisses! He reached in his duffel bag and pulled out the little velvet box he'd packed. Cole had been operating on faith, having bought her a ring after finding out she wasn't engaged.

He pulled it out of the box and got on his knees in front of her. "Now you can open them."

When she did, he reached for her left hand. "With this ring, I'm making our engagement official. Be sure this is what you want because I won't let you give it back." He slid it home.

Her eyes had turned into moist blue pools of light. "After waiting nine years, you can be sure I'll treasure this forever." She stared at the ring. "I love this diamond. It's in the shape of Teardrop Lake."

They'd always been on the same wavelength.

"When the jeweler showed me the different cuts, I was immediately drawn to this one for that very reason and asked him to set it in yellow gold."

Her smile lit up his universe before she threw her arms

around his neck and kissed him long and hard. "I adore you, Cole."

Being with her like this had made him euphoric. He pressed her back against the pillows. When they finally came up for air he said, "If I'd run off with you long ago, I couldn't have given you a ring or offered you a life."

She burrowed her face in his neck. "Let's not think about the past."

"Agreed. We've got a future to plan. The first thing I want to do is let Sam and Louise know we're engaged. They'll be overjoyed for us."

"I believe they will, and I want to thank them for letting us stay here."

"We'll do that. When we get back to Whitebark, we'll drive to your parents' so I can ask them for your hand."

"They're old-fashioned. They'll love it."

He kissed her mouth passionately. "After that we'll get my horse trailer and go pick up your mare. She can stay in my barn. From now on let's spend all our time off together whenever possible."

Tamsin hugged him with surprising strength. "It's like a dream. I can hardly believe this is real." She held up her hand to look at the ring again, but dazzling as it was, it couldn't match the glow in her eyes.

"There's a lot more to come. I want to walk through the ranch house with you and get your ideas. By the time we're married, I want it refurbished and ready for us. Sam and Louise have always had their own apartment with us, but it's asking a lot of you. I don't know how you feel about that."

She caught his face in her hands. "They've been your family for a very long time. In time I hope they'll include me in theirs."

Overcome with emotion, Cole crushed her to him. "You couldn't have said anything to make me happier. I love them and love you for feeling the way you do."

"I already love them because it's very clear they love you."

She kissed the line of his hard jaw. "Do you think you can plan some of your work for the state to be done over weekends? If you do that, then I can go with you and help you look for elk."

"I'm planning on it."

"I wish we were married right now."

"But we're not, so I want you to get inside my sleeping bag."

"Cole?"

"I plan to be your husband when I make love to you for the first time, so don't tempt me."

"But a minute ago—"

"A minute ago I was a desperate man!" He stood up so she could get under the covers. Once she was settled, he stretched out next to her and pulled her close. "Help me to control my desire for you, Tamsin. I can live until we're married, knowing you have my ring on your finger. I just want to hold you for the rest of the night. Keep on hugging me, sweetheart. I've needed you for so long. Never let me go."

TAMSIN KNEW BETTER than to argue with this extraordinary man who'd just asked her to marry him and had given her such a beautiful ring. Cole Hawkins had more integrity than anyone she'd ever known. He'd proved it in ways that had caused her to wade through rivers of sorrow, but that was all in the past now.

She remembered what her father had once said to her after Cole had gone away. *I know it's no consolation right now, honey, but mark my words. One day the right cowboy will come along.*

Letting out a sigh, she closed her eyes and nestled as close to Cole as she could. Like Chief Black Elk, her father had been a prophet, too.

Twelve hours later she reminded her father of those words after she and Cole had arrived at the ranch. When they pulled up to the house, her dad was just helping her mother out of the car. It looked like they'd just come home from church.

Tamsin got out of Cole's truck carrying a couple of small

packages and ran over to hug them. He followed her. "I'm so glad you're home!" Tamsin cried.

"How are you, honey?"

"Wonderful, Mom."

"Cole? It's good to see you." They shook his hand. Her parents had kept their opinions about Cole to themselves, but she knew deep down they were anxious for her now that she'd gone on an overnight with him.

"Did you have a good time in Lander?"

"It was an incredible experience. Sam and Louise's teenage grandson is becoming a top bull rider, just like Cole."

"That's really saying something," her father responded.

"They also have a daughter, Doris, who is a fabulous artist. She sells her artwork at a shop in town. Cole and I stopped by there on our way home. I bought the two of us some of her pottery and a doll for Sally to give the baby when she's older. Doris made it from buckskin with a beaded dress and high-top beaded moccasins. I can't wait for you to see everything."

Her mother lit up. "This is exciting! Let's go in the house so I can see it. I'm afraid Sally and Lyle are over at his parents' house with the baby this afternoon, but they'll be back soon." The news filled Tamsin with relief. It meant Dean wouldn't be anywhere around.

Once they'd gone into the living room, her father said, "Welcome back to Whitebark, Cole. It's been a long time."

"Too long. There's no place like home."

"Indeed there isn't. You're all grown up. I'm glad I finally have a chance to thank you for helping save the ranch house from catching fire. Wouldn't you know those arsonists did their worst while we were away on a trip?"

"They have a way of knowing when to strike. I was so relieved that no one was hurt."

"You can say that again."

"Tamsin said you're taking precautions in case they try to cause any more trouble."

"I read that brochure you brought to the house. We're on the watch for them."

"That's good to hear. We've been asking every rancher near the Bridger Wilderness to be extra vigilant."

Tamsin put Sally's package on an end table and handed the other one to her mother. "Here, Mom. Open it."

Inside was an eight-inch turquoise watering pot shaped like a bird with a yellow comb and a picture of a yellow sun on both sides with the rays trailing. The pot had little yellow feet.

"That's the cutest pot I've ever seen!"

"I think it is, too. I bought a watering pot shaped like a dark red buffalo with yellow feet and yellow drawings on the sides. She makes all her own pottery. You should see the tepee around the back of their home. Doris painted all kinds of horses on the elk skin. Each one is a work of art.

"In her house she's painted a wall hanging I covet." Tamsin flashed a private message to Cole. "I want one just like it."

A half smile broke at the corner of his mouth. "Maybe that can be arranged."

Her mother put the pot down on the coffee table. "Have you two eaten? You're welcome to have dinner with us."

"We'd love to, but Cole needs to get back to his ranch. Before we go, we have something important to tell you."

"It couldn't have to do with that diamond on your finger, could it?" Her dad didn't miss much.

"What?" her mother cried.

Tamsin held out her hand. "Cole asked me to marry him last night."

The man standing next to her slid his arm around her waist and pulled her close. "I've loved her from the first moment we met in high school. We'd like your blessing."

Her parents looked stunned. Tamsin knew what was going through their minds. Only days ago they'd supposed she and Dean might end up together.

"Of course you have it!" her mother cried and hugged both of them. "How soon should we be planning your wedding?"

"We're still working that out," Cole explained. "It can't be soon enough for me."

Tamsin eyed her father through moist eyes. "There's only one thing you need to know, Dad. Whether you believe it or not, I listened to the advice you gave me nine years ago. Do you remember what it was?"

He nodded with a smile. "I told you that one day the right cowboy would come along."

She beamed. "You're looking at him."

To her joy, her father gave Cole a hug. "Welcome to the family. In a way it's like you've always been a part of us, but it has taken a hell of a long time to make my daughter's eyes shine like they used to."

Tamsin could tell her father's words had touched Cole. He put his arm around her again and squeezed her hip as her parents walked them out to Cole's truck. She waved from the open window.

"Don't forget to give Sally the doll. I'll call her later tonight and tell her our news. Love you."

As they drove away, Cole grasped her hand and kissed it. "I'm surprised your mom and dad were so accepting of me."

"If you want to know the truth, I'm positive they've gone back in the house jumping for joy. Their lovesick daughter has just been cured of a disease she came down with nine years ago. It's been touch and go ever since."

Cole's rich, happy laughter filled the cab's interior. It seemed like forever since she'd heard that full-bodied sound. But when his phone rang, she was brought back to reality knowing he had to answer it. The conversation didn't last long before he hung up.

"Which work needs you most?" she teased.

"There was another fire last night, this time at the Naylor ranch. He owns more property than anyone else around and has that private runway on his ranch that brings in elk hunters from all over the country. The arson commander has called a meeting with the brass. In fact, it has already started. Chief Powell took a chance I was back from Lander. I have to be there."

"Let's go to the station right now. I'll drive to the apartment. When you're through, call me and I'll pick you up."

"Thanks for understanding. If it doesn't last long, we'll drive to the ranch for my horse trailer. I'd like to bring your mare back tonight."

"That can wait. We'll do it after my work tomorrow."

He nodded and drove fast to reach the station. The ladder truck was out in front, ready for the next run. After pulling to a stop in front, Cole reached across the seat to kiss her. "I love you," he said before levering himself from the cab. By the time she got out and walked around to climb behind the wheel, he'd disappeared inside.

Tamsin was glad the department was having another meeting. The sooner they caught the arsonists, the sooner he would give up firefighting and they could get married.

COLE WALKED INTO the conference room while Holden Granger was talking and found an empty seat in the back. The chief nodded to him.

"With the help of Norm Selkirk, head of County Law Enforcement, we've discovered the name of one Sublette County rancher who has made many trips to the eastern border of Wyoming this year and last to buy gasoline. Norm saw a pattern and started checking all the towns from Gillette and Newcastle to Lusk and Cheyenne. The rancher's actions are highly suspicious since he has to cross the state each time, but I'll ask Norm to give you the details."

The other man stood up. "Thanks, Holden. We've pinpointed this man because he made all his purchases in February and March of both years. He's been very clever to only go once to any one station. We've discovered he used a silver 2010 Dodge

Ram 3500 one-ton truck with a fifty-gallon auxiliary tank an arsonist could use. But consider that it was three years ago."

That sounded about right to Cole. One of those ugly duallies.

"What makes this case so difficult is that none of the ranchers whose property was targeted ever saw anything suspicious. So how did this arsonist spread the accelerant so fast without anyone being aware?

"I talked to a convenience store clerk in Torrington who remembered the guy because the machine outside couldn't read his credit card. He had to bring it inside and while they chatted, the clerk said the man mentioned he needed gas for his generator in case the power went out.

"We know who this cattle rancher is, but his identity has been protected by state law. After some further investigation, we've learned more. Three years ago, brucellosis was confirmed in his herd of cattle and his ranch was put into quarantine, but it was kept quiet."

Cole could relate. The news often set off panic amongst other ranchers.

"Those cases stemmed from exposure to diseased elk, of course. I was able to talk to the state veterinarian. She was able to identify the prevalence of brucellosis.

"The quarantine held until the positive cattle were identified and euthanized. After three different inspections of the rest of the cattle that turned up negative, the quarantine was lifted. We have reason to believe this man had a strong revenge motive and is the one responsible for committing arson along with some helpers. But we don't have proof until we catch him in the act."

He sat down and Holden took over once more. "We've identified the other cattle ranches in our area near the Bridger Wilderness that could be their next targets. Last night four sets of haystacks set on fire at the Naylor ranch are a case in point. One of them caused a grass fire that burned twenty acres."

Cole had gotten engaged last night, thus missing that fire.

He found it incredible that the arsonists had been so brazen. But it didn't surprise him.

"With the help of the forest service and other law enforcement agencies from the bordering counties of Lincoln and Teton who can add manpower over the next month, we're doubling patrols of the vulnerable areas here. I'll leave the last word to Commander Rich."

The older man stood up. "I can't tell you how important it is that we stop this man in his tracks. You men are on the front lines in this war zone. If you see or hear anything in the days to come—something that sends up a red flag—Sheriff Granger needs to hear about it immediately. He's manning our communication center."

Once the meeting disbanded, Cole phoned Tamsin to come and get him. Until she arrived, he chatted with some of the guys out by the ladder truck. While they were discussing what Norm had told them, an idea came into his head and it wouldn't let go. He couldn't wait to get out of there and do some investigating on his own.

When Tamsin pulled up in front, he climbed in the passenger side and leaned over to kiss her cheek. "Will you drive us to your apartment? I want to spend the rest of the evening with you more than anything, but something came up at the meeting I have to take care of, so I'll drop you off. Tomorrow when you're through with work, we'll grab a bite to eat and get your horse stalled in my barn."

Much as he would like to share his thoughts with her, he couldn't. No one could know what he was up to.

"I should have known our little holiday was too good to last, but I'm not going to complain. You've made me too happy."

"Tell me about it." He caressed the back of her neck beneath her silky hair. Cole wanted her for his wife and needed to solve this arson case ASAP.

"I talked to Sally while I was waiting for your call. She told me she always knew I would end up with you."

He grinned. "Do you think there's a chance she'll stop hating me one day?"

"If you asked her that question to her face, she would tell you she wished she could have hated you all these years. It would have been a lot easier than having a crush on you from a distance."

"You made that up."

She laughed. "No, I didn't. She said to tell you welcome to the family at long last."

He chuckled. "Did you talk to Lyle?"

She shook her head. "I decided it was better she tell him first. He'll know what to say to Dean. By the way, Sally adores the doll I bought for the baby. She wants me to take her to that shop one day soon."

"We'll plan on it."

Too soon they pulled up in front of her apartment. Darkness had crept up on them and clouds obscured the moon. Cole jumped out and hurried around to lift her from the driver's seat. This way he could envelop her in his arms and kiss her thoroughly before he let her go.

"Call me tomorrow when you get a minute," he whispered against her lips. "I'll be out mending fences with Sam."

"I'll need your new phone number, remember?"

"Amazing that we've managed this long without them." After another deep kiss, they programmed their cell phones and she hurried up the steps to her apartment. He waited until she was safely inside to turn on lights and had come back out to wave him off.

He waved back and sped through town to reach the ranch in record time. Sam's truck was parked around the side. They must have come back earlier and left a light on for him.

As soon as he unloaded his gear from their trip, Cole rushed inside to the den and got on his desktop computer. Because of his work with brucellosis, he had a security password to access certain files at the state lab. It was almost midnight when he found the case he knew in his gut was the one to which Norm had referred.

Quentin Ellsworth. He lived on a small spread seven miles out of town off the highway leading to Cora.

Cole knew the Ellsworth name well enough because the rancher had two sons. Both had gone to the same high school as Cole. The one named Silas was Cole's age, a long-distance runner who went to college in Arizona on a track scholarship. The other son, Ezra, was Sally's age. He'd done some bronco riding in the teenage rodeo. Over the years Cole had lost track of both of them.

So it was the cattle on the Ellsworth ranch that had gotten hit with the disease and made Cole believe Mr. Ellsworth could be the culprit wanting revenge. According to the file, one hundred and twenty cows out of the six hundred had to be put down three years ago. Losing that many animals would have set him back a lot financially, especially when the whole herd was under quarantine. The same thing had happened to Cole's father.

His thoughts raced ahead. What if Quentin's anger had been so great, he'd talked his sons into helping him get his revenge? Kept it all in the family. The more he thought about it, the more he had to do some investigating on his own. Why not tonight? Right now would be the perfect time to drive by his ranch and take a look around.

He went to his room for his special goggles. The NVM14 monocular multipurpose system was one of the most adaptable multipurpose night vision devices ever made, and could be used in the daytime while he was searching for elk.

After tucking his tiny notebook and pencil in his shirt pocket, he took off for the Ellsworth ranch. Norm had given them a description of the truck, but Ellsworth could have sold it by now and bought a new one. Like he'd said, they needed proof.

Traffic was light as he drove out of town toward Cora. He used his Garmin GPS to zero in on the ranch in question. He passed a small motel with a truck stop and diner before he came to the ranch turnoff.

Cole made a U-turn and stopped alongside the fencing. He could have driven inside, but chose to take a look through the special goggles. The brown-and-yellow ranch house, probably three or four bedrooms, was on the small side with an addition of a second story on one end. He could see a corral, a barn and a two-horse trailer.

Cole backed up several hundred yards to the end of the fencing, probably marking the end of the man's property. He parked his truck as far off the road as possible, then got out and followed the fencing that enclosed the front area. Lowering his head, he ran along until he was able to see the back of the ranch house.

There he caught sight of a dark blue four-door Toyota. Next to it was a red 2014 Ford one-ton truck, but no sign of the Dodge truck. He zoomed in to get the numbers of both license plates, which he copied in his notebook.

Cole would give the information to Holden who would get the names of the owners and do the research to find out where the Ford truck was purchased. If Ellsworth had turned in his Dodge for a down payment, they'd be a step closer in the investigation.

Having done as much as he could for tonight, he doubled back and took off for home. After he'd taken his shower and got into bed, he saw that Tamsin had texted him while he'd been out prowling around.

You'll be sorry I have your new phone number. Now I'll never leave you alone. Good night, Cole. I love you.

He smiled and sent her a message.

I never want to be left alone, sweetheart. We'll be together tomorrow. I don't know about you, but I can't wait!

Chapter Eight

After an amazingly sound sleep, Cole awakened with a brand-new sense of well-being and stopped in the kitchen for coffee. Louise had made some fresh and he told her how much Tamsin and her mother had loved Doris's gifts. He thanked her, grabbed a piece of toast and took off for town.

The first person he needed to talk to was Holden and he headed for the police station. There was always a lot of activity going on inside. He waited until the desk sergeant told him to go on in to Holden's private office.

The sheriff lifted his head. "What brings you in here first thing?" he asked with a smile.

"I realize Norm couldn't tell us the name of the rancher he's tentatively identified as the arsonist, but I'm sure you know who it is. I wanted to know, too. So I did a little investigating and snooping last night and found the name I was looking for. I'm afraid I did something unethical, if not illegal."

"I guess that's the researcher in you."

"Maybe. Can we talk strictly off the record?"

"What do you think? Pull up a chair."

Cole tore the paper with the license plate numbers out of his notebook and put it in front of Holden. For the next few minutes he explained what he'd done last night after leaving the meeting at the fire station.

"I'm hoping with your resources you can find out the dealer who sold Quentin Ellsworth the Ford truck I saw parked out in back of his ranch house. Maybe he turned in his Dodge truck for the down payment to get rid of the evidence. It's a long shot, but if so, it could mean he's tried to cover up his tracks."

Holden whistled. "I think you're in the wrong line of business and should join the police force."

"My fiancée would never go for it."

He sat back in the chair. "Fiancée—"

"Yup. On Saturday I drove Tamsin Rayburn to Lander with me to see the rodeo. One thing led to another and I proposed. She accepted, but we're not getting married until I give up firefighting. I told her I'd help until the arsonists are caught. If I suddenly suggested that I'm joining the police force instead, she'd never forgive me."

A huge grin broke out on Holden's face. "Congratulations, Cole. She's one beautiful woman and smart. Tamsin audited the books last year. You're a lucky man."

"You have no idea. I guess you've heard our story."

He nodded. "Word gets around. I'm really happy for you, but Chief Powell will have a coronary when you quit. Without your insight, I don't know how long this case would have gone on without any major clues to understanding the problem."

"I never dreamed my career as a biologist would help solve an arson case. But I'm not saying a word to the chief until we've caught this guy."

"I hear you. Let me put these numbers into the database while you tell me more of your theories. You say you remember his sons?"

He nodded. "What if he and his two boys, both in their twenties, have been helping him? Ellsworth might not have gotten any other ranchers involved. Can you find out if they still live at home?"

"Of course. What are their names?"

Cole told him everything he knew. Before long they had feedback on the license plates.

"The blue Toyota belongs to Quentin. The Ford truck is owned by Ezra Ellsworth."

"He's the twenty-five-year-old. Maybe he still lives at home. I wonder about the other son, Silas. And what about Quentin's wife? I wonder if she knows about all those trips he took for gas. If she does drive, where was her car last night?"

Holden eyed him directly. "Thanks to you I've got a lot of investigating to do now. For the time being I'll keep all the information you gave me to myself. Maybe Quentin sold the Dodge truck to Silas. We need to track it down and find out where both sons live."

"Agreed. There's something I'm going to tell you that no one else will know, not even Tamsin. This evening I'm going to switch trucks with Sam. I'm sure you know he's the foreman on my ranch and drives a tan Silverado. Instead of going up in the mountains on my job in the morning, I plan to leave before the sun is up and hang out around the Ellsworth ranch out of sight for three days and nights. That way I can watch the comings and goings without anyone being suspicious."

Holden's gaze narrowed. "Be careful, Cole. This guy plays for keeps."

"Don't worry. I'll pretend I'm a wildlife photographer and stay in one of those rustic little cabins at the Big Horn Motel across the highway. If I see anyone leave, I'll let you know so you can put a tail on them."

"That's a great cover."

"We'll see."

"I'll make sure some patrol cars are right around there. Stay in close touch."

"I'll give you regular updates." He got to his feet. "Let's hope my plan pays off."

TAMSIN RUSHED HOME from the hospital to change into riding clothes. She put on her cowboy hat and hurried outside to Cole's truck, this time with the horse trailer hooked up. Her drop-dead gorgeous cowboy had just gotten out of the cab.

Being engaged to him had changed her whole life. Her feet hardly touched the ground as she ran into his waiting arms. "It feels like a lifetime since last night."

His response was to kiss her harder. Someone driving by let out a loud wolf whistle. Cole only held her tighter. "Are you ready to go bring Flossie to her permanent home?"

"I love the sound of that." She covered his face with kisses before he let her go long enough to climb in the passenger side. After they drove away she turned to him. "I stopped at the office first thing this morning and showed everyone my ring. Heather's going to plan a bridal shower for me. I never thought I'd see this day."

He reached for her hand and intertwined their fingers. "I had a meeting with Holden Granger earlier and told him we're engaged. He told me I was lucky to be marrying such a smart, beautiful woman."

"Even if that's a lie, it's nice to hear."

"Not from Holden. He calls it as he sees it."

Cole drove them to Hilda's and parked along the fencing, out of the way of both cars. "I'll run inside to get our food. Do you want another taco and cola?"

"No. I think I want a hamburger with mustard, pickles and a fresh limeade."

"Got it."

She wondered what made him break out in such a big smile as he walked away from the truck. While she waited for him, she put in the CD from the glove compartment and listened to "Wind River Lovin'." Tamsin loved his music.

When she saw him come back, she turned it off and they ate dinner before starting out again. "My aunt Grace in Afton phoned me at work to congratulate me. She along with Mom and Sally will be planning a shower for us, too. She remembers you from a long time ago when she and Uncle Richard were staying with my folks. She'd been a barrel racer in her late teens and said she could see why I'd never found another cowboy. You were impossible to match. That's high praise coming from her."

"That's because she loves you. I've been thinking about our wedding, sweetheart."

"So have I. Can we be married at the church where you held your father's funeral? It's where he would have wanted to see you take your vows."

"I was hoping you would say that. It would have been Mother's choice, too."

"Of course."

"But where we have the reception is up to you."

"My parents have already asked if we'll hold it at the house. I know it will mean the world to them. I let them know we won't set the date until the arsonists are caught and you're free from responsibility."

"Good. All I want is your happiness. This morning Louise told me she and Sam want to host a party for us at their house in Lander."

Tamsin studied his handsome profile. "They love you like a son. I can't imagine anything more wonderful."

As they talked, the Ingram ranch came into view. "We're here."

She nodded. "I let Roy know we were coming to pick up Flossie. Just drive down the road and park in front of the barn. I'll bring her out."

Roy was there to greet them and opened the doors. Tamsin hurried inside and ran over to her mount. "How's my Flossie?" She hugged her neck and tousled her forelock. The horse neighed.

"She's missed you," Roy commented.

"It hasn't been the same without her. We can't thank you enough for letting us keep our horses here. The new barn is going up and it won't be long now before Dad comes for the other horses. We're very grateful."

"You'd do the same for me."

"Anytime."

Tamsin gave her horse a treat, then put on the halter and led her out to the trailer. Cole had opened the door so she could lead her to one of the stalls with a full hay net and water. "We're going to our new home, Flossie. It's not far away. You're going to love it. Cole has half a dozen horses who are going to become your friends."

Cole followed with her gear and saddle. After stowing everything, he came up behind her and put his arms around her waist. "I've been waiting for the day we'd be able to ride together whenever we wanted."

She turned to him. Once again he started kissing her and didn't let her go until she was gasping for breath. Color flushed her cheeks as she walked back outside past Roy and got in the truck. She opened the window to wave at him before they drove off.

It hit her hard that they were going home to Cole's ranch. One day soon it would be *their* home.

Within a half hour she'd walked her around the corral behind the ranch house to let Flossie get used to her new surroundings. Cole brought out her blanket and saddle. Tamsin took over and mounted her while he left her long enough to unhitch the trailer and enter the barn. In a minute he entered the corral on his gelding.

She stared in surprise. "You didn't buy another Arabian."

"Nope. Meet Samson. Strong like his namesake. He's a Missouri Fox Trotter, the most sure-footed animal I've ever ridden in my life when I'm on the trail, let alone in the mountains."

Tamsin led her horse toward his. "Well, hello, Samson. I can tell you're really something. Meet my Flossie." Her roan bay nickered and moved closer. Samson nickered back, causing both her and Cole to laugh. "Don't you have the most gorgeous chestnut coat!"

"Almost the color of your hair," Cole said in an aside that

thrilled her. "They're well matched. Let's take them out by the pasture. Samson needs the exercise."

"So does Flossie."

They left the corral side by side. To be in the saddle next to him, knowing this life was going to be forever, caused a wave of excitement to sweep over her. She cast him a sideward glance and discovered he was looking at her. The expression in his eyes told her everything words couldn't. Neither of them could wait until they were married.

By tacit agreement they broke into a gallop that took them out where the cattle were grazing. Cole waved to the stockmen. She slowed her horse. "How many head of cattle do you have?"

"Forty. It's a manageable size for us with so little help."

"We can use my savings to build the herd."

His devastating smile took her breath away. "You want to know how much your future husband is worth?"

"I already have a rough idea." A ranch this size brought in somewhere between eighty and a hundred thousand dollars a year depending on the health of the cattle. "I could buy more land for us. Between my salary and the one you receive from the state, we could build our own little empire."

"That's a compelling thought. I love the way you think. If a baby comes along soon, will you want to keep working?"

"I'm sure I could do it part-time. I guess I never told you I was planning to leave the firm one day and branch out on my own."

"That sounds ambitious."

She frowned. "Too ambitious?"

"If that's how it sounded, you couldn't be more wrong. I'm glad you love your work. Don't you realize how proud I am of you? I'll back you in anything you want to do."

"Sorry I got so sensitive."

"Why did you?"

She let out a sigh. "I guess it's because Lyle asked Sally not to work after they were married."

"What was she doing when he met her?"

"She went to junior college before working as a secretary at Witcom-Dennison Oil. That's how they met."

"Did she want to keep working?"

"She never said, and I was afraid to ask because it was Lyle's dream to provide for his family. The Witcoms have always had money."

"Well, that's not my dream! I'm going to need all the help I can get."

"I'm so glad you said that!"

"Good. That's one problem we don't ever have to deal with. Race you back to the house, sweetheart."

He took off like a tornado. She tried hard to catch up, but it was impossible. Samson was too fast. By the time she rode into the barn, he was there waiting for her and pulled her off Flossie into his arms.

She came laughing and everything got smothered because he started kissing the daylights out of her. Night had descended by the time they'd put the horses to bed and walked out to his truck.

"I don't want to take you home, but I'm going to have to because I have to leave the ranch at first light. If I take you inside, it's all over and every promise I made to myself and you will go up in smoke."

Once they both got in the truck, she turned to him. "Will you be called out tonight on a fire?" She could hear the anxious throb in her voice.

"No. I always let the chief know when I'm available."

Thank goodness he wasn't going to be doing anything dangerous tonight. "How long will you be gone this time?"

"I'll be back on Friday. I'm planning to take you to a fabulous dinner and dancing. We'll get dressed up and officially celebrate our engagement."

"Ooh. In that case I'm going to shop for a beautiful dress and get my hair done."

"That's fine, but leave it long for me."

"You don't like it when I sweep it up?"

"How can you ask me a question like that? I love you no matter how you wear it. But when you put it up, it only makes me want to pull it down and run my fingers through it."

She laughed all the way back to the apartment.

"Don't worry about Flossie. When you're not there, Sam and Louise will take good care of her. Part of the day they'll walk her out to the corral with the other horses."

At the door to her apartment Tamsin clung to him. "You're too good to me."

He kissed her long and hard. "I only ask one thing of you."

"Anything."

"Stay safe and be here when I get back."

She fought tears. "My greatest wish is that you come home whole and alive for me to love."

"That's a promise."

Tamsin was in agony as she watched him walk back down to his truck and drive away. Even though she knew he loved her and would always come back, she had the horrible premonition that she would always be in agony when he had to leave her. Such was her destiny for loving Cole Hawkins.

WHEN COLE GOT back to the ranch, he found Sam in the kitchen and explained his top secret plans. "Only Holden Granger knows what I'm doing."

"He's a good man. You remember to call me anytime if you're in trouble. You know where I keep the rifle if you need it."

"Yup. You're the best, Sam."

They hugged before exchanging keys to their trucks. Cole gathered everything he needed and packed up the Silverado before going to bed. Tamsin had left another text message on his phone.

How soon do you want to start a family?

He didn't have to think about it.

Immediately.

Her answer came right back.

Good. That's another problem we won't ever have to deal with. Sweet dreams, Cole.

He smiled.

I guess you know you're the star. Need I say more?

After setting his watch alarm, he climbed into bed, but four thirty in the morning came around sooner than he would have liked. He dressed in Levi's and a cream-colored polo shirt before stealing away from the ranch. With his cowboy hat pulled down low over his forehead, anyone who recognized the truck would assume it was Sam at the wheel.

There were several eighteen-wheelers out on the highway driving both ways. At this hour of the morning, he loved the smell of the sage coming off the hills. In the distance he could see a large group of pronghorn moving swiftly on their limbs. They had a reputation for being the fastest animal in the Western Hemisphere. Tourists came from all over to watch them run.

Another mile and he passed a pack of mule deer crossing the road. Whitebark was renowned for its native animal life that outnumbered the residents ten to one. He loved this world and could never live anywhere else. Thank Heaven Tamsin was a product of it, too.

When he reached the truck stop, it was already busy. He waited behind a semi until it was his turn to load up with gas, taking inventory of every car and rig. With that accomplished, he drove over to the twenty-four-hour diner.

Cole went inside and ordered a full-size breakfast that would hold him for half a day. He sat at the window where he could see the traffic along the highway. At seven thirty he walked over to the motel and checked in for a three-night stay.

The older man handed the credit card back to him. "You here on business?"

"You might say that. I'm a freelance wildlife photographer and am anxious to get some good shots out here in the hills. A few minutes ago a herd of pronghorn raced by. That was a sight any wildlife magazine would pay a lot for. I'm going to watch for them over the next few days."

"They're a sight all right. Stick around this evening and you'll see a family of moose and later on some black bears. They come down to the back of the motel where the tourists wash off after they've gone fishing at the river, hoping for food."

"Can't blame them."

The older man chuckled. "No indeed."

"Thanks for the information. I'll remember to check it out."

He took the key and drove his truck to Cabin Eight. Once he'd taken his gear inside and locked the truck, he carried his special goggles and a bottle of water in a flight bag and walked out to the highway. The summer traffic was picking up. He crossed over to the other side.

It was a good thing the undeveloped property with clumps of good-size bushes on the other side of the Ellsworth ranch didn't have any buildings he could see. No one would notice him as he retraced his path along the fencing and hid behind one of the largest bushes. From there he had a perfect view of the parking area behind the ranch house. The same vehicles were still there.

Cole sat on the ground and trained his handheld special goggles on the Ellsworth property. He was looking for movement of any kind. After he'd been holding vigil for an hour, he saw a woman, maybe in her midfifties, come out the back door and get in the blue car. She backed around and drove out to the highway. If he could find out where she was going, that would be a start.

He phoned Holden and gave him a description of the woman

and the car. A few minutes later he saw whom he supposed to be Quentin Ellsworth come out and climb into the Ford truck. Cole made another call to Holden as the man backed around and drove out to the highway.

Five hours later nothing had happened. No more movement. Cole hurried back to the motel to freshen up. He waved to the older man who was outside talking to some people. When the way was clear, he grabbed a late lunch at the diner and texted Tamsin.

Wish you were with me. Today the foothills are teeming with pronghorn and white-tailed deer.

He received an instant response.

Am living for the time I can go with you. I hate texting when I'm dying to hear your voice. I'm halfway through hospital audit. Should be done by Friday. If you can, call me when you've set up camp tonight. Stay safe.

That would be easy.

Till tonight. Love you, sweetheart.

Chapter Nine

Instead of going back out there, Cole drove his truck to an area of the truck stop closest to the highway. With his special goggles he could watch for anyone turning toward the Ellsworth property.

At four thirty his vigil paid off when he saw the silver Dodge Ram pass in his line of vision and caught sight of the driver. Silas Ellsworth looked a good fifteen years older than when Cole had last seen him, but his features were unmistakable.

Another twenty minutes and he saw the red truck Ezra drove turn onto the property. Did this mean both sons still lived with their parents, or was this a gathering place while they made plans?

At six, the woman he assumed was Mrs. Ellsworth returned. Cole would wait until dark and then return to the spot behind the bush to see what was going on. This would be the best time to eat dinner and send a text to Tamsin. He had a feeling he wouldn't have time to get in touch with her later tonight, not if he needed to keep a close watch on the Ellsworth ranch part of the night.

Once he'd eaten, he drove his truck back to the motel and would wait until dark to go out again. After Cole came out of the shower, his cell rang and he recognized the caller ID.

"Holden? Any news yet?"

"Yeah. You'll be interested to know that Mrs. Ellsworth is the owner of Lindquist Dry Cleaners in Whitebark. She inherited the business from her family five years ago and reports there on a regular basis."

"So she works outside the home... You wonder how much she knows. That income would have helped their family financially when they went through the brucellosis scare three years ago. Get this—the Dodge truck wasn't sold after all. Silas Ellsworth is driving it and he turned into the Ellsworth ranch at four thirty this afternoon."

Holden whistled. "That means Quentin probably gave it to Silas or else they share it. I've learned that Quentin cosigned on the loan when Ezra bought the Ford truck last winter. Ezra's address is listed as the Ellsworth ranch and he shows no other place of employment. Interesting that both trucks are duallies that can carry fifty gallons of gas."

"Yup. I'm thinking both sons still live at home and have been helping their father set fires for the last two years. Tonight I'll get the license number off the silver truck and send it to you. If you learn Silas has listed the ranch as his home address, it could mean the boys help their dad with the cattle ranching during the day and carry out all the dirty work at night."

"But we still need proof."

Cole was thinking hard about that. Once the arsonist poured enough accelerant, all he needed were matches rather than an ignition device like a Molotov cocktail. Setting hay on fire whether inside a barn or outside on the property made a conflagration easy because oxygen was plentiful. The hard part was carrying the gas to the area to be burned without being seen.

"Give me a few more days and nights to look inside the truck beds for stashes of gas."

"If only it were that easy."

"I'll figure it out."

"Watch your back, Cole."

"Don't worry. Talk to you soon." They hung up.

Cole had his work cut out and needed to get it done fast. Earlier tonight Tamsin had texted him that she was going to go shopping for a wedding dress while he was away. Their marriage couldn't come soon enough for either of them.

"WHAT DO YOU THINK, Mom?"

Wednesday evening after work, Tamsin had met her mother at Sybil's Bridal Boutique and had tried on three or four dresses. The ivory organza ball gown with the scooped neck and cap sleeves had caught Tamsin's eye and she kept going back to it.

"With the lace overlay on the bodice, it's absolutely beautiful on you, honey."

"I like it the best of the ones I've tried on. I want it to be perfect for Cole."

Her mother rolled her eyes the way Sally did sometimes. "You know what your father says. The wedding is for the bride. The groom is only marking time until it's over."

They both laughed. "Sounds like Dad." She smoothed her hand over the material. "I'll put this dress on hold until tomorrow. After work I'll ask Sally and Heather to come and give their approval."

"I'll tend the baby. She's the sweetest little angel I've ever seen."

"I know. I can't wait to have one just like her."

"First things first," her mother teased, winking at her.

First things first was right! Tamsin was going to have a coronary if there wasn't a wedding night soon.

That evening she texted Cole.

I've found the dress for our wedding. It's on hold until tomorrow. I can't wait to get it. I can't wait for you to come home.

She didn't have to wait long for a response.

Ditto, sweetheart. Be thinking about a honeymoon. Where are you dying to go?

Tamsin wanted him to make the decision.

Someplace neither of us has been.

His answer made her chuckle.

That covers a lot of territory.

She got excited.

How about outside the US? Remember when we used to dream about flying to Australia and swimming in the Great Barrier Reef?

It took him forever to answer.

Shall we discuss a household budget first?

How unromantic of him.

No!

His final answer didn't give her much hope.

Let's talk about it when I get back on Friday. I can hear activity around my camp. Got to run. Love you.

With no more contact from him, Tamsin had to let it go for now. She'd been so full of herself and her plans, she hadn't even asked him how his work was going.

Before she went to bed she made phone calls to Sally and Heather to meet at Sybil's Bridal Boutique at five tomorrow.

She wanted their opinion on a veil to go with her gown, too. Tamsin was so excited, she had trouble getting to sleep.

By Tuesday afternoon she'd finished the hospital audit. After saying goodbye to the administrator, she left for the bridal shop. She'd been on a countdown all week. Tomorrow Cole would be back .

Soon after Tamsin got there, Sally arrived. Heather hadn't come yet, so her sister helped her get into the wedding dress she'd picked out. They picked a shoulder-length lace veil that suited her and the dress to perfection.

Sally was all smiles. "No doubt about it. Cole won't be able to take his eyes off you in this."

"That's the idea, but as Mom reminded me, Cole won't care what I'm wearing."

"Too true," Sally agreed. "Lyle was much more concerned what I'd packed for our honeymoon. The less the better."

More laughter ensued. "Did you love the beach?"

"It was great."

"Last night I told Cole I wanted to go to the Great Barrier Reef for our honeymoon."

"How did that go over?"

Tamsin shook her head. "Not well."

"He's a mountain man."

"I know, and I wouldn't change him."

"I know a man who'd give anything to be in his place."

They hadn't discussed Dean until now. "Did Lyle tell him I'm engaged?"

"We both did. It'll take time, but I'm sure he'll get over it. You were wise not to lead him on any longer."

She looked at Sally. "It wasn't wisdom. I just didn't have strong enough feelings for him. Blame it on Cole."

"Oh, I do!"

Their laughter filled the dressing room before Tamsin's phone rang. She saw the caller ID and picked up. "Heather?"

"I'm sorry, Tamsin. Silas asked me to meet him for an early

dinner because he's leaving town tonight and won't be back until Sunday. Will you forgive me?"

"There's nothing to forgive. Sally's here and I'm going to buy the dress. When you can, come over to the apartment one evening soon and I'll model it for you."

"Thanks for being so nice about this."

"Have fun with Silas at dinner. I'll see you at work on Monday."

She hung up and turned to Sally who said, "Is Heather dating Silas Ellsworth by any chance?" Tamsin nodded. "I haven't seen him since he left after high school to go to Arizona on a track scholarship. He was a really fast runner. I wonder what he's doing now?"

"I don't know, but she's seeing a lot of him lately."

"Maybe another wedding is coming up?"

Tamsin smiled. "Maybe." She turned her back to her. "Help me get out of this and I'll take us to dinner before you have to go home."

"*Have* to go being the operative word since I'm nursing Kellie."

"You lucky woman."

"Don't I know it. When will Cole be back?"

"Tomorrow."

"You must be sick of waiting around for him."

"But not for long. Once we're married, we're both going to arrange our schedules around long weekends so I can go with him. At least I'm saying that now. I have to talk to my boss first."

Sally undid the last button on the gown. "That sounds fantastic, but you *can't* go on the fire truck with him."

"Nope. If I tell you a secret, you can't tell a single soul, and that includes Lyle. Please don't promise me if you know you can't keep it."

"I'll have to think about that."

"That's what I thought. Come with me while I take care of the dress."

They left the fitting room and walked up to the front of the store. "Your secret is really that important?"

"Yes."

"Then don't tell me."

"I won't."

"Tamsin—"

AT ONE IN the morning, all was quiet in the back of the Ellsworth ranch house. The lights were out and the two trucks and car had been parked for the night. Cole had been around long enough to know they didn't keep a dog on the premises. A slight cloud cover helped.

It was now or never if he was going to find the gas cans that were necessary to carry out their arson activities.

After lowering his flight bag to the other side of the fence, he climbed over it and took off for the trucks parked in the near distance. At first sight he only saw a couple of bales of hay in each truck bed. There were tool kits along with spades and equipment for repairing fences, but nothing else.

He hid behind the car, but didn't see anything set near the house to draw his interest. The place appeared to be clean of incriminating evidence.

One more look around brought the medium-size barn into view. The barn was the only place he could think of that might hide what he was looking for. Thankful for the cloud cover, he hurried toward it.

Damn. It was locked.

Not everyone locked their barns. That in itself made him suspicious. He walked around the side to a small window and used his special goggles. All he saw was the inside of the tack room. To his frustration, he only spotted gear for the horses. No gas cans.

He moved with care around the end of the barn to the other side. This side contained a larger window. Again he used his goggles. Most of the barn was taken up with horse stalls. He counted four horses. Near the front it looked like farm machinery—maybe a tractor—had been parked, but it was covered with a big tarp. While he considered breaking the window so he could get inside to look around, he heard a noise.

Cole extinguished the light and flattened himself against the timbered wall. Someone was opening the barn doors. He crept closer to the front of the barn, still staying out of sight. That was when he heard someone start an engine. It sounded like a car or truck engine, not a tractor. He knew the difference.

With stealth, Cole reached in the bag for his goggles and waited until the vehicle emerged from the barn. What he saw was a Ford F-150 in that hospital mint-green color with a US Forest Service logo on both sides of the doors. No doubt it was loaded with gas cans and ready to go, but he couldn't get a fix on the license plate.

Bull's-eye!

He pulled out his phone and called Holden. "I've got news!" Cole told him everything he knew.

"I'm on it, Cole. Great work! Stay in touch."

Within a minute the truck made a stop at the rear of the ranch house. Two people came outside and got in. Everything Cole had suspected had come true about the Ellsworth family. But what he wanted to know was how they'd gotten hold of a US Forest Service vehicle in the first place.

When the truck disappeared from sight, Cole hurried around to the front of the barn. Silas had left the doors open, no doubt to save trouble when they'd gone on another raid and needed to hide the truck in a big hurry.

Once inside, Cole turned on the flashlight and looked around the area where the tarp had been removed. He spotted a workbench and beyond it a spray-painting machine with several empty cans of various green paint. How old everything was he didn't know, but it was all here. They'd turned the barn into a workshop, maybe as far back as last year when they'd started the first set of fires. He had no idea how they'd manufactured the logo.

But everything made sense. They could drive to the various ranches carrying cans full of gas. No one would suspect a US Forest Service truck being on the off-roads checking for fires and the like in the middle of the night. That was why they'd never been caught!

Cole took pictures of everything with his phone, then shut off the flashlight. Before any more time passed, he ran outside to the fencing and raced toward the highway.

In a few minutes he reached the motel and checked his watch. At two thirty in the morning, somewhere in the county another fire was about to be set. But this time Holden had a lead and before long the police would spot the truck and it would be pulled over.

After packing up, he left the key to the room on the table and took off for Whitebark. En route, he called Holden again, but got his voice mail. Cole left a message about the spray-paint paraphernalia and evidence sitting in the Ellsworth barn. He also sent picture attachments.

Having done everything he could, he headed for the fire station. Not only did he want to help if another report of a fire came in, Cole needed to hear the moment the Ellsworth family were caught red-handed.

The ladder truck was gone when he drove around the back. When he walked inside, Steve, one of the crew looked surprised when he saw him. "I didn't know you were on tonight."

"I'm not. I just got back from my other job."

"It's supposed to be my night off, but I just got a call from the chief. He asked me to come in and help man the skeleton crew who are out in front."

"Is the chief here?"

"Nope."

"That's unusual."

"Agreed. Something must be going on."

"I'll find out from dispatch." He walked through the station to the room where Julia Humphrey was on duty, manning the call center.

She looked up at him and cried out in surprise. "Cole—what are you doing here?"

He frowned. "What do you mean?"

"A call came in twenty minutes ago from someone who said the barn on your ranch was on fire."

His barn?

The horses! Tamsin's horse!

Shocked to the core, he tore out of there to his locker and dressed in his firefighting gear. Then he raced to his truck and drove like a crazy man to his ranch. In the time he'd spent taking pictures and getting back to the motel, the Ellsworths had reached their destination without being stopped and had done their damage to Cole's property.

He broke out in a cold sweat. Was it Sam or Louise who'd called the fire department? The pit in his stomach enlarged. Were they all right?

His body was shaking as he neared the ranch and saw flames billowing in the night air. He could have been looking at the fire on the Rayburn ranch that had been set earlier in the month. Talk about déjà vu.

A huge crowd of neighbors had gathered. He parked along the private road and raced toward the guys working the ladder truck, unable to spot Sam or Louise. The tender truck was around the side. His eyes fused with the captain's.

"How bad is it?"

"There's still one horse inside, but the fire is becoming fully involved. It's too dangerous to go in there now. The roof's going to cave in any second."

An image of the Ellsworths sneaking onto his property made him wild with fury. "I can't leave it. I'm going in."

"No, Cole—"

But he ignored the captain and ran inside the fast-growing

inferno. He could hear the horse screaming in the rear stall. It was Louise's gelding Jimuta and sounded eerily human.

He reached for a rope in the debris that covered the floor and tied it around the Arabian's neck. "Easy, Jimuta. It's Cole. Come on. Let's get you out of here."

Inch by inch he made his way toward the opening, pulling the terrified horse behind him. He imagined this was like being engulfed in a volcanic eruption. A vision of Tamsin swam before him.

Come back whole and alive for me to love.

He remembered those words before a wave of hot air swept down on him. It seemed to burn his lungs before everything went black.

THE PHONE AWAKENED Tamsin at eight on Wednesday morning.

Cole!

She'd arranged to take today off of work so she could be with him after he got home. Without looking at the caller ID, she reached for it on the bedside table, ecstatic because it meant he'd come back to town. She couldn't wait to see him.

"Hello, Cole?" she cried with excitement.

"I'm sorry, Tamsin. This is Louise."

Louise?

Panic gripped Tamsin. She held her phone tighter and slid out of bed. "By the tone in your voice, I can tell something's wrong." Maybe he was still in the mountains. His truck could have had problems.

"Someone set fire to Cole's barn during the night. Sam called the fire department."

Paralyzed by what she'd just heard, Tamsin sank back down on the side of the bed. "He's been up in the mountains. Does he know?"

"Yes. The firefighters got all the horses out except mine. Cole rushed in to save Jimuta."

"I—I don't understand." Her voice faltered. "Was Cole home?"

"He'd just returned from his trip. When he found out Jimuta was trapped inside, he ran in to save him. As he came out with my horse, part of the roof collapsed and hit Cole on the arm."

Tamsin knew she was going to faint. "You don't mean he's—"

"No, no. He was dragged out and is being treated for smoke inhalation and some burns on his one arm, but he's going to be fine."

Thank God.

"But you need to come to the hospital as soon as you can because Cole is asking for you."

"I'm on my way. Bless you for letting me know, Louise."

The next hour was a blur while Tamsin dressed and drove to the emergency entrance. Her heart pounded so hard, she had trouble breathing. To make things worse, she had to park at the other end of the visitor parking because so many police cars and fire van units from the county blocked her way to the doors. She noticed vans from two television stations.

"Over here, Tamsin!" She turned her head as Louise came running up and put her arm around her. "He's going to be all right, Tamsin. Sam's with him. I've notified your family. They didn't answer, but I left a message."

"Thank you." In a daze, she followed Louise inside. The emergency room reminded her of a nightmarish war zone in a film. It was noisy, chaotic. A baby was crying. Firefighters were being treated along with other patients. Police had assembled. Tamsin heard one of the staff telling a doctor they had a gunshot wound victim in the trauma center, but all she could think about was Cole.

"You have to check in first." Louise guided her down the hall to one of the rooms where the triage nurse was putting information in the computer. "They're identifying everyone coming into the emergency room."

Tamsin understood, but they had to wait until it was her

turn to give her name and phone number. Because arson was a criminal activity, she knew this was a police situation and everyone was being investigated. But she needed to be with Cole and every second away from him was agony.

A few minutes later, an older man who looked like one of the brass Cole often talked about walked in. He nodded to her. "My name is Norm Selkirk. I'm the head of Sublette County Law Enforcement." Cole had talked about him. "If you and Mrs. Speakuna will come in the next room with me, I'd like to ask you a few questions."

It was obvious he'd already talked with Louise. The two of them went with him to the next room down the hall. He invited them to sit down. "Would you tell me your reason for coming to the emergency room, Ms. Rayburn?"

She tried to stay in control. "Cole Hawkins is my fiancé. Mrs. Speakuna phoned and told me that he'd been hurt in the fire set on his own property. He was asking for me, so I came as soon as I could. Please, I need to see him."

"You won't be able to do that for a little while, but don't worry. The doctor is with him."

Don't worry... She had to fight her hysteria.

Louise patted her arm.

"Did you know your fiancé's whereabouts before you heard about the fire?"

Why would he ask a question like that? "Yes. He was up in the Winds doing his work tracking the elk. What is this all about? I want to go to him now!" she cried.

"I wish you could, but we're following up an investigation. It won't be long before you're free to see him. For the moment I need to ask you a few questions."

"I don't understand."

"Are you acquainted with Heather Jennings?"

What on earth? "Yes. She and I are both CPAs at the Ostler firm."

"Coworkers, or more?"

"We're close friends."

The man nodded. "Have you met her alleged boyfriend, Silas Ellsworth?"

"No. I mean, I have met him, but not recently." Tamsin was ready to scream.

"Explain what you mean."

"He went to the same high school I did. That was nine years ago. I haven't seen him since."

"Do you know how long she's been dating him?"

She took a deep breath to calm down. "I'm not sure. Maybe for a month. Can I go now?"

"One more question. How well do you trust Ms. Jennings?"

Tamsin jumped to her feet. "I'd trust her with my life. Why are you asking me that?"

"Because she was seen having dinner in Silas Ellsworth's company a few nights ago. Ms. Jennings would have known about the fire on your father's property through you, Ms. Rayburn. We're trying to ascertain if she was using your association with Mr. Hawkins to gather information on him and learn when he was in or out of town."

Tamsin frowned. "You honestly think she was being my friend to get information?"

"I'm only asking the question."

"For what reason?"

"So she could feed her boyfriend what information Mr. Hawkins had told you since he's been a member of the fire department."

Tamsin was incredulous. "I've never discussed Cole's work with anyone. Furthermore, Heather has never asked. We were close long before she ever met Silas. And why would he be so vitally interested in anything Cole does? I still don't get it."

"He and two others are the alleged suspects in custody at this hour for committing the arson that has plagued the ranchers in this county for two years."

Her heart leaped. She stared at him in disbelief. "They've been caught?" He nodded. "Does Cole know?"

"You'll find out when you're allowed to visit him. Thank you for your time. Wait here and someone will let you know when the doctor says you can see him."

Chapter Ten

Overjoyed by the news that the arsonists had been arrested, Tamsin gave Louise a hug. "It's over."

"Yes. He's been through enough."

"So have you and Sam." *So have I.* Cole had promised that once the case was solved, he'd resign from the fire department and they'd get married.

For the next fifteen minutes they talked about the fire until someone on the staff came in and told them they could see the patient. Tamsin literally ran out of the room with Louise, who led the way to another room farther down the hall and around the corner. The sight of four grubby, foul-smelling firefighters standing around the opening while they laughed warmed her heart.

She heard Cole's voice before peeking inside.

"Get out of here, you guys."

"We're going."

Tamsin recognized Wyatt Fielding, a guy she knew from high school. She also recognized Captain Durrant, who grinned and patted Cole on the shoulder. One by one the other three gave a physical manifestation of their affection and relief by a nudge or some other gesture. Tamsin stayed next to Louise.

She knew Cole had developed deep friendships with his crew

back in Colorado. He'd explained that the bond between them was as strong as any blood ties could be. Judging by the behavior of these men here, she could tell how much they cared about Cole already.

This was a part of his life Tamsin had nothing to do with. She knew a moment's feeling of being excluded from a fraternity that could never include her. But it didn't matter. All she cared about was that he'd escaped death from the collapsed roof.

To her overwhelming joy and gratitude, Cole was sitting on the end of the hospital examining table, dressed in jeans and a polo shirt and hooked up to an IV.

The attending physician stood there treating him for smoke inhalation with oxygen. His lower left arm had been bandaged to the wrist. But as far as she could tell, nothing else seemed to be wrong. The man was fearless.

Wyatt made his parting shot. "Try to stay out of trouble for a while, Hawkins!"

"Mr. Hawkins won't be reporting for work for at least a week," the doctor explained. "That burn needs time to heal."

"I'm going to make sure it does!" Tamsin spoke up as she entered the room, because she knew something neither the doctor nor anyone else knew.

"Oh, boy. You're in for it now," Wyatt called out with a gleeful smile. The guys hooted and hollered all the way down the hall.

Her gaze met Cole's. The oxygen mask covered his nose and mouth, but she could tell he was smiling. "You're a sight for these bloodshot eyes," she heard him say. Her heart turned over on itself. "Come closer, sweetheart."

"I'm afraid I'll hurt you."

His deep chuckle thrilled her.

The doctor smiled. "Just make sure he keeps breathing the oxygen. I'll be back in a minute."

Sam left with the doctor, giving her a hug on the way out. Louise followed them, leaving Tamsin alone with Cole at last.

When she ran to her dark blond cowboy, he threw his right arm around her with surprising strength. Worried for him, she eased away enough to cling to his right hand. The tears dripped down her cheeks. "When Louise told me part of the roof collapsed on you, I almost died. You should never have tried to rescue Louise's horse!"

"Jimuta is a special Arabian, named for one of the Arapahoe sun gods and blessed by the chief of their tribe for its remarkable powers. I knew he was frightened, but hoped he would let me get him out because he knew me and my voice."

Tears welled up in her throat. "So many times you've told me you could never thank Louise enough for taking care of your father near the end. I would say that saving her horse has done more to show your love for her than anything else you could ever do. She was the one who called to let me know you were in the hospital."

"Louise is so modest she would never tell you that Sam risked his life to get the horses out in spite of the flames. I couldn't bear it if anything had happened to them or Flossie. Sam and the stockmen have been taking turns guarding the property at night."

"How did he know about the fire?"

"He'd just come in from his stretch when he thought he heard the horses neighing. He assumed a skunk or a raccoon had gotten in the barn and went out to investigate. That's when he saw the flames and called the fire department."

Tamsin shuddered and gripped his hand harder. "I love them both for their devotion to you and your family. Oh, I wish I could hug you."

"So do I. The doctor says I have to stay in the hospital tonight so they can treat my burn. If everything looks good tomorrow, he'll release me and we can go home where I can hold you in my arms for as long as I want."

Another night of waiting. "Are you in horrible pain from your arm?"

"No. They've given me a painkiller in the IV. My throat is sore, that's all."

"You breathed in too much smoke. I can't believe this happened to you."

"But it's over now and my injury isn't life-threatening. Let's concentrate on our wedding."

She had so much she wanted to talk about, but the doctor came back in followed by the orderlies wheeling a gurney. "We're moving you to the fourth floor." He eyed Tamsin. "If you'll go out to the desk, they'll tell you which room. Give us fifteen minutes."

"Of course. See you soon, my love." She kissed the palm of Cole's hand one more time before hurrying out in the hall where Sam and Louise were waiting. Without hesitation, she hugged them both and broke down weeping for joy that everyone was alive.

AFTER COLE WAS wheeled to the fourth floor along with his IV drip, the nurse helped him into a hospital gown and he was settled in a regular bed. To his relief the doctor had fitted him with an oxygen tube that wasn't as cumbersome as the mask.

While he waited anxiously for Tamsin to come in, knowing this situation was the very reason she wanted him to give up firefighting, he had visitors. The big brass had assembled. Norm, Chief Powell, Commander Rich and Holden walked in and stood around his bed.

Commander Rich cleared his throat. "We know you need rest, but we want to give you a quick update. Because of your heroism for going beyond the call of duty, you'll be getting an award, but it will be given at a later date when your wounds have healed."

"That's not necessary, Commander."

Norm moved closer to the bed. "Every arson victim in Sublette County owes you a debt of gratitude they can never repay."

"Neither can the firefighters," Chief Powell chimed in. "Our courageous men have answered every call to put out those fires. To know the culprits have finally been caught is a gift to all of us. Everyone will sleep better tonight because of you."

A lump had lodged in Cole's throat. "You give me too much credit, gentlemen."

Holden moved over to his other side. "That's not true and you know it. If you hadn't sacrificed yourself to stake out the Ellsworth ranch and discover what was hidden in their barn, we might not have caught up to them for another year, maybe never."

"He's right," Norm muttered. "You could have gotten yourself killed, Cole. They were carrying a rifle. Gunfire was exchanged with Ezra before he was hit and brought in to the hospital. They're treating the gunshot wound to his thigh before he's put behind bars."

"There's more," Holden asserted. "Let's not forget that *you* found the link to the diseased elk and cows that explained the motive for the arson. I'm only sorry we didn't catch the Ellsworths until after they'd set your barn on fire. One of your stockmen told me he saw a forest service truck in the distance, but didn't connect it to the fire. That was all I needed to hear."

"The Ellsworths were very clever," Cole murmured.

"Yup. But one of the guys on patrol spotted the truck returning to their ranch. Once it was pulled over and they exchanged gunfire, the gas cans provided the rest of the evidence. We can all thank God no lives were lost tonight." Holden smiled. "Now we'll get out of your hair. Someone outside is dying to get you to herself."

Cole sighed and lay back against the pillows while the nurse came in to check his vitals and record them in the computer. After she left the room, Tamsin rushed inside looking beautiful in that apple-green summer suit he loved. To his delight she'd left her glossy hair down so it brushed against her shoulders.

"Cole—" She hurried over to the bed and gently caressed

the side of his jaw. Her blue eyes traveled over his features. "Can I kiss you?"

"Please." He half groaned the word. She lowered her mouth to give him a tender kiss on the lips beneath the oxygen tube. "I keep thanking God you're alive. Oh, darling—I love you so much."

He cupped the back of her neck with his right hand to give her another one before letting her go.

"Mom and Dad will be here in a few minutes."

"That's good. Now we can set the wedding date. Any time you say."

A troubled look broke out on her gorgeous face. She clung to his hand.

"But you haven't had time to tell Chief Powell you're leaving. Or am I wrong?"

"No. I plan to tomorrow."

She smoothed some tendrils of hair from his forehead. "I was standing outside the door waiting for the men to leave. When they came out, Commander Rich congratulated me for being engaged to a hero who has done a great service for the State of Wyoming."

"He had to say that."

"No, Cole. They all said it. He informed me that he expected me to be at your side when the governor awards you the International Association of Fire Chiefs' Medal of Valor. He said the ceremony would be held next month in Cheyenne for service beyond the call of duty."

"All the firefighters should get one."

Tamsin shook her head. "You never could accept a compliment, but this is one time when you're going to have to!"

"Yes, ma'am."

She kissed his cheek. "After he told me that, Chief Powell shook my hand and said you're a role model for all the men and women who are eager to join the department. He's thrilled you're on the force and hopes you'll be on it for many years to come."

Her eyes teared over. "They're so proud of you. I am, too! After hearing their accolades, I don't know how you're going to tell them that you're leaving the department."

"Tamsin," he whispered, "I gave you my word that we would set the date as soon as the culprits were caught. That day has come."

"But—"

"No buts, sweetheart," he broke in on her. "After tomorrow, this will all be behind us. It'll be a mere formality. No looking back. I wanted to marry you nine years ago and have waited long enough. This is it."

He heard a knock on the door. "That's probably your parents. Tell them to come in."

She walked over and opened it. After hugging her, they moved to the end of his bed while Tamsin came back to his side and grasped his hand.

"What a blessing that you are all right, Cole," her mother said in a tear-filled voice. "Our hearts almost failed us when we heard you were in the hospital. The thought of losing you... You'll never know what we went through."

Moved by her words he said, "Last night was a close call, but today everything's perfect."

"We're so proud of you, Cole."

"We are," Tamsin's father concurred in a solemn voice. "Word that the arsonists plaguing the ranchers in Wyoming for the last two years have finally been caught has gone out over local and national news. They're praising the heroics of one local firefighter from Whitebark named Cole Hawkins who cracked the baffling case for law enforcement."

Tamsin's mother put a hand on his arm. "You're an amazing man, Cole. Tamsin has told us of your sacrifices to help your father years ago when you left to earn a living for the family. If your parents were alive, they'd be ecstatic to tell the world you're their son. We're overjoyed you're engaged to our daughter and feel privileged that one day soon we can call you son."

Overwhelmed by her outpouring of emotion, Cole had to clear his throat. "Thank you. That means a lot," was all he could get out when his heart was so full.

"Whatever we can do for you."

He looked at Tamsin. "We want to plan our wedding, the sooner the better. How about three weeks from tomorrow? Will that give you enough time?"

Tamsin's father chuckled. "My daughter's been ready forever," he teased. "The question is, will you be recovered?"

"I'm fine *now*."

"No you're not!" Tamsin squeezed his hand.

"What about that arm?" her mother asked.

"The doctor says I have a second-degree burn. They're filling me with painkillers and antibiotics to prevent infection. In three weeks I'll be more than fit."

She looked at her husband. "Then I don't see why we can't have a wedding by then. How about Saturday, August 1? But we're going to have to hurry to get the invitations printed and sent out in the next few days. Come on, Howard. We've got things to do. We'll be back tomorrow to see how you are."

"I won't be here," Cole informed her. "The doctor said he'd release me in the morning. But I'd love you to come to the ranch whenever you can."

"We will, but you mustn't try to do anything for a while."

"Don't worry about that, Mom. I'll be watching him like a hawk," Tamsin said in that determined voice. "So will Louise."

"See you later." As they left the room, the nurse came in carrying a foot-long red fire engine filled with a huge arrangement of red, yellow and orange flowers.

"Oh, Cole—look what you've been sent!"

With a smile, the nurse put the flowers on one of the side tables. "Compliments of the Whitebark Fire Department."

The flowers represented flames. How creative was that? Cole

would have burst into laughter if his lungs and throat didn't hurt so much.

"They must love you a lot, Mr. Hawkins. I hear you guys are like brothers." Before she left, she handed him the card so he could read the message.

Did you have to go to so much trouble to get out of work? Don't plan on joining the bull-riding circuit anytime soon, cowboy. We need you back, pronto!

Wyatt had to have been the one responsible for all this. Cole had to admit the camaraderie with the crew was something he was going to miss. They went through a lot together every time they had to go on a run. Nothing got the adrenaline surging like the beeper going off. You never knew what was waiting for you, but one thing was always certain: the guys had your back.

Much as Cole loved his work in the mountains, he'd learned to love firefighting when he'd first started out in Colorado. In his gut, he knew it would always stay with him. While he contemplated the step that would take him away from that career, exhaustion took over. He fought to stay awake for Tamsin's sake, but it was a losing battle.

TAMSIN STAYED AT Cole's side while he slept and studied the card for a long time. *We need you back, pronto.*

She'd seen the expression in his brown eyes earlier and would never forget the look of loss and regret registered there. Right then his thoughts had been far away from her and she knew why.

The nurse had spoken the truth. They *were* like brothers. Tamsin had felt it while she'd been outside the emergency room cubicle earlier listening to their banter. Cole had promised to give up firefighting so she would marry him. But she couldn't shake off the feeling that he would be giving up something so important to him, it might affect him in ways she hadn't considered.

Tamsin stayed with him until evening. The nurse took out the IV and they ate dinner together. He was given soft foods he could tolerate. She knew his throat was sore. Tamsin didn't encourage him to talk. Instead she turned on the TV to watch the news. Cole featured prominently, but the names of the arsonists hadn't been released yet.

"I can't believe that the Ellsworths were the ones responsible. They were both really nice guys in high school." Her body quaked. "I'm still trying to digest the fact that Ezra got shot trying to kill a state trooper."

"Their father lost too many cows to the disease and none of them could get over it."

"You wonder if his wife knew."

"Probably."

"How awful."

"First-degree aggravated arson means they'll all do time in prison."

She moaned. "Commander Rich interrogated me this morning." Cole looked at her with a startled expression. "He was trying to find out if my friend Heather was involved in any way because she's been dating Silas. The idea was absurd, but it's so sad. I can tell she really likes him. Now I know why she couldn't meet me at the bridal shop on Thursday."

"What happened?"

"She said Silas was leaving town and wanted to have an early dinner with her. To think he was planning to burn your barn before the night was over. I can't comprehend it that they have set so many fires with no remorse."

"Including your father's barn."

Tamsin nodded. That was a night she'd never forget, but that was because Cole had come home and the shock of seeing him again had brought her so close to a faint, she'd slumped against Dean.

"Poor Heather's going to be devastated when the police release their names to the press."

Cole sounded resigned when he said, "It wouldn't do any good to ask you not to think about it, so I won't. Your fears for me really came to fruition, didn't they, sweetheart? But no more on that score from now on."

Somehow that didn't make her happy. Not at all. She turned off the news and got up to kiss his lips. "You're exhausted. I'm going to leave for the apartment so you can get your rest. We'll text all night if you want. I'll be here first thing in the morning and drive you home when it's time."

"I don't want you to go."

"Yes, you do. You just don't want to hurt my feelings. It's because that's the way you're made. But when the doctor came on rounds, he checked your burn, put on a fresh dressing and told you to get a lot of sleep. I heard him say he's keeping you on oxygen until morning. That means it's time for me to leave. Good night, my love. Sweet dreams."

"One more kiss."

Against her better judgment she pressed a quick one to his lips and hurried out of the hospital room. She drove home exhausted and eager for a shower. When she was ready for bed, she phoned Sally and they talked for at least an hour about everything, including the Medal of Valor Cole was going to receive.

"Your husband-to-be has become a celebrity in every sense of the word. The news said he cracked the case. How did he do it exactly?"

"I don't know yet. All that smoke bothered his throat. Maybe tomorrow it'll feel better and he'll be able to tell me what happened behind the scenes. Mr. Selkirk praised him to the skies. That lets me know there's a lot Cole hasn't told me."

"He's a dark horse, that one."

"If you want to know the truth, Cole is so impossibly honorable at times, it's scary."

"That's an odd thing to say."

"Not if you knew what I know."

"What *do* you know?"

"A lot. There is one thing I could tell you, but it would be for your ears only. No sharing with your husband."

"You're kidding—"

"I knew it! You can't keep anything from him, so I'll say good-night."

"Tamsin—tell me. I swear I'll never repeat it."

"Then I'll trust you. When I told Cole I couldn't marry a firefighter, he said he would give it up because he didn't want to lose me. He promised that once the arson case was solved, he would turn in his badge. That's why we've set the date for three weeks from Saturday." A lump lodged in her throat. "That's the kind of honorable I'm talking about."

For once, silence reigned on the other end. "Sally? Are you there?"

"Yes," she answered in a quiet voice.

"What's wrong?"

"I was just thinking how hard it might be for Cole to give up firefighting, but Lyle is just coming in," she whispered. "I'll have to talk to you tomorrow. Bye for now."

The line went dead.

Tamsin hung up, then sent Cole a text telling him she loved him. Afterward she went to bed. He'd probably gone to sleep and that was why he didn't respond.

For most of the night she tossed and turned, troubled by her own thoughts and her sister's comment about Cole giving up firefighting. At five in the morning, she sat up in bed with a gasp, recognizing what was wrong. Her unrest had started at the hospital when she'd heard the fire crew joshing with Cole in the emergency room. The strange feeling attacking her had never left.

Instead it had grown much worse until she realized she had to do something about it. Sally's silence had only put the punctuation point on it. Armed with a plan, Tamsin got up and took time to do her nails and curl her hair. She wanted Cole to take one look at her and fall in love with her all over again.

After going to her closet, she found the summery dress she was looking for. It was a blue-and-white print with short sleeves and a scooped neck. She chose white high-heeled sandals to go with her outfit.

For a final touch she wore the adorable little enamel blue-bell-shaped earrings he'd given her in high school for Christmas. They'd stayed in her jewelry box all these years, her one keepsake from him she could never part with. Thankful that she hadn't, she went in front of the bathroom mirror to put them on. They matched the color in her dress to perfection. Would he even remember them?

By eight o'clock she was ready and drove to the hospital. She was so excited to see Cole, she was feverish. After reaching the fourth floor, she hurried down the hall to his room. She noticed the orderlies delivering breakfast trays. Her beloved was probably still on soft foods.

But when she reached his door there was a sign that said Do Not Disturb. Nervous that something was wrong, Tamsin rushed down the desk to inquire about him. The charge nurse looked up.

"The doctor should have taken the sign down after his rounds. You can go in."

Relief washed over Tamsin. She raced back to his door. When she walked in, she found him sitting up in his bed watching the news. The oxygen tube had been removed and he looked wonderfully normal to her. Their eyes fused before he turned off the TV.

"I thought you'd never get here." His voice sounded stronger.

"I was afraid to come any sooner and disturb you."

"You can always disturb me. Come here."

She ran around to his right side. He reached for her with his free arm. Once their mouths met, they kissed long and passionately.

Tamsin heard him moan. He finally took a breath. "You smell and look divine. That must be a new dress. What are you trying to do, give me a heart attack?" He smoothed a tendril behind her ear and she heard him draw in his breath.

"You're wearing the bluebell earrings I gave you. I didn't know you kept them. They're the color of your eyes."

"Your gift made my Christmas. I could never part with them. Don't you know I loved you to death even then?" She kissed him harder. "The nurse told me the doctor has already been to see you. How's the burn?"

"Good. He has released me to your care and I've eaten breakfast. Are you ready to take me home?"

"I think you know the answer to that question."

"Yeah. I do. I'll ring the nurse."

Within a few minutes one of the orderlies appeared with a wheelchair for Cole. The nurse handed him a bag that held his belongings and some medication from the pharmacy. Tamsin reached for the flower arrangement. "I'll carry this down."

"We'll save the engine for our first boy to play with."

She laughed. "Girls like fire engines, too."

His smile disappeared as he stared at her. "Not all girls."

With those piercing words, her excitement faded because she was the person responsible for producing that remark from him.

She tried not to show it, but by the time they got settled in her truck with the flowers put in the back seat on the floor, Tamsin knew it was time to have the most important talk of their lives. The muggy hot morning portending rain later on seemed to close in on her. Until she said what was on her mind, nothing would be right.

After they started through town, she couldn't hold her feelings back any longer. "Cole—there's something I have to say to you."

Because of the wound on his left arm, he didn't try to touch her as they drove. "It must be serious. You look like you've just lost your best friend. Where has the most gorgeous woman on the planet suddenly disappeared to?"

She had trouble breathing. "That woman needs to ask your forgiveness for something unforgiveable she's done."

He smiled, trying to lighten the mood. "You've never done anything that's unforgiveable."

"That's not true. We both know I have." Her hands clung to the steering wheel as she drove toward his ranch.

"Sweetheart—tell me what's wrong. As long as you're not going to remove the ring I gave you, I can handle anything."

By the time they reached the parking area of his property, she was a nervous wreck. "Maybe you'd better stop the truck before we have an accident."

Chapter Eleven

Tamsin came to a halt with a jerk, almost skidding into his truck. She managed to shut off the engine before burying her face in her hands. "I should never have asked you to give up your career as a firefighter. It was wrong of me. Selfish. I was only thinking of my own wants and needs, never once considering what I was asking of you. I've been so unfair to you."

By now the tears were gushing down her cheeks. "I'm ashamed of how I've acted and what I've put you through." She lifted her head to look at him. "When the flowers came and I saw that look in your eyes after you read the card from the crew, I could see what the cost would be for you to give it up. I knew then it was the last thing you wanted to do.

"Cole—for you to turn your back on something you love so much in order to marry me would kill me. I couldn't bear to be the reason you go through life feeling robbed of something so important to you. What I'm trying to say is that I don't want you to give up firefighting. I *won't* let you do it!"

His features suddenly hardened into an expressionless mask. "I'm afraid it's too late for that. Before you arrived at the hospital this morning, Chief Powell phoned to check up on me. That's when I told him I was resigning and why. The deed is done."

"No—" Her horrified cry rang out in the cab.

"No?" By now his face had lost color. "Less than a month ago, I recall you telling me you couldn't marry a firefighter, not under any circumstances. Since marriage to you was more important to me than anything else, I made the decision to get out.

"Now that I've honored my commitment to you and followed through on my part, I'm hearing something else. I don't seem to be getting this right no matter what I do. Why don't you just tell me the truth, Tamsin Rayburn? What you're trying to say is that a marriage between us isn't going to happen under any circumstances. Maybe you're more hung up on Dean Witcom than you realized."

"Cole—"

But he ignored her and got out of the truck. Grabbing the bag from the back seat, he started walking toward the front porch of the ranch house.

*"Wait—your flowers—*I'm coming in with you so we can really talk!"

He wheeled around with a wintry expression. "But I'm finished *really* listening to you. Keep the flowers and the ring. When I wrote 'Doomed to Love Her,' it turns out I was a prophet after all."

The air left her lungs as she watched him disappear inside the house. He hadn't given her the chance to express everything that was in her heart. Right now she saw no way of reasoning with him. There was only one thing she could think to do. Taking her courage in her hands, she backed around and headed for town.

When she neared the fire station, she found a parking place along the street and got out. With no ladder truck in sight, she imagined they were out on another call. Thank Heaven it wasn't the arsonists this time!

Tamsin hurried inside and approached the man at the desk. The sign said Sergeant Perez. He looked up at her, but she didn't recognize him. "May I help you?"

"I hope so. Would it be possible to speak to Chief Powell?"

"I'm afraid he's in a meeting."

She bit her lip, fearing that he was already telling the higher-ups about Cole's resignation. "Do you have any idea how long it will last?"

"Sorry."

"Do you mind if I wait?"

"What's your name?"

"Tamsin Rayburn. This is of life and death importance." She wasn't lying about that.

"Just a moment."

He left his desk and walked down the hall. A few minutes later he returned with Chief Powell.

"Ms. Rayburn. I understand you wanted to see me."

"If I could. You have no idea how badly I need to talk to you."

"Then come with me."

"Thank you."

She followed him down the hall to his office. He walked behind his desk and indicated she should take a chair.

"I'm surprised to see you here. I thought you'd be with your fiancé. He was supposed to go home from the hospital this morning, wasn't he?"

"Yes. Actually I just drove him to his ranch. But something came up on the way. Something awful, and only you can fix it." She stared at him through her tears. "Please tell me you'll help me."

"If I can."

"Cole told me he talked to you earlier this morning and turned in his resignation."

"That's true."

Her heart sank. "Did he tell you why?"

"He said it was for personal issues, but he didn't go into specifics." That sounded like Cole. Honorable to the end. "For a man who's as suited for this kind of work as he is, Cole must have had a very strong reason."

"He did," she said softly. "A month ago I told him I couldn't handle being married to a firefighter and I turned down his proposal," she stammered. "You see, nine years ago there was a terrible fire in the Bridger Wilderness and my best friend's father was burned to death along with some other firefighters."

"I remember," he murmured.

"It was so awful. When I saw the pain his family went through, I knew then I could never be married to one and told Cole how I felt."

"Ah."

"He came back at me with a compromise and said he'd give it up, but not until the arsonists were caught. Once they were identified and brought down, he'd quit the department and we'd get married."

She wiped the moisture from her cheeks. "I was out of my mind at the time and agreed to that compromise so we could be married. I loved him so much and have waited so long for him to come home from Colorado, I wasn't thinking about what he'd be giving up to marry me.

"But I know now that Cole will never be really happy again if he can't do what he loves. He's the most amazing guy. I've never known a man so outstanding at everything he does. He plays guitar, composes music, and was one of the top bull riders on the circuit. You name it, Cole can do anything. When gifts were handed out, he got most of them. Sometimes I think he's too good to be true." Her voice wobbled.

The chief nodded with a smile. "I agree. Has he told you how he cracked the case?"

"No. His throat hurt too much and I didn't want him to talk. But he'd never tell me anyway because he's too modest."

"Then let *me* tell you."

Tamsin sat there in amazement while she learned where Cole had really been the night he said he was heading to the mountains.

"He'd figured out through his work as a biologist that Quentin Ellsworth had been the rancher to lose a lot of calves to brucellosis. Cole put two and two together and knew Ellsworth had a strong motive for committing arson."

"Just like he figured out why some of the ranchers were being targeted."

"Exactly. On the night in question, he stayed at a motel across from the Ellsworth ranch, and sneaked into their barn where he discovered a truck they'd painted up to look like it belonged to the US Forest Service. When they left to go light a fire on Cole's property, they rode in that truck so no one would be suspicious."

She shook her head. "It's a miracle they didn't shoot him."

"Cole was too careful. He took pictures and sent us the information about the spray-paint machine. He took the Ellsworths on single-handedly and risked his life to get the news to the sheriff. Without his smarts, we might never have found out who was lighting those fires. The last thing we want is for him to leave the department."

Tamsin leaned forward with her hands clasped. "Then will you call him and tell him that you won't accept his resignation? I want him to stay on so he'll be happy, but he won't listen to me."

"You're a very wise woman who knows there's nothing worse than a firefighter who doesn't have the support of his wife. So I'll tell you what I'm going to do. We'll both drive out to his ranch right now and I'll reinstate him."

She jumped to her feet. "You mean it?"

He smiled. "It will be my pleasure. I've learned a little wisdom in my older age. A firefighter with a bad heartache is no good at all. Cole came back to Whitebark for you. Let's put him out of his misery once and for all, shall we?"

Tamsin loved him so much for saying that, she ran over and hugged him.

"COLE?" LOUISE'S VOICE. Since taking a shower and changing into clean jeans and a T-shirt, he'd been working on the computer.

"What is it?"

"I know you wanted to be left alone, but you've got company."

"I'm trying to catch up on data I need to send into the lab."

"Shall I tell Chief Powell that?"

His head jerked back. "*He's* here?"

"Yes."

Why the devil had he come over? "I'll be right out."

He left the den and walked out to the living room, but stopped dead in his tracks. In his line of vision he saw Tamsin, the chief and the flowers placed on the coffee table in that order.

"Chief Powell?"

"You look good for someone just released from the hospital. Since our talk on the phone this morning, I had a visit from your fiancée."

Tamsin stood next to the chief. In that stunning blue-and-white dress, her beauty only exacerbated his anger that she'd dared to come near him.

"What's going on?"

"I'm here to tell you that I won't be accepting your resignation under any circumstances. I didn't know all the facts when we spoke earlier, but Ms. Rayburn has filled in the blanks to my complete satisfaction."

Cole shook his head in shock.

"When you get back from your honeymoon, let me know when you're ready to report for duty. By then you'll be a husband. We'll work out a schedule that will be compatible with your elk research activities and still give you time to enjoy this wonderful woman you're about to marry. After what she revealed to me, she gets what you're all about. They don't come any finer."

He felt his heart start to pump blood again. His gaze shot to hers.

"Get well now and take care of that burn. The next time I see you will be at the wedding. The crew can't wait, but they'll have to come in shifts."

After the chief left the house, Tamsin walked toward Cole. "If you hadn't gotten out of the truck so fast, I would have told you that I won't marry you if you don't stay with the department. You survived the fire the other night. That gives me faith that you'll do it again and again. I love you, Cole. Your happiness is all that matters to me."

Bursting with emotions he couldn't contain, Cole reached for her and pulled her into his arms, being careful with his left. He kissed every inch of her face. "If you hadn't come back…"

Three weeks later

THE DESK CLERK checked his computer. "Mr. Hawkins? Welcome to Kauai." He handed Cole the card key. "We hope you and your wife enjoy your stay while you're in Hawaii. If you'll follow the porter, he'll carry your luggage and show you to your condo. It's right on the beach as you requested."

Now that Cole's left arm had healed to a great extent, it was wonderful to put it around Tamsin's shoulders without wincing. They left the lobby and followed the path around flowering gardens and grassy grounds to their honeymoon suite.

The gentle surf in Poipu, plus the swaying palms, had a magic feel this time of night. Tamsin clung to him. "Everything looks so perfect, it's like walking into a picture postcard. But that's because I'm with you and I'm afraid I'm dreaming that we're actually here."

The porter opened the door of their bungalow and set their bags down in the little sitting room. Cole gave him a tip and the man left.

Tamsin wandered over to the window where the breeze came through off the ocean. "I love this temperature." She turned to him. "Isn't this paradise?"

"The air is like velvet." He walked over and cupped her face. "I'm sorry it's not the Great Barrier Reef, but we didn't have time to get passports."

"It doesn't matter. We can go there someday. As far as I'm concerned, we had the perfect wedding. My parents love you, Cole. Everyone does. To be honest, I'm happy to get you away from the crew and be alone with you at last. I don't want to share you with anyone, and I think Kauai could easily be the Garden of Eden."

"Lucky Adam if Eve looked like you."

She kissed his lips. "If you want to know the truth, I feel sorry for Eve. Adam could never measure up to you."

"How do you know?"

"Because she'd never seen him master a bull or muster cattle on his horse. She never knew what it was like to hear him play his guitar and compose songs to her."

"I'm sure he did many things that impressed her. Don't forget. All they had was each other, which meant they had to be creative. That's the part I like best." He began kissing her, knowing he never had to stop.

"When I walked down the aisle with Daddy and saw you standing at the altar in your tux, my legs almost gave away. It was a good thing I had him to hold on to."

"That was pretty exciting all right. Sam asked me if I was okay. He knew my heart was pounding out of control, like it is right now. Will you make love to me, Tamsin?"

"You don't have to ask me that. I was ready the night we got engaged. You were the one who said we had to wait."

"Are you sorry?" He picked her up and carried her into the bedroom.

"I don't know. I'm a little scared. Maybe this is how Eve felt the first time. If she was like me, she wanted to be all things to the spectacular, incredible man she'd married. What if she couldn't measure up to his expectations?"

"Men have the same fears, sweetheart."

"Not you. You're not afraid of anything."

"Only once was I truly afraid. It was the night of the fire on your property. I found out one of the Rayburn girls was married. That's the night I came close to losing it, until Wyatt told me it wasn't you. Now you're married to me and I don't want to talk anymore."

IN THE EARLY morning hours, Tamsin awakened, hungry to know her lover's possession again even though they'd made love throughout the night. Cole had taken her to heights she'd never even dreamed about. It was a revelation to her. He made her feel immortal. She wanted to know that feeling over and over again.

Though he was sleeping, she started kissing his throat and inched closer to his lips, willing him to wake up enough to thrill her once more. Tamsin knew she was being shameless, but she couldn't help it. He'd awakened the passion in her. She was on fire for him. Unable to handle it any longer, she covered his mouth with her own.

Before long she felt his powerful legs stir. Soon he was running his fingers through her hair and then it was Cole rolling over to trap her body. "I know I've died and gone to Heaven," he spoke against her lips.

Heaven was right. Four hours later they both awakened with her head lying against his shoulder, a possessive arm around her hips. They looked into each other's eyes.

"Good morning, Mrs. Hawkins. How do you feel?"

She smiled. "You know exactly how I feel, Mr. Hawkins. I've never been so happy in my life, so…complete."

"That's the perfect word, my love."

"To think we had to wait nine long, agonizing years to know this kind of bliss." Suddenly the tears welled up inside her and she couldn't stop them from running out of her eyes. "I know I shouldn't think about it, but after making love with you all night, it's hard not to resent all the time we lost, all the pain we had to endure."

He kissed her mouth quiet. "Why don't we make a pact and never look back. Today is the start of our new life together. Let's make up for lost time and fill it."

"I want that, too, Cole. I'm sorry for bringing it up."

"Stop apologizing to me. I'll order breakfast and then we'll plan our day."

She traced his lips with her finger. "I know what I want to do."

"So do I." He half growled the words.

Though they'd flown all this way to Hawaii, they only left their bungalow to go out for a swim in the ocean. Then they came back to their haven, never seeming to get enough of each other. Maybe it was because they'd had to wait so long to be together, they weren't that eager to do anything but just express their love. Maybe it was the fear that their happiness could be snatched away.

All she knew was that when it came time to fly back to Wyoming, Tamsin wasn't sorry. She couldn't wait to live with Cole and make the ranch house their own home. It had been a dream of hers for such a long time.

After Sam and Louise picked them up at the airport in Jackson Hole, they drove straight to Lander for the barbecue they'd planned for the newlyweds. Many of their friends from the tribe had gathered behind Doris and Riley's house.

The warm August night couldn't have been more perfect. Cole pulled her down on the grass with him while they watched the grass dance and the hoop dance accompanied by drums, rattles and bells.

Tamsin loved the grass dance performed by the men. They wore tassels of grass that swayed with their movements, imitating the wind whistling through the grass on the plains. The hoop dances were creative versions of the animals of the plains. The night seemed enchanted, especially when Cole kept kissing her at every opportunity.

The tepee stood tall against the sky, symbolic of the great Arapahoe nation that was here before the white man. Though Tamsin had loved being in Hawaii, she'd never known a more romantic night than this one with Sam and Louise's family and people.

They celebrated until far into the night. When Cole finally helped her to her feet, Tamsin's heart pounded hard as he led her to the tepee for the night. She could easily pretend she was an Indian maiden following her warrior lover to his tepee.

Knowing what awaited her during the night, she could hardly contain her excitement. Cole lit the lantern and spread out the double sleeping bag.

"Sweetheart? Tonight we're going to do it the Arapahoe way."

"What do you mean?"

"Don't wear anything to bed." He removed his clothes and got under the covers. "Now it's your turn." He was still sitting up. She hesitated for a moment. "Surely you're not shy around me after what we experienced on Kauai."

"Is this really the custom?"

He let out a deep laugh that filled the tepee. "I have no idea. I haven't asked Sam."

"Oh, you!"

She disrobed with maidenly modesty and slid under the covers next to him.

To her surprise he pulled something out from under the covers. It looked like a roll of wrapping paper, probably two and a half to three feet in length. He handed it to her.

"What's this, darling?"

"Open it and find out."

Her hands fairly shook as she took off the paper, hoping not to tear anything. In a minute the whole paper came off to reveal a wrapped-up skin. Cole helped her open it all the way.

A gasp fell from Tamsin's lips when she realized what it was.

Everything an Indian does is in a circle, and that is because the power of the world always works in circles, and everything tries to be round. The sky is round and I have heard the earth is round like a ball, and so are all the stars. The wind in its greatest power whirls, birds make their nest in circles, for theirs is the same religion as ours. The sun comes forth and goes down again in a circle. The moon does the same and both are round. Our tepees were round like the nests of birds. And they were always set in a circle, the nation's hoop. Even the seasons form a great circle in their changing, and always come back again to where they were.

—Chief Black Elk

"Doris made this painting for us!"

He nodded. "She likes you very much, or she wouldn't have gone to this kind of trouble and used an elk skin. It's a great honor, Tamsin."

"I know it is. We'll put it wherever you think it should go in our home."

"Our home." His brown eyes shone with a luster she'd never seen before. He moved the skin away from their bag and put out the light. "Come here, sweetheart. I want to relish this night with you in my arms."

Tamsin nestled against him. "It feels so surreal to be in this tepee sleeping out under the stars. Everything seems so right. Sam and Louise are wonderful people with such a rich heritage. I'm grateful to be able to share it."

"That's how I feel about you. Blessed beyond belief to realize you're my wife."

She kissed him with longing. "We're going to have the most wonderful life. I can't wait until we have a baby."

"I think we've done a pretty good job of working on it so far. But until our first one arrives, let's just savor the two of us having this time together. You have no idea how jealous the guys are who aren't married yet. I hate to tell them they'll never find a woman like you."

"Like I said, I feel sorry for Eve, but I guess it's true that what you *don't* know can't torture you."

More laughter rumbled out of Cole before he reached for her and taught her a new meaning for the word *ecstasy.*

Chapter Twelve

"Sally?"

Tamsin ran through Sally and Lyle's new home at noon and found her in the nursery.

"Shh." Her sister turned to her. Tamsin looked in the crib. Their precious four-month-old, Kellie, was asleep, curled up in one corner clutching her blanket.

"Sorry." She mouthed the words. They walked out and down the hall to the front room.

Sally smiled at her. "What went on in the mountains to make you look and sound this excited?"

"It's what happened when we got back this morning. I just came from seeing your OB. We're expecting!"

The two sisters hugged each other in happiness. "Does Cole know?"

"Not yet. I came here first."

She cocked her head. "Don't you think he'd want to know first?"

"Yes, but because you suspected I was pregnant last week before we left on our last trip, I decided to tell you first. You've always had an uncanny knack for knowing what was going on with me. Have I told you how much I love you for seeing into my heart and urging me to be honest with Cole? I'm so happy every minute of my life with him, I'll be forever indebted to you."

Sally shook her head. "Even if you made it hard for him, he wouldn't have given up. You two were meant to be together."

"I know we are." But her smile faded. "Tell me one thing. How's Dean been since he moved to Riverton?"

"Believe it or not, Lyle says he's met someone."

Tamsin's heart clapped for joy. "Oh, I hope it's the real thing for him. I'll always love him in my own way."

"I think he knew that. I love him, too. It would be great if this was the real thing." She grabbed Tamsin's hand and pulled her over to the couch. "I want to hear details about the baby."

"I'm six weeks pregnant."

"Knowing you, you've got names picked out already."

"If it's a boy, I want to name him after Cole's father. He worshipped that man."

"And if it's a girl?"

"Cole will probably have his own ideas on that."

"What do you bet he writes a dozen songs about him or her before the baby's born."

Tamsin nodded. "Would you and Lyle come to the ranch for a surprise dinner tonight and bring Kellie? I've already invited Mom and Dad. Sam and Louise will be there as well as Doris and her husband. We'll have a big family celebration. I'm going to make a cake that says 'Proud Papa.'"

"Cole will die."

"That's the plan, figuratively speaking. I swear, Sally. If anything ever happened to him…"

"Hey—I thought you were over thinking like that. You're going to be a mother. Concentrate on the family you've started. Another Hawkins is on the way. It'll either be a barrel racer or a bull rider. Frankly, I hope it's a girl for Kellie to play with. Have you seen the little tiny baby cowboy boots at the shop in town? They're so cute!"

"What's so cute?"

Lyle had just walked into the living room.

"Oh, honey—Tamsin has the best news on earth!"

"I already knew that."

"How do you know?" Tamsin asked.

"My wife told me last week. Congratulations." He walked over and hugged her.

The three of them broke down laughing and suddenly they could hear the baby crying.

Lyle headed out of the room. "You two go on plotting while I get her. You and Cole have no idea what you're in for now."

Tamsin couldn't wait. She jumped up from the couch. "I've got to go home and get ready for Cole. Tell Lyle goodbye for me. See you tonight."

She raced out of the house to her truck, unable to get home fast enough. A bright new future awaited them. He just didn't know it yet.

* * * * *

Falling For The Rancher

Tanya Michaels

Tanya Michaels, a *New York Times* bestselling author and five-time RITA® Award nominee, has been writing love stories since middle school algebra class (which probably explains her math grades). Her books, praised for their poignancy and humor, have received awards from readers and reviewers alike. Tanya is an active member of Romance Writers of America and a frequent public speaker. She lives outside Atlanta with her very supportive husband, two highly imaginative kids and a bichon frise who thinks she's the center of the universe.

Books by Tanya Michaels

The Best Man in Texas
Texas Baby
His Valentine Surprise
A Mother's Homecoming
My Cowboy Valentine
"Hill Country Cupid"

Hill Country Heroes

Claimed by a Cowboy
Tamed by a Texan
Rescued by a Ranger

The Colorado Cades

Her Secret, His Baby
Second Chance Christmas
Her Cowboy Hero

Texas Rodeo Barons

The Texan's Christmas

Cupid's Bow, Texas

Falling for the Sheriff

All backlist available in ebook format.

Visit the Author Profile page
at millsandboon.com.au for more titles.

Dear Reader,

One of my favorite things to do as a writer is revisit communities (like Cupid's Bow) and characters that I've already created. It's like spending time with old friends.

Physical therapist Sierra Bailey started out as a minor character in my 2014 book *The Texan's Christmas*. She was only in a few scenes, but I loved her feisty spirit. She proved to be the perfect heroine for this book, helping to heal not only her teenage patient, Vicki, but Vicki's older brother, guilt-stricken rancher Jarrett Ross.

Up until a few months ago, Jarrett lived an adrenaline-fueled existence that centered around rodeo wins and pretty women. But when he stood his sister up for dinner and she was in a horrible car accident, Jarrett came home to help take care of her and the family ranch. He's sworn off dating for the moment, and no woman is more off-limits than the beautiful physical therapist spending the month with them. Yet Sierra's determination, humor and heart are even more irresistible than her red hair and gorgeous curves.

Jarrett can't stop himself from falling for Sierra, but can he convince the woman who's only here on temporary assignment that her future could be in Cupid's Bow... with him?

This is the second installment in my Cupid's Bow, Texas series, and I hope you'll follow me on Twitter, @tanyamichaels, or Facebook (authortanyamichaels) to learn about my future Cupid's Bow books.

Happy reading,

Tanya

While I was writing this book that features someone in health care, my daughter actually had quite a few medical appointments. Thank you to her nurses—and nurses in general—for their time and effort in a demanding profession.

Chapter One

It was surreal, staring at a photo of himself and feeling as if he were looking at a stranger. No, that wasn't exactly right, Jarrett Ross amended, studying the framed rodeo picture on the wall of his father's home office. The word *stranger* implied he didn't know the dark-haired cowboy, that he had no feelings about him one way or the other.

A wave of contempt hit him as he studied the cocky smile and silvery, carefree gaze. *Selfish SOB.* Six months ago, his only concerns had been which events to ride and which appreciative buckle-bunny to celebrate with after he won. A lot had changed since then.

Six months ago, Vicki wasn't in a wheelchair.

"Jarrett?"

He turned as Anne Ross entered the room. He'd been so mired in regret he'd almost forgotten he was waiting for his mother. Dread welled as she closed the door behind her. Did they need the privacy because there was more bad news to discuss? He wanted to sink into the leather chair behind the desk and bury his face in his hands. But he remained standing, braced for whatever life threw at them next.

"How did Dad's appointment go?" Jarrett hadn't been able to accompany his parents to the hospital this afternoon. There was too much to do at the Twisted R now that he was the only one working the ranch. But even without the countless tasks necessary to keep the place running, he would have stayed behind in case Vicki needed him—not that his sister voluntarily sought out his company these days.

"You know your father. He's a terrible patient." Anne rolled her eyes, but her attempt to lighten the situation didn't mask her concern. "Overall, the doctor says we're lucky. He's recovering as well as can be expected from the heart attack and the surgery. The thing is…"

Jarrett gripped the back of the chair, waiting for the other boot to drop.

His mother came forward and sat down in the chair across from him, the stress of the past few months plain on her face. Even more telling was the slump of her shoulders. She'd always had a ramrod-straight posture, whether sitting in a saddle or waltzing across a dance floor with her husband.

"I have to get your father off this ranch," she said bluntly. "I've been after him for years to slow down, to get away for a few days. I even tried to talk him into selling the place."

That revelation stunned Jarrett. He'd never realized his mom's complaints about the demands of ranch life were serious. He'd thought her occasional grumbling was generic and innocuous, like jokes about hating Mondays. People griped about it all the time, but no one actually suggested removing Monday from the calendar. It was impossible to imagine Gavin Ross anywhere but at the Twisted R. Not sure how to respond, he paced restlessly around the office. Despite the many hours he'd spent here over the past month, it still felt like trespassing. As if his father should be the one sitting behind the desk making the decisions that would affect the family.

"Your dad refuses to accept that he's not in his twenties anymore," his mom continued. "At the rate he's going, he'll work himself to death! And after the added stress of Vicki's accident…"

Guilt sliced through him. Was his dad's heart attack one more thing to trace back to that night in July? His mind echoed with the metallic jangling of the keys he'd tossed to his younger sister. He hadn't gone with her because a blonde named Tammy—or Taylor?—had been whispering in his ear, saying that as impressive as he'd been in eight seconds, she couldn't wait to see what magic he could work in an hour's time.

Jarrett pushed away the shameful memory. "So you and Dad want to take a few days of vacation?" he asked, leaning against the corner of the desk closest to her.

"A few weeks, actually. I haven't discussed it with him yet, but Dr. Wayne agrees that it's a good idea. My cousin has a very nice cabin near Lake Tahoe that she's been offering to let us use for years, and Dr. Wayne said he could give us the name of a good cardiologist in the area. Just in case."

When you were recovering from open-heart surgery, "just in case" wasn't nearly as casual as it sounded.

"Your father is mule-headed. Now that he's starting to feel a little better, he'll try to return to his usual workload. I can't let him do that. He may seem larger than life, but he's not invincible." Her gaze shifted downward. "And...without us as a buffer, Vicki would naturally turn to you for company and assistance."

The soft words were like a pitchfork to the gut. His sister, younger than him by almost seven years, had grown up idolizing Jarrett. Now his parents had to evacuate Texas just to force her to speak to him again.

"She's going to forgive you." Anne reached over to clasp his hand. "The drunk driver who plowed into the truck is to blame, not you."

He wanted to believe her, but it was his fault Vicki had been on the road. They'd had plans to grab a late dinner. Between his travel on the rodeo circuit and her being away for her freshman year of college, they'd barely seen each other since Christmas. But instead of catching up with his kid sister as promised, he'd ditched her in favor of getting laid. Vicki had been trapped amid twisted metal and broken glass when she should have been sitting in some restaurant booth, debating between chicken-fried steak and a rack of ribs. She'd always had a Texas-sized appetite, but her athletic hobbies kept her trim and fit.

Past tense. She no longer had much of an appetite. And although the doctors assured her that, with physical therapy, she would walk again, it would be a long damn time before she played softball or went to a dance club with her sorority sisters. She hadn't even been able to return to campus for the start of the new semester in August, another consequence that ate at him. Unlike Jarrett, who'd earned a degree with a combination of community-college courses and online classes, Vicki had been accepted into one of the best universities in the state. How much academic momentum was she losing?

Anne blamed Gavin's heart attack on years of working too hard and his stubborn insistence that "deep-fried" was a valid food group. But it was no coincidence that the man had collapsed during one of Vicki's multiple surgeries. The stress of his daughter's ordeal had nearly killed him.

"Jarrett." Anne's scolding tone was one he knew well from childhood. "I see you beating yourself up. You have to stop. If not for yourself, then for me."

"I'm fine," he lied. She was shouldering enough burden already without fretting over his well-being, too. "I was just processing the logistics of running the Twisted R while taking care of Vicki. I'll figure it out. You and Dad should definitely go."

"Thank you. Be sure to voice your support when he objects to the idea." She pursed her lips, considering. "We probably have a better shot at convincing him if you're *not* handling Vicki and the ranch by yourself. What if we found a part-time housekeeper who could act as her companion? Or, ideally, even someone with medical experience. My friend Pam's a retired nurse. I can ask her about home health care."

"Are we sure that's in the budget?" The mountain of medical bills was already high enough that Gavin had recently let go of their sole ranch hand after helping him find a job on another spread. Gavin insisted the Twisted R could function as a father-and-son operation if Jarrett was available to help full-time. No more rodeos for the foreseeable future.

Or ever. He hadn't competed since the night of Vicki's accident, and it was hard to imagine enjoying it again. Everything he'd loved—the adrenaline, the admiration of the spectators—seemed shallow in light of what his sister and dad had suffered.

"I'm not suggesting we hire a long-term employee," she said. "Just some help for a month or less. We have plenty of space. Maybe with Pam's help we can find someone temporarily willing to accept low pay in exchange for room and board. There could be someone young who needs the experience and a recommendation."

His mother made it sound almost reasonable, as if there were lots of people who would work practically for free and wanted to move in with a surly nineteen-year-old and a rodeo cowboy who'd taken early retirement. *What are the odds?*

Then again, they had to be due for some good luck.

"Okay," he agreed. "Call Pam and see what she says."

Meanwhile, he'd cross his fingers that his mom's friend knew someone who was truly desperate for a job.

"WHAT THE HELL do you mean I'm out of a job?" In her head, Sierra Bailey heard the familiar refrain of her mother's voice chiding her. Unladylike language was one of Muriel Bailey's pet peeves. *I just got fired. Screw "ladylike."*

Eileen Pearce, seated at the head of the conference table, sucked in a breath at Sierra's outburst. It was too bad Eileen and Muriel didn't live in the same city—the two women could get together for weekly coffee and commiserate about Sierra's behavior. "The board takes inappropriate relationships with patients very seriously, Ms. Bailey."

"There was no relationship!" Except, apparently, in Lloyd Carson's mind. Bodily contact between patient and physical therapist was a necessity, not an attempt at seduction. Sierra had never once thought of Lloyd in a sexual manner, but he'd apparently missed that memo. The man had unexpectedly kissed her during their last session. Which, in turn, led to his wife angrily demanding Sierra's head on a platter.

Taking a deep breath, Sierra battled her temper. "Patients become infatuated with medical professionals all the time. It's a form of misplaced gratitude and—"

"Yes, but in the year you've been with us, we've had multiple complaints about you. Granted, not of this nature, but your track record is flawed. Perhaps if you'd listened on previous occasions when I tried to impress upon you the importance of professional decorum..." Eileen paused with an expression of mock sympathy.

Comprehension dawned. This wasn't about Lloyd Carson and his romantic delusions. The board of directors had been looking for an excuse to get rid of Sierra. She felt foolish, not having seen the dismissal coming, but she truly believed she was good at her job.

Was she mouthy and abrasive? Occasionally.

All right, regularly. One might even argue, frequently. But sometimes PT patients needed a well-intentioned kick to the rear more than they needed to be coddled. *Lord knows I did.*

At twelve years old, Sierra had been a pampered rich girl whose parents treated her with a much different standard than her three rough-and-tumble brothers, as if she were fragile. Dr. Frederick Bailey and his wife, Muriel, had raised their sons with aspirations of global domination; they'd raised their daughter with the promise that she'd be a beautiful Houston debutante someday. No one had challenged her until the gruff physiotherapist who'd helped her after she'd been thrown from a horse.

He'd taught her to challenge herself, a lesson she still appreciated fifteen years later. The side effect was that she also tended to challenge authority, a habit the hospital's board of directors resented.

Given the barely concealed hostility in Eileen's icy blue gaze, it was a miracle Sierra had lasted this long. *You're partially to blame here, Bailey.* While she'd deny with every breath in her body that her conduct with Lloyd Carson had ever been flirtatious or unprofessional, Sierra could have been more of a team player. She could have made an effort to care about occupational politics.

As Eileen went over the legal details of the termination, Sierra's mind wandered to the future. Her savings account was skimpier than she'd like, but she was a trained specialist. She'd land on her feet. It was a point of pride that she'd been making her way for years, without asking her parents for money.

You'll find a new position. And when you do? Stay under the radar instead of racking up a file of grievances. In the interests of her career, Sierra could be detached and diplomatic.

Probably.

Chapter Two

"Darling, you're being needlessly stubborn," Muriel Bailey chastised through the phone. "Coming home for an extended visit would be a win for everyone. Since you aren't busy with work—"

"I'm busy looking for a job." Word had spread through the medical grapevine from Dallas to Houston that Sierra had been fired. Ever since Muriel had learned about it last week, she'd been relentlessly campaigning for Sierra to move back to Houston. *There's a better chance of my being elected president and moving to the White House.*

Her mother sighed. "But it's always difficult to get vacation time approved after starting a new position. What if they won't give you the days off for your brother's wedding?" According to Muriel, Kyle's December nuptials would be The Social Event of the Decade. "I need you here so you can help me with the millions of details! Then you'll start job-hunting again after the holidays. New year, new career."

Trapped under her parents' roof from September until January? Little spots appeared in front of Sierra's eyes, and she gripped the edge of the granite-topped kitchen island for support. "I'll be sure to mention that my brother is getting married during interviews and give prospective employers a heads-up." Assuming she got any more interviews.

By affronting the hospital's board of directors, she seemed to have damaged her options here in Dallas. Only two people had been willing to meet with her so far—a sleaze who'd ogled her breasts throughout the entire conversation and a sycophant who'd gushed about what an honor it was to meet the daughter of esteemed Chief of Neurosurgery Frederick Bailey. She didn't want to take a job that was offered because of who her father was, but if nothing better materialized...

"Sierra, are you even listening to me?"

"Um." Not for the past five minutes or so. "I may have missed that last part."

"Douglas Royce has been asking about you. He can't wait to see you at the wedding."

Oh, for pity's sake. Her mother couldn't possibly think there was still a chance Sierra might one day become Mrs. Douglas Royce? Opening the fridge, she searched for a bottle of wine. *Damn.* The downside of no paycheck was a serious lack of groceries. "We broke up years ago."

"Yet you haven't had a serious relationship since! Perhaps because, deep down, you—"

"Paul and I were plenty serious." Just not transcontinental serious. When Dr. Paul Meadows had left a couple of months ago to do medical work in Africa, they'd shared an affectionate goodbye. It was true she hadn't dated much between Douglas and Paul, but three years of grad school and twelve months of residency hadn't left much free time. "You're conveniently forgetting, I never loved Douglas half as much as you and Dad did. So you're not going to use him to lure me home."

"Parents shouldn't have to 'lure' their own flesh and blood. Where's your sense of familial duty?" Muriel huffed. "Who's going to help me with this mountain of wedding tasks?"

Sierra supposed it would be sheer lunacy to suggest the bride. Was poor Annabel getting *any* say in her big day? *I warned Kyle they should elope.* "Don't be afraid to delegate to the zillion-dollar-an-hour wedding coordinator, Mom. That's what Annabel's family is paying her for. I hate to cut this short, but I have a phone interview this evening." Could her lie have sounded less convincing?

"Really? With whom?"

"Um…" Sierra rubbed her temple. "Oh, I think that's my other line. Gotta go, love to Dad, 'bye!" She disconnected before her mother could respond, poured a glass of water and went to the living room, where her laptop sat on the couch. For a moment, she considered checking flights to Africa. Maybe she should follow Paul's example—go help people in another part of the world and put an ocean between her and her parents.

Instead, she checked email to see if her job search had netted any new responses, then fired off a quick note to Kyle.

Subject: Our Mother Is Off The Rails
Annabel must REALLY love you to put up with Mom. Hope you know what a lucky guy you are. See you in December—and not a single day sooner! S.

Her brother never replied to any of her messages. No doubt he was too busy plotting corporate takeovers.

She started to close her email, but her gaze lingered on a name in her inbox. Daniel Baron. He'd written to her two days ago, but she still hadn't decided whether to act on the information he'd passed along.

Daniel was a former bull rider and past patient. She'd reached out to him last week when it became clear she needed more references. Not only had Daniel been happy to hear from her and more than willing to endorse her, he'd learned of an unusual job posting through a friend of a friend. He'd told her about a family in Cupid's Bow, Texas. She'd almost rolled her eyes at the town name, but she supposed it was no quirkier than Gun Barrel City, Texas. Or Ding Dong, Texas.

According to Daniel, the teenage daughter of the family had been in an accident, and the Rosses were looking for someone to live on the ranch and work with the kid for about a month. A ranch...where there were horses. She shuddered.

I am not a small-town person. But she prided herself on being tough when she needed to be, and it wouldn't be a long-term situation. With a guaranteed roof over her head, she would have time to investigate other opportunities. Three and a half weeks could make the difference between finding a position where she truly fit and simply accepting a paycheck so she could continue indulging in luxuries like food and water.

After she'd first read Daniel's email, she'd looked up Cupid's Bow online. It was tiny. Her parents' country club probably had a higher population—ironic, since the club worked at actively excluding people. Sierra doubted there were any symphony performances or science museums in Cupid's Bow. But worse than a potential dearth of culture or even the presence of horses was the possibility of nosy neighbors. Weren't people in close-knit communities subject to scrutiny and gossip? Given her parents' wealth and high social standing, Sierra had spent her teen years feeling conspicuously visible. People who'd never even met her had opinions about who she was and who they thought she should be. She detested feeling as if she had to answer anyone.

All right then, don't *call the Rosses. Stay here and get a job waitressing. With your gracious nature, you're sure to make enough tips to pay off those student loans.*

Lord. No wonder she couldn't get a job—she even gave herself attitude.

Decision made, she pulled her phone from her pocket before she could change her mind. As she dialed, she reminded herself there was no guarantee the Rosses would hire her. If they did, she'd survive roughing it in Cupid's Bow one day at a time. How many times had she lectured patients on the necessity of breaking down tasks into less intimidating chunks?

"Quit looking at it as months of PT," she'd tell them. *"Just get through each set of exercises, one day at a time. This first*

set's only ten minutes. It may be uncomfortable, but you can handle ten measly minutes. Don't wuss out on me now..."

She cajoled, encouraged and berated people into cooperating. The least she could do was take her own advice.

The phone rang, and she inhaled deeply. After a couple more rings, she began mentally rehearsing the message she would leave on the voice mail. But then a man answered.

"Hello?" The irritation in his deep voice made the word less a greeting and more a challenge.

She hesitated, but for only half a second. Tentativeness wasn't in her nature. "May I speak with Jarrett Ross?"

"You got him. But if you're selling something—"

"Only my professional services." Someone should tell Mr. Ross that anyone who placed a Help Wanted ad should curb his hostility; it made people not want to help. "My name is Sierra Bailey. I'm a physical therapist, and Daniel Baron, one of my former clients, gave me this number. He mentioned your family is looking for someone with PT experience."

"Oh! Yes. God, yes. Sorry, you just caught me at a bad time. Of course, that describes all of the time lately, but— Sorry," he repeated. "I wasn't expecting applicants to call me. Most of them have been phoning my mother."

"Ah. You're not the girl's father?" Daniel had given her a name and a number. He hadn't outlined the family tree.

"Definitely not. I'm Vicki's older brother. But I might as well talk to you. After all, you and I would be the ones living together while my parents are away."

Living together. The words gave her an odd jolt. Although Paul had spent enough nights at her place to warrant his own dresser drawer and a sliver of counter space in the bathroom, she'd never technically lived with a man. *You wouldn't be living with this one, either.* Not in any personal way.

"My parents' trip is why we're seeking the extra help with Vicki," he continued. "Not only could she benefit from physical therapy here at the house, we could use someone to keep her company while I'm working the ranch. If she needs something, I'm not readily accessible on the back forty. What was your name again?"

"Sierra. Sierra Bailey."

"And Daniel Baron gave you my number? He's a good guy. I used to compete against him and his brothers all the time."

"Ah. So you're a rodeo rider." She hadn't meant to sound judgmental. It just wasn't a lifestyle she could wrap her head around. She worked with so many people who were injured through no fault of their own that it was hard to understand anyone deliberately pursuing such a potentially dangerous career.

"I was," he said tightly, "but not anymore. I'm committed to the ranch. And to Vicki's recovery."

The patient. Here was comfortable ground. In her other interviews, she'd had to talk about herself, which made her prickly. It was easier to sound competent and professional while discussing the person she'd be treating.

She asked about the girl's age—nineteen was older than she'd expected—and injuries. There was a pause before Jarrett began describing them. When he started talking again, the words came in an uncomfortable rush, as if he wanted to get through the list as quickly as possible. His younger sister was healing from several injuries, including a broken wrist, but the major issue was that her pelvis had been crushed in the accident.

Sierra winced. It was the kind of pity she'd never show in front of a patient because pity made a person feel weak. But the young woman had a rough time ahead of her.

"You obviously know your field well," Jarrett said after they'd spent a few minutes discussing medical specifics. Yet he sounded more grim than impressed. Wasn't her expertise a *good* thing? "To tell you the truth, Ms. Bailey, you may be overqualified. We were thinking more in terms of a semiretired therapist or a home health care assistant who might not mind some light housekeeping and making sure Vicki gets dinner if

I'm working past sundown. I don't know if Daniel mentioned salary, but—"

"He did." Calling that sum a salary was a generous overstatement. "It's below what I would normally consider, but honestly, I'm taking some time off to decide between several future options." Yeah, like whether to waitress at a steak house or bartend at a West End nightclub. "This gives me time to carefully evaluate my choices." *Well done, Bailey.* She'd managed to make herself sound methodical, not desperate.

"So you're all right with our terms?"

"Well, I won't argue if you decide after a week that I deserve a raise, but what you're offering is at least worth my driving to Cupid's Bow for a face-to-face meeting."

"That's fantastic." It was the happiest he'd sounded during their entire conversation, and it highlighted how dour his mood had been—from his tense tone when he'd answered to his obvious discomfort discussing his sister's accident to his doubt Sierra would deem the job worth it. Jarrett Ross clearly wasn't the president of the Cupid's Bow Optimists Club. "I just wish my parents hadn't already booked their flight. They're leaving in two days, so unless you can be here tomorrow, they won't be available to sit in on the interview."

"Sorry, tomorrow's full." Since she hadn't known where and when she'd be working again, she'd scheduled a number of personal appointments, taking advantage of the time left before her health and dental insurance ran out. "I can manage the next day, though."

They agreed on a time, and he asked for her email address so he could send her directions. "GPS or internet maps will get you most of the way, but we're a bit off the beaten path."

Which didn't bolster her enthusiasm for making a temporary home in Cupid's Bow.

Then again, if the town could evade the reach of an orbiting satellite system, she should easily be outside the meddling reach of Muriel Bailey. Ever since Sierra's last relationship ended, her mother, undaunted by living three and a half hours away, had tried arranging meetings between Sierra and Dallas's most eligible bachelors. The good news about a town the size of Cupid's Bow was that there couldn't be many men who met her mother's exacting standards.

So when she ended her call with Jarrett by saying "I look forward to meeting you," she very nearly meant it.

Chapter Three

"Knock, knock," Jarrett said tentatively, unsure of his welcome as he stood in the doorway of his sister's room. His voice seemed to echo unnaturally. The house had been damned quiet in the hours since their parents had left at the crack of dawn. According to his mother, Vicki had barely said a word when they came into her room to exchange goodbyes. Did she feel like the Rosses were abandoning her?

His mother was excited that Jarrett was interviewing another candidate this afternoon. Until Sierra had called, the family had decided to offer the position to local retired nurse Lucy Aldridge, a grandmother of five. Lucy was kind, if a bit absent-minded, but she was also more than three times Vicki's age. Anne Ross had worried Vicki wouldn't relate to her. Jarrett didn't know specifically how old Sierra Bailey was, but judging from the credentials she'd emailed, she'd been out of med school for only a couple of years. And she certainly hadn't sounded like a woman approaching seventy. When they'd spoken, Sierra had sounded... *Feisty* was the word that sprang to mind.

"Did you need something?" Vicki asked, her voice empty of inflection. Her wheelchair was pulled up to her desk, and he couldn't tell if she was looking at her laptop or simply staring out the window. This used to be a guest suite, but since it was on the first floor, they'd relocated Vicki after the accident. All the essentials were here, but she'd said not to bother with miscellaneous belongings, like the posters that hung on her walls upstairs. Or the gleaming softball trophies that sent blades of guilt through him whenever he saw them.

Her blond hair hung crookedly in a limp ponytail. She was able to shower by herself in the remodeled bathroom, but she only bothered to brush her hair when her mother said something about it. And the last time she'd applied makeup was when her boyfriend, Aaron, had visited weeks ago.

"I just wanted to remind you that Sierra should be here in an hour or so." When Vicki didn't respond, he prompted, "Sierra Bailey, the potential therapist. I thought you might like to meet her."

She hadn't sat in on any of the interviews, dismissing it as unnecessary. All of the candidates had been local, which meant she'd met them all at least in passing. Anne hadn't pushed the issue, since she'd already had her hands full convincing Gavin to leave the ranch. Jarrett was surprised by his sister's apathy. Vicki had always been opinionated. Surely she wanted to have a say in who was chosen to be her companion?

"I'll pass," she said. "I was about to take a nap. I'm exhausted."

From all the energy it took to stare out the window? *Don't be an ass. You don't know anything about the effort it takes her to perform daily tasks you take for granted.* Besides, fatigue wasn't always physical.

He attempted a compromise. "If she seems like a good fit for the job, do you want me to wake you up before she leaves? Then you could—"

"No." She shot a glance over her shoulder. It was jarring how her dark eyes flashed with so much emotion while her clipped words held none at all. "Makes no difference to me who pushes my wheelchair."

Nobody pushed the chair. They'd rented an electric one to make her as self-sufficient as possible. "Vicki—"

"I don't care who you hire, just make it clear she's not my babysitter. And anytime Aaron visits, we want our privacy."

He clenched his jaw, conflicted about his little sister's "alone time" with her boyfriend. *Hypocrite. Like* you *were celibate at nineteen?* Hell no. He'd always been ready and willing to hit the sheets with a pretty lady—a character trait he deeply regretted. If he'd had any self-discipline, Vicki wouldn't be in the wheelchair. Or in this room. She'd be at college with Aaron and her friends.

"Close the door on your way out," she said woodenly.

"Okay." As conversations went, he couldn't call this one a rousing success. On the other hand, it was the most sentences she'd spoken to him at one time all month. Maybe his mother was right about his parents' trip forcing Vicki to deal with him. Jarrett just wished his sister would let loose and scream at him. Call him an irresponsible ass. Maybe even hurl something at him with that pitcher's arm of hers. She'd broken her left wrist, but her right was undamaged.

He went to the kitchen, where he pulled a casserole from the freezer for its two hours in the oven and brewed iced tea for his expected guest. He'd briefly spoken to Daniel Baron this week about Sierra. The man sang her praises. Daniel had worked with her after the bull-riding injury that made him quit rodeo for good, not that he sounded disappointed about his new lifestyle. He was happily married in San Antonio with twin toddlers. If Sierra was under fifty and even half as promising as Daniel made her sound, she had a job.

While he waited for Sierra to arrive, Jarrett caught up on emails and the paperwork that accumulated while he spent most of his time outside. In addition to taking care of the cattle and preparing to plant the winter crops, he generated income by offering riding lessons and equine therapy. He was happier doing physical work than crunching numbers, but it was on his shoulders to make sure nothing fell through the cracks while his father recuperated.

He'd just finished entering some figures in the banking spreadsheet when the doorbell rang. If either the golden retriever or shepherd-Lab mix had been close to the house, he would have heard barking long before the visitor reached the front porch, but in pretty weather, the dogs enjoyed the wide-open spaces of ranch life.

In case his sister had been genuine about needing sleep, he hurried to the door to make sure Sierra didn't ring the bell a second time. Mentally crossing his fingers that the woman on the other side was everything Daniel said, he swung the door open.

He felt his features freeze midsmile. Shock made it momentarily difficult to form words, even one as basic as *hello.* He'd been hoping for younger than fifty, but the stunning redhead appeared to be in her twenties. And, although his mama would smack him upside the head for the stereotype, she looked more like a lingerie model than a med school graduate.

Well, technically, she was probably too short to be a model, but that body... "Sierra Bailey?" he asked, half hoping she wasn't.

She nodded. "Jarrett Ross?"

"One and the same." As he ushered her inside, he tried to recover his composure. The view from behind wasn't helping. Her slim-fitting suit skirt fell just below her knees, modestly professional, but the material lovingly cupped the flare of her hips and shapely butt.

Squeezing his eyes shut, he spared a dark thought for Daniel Baron. His friend should have warned Jarrett what to expect. Daniel was so head over heels in love with his wife, Nicole, that other women probably paled in comparison, but the man wasn't blind.

The irony would have been laughable if Jarrett's sense of

humor weren't dormant. He hadn't had sex in months. He'd ignored flirty texts and used the isolation of the ranch to avoid temptation, but that hadn't been penance enough. Karma had sent him a gorgeous woman whose green eyes flashed intelligence and whose curves would make a centerfold envious. His past self would have found sleeping down the hall from her a tantalizing prospect.

Hell, the old Jarrett would already be working to seduce her. But he was a recovering ladies' man and, potentially, her employer. *You will not so much as look at Sierra Bailey.*

Too late.

IT WAS TOO soon to tell whether this interview would be an improvement over her others, but, so far, it was certainly *weirder.* Sierra had entered the house ready to apologize for being late. She'd got lost twice, not that she'd been able to call Jarrett Ross and tell him because she'd apparently been driving through a cellular dead zone. She'd finally happened across a tiny gas station where a friendly guy with elaborate tattoos gave her directions to the Twisted R.

She knew it was bad form to show up tardy to an interview, but before she'd had a chance to explain, Jarrett had suddenly declared, "Tea!" the way a scientist might shout "Eureka!" Then he'd pointed her into a wood-paneled study and bolted in the opposite direction. Presumably, to fetch tea.

Her first impression of the rancher was that he was tall— although, from her perspective, lots of people were. More specifically, he was hot. His dark hair, threaded with a few sun-streaked threads of gold, contrasted dramatically with pale silvery eyes. He had a chiseled jaw and defined cheekbones.

And abs worthy of inspiring legend.

That highly unprofessional observation struck as she caught sight of a framed picture among the dozen or so that hung on the far wall behind a massive desk. In the photo, a shirtless Jarrett stood on the shore of a river, displaying a fish he'd caught. She was already moving in for a closer look before she realized what she was doing, as if mindlessly drawn in by a tractor beam. *Tractor abs.* Plus, sculpted shoulders and arms that—

Bailey! What the hell happened to being professional?

Right.

It was ironic that she'd been fired over Lloyd Carson, given that she'd never entertained a single thought about him half as improper as what she'd just been feeling for Jarrett Ross. *Get your act together.* She moved on from the shirtless picture to the other shots decorating the wall. Several had been taken at rodeos, and while she'd never understand bronc-riding as a career choice, she had to marvel at the raw grace displayed in one action shot. Repressing the memory of her own horrific fall from a horse, she wondered how Jarrett managed to stay in the saddle. For that matter, how was the black cowboy hat staying on his head?

Next to that photo was a snapshot taken right here on the house's front porch. Jarrett's arm was casually draped around a blonde girl's shoulders. Sierra was willing to bet money that the young woman was his sister, Vicki. Their coloring was reversed—the girl had light hair and brown eyes—but the similarity of their features was unmistakable. As was the affection between them.

Sierra glanced from Vicki's face to Jarrett's. His expression was so self-assured. He was grinning as though he didn't have a care in the world, and his eyes sparkled with mischief and confidence—a far cry from the somber man who'd opened the door to her.

She supposed no one chose to display family photos where the subject was scowling or looked troubled, but his image was the same in every picture—the self-satisfied lord of all he surveyed. Was it Vicki's accident that had changed him? Sierra knew a lot of siblings were closer than she was to her own brothers. Jarrett had been notably tense while detailing his sister's injuries over the phone, as if he felt her pain.

Vicki may be the one in the wheelchair, but apparently she wasn't the only one who needed to heal.

Chapter Four

Sierra shifted her position in the leather chair and sipped her sweet tea, waiting for Jarrett to say something. They'd reached the end of his list of questions, and she assumed he was mulling over her responses. He hadn't said anything in several seconds. He'd been terse throughout the conversation, lending credence to the strong, silent cowboy image, but, on the bright side, he hadn't mentioned her family connections or leered at her. He'd barely looked at her at all, either focusing on the pad of paper where he was jotting notes or staring at some point just over her shoulder.

The interview had reached its logical conclusion. All that was left was for her to talk to the patient and assess for herself the work that needed to be done. Jarrett had handed her a folder of medical records after joining her in the study with two glasses of iced tea, but X-rays told only part of the story.

Sierra set her glass on the desk and cleared her throat. "When can I meet Vicki?"

His head jerked up, his eyes almost meeting hers before he resumed that unfocused gaze into the beyond. "Oh, uh, that won't be necessary. She's sleeping now and authorized me to make the decision on her behalf. And I'm happy to say, the job is yours. If you want it."

Fantastic. She was employed again—by a laconic cowboy who lived at the butt-end of nowhere and kept staring eerily into space as if he were about to have a psychic vision. "Thank you for the offer. I'll be able to give you my answer after I meet your sister."

He frowned. "I told you, she's sleeping."

She rose from her chair, eager to escape the awkward confines of the study. "So we'll need to wake her up." Every patient case she'd ever worked had started with an evaluation. And this wasn't just any case—she'd be living with these people! No way was she packing her bags and relocating before meeting both of her new roommates.

Jarrett's gaze locked with hers, and the sudden connection was like an electric current that ran all the way down to her toes. The masculine energy in his rigid body language caused a wholly inappropriate tingly sensation. She could almost understand how a stupid cliché like "you're beautiful when you're angry" had originated.

"Vicki expressly asked not to be disturbed," he said, his sharp tone matching the metallic glint in his eyes.

Sierra lifted her chin, determined to make him see reason. "Is she ill?" If the girl was sick, then Sierra would come back another day to meet her—especially if Vicki was contagious. Otherwise…

"You mean like with a cold or something? No. But, as a professional, you must know that people recuperating from such serious injuries need plenty of bed rest and—"

"It's been a couple of months since her accident. Too much bed rest leads to atrophy. I've been here over an hour," she said with a glance at her watch. "That's adequate for a nap. Sleeping the day away can also be a sign of depression. Part of my job will be keeping Vicki engaged, whether she likes it or not."

"You mean bullying her?" he asked. The way he shot to his feet, as if preparing to physically protect his sister, might have been endearing under other circumstances.

"I wouldn't say 'bullying.'" *She* might not put it that way... but a few of her patients had. Bully. Drill sergeant. Hard-ass. Daniel Baron, sweating through a session with his handsome features contorted into a grimace, had once called her a demon tyrant with no soul. But she was pretty sure he'd meant it as a compliment.

"Look, I'm good at what I do," she asserted. "If you want me to take this job, you have to trust me."

Nice going, Bailey. Three minutes after he offers you the position and you're already giving ultimatums. What happened to demure and diplomatic and all that other crap?

He clenched his jaw, and she wondered uneasily if he would throw her out. Then he shoved a hand through his hair, the anger in his expression fading. "She's my responsibility." It didn't sound like a protest, more like...a plea.

Her heart twisted at the jagged vulnerability in his voice. She added "lack of professional detachment" to her list of today's sins.

Jarrett sighed, rounding the desk toward her. "Come on. Let's get this over with."

LAST SPRING, JARRETT had subdued a towering drunk intent on a bar fight until Sheriff Trent and Deputy Thomas could get there. During the summer, he'd calmly faced an angry bull and the occasional venomous copperhead. But women? They were scary.

Caught between Vicki's inevitable displeasure and Sierra's implacable resolve, he held his breath and knocked on the closed bedroom door. Normally, he did just fine with ladies, but now he was trapped in a house with two females he couldn't charm. His sister was immune, and flirting with an employee was unethical.

A rebellious part of his brain that didn't care about ethics wondered, if he *were* free to flirt with Sierra, how would she respond?

She was tough, with an unyielding force of will, hardly a woman who batted her lashes and giggled when a guy looked in her direction. Yet there'd been a sizzling moment in the study when their eyes met and— He broke off the thought. What had happened to not allowing himself to lust after the therapist?

Annoyed at his lack of discipline, he banged his fist against the door a bit harder this time. Still no response.

"She's not answering." From behind him, Sierra stated the obvious. Her palpable impatience was a vibration in the air. He could just imagine the nuclear confrontation when her hard-headed personality clashed with his sister's. Was it a mistake to hire the redhead instead of sweet-natured Lucy Aldridge, who would affectionately fuss over Vicki as if she were an honor-ary grandchild?

"We should go in," she urged.

Nearly a month of this woman bossing him around? Jarrett ground his teeth. "I'm not in the habit of invading her privacy."

Sierra's hand curved over his shoulder, surprising him, and when he turned to meet her gaze, he saw genuine concern. "You'd be checking to make sure she's okay. The way you've described her state of mind…"

He turned the knob and shoved the door open a few inches. "Vicki?"

She was lying on her back with her eyes closed, but her fea-tures were creased with aggravation. "I'm *trying* to sleep. Go away."

Sierra squeezed past him into the room. "Since you're awake, I was hoping we could talk."

At the unfamiliar voice, Vicki opened her eyes. "Now's not a good time." She glared past the redhead at her brother. "I'd appreciate you not letting strangers into my room."

"I—"

"Not a stranger for long," Sierra interrupted cheerfully. "I'm your new physical therapist. Sierra Bailey. Pleased to meet you."

Jarrett wasn't sure when she'd officially accepted the job, but he didn't undermine her authority by asking the question out loud.

Sierra took a step closer to the bed, nodding toward the brace that covered most of Vicki's forearm. "Are you regularly seeing a therapist about your wrist?"

Vicki grunted a sound that was more or less agreement.

"How much have you been working at home?" Sierra asked, switching to a question that required a more specific answer.

"When I can. It hurts."

"The more you build your strength—within medically approved parameters, of course—the faster you'll heal. What exercises have you been doing?"

"You're the one who needs this job," Vicki snapped. "Shouldn't *I* be doing the interrogating?"

Folding his arms across his chest, Jarrett waited to see how Sierra dealt with his sister's uncooperative attitude. He knew from their exchange back in his dad's study that the redhead had a temper.

Yet Sierra's tone was only one of mild reproach when she said, "I didn't realize you had any questions for me. According to your brother, you willingly forfeited any say in the decision-making process." She paused. "But if there's something you'd like to ask, fire away."

"Have you even been a therapist long enough to know what you're doing?" Vicki raked her over with an expression that made it clear she wasn't impressed with what she saw. "You barely look old enough to buy beer."

Despite the younger woman's sneering, Sierra smiled broadly. "Twenty-seven in November. But if you keep up the flattery, I might make it the whole time I'm here without trying to smother you."

Jarrett bit the inside of his cheek to keep from laughing. Technically speaking, it was poor bedside manner to threaten one's patients. But Vicki's outraged expression was downright encouraging. It reminded him of fights they'd had in years past, when she'd been whole and spirited. He'd take her anger any day of the week over the hollow-eyed stare she'd developed.

Although he'd wanted to gauge how the two females inter-
acted without his interference, now he spoke up on Sierra's behalf, defending his hiring decision. "Ms. Bailey's well qualified
for her job—educated and experienced. According to Daniel
Baron, she's one of the best in the state of Texas."

Sierra glanced back, looking surprised by the endorsement.
The smile she flashed him decimated his vow not to notice how
attractive she was.

"Thank you. But it's silly to call me Ms. Bailey. We should
be on a first-name basis since we'll be living together. Who
knows—by this time next month, we'll probably all have nick-
names for each other."

"I have a few ideas," Vicki muttered.

"So do I. As for my qualifications, I graduated college early
and finished my med school program at the top of the class.
Before that, I logged hundreds of volunteer hours in clinics and
my high school athletic department, learning from the train-
ers. I've been learning everything I can about physical therapy
since a PT helped me after I fractured my spine. You're not the
only one held together with screws and plates," she added softly.

Jarrett was caught off guard by this revelation. During their
conversations on the phone and in the study, she'd never volunteered why she'd chosen the field. He hadn't thought to ask.
With the knowledge that they'd faced similar obstacles, maybe
Vicki would—

"We're not gonna be besties just because we've both had
surgery," his sister said.

"Definitely not," Sierra agreed. "I don't do 'bonding.'"

Oddly, the disdainful words seemed to mollify his sister.

Vicki was quiet for a long moment. "You've only asked me
about my wrist. Why not the big thing?"

"You mean the fact that you're in a wheelchair? Don't let
that loom large in your mind as The Big Thing. In principle,
the broken pelvis is just like the broken wrist. Both are physi-

cal challenges you can overcome with time to heal and lots of hard work. The question is, are you willing to do the work?"

When Vicki slowly nodded, something like hope shining in her dark eyes, Jarrett knew he owed Daniel Baron a debt of gratitude. Sierra Bailey was definitely the right woman for the job.

DINNER THAT NIGHT was quiet, and as he washed off the plates, Jarrett found himself anxiously awaiting Sierra's return in two days. He'd always loved the spacious ranch house, but with just him and his sullen sister, the empty space around them magnified the silence. That wouldn't be the case when Sierra moved in. Despite being a petite woman, she somehow filled an entire room with her energy.

Jarrett had invited her to stay for supper after her conversation with Vicki, but she'd insisted she needed to get going as soon as possible.

"The sun's setting earlier every day," she'd pointed out, "and I need to get at least somewhere *close* to civilization before it's completely dark. If I never return, it's because I got lost on one of your meandering, quaintly unmarked roads. Seriously, is there like a town ordinance against signs?"

In the short time she'd been at the ranch, she'd made several comments suggesting Cupid's Bow was not her ideal location. Thank God she'd agreed to take the position anyway. He glanced to where Vicki sat at the table, trying to touch her thumb to her finger. It was one of the exercises Sierra had insisted Vicki do.

"You follow this regimen exactly until I get back," Sierra had said, handing over a sheet of paper. "Or incur my wrath."

Vicki had rolled her eyes. "You really scare me, shorty."

Was it wishful thinking on Jarrett's part or had there *almost* been a smile in her voice? Even though parts of his sister's encounter with Sierra had been contentious, it was still the most animated he'd seen her in weeks—not counting the infrequent times her doofus boyfriend bothered to phone.

Jarrett had no real reason to dislike Aaron, but seeing how

much those short conversations meant to his sister, he resented that the guy couldn't make time in his busy college schedule to call more often. *Or maybe Aaron's inattention makes you feel guilty because you know damn well there are women who probably expected a call from* you *that never came.*

He balled up the dish towel and threw it on the counter. "You ready to try that rice thing?" Sierra had left instructions for Jarrett to fill a bucket with dry rice and for Vicki to place her hand inside and try to rotate it. The rice would provide resistance.

The physical therapist had arched an eyebrow at Vicki. "Resistance is right up your alley, yeah?"

Jarrett went into the walk-in pantry for a bag of rice without waiting for his sister's answer—these days, he couldn't always count on her to give him one. When he joined her at the table, she was still doing the first set of exercises, wincing in visible pain. He desperately wanted to say something helpful, but what? The closest he could come to empathizing with what she was going through were the many bruises and sore muscles that came with riding rodeo. He'd voluntarily endured those because he liked to win. There was nothing voluntary about her suffering.

As she slid her left hand into the bucket, he tried to sound encouraging. "Sierra is highly recommended. Follow her advice, and I'm sure all of this will get easier." Eventually.

Beads of sweat dotted Vicki's forehead as she attempted to turn her wrist. "She's pretty, too. Like, obnoxiously pretty." She pinned him with her gaze. "Don't you think so?"

The question felt like a trap. Saying he hadn't noticed Sierra's appearance would be a ridiculous lie and an insult to his sister's intelligence. But survival instincts warned that admitting Sierra was beautiful would only increase the household tension. "I'm not sure what 'obnoxiously pretty' means."

"Well, she's way more fun for a guy to look at than old Lucy Aldridge."

The realization of what she was suggesting bit into him like barbwire through the skin. Shame bubbled to the surface instead of blood. His sister truly believed he was so selfish that he would hire the woman in charge of her well-being based on sex appeal? *Of course she does.* He had a track record of putting pleasure before loved ones or responsibility.

He clenched his hands into fists, and the reflexive action only heightened his guilt. He could move all ten of his fingers with no effort at all, while Vicki had gone pale in her wheelchair from trying to stir around grains of rice.

"Vic, I would have hired a wart-covered, hunchbacked troll if I thought she could get you better faster. Maybe some guys would find Sierra Bailey 'fun to look at,' but I won't be looking at her. I'll be working the ranch and staying out of her way so she can focus on you. Your recovery is all that matters to me."

She cast him a brief, skeptical glance before ducking her gaze without comment. The little sister who'd once idolized him no longer trusted him.

Why should she? He'd given her reason to doubt. *I know I let you down, Vic, but I swear it won't happen again.*

Chapter Five

Even though she'd packed up her car with luggage and turned off all her utilities, accepting the job with the Rosses didn't feel real until Sierra drove past the Welcome to Cupid's Bow sign on Saturday. *Sure, the town welcomes you—then they hide all the other road signs so you can never find your way back out.* Cupid's Bow, Texas. Come for the home cooking, stay for…ever.

On the phone last night, Muriel had asked, "Are you sure about this, darling? Living in some backwater town for a month when you could be at home with your loving family?"

If Sierra hadn't already been convinced that she should take the job, that would have done the trick.

Now, alone in the car, she reiterated what she'd said to her mother. "This is where I need to be right now." So why the nervous butterflies in her stomach? Anxiety that Vicki Ross would be a difficult patient?

No way. I am Sierra Bailey, and I eat difficulty for breakfast. I pour it into my coffee to give it that extra kick.

And yet…tummy flutters. She refused to even consider that they might be a reaction to seeing Jarrett Ross again. Sure, the rancher was good-looking, but she'd spent many hands-on hours working with hot athletes. She was *not* jittery about moving in with a tall, gray-eyed cowboy. The more likely explanation for her apprehensive stomach was that breakfast hadn't agreed with her.

There was a grocery store up ahead. She could stop for antacids and other essentials she'd want to have on hand for the next few weeks. Plus, Jarrett had mentioned that grocery shopping and meal preparation would be part of her job. Might as well investigate the supermarket's selection and get her bearings.

Fifteen minutes later, she'd discovered that the local produce prices were fantastic and that she didn't own enough denim to fit in around Cupid's Bow. The two pairs of jeans she did own were in a suitcase in her car; she felt conspicuous in her circle skirt, swirled with autumn colors, and green chenille V-neck sweater. The only people she'd seen who weren't wearing jeans either wore denim shorts or overalls.

Rounding an endcap, she pushed the cart into the pharmaceutical section, gratified to spot a blonde woman, her hair pulled back in a loose French braid, wearing a sundress not made of denim. The bright geometric print and pattern of straps holding the bodice in place made the outfit fashionable without looking ostentatious.

"Love your dress," she said impulsively.

Turning from the shelf of vitamins she'd been contemplating, the woman flashed her a bright smile. "Thank you. All that jazz."

"I… Pardon?"

"The boutique just off of town square," the woman clarified. "All That Jazz. Run by Jasmine Tucker?" She grinned at Sierra's blank expression. "You must not be from around here."

At that moment, a teenage boy with a little girl in tow barreled toward them. They weren't running, exactly, just moving at the uninhibited speed of childhood. "Mom! They didn't have the brand you normally get," the boy announced, skidding to a stop by his mother's cart. "Will one of these work?" He held up two different boxes of cake mix.

Before the woman could answer, the little girl in the unicorn T-shirt tossed a box of crayons into the cart. "I need these."

"Doubtful," the boy scoffed. "You own more crayons than anyone else in North America, Aly."

"These are *scented*. I don't have scented." At Sierra's chuckle, the girl looked up, registering her presence for the first time. "Hey, we don't know you!"

Sierra shook her head. "Nope. Today's my very first day in town."

"Welcome to Cupid's Bow," the blonde said. "I'm Kate Sullivan. This is my son, Luke, and my future stepdaughter Alyssa."

"She's marrying my daddy!" From the huge smile on Alyssa's face, she was obviously excited about the upcoming nuptials. "Me and my sister get to be flower girls, and we're gonna wear poofy dresses that—"

"How about you go with Luke and return the cake mix we don't need?" Kate interrupted, taking one of the boxes from her son's hand. "And don't run, okay?"

"Okay," the kids chorused without looking back at her.

"And they're off," Kate said with an affectionate sigh. "I came to the vitamin section to get more gummies for the girls, but, honestly, maybe I should be looking for a supplement for *me* so I can keep up with all of them. Let's try this again, with fewer interruptions. I'm Kate Sullivan." She extended a hand. "Nice to meet you."

"Sierra Bailey," she said as they shook hands.

"I'm so delighted you're moving here." Kate grinned. "With you around, people will have to stop referring to me as 'the new woman in Cupid's Bow.' It's been months!"

"Happy to help," Sierra said, "but I'm not moving here, exactly, just working for a few weeks at the Twisted R." Assuming she could successfully locate the ranch again.

"Oh!" A female voice from the other side of the shelf cut into their conversation and an elderly lady peeked over the top, only her tightly rolled white curls and gold spectacles visible. "Are you working with that poor Victoria Ross? Such a tragedy what happened to her. Hello, Kate, dear."

"Hello, Miss Alma. This is Sierra Bailey."

"I heard. My new hearing aids are a miracle. I hope you enjoy your stay here in Cupid's Bow, Sierra. You tell poor Vicki that the whole town's pulling for her." She clucked her tongue. "Absolute tragedy." A minute later, she pushed her cart away and disappeared down the bread aisle.

Kate smiled after her. "Not everyone is as active an eavesdropper as Miss Alma—she's almost ninety and says living here almost a century gives her a vested interest in local events—but this is a small town. We all heard about Vicki's accident. The Ross family hasn't been the same since."

"I haven't met her parents." She only knew they were traveling for "health reasons." "Just Vicki and her older brother."

"Jarrett. A real charmer, that one."

"He's…attractive," Sierra said neutrally. "But charming? For the first hour of my interview, he read questions verbatim off a legal pad and barely said anything else. I can count on one hand the number of times he even looked up at me."

The corners of Kate's mouth turned down, and sympathy filled her amber eyes. "After his dad's heart attack, I took some meals to the family. Jarrett was so shell-shocked, not himself at all. I haven't seen him recently, but I was hoping that with his father and Vicki both doing better… Well. I suppose we all cope in our own time, don't we?"

Sierra nodded. She'd witnessed patients and their families handle crisis in dozens of ways. Sometimes, catastrophes brought people together; other times it drove a wedge between them. There were patients who spiraled into a dark place and needed help finding their way back; others rebounded with astonishing resiliency.

Kate gave a small shake of her head, as if brushing away her moment of melancholy. "I live near the Twisted R—at least, I do until my wedding. My fiancé, Cole, and I are having a house built that won't be ready for months. Meanwhile, Luke and I are staying on my grandmother's farm, which is out the same direction as the Ross place. If you ever need anything, we're much closer than town. I'll give you my number. Maybe we can get together if you have an afternoon off."

"Thank you." Given Vicki Ross's surly attitude, Sierra might need to occasionally escape the ranch to keep her sanity intact. "I'd love to visit that boutique you were telling me about."

They had just finished exchanging cell-phone numbers when the two kids returned.

"Sorry we took so long," Luke said, jamming his hands in the pockets of his jeans. "I—"

"He was talking to a *girrrlll*," Aly reported, making the last word three syllables.

He shot her a sidelong glare. "I ran into a classmate—"

"A girl classmate!"

"—who had questions about Friday's math assignment."

"No problem," Kate said. "Sierra and I were busy chatting, too. But I guess we should dash if I'm going to get these groceries to Cole's house for lunch. He and Mandy are probably starving. Call me soon, Sierra!"

"Will do."

As she finished her own grocery shopping, Sierra felt a little smug. She'd been told more than once that she didn't play well with others and that some people mistook her independent nature for aloofness. Yet she hadn't been in town an hour, and already she'd made her first friend.

Maybe Cupid's Bow wouldn't be so bad after all.

JUST WHEN SIERRA was starting to think she'd driven too far, she spotted the intersection where she needed to turn for the Twisted R. On her first trip out to the ranch, she'd been irritable because she was late for her interview. This time around, she could appreciate the scenery more.

The wide-open space was both tranquil and somehow humbling. Picturesque pastures dotted with clusters of Queen Anne's lace and mesquite trees framed the road, and she'd never seen a clearer blue sky than the one overhead. A deer lifted its head from the plants it was lazily munching to watch her pass, and she half expected that if she glanced in her rearview mirror she'd find animated woodland creatures singing some kind of welcome song behind her car.

It was all very bucolic. But she still couldn't imagine living in a place where the closest store was half an hour away. *The land that delivery food forgot.*

She turned left onto a winding road barely wide enough for two vehicles to pass each other and saw the sprawling white house atop the hill ahead. She liked the Rosses' place—it wasn't as linear and pristine as her parents' three-story mansion with its pretentious columns in the front and a detached garage in the back. Jarrett's home was endearingly lopsided, with one corner that seemed out of proportion to the rest of the house— probably a room that had been added on long after the place was originally built. The roof was all crazy angles, hinting at slanted ceilings and interesting attic space. A carport was linked to one side of the house, a screened deck jutted out in the back and there was a generous porch that began within a foot of the front door and wrapped around the opposite corner of the house.

A moment later, she passed beneath the Twisted R sign, her car jostling over the metal grid that kept cattle from wandering out through the entryway between fences. By the time she parked, two dogs had come to greet her. A golden retriever gave an amiable woof as Sierra opened her door; a slightly smaller dog hung back a few feet. It was mostly black with gold paws and a white throat.

"They're friendly," Jarrett called from the porch steps. "But they probably have muddy paws, so if Sunshine looks like she's about to jump on you, tell her no. She'll listen—she just likes to test boundaries."

Sierra grinned down at the retriever, scratching behind her

ears. "Fellow boundary-pusher? You and I should get along just fine." She looked up to see Jarrett closing the distance between them with rangy strides. The lighter streaks in his dark hair gleamed in the sun, and the way his jeans fit made her take back any snarky thoughts she'd had about denim.

She spun on her heel toward the back of her car, seizing the distraction of luggage to keep herself from staring at her new boss.

"Can I give you a hand?" he asked from right beside her. Since he was already reaching into the car trunk, the question seemed rhetorical.

She blinked up at him. "You move deceptively fast."

"Long legs." He hefted a suitcase. "We'd just finished lunch when I heard the dogs barking. Have you eaten?"

"I'm good, thanks." She didn't share that her stomach was twisted in knots. Despite the bravado-filled pep talks she'd given herself during the drive, now that she was here, she acknowledged that moving in—even temporarily—was unnerving. She was used to having sole dominion over things like the television remote and the thermostat. Sharing a living space would be an adjustment, no matter who her roommates were. How much would Jarrett's appeal complicate the situation? And then there was Vicki's hostility.

Before Sierra had left the other day, the two women had reached an understanding, but physical therapy was tough. When Vicki was in pain, Sierra would be an easy target for anger. It came with the territory. Sierra was accustomed to dealing with a range of emotions from her patients. But usually she was able to retreat home at the end of a long day and leave the stress of a contrary client behind. Now the contrary client would be sitting across from her at the dinner table.

Good thing I like a challenge.

She passed a large duffel bag to Jarrett, appreciating the ripple of muscles in his forearm as he resituated everything he was carrying. Once they were both loaded down like a couple of pack mules, she followed him up the porch stairs and into the blessedly air-conditioned house. September wasn't as brutal as July or August had been, but the Texas heat was still enough to make her regret the short-sleeved sweater she wore.

They went through the entry hall and past the study, kitchen and Vicki's room. At the end of the hall was a living room decorated in Southwest tones and worn but comfy-looking furniture. A spiral staircase in the far corner led to the second story.

Jarrett flashed a sheepish look over his shoulder. "It's a bit of a climb."

She gave a one-shouldered shrug to show she didn't mind. "It'll help keep me fit."

His gaze swept over her body, and for a second, she thought he might say something. But he turned around without further comment.

The steps were narrow, and she had to concentrate on not letting her luggage scuff up the walls. At the top, Jarrett gave her the lay of the land. "That's the master bedroom, and that one is—was—Vicki's." He ducked his gaze, his tone flat. They both knew it would be a long time before Vicki Ross climbed those stairs again. "I'm at the other end of the hall, along with the guest room where you'll be."

He gestured for her to go ahead, and Sierra chuckled as she got her first good look at her room—the Island of Misfit Furniture. If she had to guess, she'd say that anytime a room in the house had been remodeled and there was a perfectly good piece of furniture they hadn't wanted to get rid of, it had been shoved in here. The king-size bed was too big for the space. The pink vanity in the corner had probably been Vicki's when she was twelve. The brass headboard was unlike any she'd seen before, a series of whimsical curlicues that curved around the edges of the bed, hugging the mattress.

A few steps into the room, Jarrett had to duck. Because of how the roof slanted down at the edge of the house, there were places where she could probably touch the ceiling if she stood on her toes.

Jarrett frowned. "I haven't been in here since I helped Mom move that old wardrobe. I forgot how claustrophobic it is."

"Not so claustrophobic when you're five foot one."

He set down a suitcase. "Would you rather stay in my parents' room? With as little as we're paying you, the least we could do is offer you comfortable accommodations."

She wasn't her mother, who insisted she couldn't sleep in sheets with less than an eight hundred thread count. "I like the funky vibe. And the wardrobe reminds me of one of my favorite books when I was a kid." Stifling the urge to climb inside and look for magical portals, she turned and ran her hand over the lacy vintage comforter. As long as the mattress was comfortable, even Muriel would have to call this bed luxurious. It was freaking huge. Sierra sat on the edge, bouncing slightly to test it. "This bed's almost too big for one person."

There was a sudden heat in his gaze that made her skin prickle. He looked away, but not before she realized his mind was in a different place than hers. *Great start to the first day— telling your boss you don't want to sleep alone.* Now he was staring fixedly at the wall, as if embarrassed by his wayward thoughts.

She stood, brazening through the moment by making a joke of it. "You don't mind if I host wild orgies on my nights off, do you?"

For a split second, he didn't react. But then his lips quirked in a slow smile. "Orgies, huh? Call me old-fashioned, but I think if one guy can't make you happy, he's not doing it right."

Her heart clutched—not at the outrageous teasing, which she'd started, but at how that grin transformed his face. In town, Kate Sullivan had called Jarrett a charmer. The word didn't fully capture the wicked glint in his eyes or the thrill Sierra got from having coaxed a playful moment. She'd already been drawn to

Jarrett more than was appropriate, given their circumstances, but now that she knew about that dangerously tempting smile and his sense of humor?

For the first time since they'd met, she was the one who lowered her gaze. "I should get settled in," she said, striving for an efficient, professional tone. "The sooner I unpack, the faster I can start helping Vicki."

He flinched. "Vicki. Of course. I'll...see you at dinner."

With that, he was out the door. She honestly didn't know if she was sorry to see him go or relieved.

AT THE RISK of being overly optimistic, Sierra thought that her first hour of PT with Vicki had gone quite well. The young woman hadn't made a single bitchy comment. Granted, she was glaring as if she wanted to kick Sierra's ass, but the good news was, if she ever managed to achieve that, Sierra would know she'd done her job even better than anticipated.

They'd wrapped up a set of exercises, and Vicki was glowering over the top of the water Sierra had handed her.

Sierra slid one of the chairs away from the kitchen table and spun it around, straddling it. "Did your post-surgery therapist talk to you about imagery?"

"No, but my Freshman Lit teacher did. Want to discuss symbolism in 'The Yellow Wallpaper'?"

"I'm talking about positive thinking and having a mental picture of exactly what you want to accomplish, something specific and concrete." At Vicki's disdainful look, Sierra added, "There have been actual medical studies concluding that imagery can help accelerate the healing process."

"So your clinical approach is for me to close my eyes and chant 'I think I can, I think I can'?"

Well, it had been too much to hope that Vicki's sarcasm was cured forever. "Yeah," Sierra drawled, matching the young woman's scathing tone, "that's exactly what I said. To hell with the carefully researched exercises and the grueling muscle stretches. Let's just hold hands and hope for the best."

The corner of Vicki's lips twitched. "I'm not holding your hand."

"You will if I tell you to," Sierra said mildly. "You're missing the big picture—everything I do is for your benefit. My only goal here is to help *you* make progress." Her only primary goal, anyway. She had secondary objectives of figuring out her future after Cupid's Bow and repressing her attraction to Jarrett. "Look, Vicki, try to keep an open mind and trust that I have the experience to do my job well."

When she didn't respond, Sierra decided to take the silence as acquiescence.

"All right," she continued, "we want to come up with a specific image that you can focus on during sessions, something that will help keep you motivated when you want to quit."

Anger flashed in Vicki's brown eyes. "I'm not a quitter."

"Good. Me neither. So let's harness our collective stubbornness and work together. What is it that you want?"

"To walk again. Without a walker or crutches or anything that makes me feel—" She shook her head fiercely, unwilling to voice her frustration and fear.

"You'll get there," Sierra promised. "Not all the way there in the three weeks we have, but eventually. But if you could walk right now, no limitations, what would you most want to be doing? Think in terms of sensory details. Build a clear goal in your mind. Hiking outside and feeling the warmth of the sun on your face? Strolling through your favorite store and looking for great sales items?"

"Dancing with Aaron." A smile lit her face. "Aaron Dunn is my boyfriend. There's a dance hall near campus that we love to visit. Aaron's a great dancer. He was teaching me how to jitterbug before last semester ended."

"Perfect. So close your eyes and imagine everything—the song you're listening to, the clothes you're wearing, the smell of beer—er, Aaron's cologne," she amended for her underage client. "Got it?"

Vicki nodded.

"Then let's get to work."

Chapter Six

Jarrett came in through the mudroom that connected the carport and the kitchen. As he pulled off his boots, he heard the sound of female voices arguing on the other side of the door. *Damn.* Maybe it had been irresponsible of him to leave Sierra and Vicki alone all afternoon, but there was so much that needed to be done on the ranch.

Plus, exercising the horses being boarded at the Twisted R and preparing soil for fall crops kept him almost busy enough to avoid picturing Sierra Bailey on that massive bed upstairs.

He groaned, wondering if he had time for a cold shower before he helped negotiate a truce between the women in the kitchen. But then Sierra laughed, a rich throaty sound, and he realized that the bickering he'd overheard was good-natured, not spiteful. He couldn't make out Sierra's words, but whatever she said made Vicki snicker, too.

He froze, trying to recall the last time he'd heard his sister laugh. Amusement had been in short supply since her accident. He'd been confident Sierra could help facilitate his sister's physical rehabilitation, but he hadn't expected that, in one short day, she could help Vicki rediscover joy, too. Gratitude struck him full in the chest. Hearing Vic sound happy, even for an instant, highlighted just how miserable and withdrawn she'd been. He wanted his lighthearted sister back, the one who had a bright future ahead of her and thought her big brother hung the moon.

Then be that guy, her hero, not the jerk who jokes about sexual prowess with the hired help.

Right. No more flirting with Sierra. That moment up in her room had been an anomaly, not proof that he was slipping back into his old habits.

Filled with renewed purpose, he opened the door and entered the kitchen. The door to the walk-in pantry was wide open, and Vicki sat in front of it, craning her head to read some of the cans and boxes on the top shelf from her wheelchair.

Sierra stood at the kitchen counter, writing in a spiral notebook. She spared a quick glance in his direction. "Hey, cowboy. Have a good afternoon milking cows and—"

"They're beef cows," Vicki corrected her. "Not dairy."

"Alrighty." Sierra tried again. "Have a good afternoon herding dogies and riding the range or whatever it is you do?"

Vicki snorted. "You've never spent time on a ranch before, have you?"

"Nah. I'm a fan of civilization—places you can find with GPS, towns with movie theaters that show more than one movie."

"I think the Cupid's Bow Cinema is up to three films at a time," Jarrett defended his hometown. "Although, they might all be from last year. What are you ladies up to?" he asked, crossing the kitchen to get a cup out of the cabinet.

"Grocery list," Sierra said. "I have an exciting Saturday night ahead of meal-planning. It's vital that Vicki gets lots of vitamin D and calcium right now. Meat's important, too, so I'm relieved she's not a vegetarian."

Contemplating a bleak, steakless existence, Jarrett made a face of reflexive terror. "We come from a long line of carnivores."

"Except for softhearted Aunt Pat," Vicki interjected. "She used to help her dad take care of their cows and got too attached.

Now she's— What do you call those people who don't eat meat except for seafood?"

"Pescatarian," Sierra supplied.

Vicki snapped her fingers. "Right. But Uncle Gus got her a saltwater aquarium for Christmas, so seafood might be out now, too."

"Fish would be a good staple for your recovery diet," Sierra said. She turned toward Jarrett. "I already went over some options with Vicki. She said she likes trout. That sound okay to you?"

He nodded.

"Have an opinion on mushrooms?"

"I'm not picky." That statement could sum up a lot about his life—big appetite but not a man of discerning tastes.

"Wish the same was true of your sister," Sierra grumbled. "She shot down half the suggestions on my list."

"You tried to get me to eat liver!" Vicki made gagging noises.

"It's high in vitamin D."

"I think you mean high in grossness."

"Well, stay on my good side," Sierra warned, "or it'll be liver seven days a week."

Vicki's eyes widened. "Wait…you have a good side?"

Jarrett didn't mean to laugh, but an errant chuckle escaped. Poking his head in the refrigerator, he reached for the pitcher of water and hoped Sierra hadn't noticed. He didn't want to incur her wrath and end up with an endless banquet of liver lunches and dinners. When he risked glancing in her direction, he found her with her hands on her hips, her posture drawing his attention to her slim waist and the full curve of her hips. Recalling his vow not to be *that Jarrett* anymore, he immediately raised his gaze to her face.

Despite her mock frown, humor danced in her eyes. "Trust me, when my bad side comes out, you'll know the difference."

And just what does it take to entice Sierra Bailey to be bad? The flirtatious words hovered on the tip of his tongue. With the uncharacteristically light mood in the kitchen, it would be so easy to tease her, to fall into the trademark banter he'd used to make time with half the single women in the county.

His grip on the pitcher handle tightened. Hadn't he reminded himself he was no longer that guy only seconds ago? Being in Sierra's presence made it difficult to remember his noble intentions. For weeks, he'd been staying out of town, away from the usual places he frequented, in order to avoid temptation. But now one of the most alluring women he'd ever met was under his roof.

His sense of self-preservation urged him to get out of the house. "I just remembered—I told some buddies I'd try to meet up with them tonight. I can help you make dinner, show you where everything is if you'd like, but after that—"

"You go on." Sierra waved a dismissive hand. "I'm sure Vicki can talk me through everything I need to know."

He nodded, looking to his sister for confirmation.

Her eyes were dark pools of disappointment. Her playful manner was gone, her shoulders slumped. Crap. Vicki hadn't exactly been clamoring for his company lately. It hadn't even crossed his mind that she might want him to stick around for the evening. *I'm doing this for you, Vic.* Staying away from Sierra would help him keep the promise he'd made to his sister.

"Unless you need me to stay?" he asked his sister cautiously.

"No, it's fine. Go. *One* of us should have a social life." Her tone was brittle, on the verge of cracking.

Jarrett rocked back on his heels. The last thing he'd wanted was to upset her. Should he stay after all? Ten minutes ago, Vicki had been laughing; now her expression was grim. *Leave. You've already done enough damage here.*

THE ONLY TRUE bar in Cupid's Bow, not counting the drink counters at the bowling alley or dance hall, was The Neon Arrow. The house specialty was cold beer at a decent price. As he crossed the gravel parking lot, mushier than usual after heavy August rains, Jarrett wondered how long he could nurse a single beer. At his size, he held his liquor well, but ever since Vicki's accident, he never got behind the wheel with more than one drink in him.

After the time it had taken him to shower, change and make the drive, it was fully dark outside. Inside the Arrow, the light wasn't much brighter. Townspeople sat at dimly lit tables or stood gathered around one of the three pool tables in the back half of the little building. He scanned the room halfheartedly for friends, not sure that he was the best company right now. Considering his mood, perhaps it would be better to—

"Long time, no see, stranger." A sudden clap on Jarrett's back made him realize solitude might not be an option.

He turned to see firefighter and longtime friend Will Trent. "Hey."

"Good to see you out and about. Finally. I was starting to seriously consider rounding up my brothers and physically dragging you off the ranch."

"Yeah. Well. Been a rough few months."

"I know." For a moment, grave understanding replaced Will's smile. "How 'bout I buy you a beer to celebrate your being back in circulation?"

"Deal." Jarrett wasn't sure how much circulating he wanted to do, but he could use the drink.

As they headed through the crowd toward the bar, one of the blonde Carmichael sisters kissed Will on the cheek. "Find me if you have time for a game of pool later," she said. "After that bet I lost last week, I want a rematch."

"Same stakes?" Will asked.

Her only answer was a naughty grin.

They made it about three feet when a brunette punched Will on the arm. "You missed your chance," she angrily declared. "I'm here with Grady Breelan. I am officially *done* waiting by my phone for you to call!" She flounced into the crowd before Will could respond.

"Who was that?" Jarrett asked. "And when did you become the local heartbreaker?" Up until July, that had been Jarrett's title. Will Trent had always been a one-woman man; he'd dated his high school sweetheart for years, then proposed to her. But she'd jilted him before the wedding.

"That was..." Will paused, pursing his lips. "Denise."

"Oh, right. Denise Baker." He should have realized that sooner—after all, they'd gone out briefly. *Very briefly.* He was lucky she hadn't socked him on the arm, too. "I didn't recognize her with short hair."

The line at the bar was considerable, and Will jerked his head toward a nearby high-top table. "We'll probably get service quicker if we sit down and let a waitress take our orders."

That proved accurate when a young woman in a denim vest showed up and asked what she could get them to drink. She was pretty in a freckled, pixie way, but she hardly looked old enough to work in a bar. If Jarrett had run into her on the street, he would have assumed she was Vicki's age. Or younger.

"Will." Her eyes warmed at the sight of the firefighter, and she resituated her tray, leaning in to give him a one-armed hug. "How are you doin' tonight?"

"Just fine, Amy. You know Jarrett Ross?"

"Not personally, but I've seen him in the rodeo ring. You're practically a celebrity," she said to Jarrett. "You riding next month over in Brazoria County?"

"No." Too bad Jarrett didn't have a drink yet. Beer, water, soda—he didn't care. His throat was painfully dry. He used to brag all the time about his wins, but now talking about rodeo made him feel as if he were gargling with sawdust. "I'm taking some time off."

Her laugh had a sad edge to it. "Wish I could afford some time off every now and then."

"You still working two jobs?" Will asked.

"Three, but who's counting?" She gave herself a shake, plastering on a bright smile. "Y'all aren't here to listen to me whine.

It's Saturday night! You should be having fun—have a little extra for me, okay?" With that, she scooted off to retrieve their drinks. She returned with a couple of frosty longnecks wrapped in napkins.

When Will tried to tip her more than the drinks cost, she protested. "You're a doll, Will Trent, but I'm no charity case."

"The money's not for you—it's for that baby of yours. Give him a hug for me."

With a sigh, she tucked the cash into the zippered pouch she wore belted around her waist. Then she kissed Will on the same cheek that the blonde had.

After Amy was gone, Jarrett asked, "You two aren't...?"

Will sat back in his chair, his expression appalled. "Hell no. I think Amy was a junior or sophomore when my younger brother graduated. She's just a kid. With a kid of her own." Frowning, he watched her clear empty bottles from the next table. "Her apartment got hit by lightning in a storm last month, and I helped put out the fire. Frankly, I'm almost glad it happened."

Jarrett's eyebrows shot up. "Because it broke up the monotony of a slow week?"

"Because Amy had to temporarily move in with her mom while the damage was being repaired. Living at home helped her break things off with her loser boyfriend. The guy's bad news. Cole's pretty sure he deals drugs but hasn't been able to prove it yet." Will's older brother was the town sheriff. "The night of the fire, Amy had a bruise on her arm she claimed was from banging into the kitchen counter while trying to heat a bottle. Except, the bruise was in the shape of fingers."

The thought of a woman being hurt made Jarrett ill. "She have a dad or big brothers to look out for her?" Maybe someone needed to have a conversation with her ex.

"Just a self-appointed, honorary brother tipping her with fives and tens when I can."

Even though Will had called the waitress a "kid," as a mother providing for her child, she was more of a grown-up than Jarrett was. He would be thirty in a few years, but up until July, he'd been dancing through life with no real responsibility.

"Speaking of siblings," Will said, "how's your sister doing?"

"She's…" He took a long swallow of beer, unsure how to answer. Certainly Vicki had improved since her days in the hospital, when she'd been pale, listless and unable to even sit up. Sierra was hoping to transition her to a walker, and he was grateful for every bit of progress. Yet it was still difficult to believe that the exuberant girl who'd always taken the front porch stairs two at a time couldn't climb any stairs at all. If going in through the carport hadn't already been an option, they would have needed to build a ramp for her.

Then there was the damage done to their relationship. How long would it take to rebuild the trust and camaraderie? When he'd impulsively said he was going out for the evening, he'd hoped Sierra and Vicki would continue to bond in his absence— maybe watch one of those mushy movies that Vicki and his mom always sniffled through but that made Jarrett restless for the end credits. But she'd been so sullen when he left, glaring with unspoken accusation. Did she think he'd pawned her off on Sierra so that he could pick up a woman and make up for lost time?

"Damn," Will said softly. "That bad?"

"We hired a therapist to stay at the ranch for a few weeks. She seems to really know her stuff, so maybe Vicki's next big milestone is right around the corner." He wondered if his smile looked as fake as it felt.

"Local buzz was that you were hiring Lucy Aldridge."

"My parents and I discussed that, but we went in a different direction." Jarrett thought about Sierra's red-gold hair and frequent warnings not to incur her wrath. *Very, very different.* He just hoped it wasn't a direction he would regret.

SIERRA ENTERED THE kitchen bright and early Monday morning. *Technically,* she thought, stifling a yawn, *dark and early.*

She was greeted by the heavenly aroma of coffee and resounding silence. The mug and cereal bowl in the sink attested that Jarrett had been there, but apparently he'd already headed out to tackle ranch chores. She'd barely seen him since his abrupt departure from the house Saturday. Yesterday, he'd taught riding lessons for most of the afternoon and told them not to wait on him for dinner. Sierra almost felt as if he were avoiding her.

Which makes you either paranoid or conceited. He could just as easily be avoiding Vicki, pained to see his sister in a handicapped state. Or maybe Sierra was overthinking the matter and he was just really busy. After all, the Twisted R was over a hundred acres, and Jarrett was taking care of everything by himself. If his daily schedule were leisurely, he wouldn't have needed to hire her in the first place.

Hours later, as she was fixing lunch, he came in through the side door off the kitchen, which made her feel silly about her unfounded suspicions.

"Hope you're hungry," she said, "because—"

"I am, actually, but I'll grab a bite in town. I'm making a run to the feed store, then picking up some lumber." Then he was gone as quickly as he'd appeared.

Apparently, he hadn't even taken the time to say goodbye to his sister before leaving the ranch. When Sierra and Vicki sat down to eat, the girl barely touched her homemade soup or grilled cheese sandwich; she was too busy glancing at the door every few seconds. Obviously, she'd expected—hoped?—that Jarrett would join them.

Sierra followed her gaze. "If you're waiting on your brother, he had some errands to run."

"Oh." Vicki's shoulders slumped.

Sierra bit the inside of her lip, wondering if he knew how disappointed his sister was not to spend more time with him. "I guess the ranch keeps him pretty busy," she said, hoping to ease the sting of his absence. "Seems like a lot of hard work."

"Yeah." Vicki dragged a spoon through her soup, making little swirls in the broth. "Must be nice."

It was one thing to envy Jarrett a night on the town, but was Vicki really jealous about the hours he spent patching fences or baling hay? *She's bored out of her skull.* Sierra was not a dull person, but not even her companionship could replace the entire sophomore class at Vicki's university.

There were gaps in the nineteen-year-old's day. As much as Sierra liked to goad her patients into giving maximum effort, overdoing the exercises would only complicate recovery. Between sets, Vicki had to take it easy. Physically, anyway. They needed to find her something more mentally challenging than daytime TV.

It would be best if Vicki had her own project during the hours when Sierra was tracking down job leads, cleaning or grocery shopping. The idea was for the two women to work as a team, not spend so much time stuck in each other's company that they got sick of each other. Maybe Vicki could take some online courses to help catch up to her classmates? Not that Sierra could authorize such an expense. She needed to discuss options with Jarrett, maybe tonight after dinner.

And if he kept making himself scarce? Then she'd just have to track him down.

Chapter Seven

Sierra squinted into the dusk, her resolve momentarily faltering. Were there snakes out there? She had no idea. But cow patties were inevitable.

So watch where you step. She was carrying a flashlight in one hand and a bagged roast beef sandwich in the other. Jarrett had missed dinner for the third night in a row; when it had become clear that he wouldn't be there, Vicki had looked as if she might cry. It was time Sierra and her employer had a chat.

Randomly wandering one hundred and fifty acres in search of him would be a fool's errand, but the light spilling from a huge barn let her know where she could find him. Marching down the porch steps, she headed in that direction and tried not to think about the coyote howls she'd heard in the distance last night. At least, she hoped they were suitably distant.

The dogs trailed along beside her, probably drawn by the smell of roast beef, and she was comforted by their presence. "You'd let me know if there was anything in the dark to worry about, right, Sunshine?"

The retriever perked up at the sound of her name.

"If the two of you keep me safe from critters," Sierra promised the dogs, "there are yummy scraps of roast beef in your future."

Despite the dimness of the evening around her, it wasn't so dark that the stars were truly visible yet. She bet they were spectacular this far from any city, and she made a mental note to stargaze one night. Might as well take advantage of the view before she returned to her regularly scheduled urban life. Who knew when she'd ever fall this far off the beaten path again? She heard a horse whinny and grimaced. *Definitely* not *my kind of place.*

There weren't any horses in the fenced paddock outside the barn. Vicki had said something yesterday about them spending daylight hours in the pastures and being stabled at night. Sierra could tolerate being near one if it was safely on the other side of a stall door. Still, when another horse nickered in reply to the first, she felt a phantom pain along her spine, tightening her lower back and making it momentarily difficult to move forward. *Screw that. You are Sierra Bailey.*

Shoulders squared, she stomped into the barn with more gusto than tact. "Are you avoiding me?"

Several equine heads turned her way, their long faces poking over stall doors, their eyes dark and huge. She swallowed hard.

A stall door to her left swung open, and Jarrett emerged, looking perplexed. "One of the mares we board is a little high-strung," he said softly. "As a general rule, I encourage people to use calm, soothing voices."

"Sorry," she said, matching his tone. She held up the plastic bag as a peace offering. "I brought you some dinner. We weren't sure when you'd make it back to the house."

His gaze zeroed in hungrily on the sandwich. "Thank you. I was so busy giving these guys hay for the night I didn't realize I was starving." After latching the stall door closed, he stripped off the pair of work gloves he'd been wearing and reached forward to take the food.

Then he walked toward the back of the stable, gesturing with a head tilt for her to follow. There was a small wooden bench built into the far wall. She took a seat while he washed his hands at a sink around the corner. Was there enough room for him to join her? They'd have to sit very close, a prospect that seemed simultaneously tantalizing and ill-advised. She was glad when he sat a few feet away on a bale of hay.

"What's this about me avoiding you?" he asked, unwrapping his sandwich.

She really should learn diplomacy someday. "Well, uh, I've been here three nights, and in that time you haven't come to the house for supper once."

"You do understand these horses don't groom and feed themselves, right?" He looked annoyed. And sweaty. And far more comfortable in his own skin than the reserved man who'd first interviewed her. In this setting, he—

What is wrong with you? She didn't like barns or horses or the smell of hay. It was completely illogical that she'd be drawn to a cowboy with scuffed boots and a streak of dirt across the upper thigh of his jeans. Realizing that her gaze had dropped to his lap, she jerked her head up, feeling as twitchy as that mare he'd mentioned.

"Let me start over," Sierra said. "I approached this wrong because I was a little jumpy about walking in the dark and—"

"Maybe you should've stayed inside the well-lit house."

"Trust me, I'm all for well-lit houses and indoor plumbing and air-conditioning. I wouldn't venture out among the mosquitoes and cow pies without good reason. And Vicki is my reason." She took a deep breath, reminding herself of her purpose. Best to focus on her patient's well-being, not Jarrett's denim-clad thighs.

He leaned forward, his expression tense. "Is she okay? Did something—"

"Nothing happened. I just needed to talk to you about her frame of mind. Maybe this isn't the ideal time and place, but for two people who live in the same house, we don't seem to run into each other much," she said wryly. Before he could turn defensive, she added, "I'm sure that's because the ranch keeps you so busy. But your sister…" She recalled Vicki's haunted expression at dinner as she once again spent an entire meal staring at the door instead of eating. "Are the two of you close?"

He stiffened. "Did she say something? About me?"

"Not specifically."

"Oh." His gaze dropped to his sandwich, but he didn't take another bite. If the Ross siblings didn't start eating more, Sierra was going to get a complex about her cooking. "There's a pretty big gap in our ages."

Was that his way of explaining why he and his sister didn't spend more time together? Sierra had dealt with her fair share of evasive answers from patients who didn't want to admit that they'd been slacking off; she knew guilty undertones when she heard them. "Age difference aside, she seems like she really misses you."

That got his attention. His eyes lit with something almost like hope, but then he shook his head. "I doubt it. And, as I said, the ranch keeps me busy."

"Are you one of those people who get uncomfortable around anyone who has a handicap?" she asked impatiently. "Because Vicki will be in that wheelchair for—"

"I assist with equine therapy for disabled kids and adults, and you don't know what you're talking about."

Oh, good—she'd misjudged her boss *and* angered him. She could just apologize and leave, except that retreating wouldn't do anything to improve Vicki's situation. She took a fortifying breath, trying not to wrinkle her nose at the prevailing horsey smell, and gave her best attempt at a conciliatory smile. "One of the things your sister did say was that you're lucky to have so much to do. I think she's bored and feeling a little useless."

"Of course she is." He rubbed his forehead with the heel of his hand. "She should be at college, not cooped up in the house. This is all my—"

He didn't have to finish the sentence for Sierra to understand that he blamed himself. Sympathy tugged at her. She'd been told

Vicki was driving alone and had been hit by a drunk driver. Did Jarrett have any rational reason to feel guilty? Then again, emotions didn't always adhere to logic. This inappropriate impulse she was feeling right now to go hug him, for instance...

She cleared her throat. "Is there some kind of project we can give her? Something truly beneficial, not busywork that makes it seem like we pity her." Patronizing her would only court the young woman's resentment. "Do you know I've heard three different people in town call her 'poor Vicki'?" Earlier, Sierra had wondered if an online class would be good for her patient. Now she reconsidered. Vicki needed something less solitary, something that would demonstrate to the people of Cupid's Bow—and to herself—that wheelchair or not, she was a smart, capable woman.

Jarrett scowled. "Surely no one would be dumb enough to say that to her face?"

"Whether they do or not, the sentiment is there. What can we do to change it? Is there some kind of local charity she could volunteer with, or—"

"There's the Harvest Day Festival," he said. "It's an annual event the last weekend in September. Basic fall celebration—hayrides, face paintings, pumpkin-carving contest. My friend Will and I were just talking about it the other night. The place where we normally hold it is out because of construction on the new courthouse in downtown Cupid's Bow."

She managed not to snicker at the idea of a "downtown" in a place that probably had only four city blocks.

"They've relocated it to a park, so—according to Will's soon-to-be sister-in-law, Kate—it's taking more planning than normal since they have to refigure the layout. Maybe Vicki could help? She's lived here her whole life and knows that park like the back of her hand. Or, the committee's always making calls asking for different donations and recruiting people to emcee the square dance or judge the Harvest Queen contest. Vicki can phone call with the best of them." His mouth tilted upward in a half grin. "Trust me, I've seen some of her cell-phone bills."

"This sounds really promising," Sierra said, feeling a burst of optimism. "Any idea who we'd talk to about getting her signed up?"

"Kate's on the committee, but Becca Johnston is probably running it. That woman is in charge of half the stuff in town. Start with her. But if she says anything to you about a bachelor auction, my answer is no. Unequivocally, emphatically *no*. I'm still not sure how the hell she talked me into that at the Watermelon Festival."

"You were in a bachelor auction?" Had he worn his standard uniform of jeans and boots, or had it been one of those charity events where they paraded the bachelors in tuxes? She studied him from beneath discreetly lowered lashes, trying to imagine the tall cowboy in a tuxedo. *Ross. Jarrett Ross.*

"Once. Against my better judgment. Never again." As if to underscore the finality of his decision, he stood. "Thanks for the sandwich, but if I don't get back to work, I'll be here all night."

"Right. Sorry."

"Don't be. You came out here with Vicki's best interests at heart, and that means a lot to me. *She* means a lot to me." He expelled a heavy breath. "To answer your earlier question, we were close. Before."

"You will be again." That was a rather ballsy statement, considering she didn't even know the cause of their rift. But Sierra's entire career—pretty much her life—was based on the belief that wounds could be healed, given sufficient time and effort. "Try to join us for dinner tomorrow?"

His silvery eyes held hers for a long moment. "I'll try."

Well. It was a start.

She took a few steps forward, subtly glancing around to see if the dogs were nearby. It was a lot darker out now than it had been when she'd arrived, and she wouldn't mind the canine escort back to the house.

"Everything okay?" Jarrett asked from behind her.

"Absolutely. Just fine. I—"

A black-and-white horse suddenly poked its head through the stall, as if curious about their conversation, and Sierra jumped, flinching away from the giant nose and flaring nostrils.

"That's Panda, Vicki's favorite. My sister has her spoiled and now Pan expects everyone to bring her carrots or pear slices. You can pet her," he encouraged, reaching up to pat the horse's neck.

"Oh, no. Thanks." She would have moved even farther away, except that would only bring her closer to the stall on the opposite side and the beast lumbering therein. Why did horses have to be so *big*? If only the Twisted R stabled ponies. Maybe those cute, super-shaggy ones. She was reasonably certain those wouldn't alarm her.

Jarrett quirked an eyebrow, looking amused. "Let me guess— you've never been around horses before."

"Actually, I have." She kneaded the muscles of her lower back, as if she could rub away past pain. "I...fell off one." Technically, she was thrown. More arrogant than experienced, she'd decided she was ready to try jumping the horse. Her mount had not agreed, balking at the last minute.

"A bad fall?"

She managed not to shudder at the memory. "Yeah."

His eyes widened. "The day I hired you, you told Vicki you'd suffered a spinal injury. Was—"

"Yeah."

"I'm sorry you were hurt," he said, stepping away from Panda, "but I respect the hell out of what you do—building from a painful experience of your own to help other people. It's... Will you laugh at me if I call you heroic?"

She was used to combating disapproval about her methods or her personality; Jarrett's earnest praise left her discomfited. Beneath his admiring gaze, her cheeks heated. Good grief. Since when did she blush? "Hero's a new one," she joked. "Most people just call me a dictator with a Napoleon complex."

"I'm serious. Your work *matters*. Some people are so damn selfish, barreling through life with no impact at all on those around them." His mouth twisted, his expression one of sheer disgust. "Except to hurt them."

She didn't know who had wounded Jarrett with self-absorbed actions, but the righteous fury in his eyes almost made her feel sorry for the guilty party. "Well. Thank you," she said awkwardly. She had that same errant impulse to soothe him that she'd had while sitting at the back of the barn, as if she wanted to go hug him.

Stupid. Not one of her brothers would appreciate a sympathetic hug—what made her think the strapping cowboy would? And, if she were being honest with herself, she wasn't sure the urge was that altruistic. Empathy aside, she couldn't deny the feminine thrill that shot through her at the idea of being that close to him, feeling the body sculpted by years of ranch work and rodeos against her own. *Get out of this barn before you start entertaining any trite roll-in-the-hay fantasies.*

With one final nod in his direction, she hurried outside. At the moment, potential critters in the dark weren't nearly as alarming as the pull she felt toward Jarrett Ross.

"You're giving me the afternoon off?" Vicki narrowed her eyes, regarding Sierra with suspicion. "Why? That's not like you."

Sierra shrugged. Chopping vegetables at the kitchen island provided a convenient excuse to turn away from Vicki's scrutiny. "Even taskmasters take the occasional break to have lunch with their friends."

"*You* have a friend in Cupid's Bow?"

"Kate Sullivan." It was a stroke of luck that the woman had turned out to be on the festival committee. "I met her my first day in town, and she's nice. Which is a welcome change from your company."

"What?" Vicki feigned confusion. "I'm delightful. Ask any-one. You must bring out the worst in me."

Sierra's lips curled in a grin. In some ways, Vicki reminded her of a younger version of herself. She wondered if her patient would take that comparison as a compliment. *Why should she? You're a pain in the ass.* True. But she was a pain with a pur-pose. When she'd called Kate this morning to ask about the Harvest Day Festival, the woman had said her timing couldn't be more perfect.

"The committee meets every Tuesday at the Smoky Pig for lunch," Kate had told her. "Are you free to join us today?"

Sierra had promptly rearranged her schedule. Jarrett had promised to come to the house for lunch, so he could eat with Vicki while Sierra went into town. She hadn't yet told her pa-tient about the festival idea. This way, if there was no pressing job open for the young woman, she didn't need to know about the rejection or worry that the other members had turned her down because they viewed her as incapable. Besides, while Si-erra and her patient had steadily been building a productive re-lationship, Vicki still had her prickly moods. Sierra would rather present the opportunity as a fait accompli than have Vicki balk at the suggestion.

"As soon as I get lunch prepared for you and your brother, I—"

"Hold that thought," Vicki declared, pulling her cell phone out of her hoodie pocket. Her eyes widened and, by the way her face lit, Sierra knew immediately who the caller was. "Aaron? Wait just a second. I'm taking this in my room," she informed Sierra. Then she rolled herself from the kitchen with speed nor-mally reserved for professional racetracks.

Watching the giddy display of young love, Sierra felt simul-taneously charmed and jaded. Had she ever cared about any-one with that much enthusiasm? She'd adored Paul, but in a more...practical way. He was a good person who shared a lot of the same values she did and didn't mind her outspoken nature. But as much as she'd enjoyed spending time with him, she'd never moped if a day passed without his calling. *Well, you weren't nineteen.*

The door to the mudroom creaked open behind her. She turned to find Jarrett tilting his black cowboy hat on his head so he could rub a bead of sweat off his jaw with the sleeve of his T-shirt. Her heart stuttered at the absent male gesture.

She gave herself a mental shake. *What happened to mature and practical?*

"Sierra? You okay?"

She swallowed, trying to bring her thoughts into focus. "Um...don't I look okay?"

He cocked his head, studying her. "You looked...intense."

"Oh. Probably because I'm busy plotting."

"Global domination?"

"Nah. I thought I'd start at the state level and work my way up." She glanced past the kitchen to make sure Vicki was well out of earshot, then lowered her voice. "I'm making lunch for you and your sister, but I won't be staying to eat. Kate Sullivan is picking me up soon. For a festival meeting."

"Great. But why are we whispering?"

"I haven't exactly told Vicki about my brilliant idea yet. Her reactions can be a little...unpredictable. So I'm going with the ethically questionable maxim that it's better to ask forgiveness than permission."

"You're going to volunteer her time without asking her first?"

"That's the plan," she said cheerfully. "Assuming you'll okay my taking a few hours off for the meeting."

"Of course. That actually works out well since I have a lot of office work to catch up on. So I can be in the house while you're gone." He paused. "Wait. You and Kate already arranged for her to come get you."

"Yep."

"But you're just now asking if it's all right. Out of curiosity, what would you have done if I'd said no?"

"Changed your mind." She gave him what she hoped was a winning smile. "I'm a very pushy person."

"I hadn't noticed," he drawled, his expression deadpan. "Do I have time to take a shower before lunch is ready?"

Since they were sharing a bathroom, it was far too easy to picture him in the generously sized shower stall with its clear door and chrome finishing. Annoyed with herself for the un-disciplined—and highly erotic—mental images, she snapped, "Make it quick."

He raised an eyebrow at her tone. "Careful, darlin'. You rush a guy, you don't always get the results you deserve."

Heat flooded her. The idea of Jarrett taking his time wasn't any safer to dwell on than the vision of him wearing nothing but a few soapsuds. Whistling under his breath, he left the room. She waited until he'd disappeared around the corner to stick her head in the freezer.

Chapter Eight

"I'm so glad you called me," Kate said as they rolled over the cattle guard and onto the road. "I was already thinking about getting in touch and inviting you to lunch sometime, but I didn't want to be pushy. I know it can take time to settle in."

Sierra pulled a pair of sunglasses out of her purse. "Not much settling to do—I'll only be here three more weeks, give or take."

"And you want to spend part of your short time here involved with the festival? Do they not have cable on the ranch?"

"This isn't an act of boredom so much as me scheming to get Vicki Ross reengaged with the community. My interest in the festival is to get *her* signed up for a job. Will you help me convince the rest of the committee? Vicki's bright and has ample time on her hands."

"Sure. I don't know her well, but she's always struck me as smart and energetic. According to my fiancé, she used to babysit the twins before she left for college. Anyone who can successfully manage Alyssa and Mandy has my respect."

The ride into town didn't take nearly as long as Sierra remembered. It probably helped that she could just enjoy their conversation—which touched on everything from Kate's search for the right wedding dress to college football—instead of worrying about getting lost. Soon, they were parking in a public lot at the end of the picturesque—if unimaginatively named—Main Street.

"From here we walk." Kate grinned. "Which gives me the chance to burn off at least a couple of calories before I stuff my face with barbecue."

They climbed out of the car, greeted by energetic gusts of wind. Sierra's polka-dot skirt whipped around in a breeze perfumed with sweet, earthy scents from the nearby flower shop. Her hair blew in her face, and she regretted not wearing it pulled back.

"When I left Gram's farm," Kate said, "Luke was decorating kites with the girls to fly in the pasture, but with the way it's picking up, this wind might be too strong for them. No clouds yet, but you can tell a storm will be rolling in." Glancing up at the blue sky, she inhaled deeply. "I love that sense of electricity in the air before it rains."

Electricity. Maybe Sierra could blame the impending change in weather for the zing that had gone through her in the kitchen earlier, for the not unpleasant way her skin prickled when she locked eyes with Jarrett. That hum she felt through her body could be some trick of barometric pressure instead of wildly unprofessional lust. *Absolutely...and Santa Claus and unicorns are real, too.* Physical attraction was one thing. If Jarrett were only a hot cowboy, without an intriguing personality to match those mesmerizing silvery eyes, she could ignore her baser instincts. But the chiseled face was paired with gallant protective instincts and his heady admiration for Sierra. He'd labeled her a hero. How was a girl supposed to resist that? And then there were those fleeting, unexpected moments of wicked teasing. If she didn't know better, she would swear he'd been flirting with her before she left.

Careful, darlin'.

Sierra's mother called everyone "darling." The way Muriel said it was impersonal, the verbal equivalent of an air-kiss. But when Jarrett drawled the word, it was rich and beguiling. An invitation.

Consider it an invitation mailed to the wrong address, she told herself. *Whatever you do, don't open it.*

"Wanna be a little bit bad?" Kate asked.

"What?" Sierra jolted, startled by the question. Could people tell just by looking at her what she was thinking? That would make dinner tonight with Vicki and Jarrett extremely awkward.

"Trying on wedding dresses has made me resolve to lose ten pounds," Kate said as she slowed beneath a striped awning and reached for the restaurant door, "but this place has the *best* desserts. I was hoping you'd split one with me after lunch. Then it's only half bad. Which is practically half good."

"So my enabling you would be my good deed for the day?" Sierra grinned. "I like the way you think."

As they walked inside, Sierra pushed her sunglasses up on her head to better see. The wood-paneled walls and exposed railing made the interior of the restaurant dark, but judging by the mouthwatering smell of barbecue, people didn't come here for the decorating.

"We're back there," Kate said, leading Sierra to where three tables had been pushed together to accommodate a group of women, ranging in age from their twenties to over seventy.

"Which one's Becca?" Sierra whispered.

Kate paused, pursing her lips. "I don't see her, which is weird. She's usually the first one here. Although, maybe today is one of the days she's meeting with her contractor. She's about to start substantial house renovations. And woe to the contractor who does not give that woman exactly what she wants."

"Is she really so scary?"

"She's nice, if you get to know her. But she's detail-oriented, with a *very* specific idea of how things should be done, and a little intimidating. Gram calls her ruthlessly efficient." As they reached the table, Kate beamed at the assembled women. "Afternoon, everyone! I brought a new recruit with me—Sierra Bailey."

"Oooh." A brunette seated in the middle flashed a teasing smile. "Fresh blood. Did you warn her what she's in for?"

"I'm actually here on behalf of Vicki Ross," Sierra said. "I've been working with her, and—"

"That poor girl," an older woman murmured.

Nods of agreement followed around the table, making Sierra want to roll her eyes.

"Everything that poor family has been through," a woman with a sleek blond bob said mournfully. "I've been meaning to go out to the ranch and check on Vicki. Maybe take her brother a casserole."

An auburn-haired woman across the table snorted. "That's not all you want to give him."

"Why, Anita Drake! That is so dirty-minded of you. And, also, true." The blonde shrugged apologetically at Sierra. "Jarrett Ross is hot."

No argument here. "Mr. Ross isn't really my concern," she said neutrally. "But I've been working as his sister's live-in physical therapist. I'm pleased to report Vicki's making great progress. Everyone in Cupid's Bow has been so sweet in their concern for her, and she wants to give back to the community. I'm hoping we can find a way for her to help with the festival."

"Which I think is a wonderful idea," Kate seconded. "I—"

"Disaster!" A woman in pearls and a pink sweater set looked up from her glowing phone screen. "Becca just texted me on her way here from the park. There's been minor flooding around the river, and with the additional rain expected this week, entire sections of the park might be underwater for the festival. Ladies, we need a new location immediately!"

"So." Sierra had been quiet for a few minutes after leaving the restaurant, needing time to process. When she finally spoke, they were halfway down the sidewalk. "That was Becca Johnston, huh?"

Kate smiled. "She can be a lot to take when you first meet her."

"I think she's my new hero." Sierra was used to being the bossiest redhead in any room, but the tall strawberry blonde had her beat. The woman was a force of nature. One glare from her and any gossiping or dissension around the table stopped immediately.

"And you haven't seen her at full strength," Kate said. "That was Becca on a preoccupied day."

The committee head had admitted as much, saying that her life was about to be turned upside down with home renovations and she needed the festival problem solved *now*. Kate had offered her grandmother's farm, which Becca dismissed as too small. Another committee member was suggesting they ask a rancher named Brody Davenport when the would-be casserole bearer who'd earlier declared Jarrett hot interrupted to say the Twisted R would be perfect. Apparently, his parents had hosted local events there in years past.

"Done," Becca had decreed. "We'll have it at the Twisted R."

Someone had wondered aloud if they should secure Jarrett's formal permission first, but Becca didn't have time for naysayers. The specifics of the conversation were fuzzy, but Sierra remembered nodding along with Becca's sound reasoning. Yes, they did need a new home for the festival as soon as possible. And hosting the festival at the Twisted R was a perfect way to involve Vicki, who could help work out where all the proposed activities should be situated.

Becca had eyed Sierra, sizing her up. "You don't strike me as the type of woman who takes no for an answer."

"Definitely not."

"Wonderful. Then you're the perfect point person to give Jarrett Ross the good news."

Climbing into Kate's car, Sierra wondered how angry Jarrett would be when he discovered his ranch had been selected without his approval. *On the plus side, at least I didn't sign him up for a bachelor auction.*

WHEN SIERRA ENTERED the house, she was surprised to find Vicki at the kitchen table doing wrist exercises.

"I've been waiting for you to get back! Can we try some chair stands?" Vicki asked. They'd discussed how they were working up to Vicki holding the back of a chair and slowly standing, getting a sense of how much weight she could actually put on her legs.

"Eager. Cooperative." Sierra rocked back on her heels. "Who are you and what have you done with Vicki Ross?"

"Guess who's coming to see me this weekend?" Her face was rosy, and she was practically vibrating with joy in her wheelchair. "Aaron! You were gone when we got off the phone, so I didn't get the chance to tell you, but that's why he called. He's going to skip his afternoon class on Friday and drive to Cupid's Bow as soon as he finishes his calculus test that morning. I can't wait to see him! I want to show him I'm getting stronger."

"Fantastic news." Obviously Sierra wouldn't have to push very hard to keep her patient motivated for the rest of the week. Plus, based on Vicki's glorious mood, today would be the perfect time to tell her that Sierra had volunteered her to help organize the festival.

Over dinner. Sierra had already decided to cook chicken and dumplings—a specialty she'd learned from her mother's housekeeper—to soften up Jarrett. She hoped the meal made him as mellow as it usually did her father and brothers. The three of them could briefly discuss the festival, and then she would change the subject to what to cook while Aaron was here. Vicki would be too excited about the latter to protest the former.

"Will you take me shopping?" Vicki asked. "We have my appointment at the hospital Thursday. Can we go to All That Jazz afterward? I want to buy something special."

"Sounds like a good plan. Kate recommended I check out the boutique while I was in town. Why not make a day of it? Your therapy follow-up, lunch—"

"And the salon!" Vicki fingered the ends of her hair. "Maybe it's time for a new hairstyle. Nothing insanely different, just... a change."

Sierra nodded encouragingly. "Change is good."

"You sound like Jarrett. He always used to say that to justify—"

"To justify what?" Sierra asked, sitting next to Vicki at the table.

"Nothing."

The urge to pry was strong. There were undercurrents between the Ross siblings that Sierra didn't understand. On the one hand, she would swear that they were closer—or, used to be closer—than she'd ever been with her brothers. But the tension between them could be overwhelming. Sierra felt as if she'd wandered into a play during the second act, unsure of the story line. She'd gleaned that Jarrett blamed himself for Vicki's accident. Did Vicki think he was at fault, too? Had they argued about it?

"Jarrett promised he'd be joining us for dinner," Sierra said.

"Okay." Vicki stared at her hand as she wiggled her fingers. She had the appearance of someone trying very hard to look as if she didn't care.

"Did the two of you talk much at lunch?" Sierra prodded.

"I told him Aaron will be visiting and that we don't need chaperones looking over our shoulders every three minutes." She met Sierra's gaze. "I want to keep up with my therapy so I can be walking on campus again as soon as possible, but when we're not working—"

"Make myself scarce. Got it. I promise not to cramp your style."

Vicki grinned. "You're not completely heinous."

"Wow. Mind if I steal that for my résumé? Sierra Bailey, Licensed Physical Therapist, Not Completely Heinous. The job offers should come pouring in."

"You really don't know where you're going after this?"

"Not a clue." Which she was trying not to let terrify her. Now that she'd secured a project for Vicki, she needed to ramp up her efforts at looking for a job. If nothing else, maybe mailing cover letters and résumés would keep her too busy to have inappropriate thoughts about her boss.

"We know some rodeo riders who bust up their ribs and get concussions and stuff. Maybe you'll decide to stay and open a practice in Cupid's Bow."

"Doubtful," Sierra scoffed. "Cute town, but more a detour for me than a destination." It was not her kind of place.

Although, after an afternoon of laughing with Kate and enjoying scrumptious food, it was hard to remember why not.

"IF THAT TASTES as good as it smells, you may be in the wrong profession." Jarrett appeared at the edge of the kitchen, barefoot in a white T-shirt and a pair of jeans fraying at the hems. Closing his eyes, he inhaled, a look of blissful anticipation settling over his face. "My plan was to keep working in the office until you called me for dinner, but I haven't been able to focus on anything for the past ten minutes except the wonderful smells wafting down the hall. What are you making?"

"Chicken and dumplings, roasted green beans, spinach salad with homemade bacon vinaigrette. And there's an apple cobbler in the oven."

"Mmm. Is this to say thank-you for having the afternoon off? Because if that's the case, you can take off every afternoon."

"Oh. Nice," Vicki said as she rolled into the room. "So we've decided that me regaining use of my legs ranks slightly below fresh-baked apple cobbler?"

Jarrett whirled around, the color draining from his face. "Of course not. I—"

"Relax." She sighed, her expression unreadable. "I was just

giving you crap. You used to be able to tell when I was kidding," she added, her voice barely audible.

The pained silence that fell across the kitchen like a shadow made Sierra's heart ache. She cleared her throat. "If you two are finished busting each other's chops, how about you make yourselves useful and set the table? Vicki, you can get the silverware."

Dinner really did smell fantastic, but, once it was served, no one dug in with much gusto. Sierra was still pleasantly stuffed from a big lunch and the carrot cake Kate had talked her into sharing. Five minutes ago, Jarrett had been starving. Now he kept casting his sister searching looks while she mostly stared at her plate, lost in thought. So much for the food putting them in a jovial mood that would make them receptive to her festival news.

Might as well get this over with. Sierra set her fork down and turned to Jarrett. "You remember my saying that sometimes it's easier to ask forgiveness than permission?"

He hesitated with a forkful of dumpling to his mouth. "Yes."

"Good. I need you to forgive me. I told the Harvest Day Festival committee that they could hold the festival here at the ranch."

"You *what*?" Surprisingly, this didn't come from Jarrett but from Vicki, who then burst out laughing.

For his part, Jarrett looked as if he didn't know what to say. He gaped at her, unblinking. "Huh. Well, you did warn me that was your approach. I just thought you were planning to ambush her with it." He jerked his chin toward Vicki, who sobered quickly.

"Wait, what? Ambush me how?"

An equal opportunity ambusher, Sierra turned to beam at the other Ross sibling. "You're going to be working with Kate Sullivan to figure out where to put everything on the ranch. They had a rough plan drawn out for the park, but since the creek's flooded and more rain is coming..." She faltered under the combined weight of their stares. "Look, guys, the meeting didn't go quite the way I imagined. I went with Kate hoping to find Vicki something to do so you're not cooped up in the house and bored. You were envying Jarrett his ranch chores the other day—chores that involve mucking horse poo out of stalls! Working on the festival has to beat shoveling poo, right?"

Vicki's lips twitched as if she were holding back a laugh. "Manure," she corrected her.

"Potato, potahto." Sierra waved a hand. Sensing that she'd appeased Vicki, she turned to Jarrett. "I had no idea they were going to need a different venue. The flooding problem came up and someone suggested the Twisted R, which Becca Johnston agreed was the best solution. After that, it's kind of a blur, but everything she said made so much sense, and she said she was trusting me to clear it with you and…"

"Oh my gosh!" Vicki's eyes twinkled. "You got Becca'd."

"Becca'd?" They'd made the head of the committee a verb?

Jarrett nodded, the humor dancing in his own gaze highlighting his resemblance to his sister. "Happens to the best of us. I'm still unclear on how she managed to rope me into the July bachelor auction, but there I was on stage." He gave a philosophical shrug. "Becca'd."

"Last year," Vicki said, "she talked me into making floats for the town Easter parade instead of going to Florida for spring break with my best friends. When they asked me why, I couldn't even really explain it. People in Cupid's Bow just don't say no to her."

"Congratulations, darlin'." Jarrett winked at Sierra. "You're one of us now."

Chapter Nine

When Jarrett finished washing up at the sink in the mudroom and entered the house Wednesday evening, he found Sierra bustling around the kitchen, her manner harried and her expression contrite.

"I know I'm the one who said it was important for you to show up for dinners," she said, "and I appreciate your punctuality. But I'm afraid I'm running late. I had a phone interview with a clinic in Fort Worth that ran long."

"No hurry." He took a seat at the table so that he was out of her way. If there was anything Sierra wanted him to do, she'd tell him. Otherwise, best not to interfere as she bounced around the room, her knee-length skirt swishing as she muttered reminders to herself.

He felt guilty about all the effort she was putting in for such paltry pay. "I appreciate you keeping Vicki fed, but you're not expected to spoil us rotten. You don't have to go all out every night. Heck, I would have been perfectly happy with leftover cobbler for dinner."

"Yeah?" She smirked over her shoulder. "Then maybe you shouldn't have finished it all at lunch."

"I regret nothing."

Her lips curved into a quick answering smile before she went back to her verbal checklist. "…sugar for the tea. Ooh, flip the fish!" She grabbed a spatula and opened the oven door. When she bent over, the silky material of her skirt lovingly hugged her butt.

Damn, the woman had a nice backside. *Which you have no business ogling.* He chivalrously shifted his gaze. Eventually.

But watching Sierra cook was a banquet of temptations. She reached above her head to grab a measuring cup from the cabinet. From the rise and fall of her breasts beneath her halter top to the smooth muscle of her calves as she stretched up on tiptoe, she was spectacular. He was fortunate enough to see breathtaking vistas every day, but the view right here was more stunning than anywhere else on the ranch.

"Vicki's watching TV in the living room," she said. "The last half of *Die Hard*, which she said is one of your favorites."

A classic. Maybe he should seize the excuse and leave before anything got harder here in the kitchen. Against his better judgment, he refused. "Now that I've sat down, it's nice to be off my feet. If you don't mind the company, I'll just stay put."

"I don't mind at all." She paused, stopping the three different things she'd been trying to do at once to smile at him. It felt like a gift. "I have to say, when I moved in, I worried about the loss of independence. I'm not used to sharing living space with anyone. But you guys make pretty good roommates. It's a lot more rewarding to cook for other people. It's really gratifying when you two compliment a meal. When I shower myself with compliments, it just feels self-aggrandizing."

He chuckled. "Even if you never lived with a significant other, haven't you ever cooked an anniversary or birthday dinner for a boyfriend?"

"Once or twice, I guess. My last serious boyfriend was a doctor, and his on-call hours were insane. Sometimes our 'dates' were watching DVRed shows together at two in the morning. Not an ideal time for a four-course meal."

She used to date a doctor. He slumped in his chair, wondering why he found that discovery so depressing. *Because it's a reminder that even if you* could *ask her out, Sierra is completely out of your league.* She was a sophisticated woman who'd gone to medical school. He was a rodeo has-been who lived with his parents.

It hadn't mattered so much when he was on the road half the time. After the Rosses' full-time ranch hand left, Jarrett and his parents agreed that it made sense for him to renovate the old bunkhouse into a place of his own. But with everything that had been happening, it was hardly the top priority.

"What about you?" Sierra asked, grating cheddar cheese into the bowl on the counter. "I've heard all about Aaron. Do you have someone special in your life?"

"No." Did he sound abrupt? He couldn't help it. His love life was the last thing he wanted to discuss. There was no version of it that wouldn't make him sound like a first-rate ass.

When the doorbell chimed unexpectedly, he took it for the reprieve it was and shot to his feet.

"Expecting anyone?" Sierra asked. "I can hold off on dinner if—"

"It's probably just one of the boarding clients stopping by to visit their horse after work. Or it could be a package delivery." Maybe one of his parents had ordered something online.

"Or someone delivering a casserole," Sierra grumbled.

That was an odd prediction. Certainly lots of friends and neighbors had brought over food and get-well cards when Vicki and his dad were in the hospital, but that had stopped weeks ago.

He crossed through the house to answer the front door and found Will Trent standing on the front porch.

"Did we make plans I forgot about?" Jarrett asked. The other night at the bar, there had been a couple of times he'd caught himself thinking about Sierra and nodding along with no real idea of what Will had just said.

Will shook his head. "Nope. I'm showing up uninvited like an ill-mannered lout. My mother would be horrified. But I brought these to make up for my rudeness." He held up a six-pack of beer. "Thought I'd come see how you were doing. If you're not too busy, we could watch a movie full of senseless violence or maybe call my brothers and play some poker. You gotta watch Jace, though. He cheats."

"Really?" That was hard to believe of a Trent.

"Nah. But telling myself that allows me to keep some dignity when the little punk takes my money."

Jarrett chuckled. "Come on in." He couldn't remember Will ever dropping by out of the blue like this. Had Jarrett really looked that grim when they'd seen each other Saturday that his friend felt compelled to check up on him? "Tell me the truth," he said, remembering how angry Denise Baker had been when she saw Will at the bar. "Did you drive all the way out here because you need sanctuary from some woman who's mad at you?"

"Pffft. Women love me," Will boasted. But then he scowled. "Except for Megan Rivers. Dang female acts like I'm—"

"Who is Megan Rivers?"

"My next-door neighbor. She moved here a couple of years ago. Probably never got on your radar because she's the mother of triplets."

Jarrett didn't get involved with single moms. He'd preferred dating women whose lives were as uncomplicated as his. *Because you're a shallow SOB.* "So Megan doesn't like you? How come?"

"Who knows? Maybe she's a hopelessly bad judge of character. Maybe her ex was named Will."

"Or Trent."

"Or maybe living with three preschoolers just makes a person really, really cranky."

That certainly seemed plausible.

"I've never seen her smile," Will said. "Ever. I tried to make her laugh once, while we were both getting our mail, and she just glared like she wanted to throw her parenting magazine at me."

"It's unlikely anyone here will pelt you with reading materials, but I can't make any guarantees. Vicki has her moody moments, and Sierra, the physical therapist, is—"

"Did I hear my name?"

Jarrett turned to see Sierra at the other end of the hall.

Next to him, Will straightened from his relaxed posture to full alert. "Hi, there. You're Sierra?" When she nodded, Will pinned Jarrett with a knowing look. "So this is why we rarely see you in town," he said under his breath. "I wouldn't leave the house, either."

"It's not like that," Jarrett hissed.

"I was hoping you'd say that." Will strode forward, offering his hand. "Will Trent. A pleasure to meet you, ma'am."

She shook his hand, glancing at the six-pack he carried. "Are you staying for dinner? I made plenty."

"My policy is never refuse an invitation from a beautiful woman."

Sierra grinned up at him and suddenly Jarrett understood exactly what it felt like to want to throw something at his friend.

FOR ALL THAT Sierra was coming to care about the Rosses, Will Trent's arrival was a breath of fresh air. With his jet-black hair, the man was tall, dark and handsome—although not quite as tall as Jarrett. Not quite as handsome, either. But Will's easy smiles and unrepentant flirting made him fun to be around. He didn't seem the type for any charged silences or brooding guilt. He nicknamed Vicki "Hot Wheels" and entertained her with impressions of townspeople while he lent a hand setting the table.

The only person who didn't seem thrilled to see him was Jarrett, which confused her. She knew from a couple of mentions this week that Will was the friend Jarrett had gone out with last weekend. Had she overstepped by inviting the man to stay for dinner? It had seemed like the obvious course of action. Frankly, she welcomed the silly banter he provided. Will lightened the mood.

Not everyone's.

She would have expected his buddy's presence to engage Jarrett in conversation. Instead, he seemed withdrawn, hardly saying three words as Sierra filled glasses with iced tea. He leaned against the kitchen island with his arms folded, looking more like the stoic cowboy who'd hired her than the one who'd caught her rearranging the pantry last night and teased her about being a control freak.

"Jarrett?" She called him to the corner of the kitchen, away from where Will and Vicki were joking at the table. "Can you help me get this serving bowl down?"

He nodded, wordlessly crossing the tile floor to where she waited. The scent of the soap he'd used enveloped her, pleasantly mingling with the muskier, masculine smell of him. She should move out of his way. But since she'd engineered the moment to ask privately whether it was okay that she'd invited Will to join them, she needed to be close for Jarrett to hear her whispered question. So she remained where she was and found herself wedged between the counter and Jarrett, his body pressing lightly against hers as he reached above her. Her breath hitched and he looked down, capturing her gaze with his own.

He lowered the bowl into her hands. His fingers, warm and a little rough, brushed over her knuckles, and she shivered. She barely remembered what she'd intended to ask. And she could not remember the last time she'd felt like this—palms damp, heart racing, her skin deliciously sensitive.

Get a grip, Bailey. The man handed you a bowl. He didn't undress you.

His eyes were molten silver. "Anything else I can do for you, darlin'?"

"I, um…" *Kiss me.* Not that she would ever voice such an insane request. Kissing Jarrett was completely out of the question.

Except, it didn't feel out of the question. He was watching her so intently, as if he could see her thoughts, and he was standing close enough his breath feathered over her skin. In that heart-beat, kissing him would be as natural as—

"Sierra?" Vicki's voice in the background was impatient. "We planning to eat before the food gets cold?"

Jarrett jerked away from her so abruptly she almost dropped the bowl he'd handed her. She'd missed her chance to ask him if it was all right that she'd asked Will to dinner, but, really, what would she do if he said no? Rescind the invitation and kick out the family friend?

It's too late, Bailey. Might as well go with it.

But that advice applied only to their dinner guest. *Not* her attraction to her boss.

"WELL, THAT WAS an embarrassing display," Vicki said from behind her.

Sierra stiffened at the sink where she was washing dinner dishes. Now that Will had gone, was Jarrett's sister finally speaking her mind about the moment earlier when it had taken far too long for one adult to hand another one a bowl? Had Sierra's riotous feelings been visible to everyone in the room?

Battling a hot rush of mortification, Sierra turned to face her patient. Should she go with flat denial, or deem it a temporary lapse in judgment that would never happen again? But once she'd spun around, Sierra saw that Vicki hadn't even been speaking to her. She was addressing Jarrett, who'd returned from seeing Will out.

He scowled down at his sister. "I don't know what you're talking about."

"Sure you don't," Vicki scoffed. "You're thick-skulled, but you've got to have *some* self-awareness. You spent all of dinner practically snarling at one of your best friends. Honestly, Sierra's a grown woman. If she wants to go out with Will, she can."

Go out with Will? Sierra blinked. He'd told her to save him a dance at the Harvest Day Festival, but she got the impression he said that to a lot of ladies. It had been an offhand comment, not a declaration of courtship.

"Sierra's going to be here for the better part of a month," Vicki said. "Are you planning to be a butthead every time some guy comes sniffing around her?"

"Hey!" Sierra objected to the "sniffing around," which made her sound like a dog's chew toy.

Neither sibling looked her way.

"Why would I care who Sierra goes out with in her free time?" Jarrett demanded. "We've covered this before. You know I don't think of her as a woman."

"Hey!"

This time, her indignation registered. Both Rosses turned to face her, looking almost surprised by her presence.

"Do you people mind not discussing my love life like I'm not even here? Actually," she backtracked, "I'd prefer you don't discuss it at all. It's none of your damn business."

"Exactly my point," Vicki said smugly. With that parting shot, she wheeled herself from the room.

The last thing Sierra wanted was to be left alone with Jarrett after his humiliating announcement that he barely saw her as a woman. Embarrassment stung her cheeks. Had she misread that moment earlier, the way he'd looked at her? *What does it matter if you did?* She'd already vowed that she would keep her hands to herself—anything else would be foolhardy and unprofessional. Jarrett's dismissive tone made it easier to squash temptation. He'd done her a favor, really. She sure as hell didn't want to kiss him now.

What she wanted to do was storm out of the room, but the dishes weren't finished. She refused to look as if she was fleeing his presence. Sierra Bailey didn't flee. Instead, she plunged her hands into the soapy water, hoping that if she ignored Jarrett, he'd leave.

"I should apologize for my sister," he began stiffly.

"You should apologize for yourself." She scrubbed a plate with vicious force. "Not a woman?"

"Don't take it personally. All I meant is that I don't have any romantic interest in you."

She flinched at the bald rejection, not turning around as he stepped closer and grabbed the dish towel from the counter.

"And you shouldn't have any interest in me, either," he said.

"Oh, *trust* me..." She shot him a withering look over her shoulder.

Standing entirely too close for her peace of mind, he started drying the dishes she'd already washed. Damn it, he still smelled good, although she hated herself for noticing. She wanted to snap at him that she didn't need his help, but it wasn't as if she could kick the man out of his own kitchen. Nor could she break a plate over his head, but the mental image was heartening.

He took a deep breath. "I won't try to stop you if you want to date Will Trent—"

"That is so generous of you," she gushed, her eyes wide. "Letting me make my very own grown-up decisions about my own life!"

He clenched his jaw. "As the person who introduced the two of you, I feel like it's my responsibility to let you know he's just looking for a good time. Will's a decent guy, but he won't offer any kind of commitment."

"Commitment?" Did the deluded man think she was hoping to find the future Mr. Sierra Bailey during the next two and a half weeks? She slammed down a plastic cup in the drying rack. "Women aren't always hunting for husbands, you know. Sometimes, all *we* want is a good time. And, for your informa-tion, I'm not naive." Will Trent was a charmer, but he seemed like a player, the kind of guy who called every other woman "Gorgeous" because he couldn't remember her name.

Sierra had made it her entire adult life without having her heart broken. She could manage just fine without Jarrett Ross's condescending guidance.

"I never called you naive. Don't put words in my mouth! God, you're—"

"I'm what?" she pressed. It was a bad idea to bait him after he'd had the good sense to censor himself, but she was too angry to care.

Exhaling a puff of air, he stared upward as if silently praying for patience. "Stubborn. Sarcastic. Infuriating." He pinched the bridge of his nose. "But you *are* a grown woman. I'm sorry I said anything about your personal life in the first place. It won't happen again."

"Good." At least he'd admitted she was a woman. Theoretically, she'd won their argument.

But the sinking sensation in the pit of her stomach and the impotent wish she could have a do-over of the whole conversation didn't feel like victory.

"You should try these on!" The boutique owner, Jasmine Tucker, handed Sierra a pair of emerald-green slacks. "I know they're a little outlandish, but with your coloring..."

Sierra humored her, adding the slacks to the selection she had draped over her arm. "I'm not really here shopping for me," she said, more as a reminder to herself than to dissuade Jazz. The clothes were great, but since Sierra had no idea where her next paycheck was coming from after this job... "I'm just Vicki's chauffeur."

The young woman was already in a fitting room; she'd stubbornly waved away Sierra's assistance. Changing clothes in such a confined space couldn't be easy, but Sierra respected Vicki's drive to be self-sufficient.

"Well, if you find something you love," Jazz said, lowering her voice to a confidential whisper, "I've been known to give some pretty sweet discounts." She sighed. "I'm never going to break any retail profit records. I love sending people home with new outfits too much. I can't help it! I had sisters and was always stuck with hand-me-downs, so new clothes are— Ooh, this dress would look great on you, too!"

Sierra chuckled, the exchange surreal. "I can't believe I'm getting personalized fashion advice from the supermodel whose face used to look up at me from magazines in the waiting room."

"Ha! I was never anywhere close to supermodel status," Jazz demurred. "But thank you."

"Do you ever miss it?" Sierra asked. "Life in New York? Cupid's Bow must be so…quiet in comparison."

"Yes, thank heavens. There's a lot I enjoyed about New York—Broadway shows, great little restaurants with funky, unexpected menus—but my life there was exhausting. I felt like I couldn't catch my breath for four years straight. Coming home was such a relief. I know Cupid's Bow is small, but it isn't boring. The people here are much too interesting for that."

Good point. Sierra thought of some of the people she'd met— nosy octogenarian Miss Alma, Becca Johnston with her take-charge superpower, a former New York fashion model. *Jarrett Ross.* He certainly wasn't boring. Unpredictable, frustrating and moody, perhaps. But not boring.

When she'd come downstairs this morning, she'd found a bud vase with fresh-cut flowers where she normally sat at the table. Next to it was a napkin with the words *I'm sorry* scrawled across it in pen. She hadn't seen him, though, to tell him she was no longer angry about yesterday's botched exchange. How could she be? In his own misguided way, he'd genuinely been trying to look out for her, as a friend.

Maybe that's what upset you. While she recognized intellectually that it was best for them to only be platonic friends, it was somewhat ego-deflating to discover that the pull of attraction was one-sided.

"You know what?" she asked Jazz. "Maybe I will splurge on something new." Finding something that made her feel good about herself would be a nice boost.

She opened the door of a dressing room and stepped inside.

A fun new purchase would be the icing on what had turned out to be a pretty great day. They'd started the day at the hospital so that Vicki could meet with her official physical therapist. Sierra had wondered if the man would resent her intrusion or question her methods, but Manuel had been thrilled to meet her. He'd invited her to take part in the session, helping to stretch Vicki's muscles and act as cheerleader when she stood from the wheelchair. She couldn't do it for long, and every single time, she broke out into a sweat almost immediately, teeth gritted as determination warred with exertion. Still, standing was a major milestone. Steps would come with time.

After PT, they'd had lunch at a quaint little deli and gone by the salon where Vicki got her hair cut into sassy new layers. Sierra had contemplated a change of style, too, but ultimately declined.

"You don't really need a new style," Vicki had said. "You're reasonably hot—for a woman pushing thirty."

"I just remembered we need to stop by the grocery store on the way home. I need to pick up some liver."

Grinning at the memory of Vicki's horrified expression, Sierra tried on a dress that was a rainbow of scarves and bandannas stitched together. Pretty. Was it casual enough for the Harvest Day Festival, or would she stick out like an overdressed thumb? She exchanged it for another outfit. The pants were so long on her they were laughable. Being petite was one of the reasons she wore so many skirts. It was difficult to find pants the right size, and she hated to bother with the hassle of hemming or custom tailoring.

When she was finished, she took the colorful scarf dress and met Vicki at the cash register. The girl looked excited about her new purchase—and showing it off for Aaron this weekend—but fatigue was beginning to shadow her face. It had been a busy day. Sierra expected her passenger to fall asleep in the car on the way back to the ranch.

But Vicki surprised her by wanting to talk. "Sierra? I'm…

sorry if I made you uncomfortable last night. After Will left. I just thought it was ridiculous how my brother was acting all jealous and possessive."

Jealous? Her ego tried to cling to the word. Jarrett couldn't be jealous over her unless he was attracted to her, right?

She sternly reminded herself that attraction was a complication neither of them needed. "I don't think it was so much jealousy as protectiveness. He sees me, temporarily, as part of his household and wanted to warn me that Will is a ladies' man."

Vicki mumbled something while looking at her window. The only words Sierra caught were "pot" and "kettle."

"But as a general rule," Sierra continued, "if you want to avoid making someone uncomfortable, maybe don't speculate on her love life? If I were to go out with Will Trent or anyone else, the idea of you and Jarrett sitting around the table and dissecting my date is a little…"

"Invasive?"

"Ooky."

Vicki laughed. "Right. I think I remember that word from the vocab section on my SATs. You're a real genius, Sierra."

"Yep. That's why your family pays me the big bucks."

SIERRA KEPT DINNER comparatively simple Thursday—salads topped with strips of steak. If the meal turned out to be awkward after last night's argument with Jarrett, at least there wouldn't be many dishes to clean. Three large salad bowls and, boom, she could escape upstairs with a good book.

But judging from the sheepish glance he gave her when he appeared for supper, their confrontation was well behind them.

"Hey." He hooked his thumbs in the pockets of his jeans. "Vicki in her room?"

"Skyping with a sorority sister about the latest pledges chosen to join. She said to let her know when it's time to eat."

"You, ah, saw my note this morning?"

Her lips twitched. "The napkin apology?"

A slow grin spread across his face. It was like watching sunrise. "Double-ply. When you care enough to leave the very best."

She laughed. "For the record, I'm sorry, too. I'm all the things you accused me of—stubborn, sarcastic. God knows my own family thinks so."

"You don't talk about them much." He pulled salad dressings out of the refrigerator. "They're in Texas, right?"

"Houston." Which felt like a different galaxy than Cupid's Bow. "I've got three brothers, one of whom is getting married in December."

"Your parents must be so proud of you."

"Um...possibly?"

His eyebrows shot up. "How could they not be?"

"I'm sure they are, in their own domineering, 'this-isn't-the-life-we-would-have-chosen-for-you' kind of way. After three boys, Mom was really excited to have a daughter. Based on baby photos, I don't think I wore anything but pink for the first year of my life."

He eyed the vintage T-shirt she was wearing with a black skirt and boots. "I can't quite picture that."

"You'll have to take my word for it. Total pampered princess."

"What happened?"

"My fall. It made Mom and Dad see me as more fragile than ever, but it had the opposite effect on me. Once I stopped feeling sorry for myself, recovering from that injury made me realize for the first time how strong I could be. We butted heads a *lot* during my teen years." She rinsed the cutting board in the sink. "I can't imagine doing what you do—working with your family on a daily basis, living with your folks."

"I don't plan to live in this house forever." Was his tone a touch defensive? "There's a bunkhouse over the hill that I'm moving into. After some remodeling."

"I wasn't judging you," she promised. "They're lucky you're here to help with the ranch and with Vicki."

At his sister's name, his expression grew shuttered. "The luck I bring isn't always good."

In moments like these, he looked so sad. "Jarrett, I..."

He turned away from her. "I'll let Vicki know dinner's ready."

Whatever words of comfort she might have found, he obviously didn't want to hear them.

VICKI WAS IN the middle of telling Jarrett all about their day in town when she suddenly gestured with her fork, stabbing it across the table toward Sierra. "Hey, I just remembered what I wanted to ask you about on the drive home! During one of my first sessions with Manuel, he gave me some big pep talk and mentioned that it was possible for patients to ride a horse even if they couldn't walk yet. Is that true?"

Sierra choked on a bite of steak. Oh, why couldn't Vicki have asked about aquatic therapy instead? Cupid's Bow was rumored to have a spectacular community pool. Coughing, she reached for her glass of ice water. "Yes, it's true." Horseback riding aided in strengthening the leg muscles; plus, the motion mimicked the sensation of walking, helping the body relearn.

Vicki brightened. "How soon can we do that?"

"Um... That might be more up Manuel's alley than mine," Sierra admitted. "Any idea if he makes house calls? I don't... I can't really—"

"Sierra doesn't ride anymore," Jarrett said. "But Cupid's Bow is full of people who know horses. We can find someone to help get you back in the saddle, Vic. But we will need a trained therapist to supervise the process. Sierra, would you be able to manage that?" From his gentle tone, it was obvious he understood how much she dreaded being around horses.

Vicki frowned, her forehead wrinkling into lines of confusion. "What do you mean she doesn't ride 'anymore'? I feel like I'm missing something."

"I rode when I was a kid," Sierra said. "Briefly. But not since then."

"Not a problem," Vicki said. "Jarrett will teach you. Who better? He gives lessons professionally! And you guys can work on that this weekend while Aaron is here, which will give us more time alone." She nodded her head, looking pleased with herself.

Riding lessons? Something that sounded embarrassingly close to a whimper escaped Sierra. She coughed again, hoping to cover it.

"I don't think Sierra's interested in learning to ride," Jarrett said. "But—"

"Wait. Are you *scared* of horses?" Vicki asked incredulously. "That's crazy!"

"Not so crazy if you fall off one and fracture your spine," Sierra said self-consciously.

"I just meant, the idea of you being afraid of anything is crazy. I can't wrap my head around it," Vicki said. "You're… you know."

Sierra smiled, touched by the flattery. "Thank you. But everyone's scared of something."

"Uh-huh." Vicki arched an eyebrow. "So your plan is to wuss out."

"Can we go back to the part where you were implying I'm an awesome badass?"

"When was the last time you let a patient wuss out of something?" Vicki challenged.

"Um…" Sierra glanced toward the head of the table, seeking Jarrett's input. He'd been pretty supportive throughout the conversation. But now he had a hand over his mouth, clearly trying not to laugh as Vicki continued.

"Isn't the expression that if you fall off a horse, the best thing to do is get right back in the saddle?"

"Not when you break your spine!" Sierra hadn't been physically able to ride for almost a year. After that, there was no chance her parents would have risked letting their precious daughter give it another chance. By the time she was an adult, she'd long since lost any urge to try again.

"But you're all healed now," Vicki persisted. "I tell you what—if you get on a horse, I won't give you any crap for a straight week."

"Counteroffer—you don't give me any crap for a week, and I won't smother you with your own pillow."

"You really shouldn't threaten to kill me in front of a witness."

"Who, your brother? I'm not worried about him turning me in. He's easily bribed with apple cobbler."

"I'm also partial to blackberry," Jarrett chimed in.

"Come on, Sierra. Please."

Sierra tossed her hands up in exasperation. "Why are you even pushing this? I'll talk to Manuel about coming out to the ranch and working with you, so—"

"I'm pushing because it's what you would do. If there was a challenge someone didn't think they could overcome, you would harangue and nag and cajole until they succeeded."

"She's got you there," Jarrett agreed.

"Damn." She sat back in her chair, knowing that Vicki was right.

"So." He grinned at her. "What time tomorrow should I expect you for your first lesson?"

Chapter Ten

Sierra was sitting next to Vicki's mat on the living room floor, helping her rotate through foot positions as she lay on her back, when the dogs began barking wildly to signal that someone was approaching the house.

"Aaron!" Vicki's body jerked as if her first impulse was to sit straight up.

"Easy, there. Slow down so you don't cause yourself any new injuries. Let's get you into the chair. Then I can go open the door."

Vicki nodded. "You let him in, and I can freshen up. I'm sure my hair's a mess." She grimaced as they worked together to shift her position.

"Are you in pain?"

"No. Just hoping Jarrett isn't close enough to the house to accost Aaron. He'd better not be giving him the lecture about sleeping on the fold-out couch and how there will be 'dire consequences' if he's found in my bedroom."

"He's just looking out for you because he loves you."

"You have brothers, right?"

"Three."

"And did you appreciate them interfering in your love life?"

"They never tried. Probably because *I* was more likely to deck a guy for making a move than any of them were."

As much as her brothers cared about her, they favored less direct forms of confrontation. If a man seriously wronged her, Kyle would probably buy up the city block where the offender lived and have him evicted; David would look for a lawsuit angle. Michael would just report the incident to their father and let him handle it.

She'd almost got Vicki into her bedroom when the doorbell rang. Sierra hadn't given much thought to what Aaron would look like, but the blond boy on the front porch wasn't what Vicki's rhapsodizing had led her to expect. Sierra knew he was a year older than Vicki, but he was so baby-faced that it probably took him a week to develop a five o'clock shadow. He was taller than Sierra—as was the average fourth grader—but about the same height as Vicki.

"Well, hello there." He gave her an appraising look over the rims of his sunglasses. "You must be Vicki's nurse."

"Physical therapist. And you are?" It was petty of her, pretending she hadn't heard plenty of gushing about him, but the kid's smirking expression goaded her.

He scowled. "Aaron Dunn. I'm expected."

"Come on in." She opened the door wider, and he entered in a cloud of expensive body spray. "Vicki will be out in a minute. Can I get you something to drink?" She stifled the urge to offer him a snack, not wanting to sound like a suburban mom serving after-school cookies.

They went to the kitchen, making small talk about the drive. She admitted that she was still struggling to find her way around Cupid's Bow, but he was unwilling to bond over the town's lack of road signs.

Instead, he gave her a patronizing smile. "Guess not everyone's born with my innate sense of direction."

Work with me, kid. I'm trying to like you on Vicki's behalf. To be fair, if Sierra were nineteen, she might be able to see Aaron's appeal. He was cute in a generic, glossy sort of way and, to his credit, an attentive enough boyfriend that he'd driven several hours to spend the weekend with Vicki. But compared to someone like Jarrett, with his rugged appeal and slightly shaggy hair and calloused hands—

"Aaron!" Vicki entered the room, her face glowing with happiness.

He gave her a wide grin. "Every time I see you, I can't believe you're that pretty *and* so smart. The total package." To Sierra he said, "She's the only reason I passed history last semester," a confession that made her like him more.

They kissed hello, but Vicki disentangled herself before Sierra started to feel too much like a voyeur. "Sierra, I got a text from Jarrett while you were answering the door. He's ready for you down at the stable."

Sierra was 100 percent certain that Jarrett had not instigated the text exchange. Rather, Vicki had probably sent him a message that said "Horse-riding lesson! Now!" in order to get Sierra out of the house.

"Sure. Just let me get my boots."

"Which leaves you and I alone." Aaron brushed back a strand of Vicki's hair, smiling down at her. "To study history."

"Don't 'study' too hard," Sierra said. "I'll be back in a little while to make lunch." With that, she hurried out of the room before the heat of Vicki's glare burned holes in her shirt.

JARRETT SAT BALANCED atop the wooden corral fence, head tilted back so he could enjoy the sunshine on his face. It was one of those sublimely perfect days where he felt blessed not to have an office job.

At his sister's imperious text, he'd led one of the gentler horses into the fenced area and tied her lead to the railing with a quick-release knot. He'd been waiting only a minute or so when Sierra came over the small hill that separated the front yard from the acres of pasture beyond. The sun glinted off her red hair, making it even more fiery and dramatic than usual. He loved watching her move; her confidence and purpose was just shy of feminine swagger. It was impressive that she carried herself with such self-assurance even when coming to face a horse, which she'd done her best to avoid.

As their gazes met, he lifted his hand in a wave. "You look good in jeans. Very good." Where had that come from? He'd meant to say hi. "I'm, ah, used to seeing you in skirts."

Her smile was wry. "Can't ride a horse in a skirt, though, right?"

He hopped down off the fence. "I don't actually plan to put you on a horse today. I thought we'd start off slow, just basic grooming to help foster a bond. No rush."

"Right." Her eyes sparkled with humor. "I vaguely recall that you're against rushing—something about not getting good results."

She was so pretty when she smiled like that, carefree and a little bit naughty. Too bad they wouldn't be riding today— helping her into the saddle would have provided an excellent excuse to touch her. He repressed a sigh. Being noble sucked.

Yeah, well, you promised your sister. And yourself. He gestured toward the mare waiting inside the fenced area. "That's Shiloh. She's a sweetheart. I know you've had some experience with horses before, but since it's been so long, I figured we'd start with the absolute basics. You want to approach horses from the front, preferably on the left side. If the ears are back, you're not welcome. That's not usually a problem with Shiloh. Approach slowly, saying hi to her, and let her smell your hand. I don't have any treats with me, but she loves being brushed, so this whole experience will be a treat for her."

"Glad it will be fun for someone," Sierra muttered.

"You can do this."

"Damn straight. No way am I going to have Vicki heckling me all night for chickening out. So let's get this over with."

"That's the spirit." He opened the gate for her and led her inside the paddock. "Don't forget to talk to her. The calmer you are, the calmer the horse will be." Although, frankly, Shiloh's default mode was pretty mellow.

"Hey, there, Shiloh. Nice to meet you." She slowly raised her hand for the horse to snuffle. "Please don't chomp any of my fingers off."

He tried unsuccessfully to smother a laugh.

Sierra glanced over her shoulder at him. "Have you seen her teeth? They're huge! Which figures. She's huge in general."

Seeing Sierra next to the horse was an almost comical reminder of her height. Her personality was so larger-than-life that it was easy to forget how petite she was.

A bag of grooming supplies hung over a nearby post, and Jarrett reached inside for the currycomb. "We're going to start with this to loosen dirt. You want to brush over the muscled parts of her body—stay away from the legs and face—in a circular motion."

Sierra slid her hands through the strap on the comb and, inhaling deeply, took a step closer to the horse. Jarrett stood in front of Shiloh, prepared to help calm her if necessary.

"I must seem idiotic to you," she said, "getting shaky over brushing a perfectly sweet horse who's standing still when you made a living by climbing on the backs of broncs who were actively trying to throw you."

"You know I don't think you're an idiot. Far from it." It would be so much easier to live under the same roof with Sierra if he had a more negative opinion of her. He could criticize her for being stubborn, he supposed. Or temperamental. Except that those qualities also made her determined and passionate. She might not be perfect, but she was a remarkable woman.

He turned away before he did something ill-advised—like telling her she was as extraordinary as she was beautiful. "Now we move on to the hard brush." He stepped closer to give her the brush. She smelled like cinnamon, from the French toast she'd made them for breakfast, and sunlight—sweet, warm, tantalizing.

Even though he could have talked her through the process as he had with the currycomb, he gave in to temptation and closed his fingers over hers, standing very close as he guided her hand. "Short, firm strokes," he said, demonstrating.

"Like this?"

"Yeah. That's good." Jarrett had taught dozens of people about caring for horses. Instructing Sierra should be automatic and perfunctory, not arousing.

Jarrett had always been very goal-oriented. It was one of the things that made him a winner in the ring. With past lovers, he'd focused on the act of sex itself, on making sure his partner enjoyed herself, but he'd overlooked how sexy even seemingly platonic moments could be. *Maybe because you never bothered to have platonic moments.* When a woman had demonstrated her interest in him, he hadn't spent weeks courting her before seducing her. In some ways, the relationship with Sierra was one of the most personal he'd ever had. He wasn't used to planning to-do lists with someone else, standing side by side as they did dishes, noting how adorably sleepy she looked at the end of a long day. Even arguing was new. His sexual encounters were usually amiable and conflict-free. *Shallow.*

When he'd vowed earlier this summer to change his ways, guilt had been a major motivator. Yet now he found himself craving a different kind of connection with a woman for reasons that had nothing to do with regret or mistakes. He felt as if he'd caught a glimpse of something in the distance—something rare and special and worth working toward.

"Now what?" Sierra asked.

Damned if I know. Then it registered that she was asking about equine grooming, not his sappy dating epiphany. "Uh, soft brush, to smooth the coat."

Once she was finished, he showed her how to care for the hooves, although he did it himself—partly in case Shiloh got antsy and partly to give himself something to think about other than dating. Even if he hadn't promised Vicki that nothing would happen between him and the physical therapist, Sierra was leaving Cupid's Bow in a couple of weeks. The thrill of a short-term fling with no future was exactly what the old Jarrett would have wanted.

"You did really well," he said once they were finished and Sierra was affectionately patting Shiloh's neck. "How about we follow the same routine tomorrow, and then by Sunday the two of you should be comfortable enough with each other that we can go rid—"

His words were cut off by the sound of an engine, and they both turned to see Aaron's truck roaring down the ranch's dirt road toward the main street.

"What do you suppose that's about?" Jarrett asked.

Sierra met his gaze, her expression perplexed. "We were done here anyway, right? I'll get back to the house. See you for lunch?"

"Okay." But as he led Shiloh back to her stall, he couldn't help wondering about Aaron's speedy exit. Had Vicki been in the truck with him? It was possible the two of them were going to eat lunch in town and the kid was just driving too fast to show off. But if she hadn't been with him, why was the visitor who'd just arrived leaving in such a hurry?

Knowing he wouldn't be able to concentrate on anything until he knew Vicki was okay, he tried texting her. When she still hadn't responded a few minutes later, he headed for the house. No doubt he was overreacting, but this way he could at least lend Sierra a hand with lunch.

As soon as he entered the mudroom, he heard his sister's raised voice.

"—left me for her. But who can blame him, really? *She* can walk," Vicki said, her tone thick with self-loathing. "And dance. And…do other things."

He clenched his fists. No wonder the loser had fled the

Twisted R. He'd probably known Jarrett would want to pummel him.

Not bothering to remove his boots, he stomped into the kitchen, where Sierra sat next to his sister, a consoling arm around her shoulders. "I say good riddance," he growled. The sight of Vicki's puffy, tearstained face made him seriously consider a road trip to the college campus. "I'm sorry he hurt you, but that jerk never deserved you. You will find someone who—"

"Has a fetish for girls in wheelchairs?" Vicki asked hollowly.

Raw helplessness scraped at his insides. He hated seeing her in pain. "You won't be in the wheelchair forever, Vic. You'll meet other guys, better guys. You'll fall in love again, and—"

"What the hell do *you* know about love? Have you even gone out twice in a row with the same woman, or is the 'relationship' over as soon as you throw the condom away?"

"Victoria!" He sucked in a breath, staggered by the crass words and the hostility in her expression.

"Vicki, that was uncalled for." Sierra's tone was soft but rebuking. "You have every right to be upset, but Jarrett's not the bad guy. He hasn't done—"

"You have zero idea what my big brother has and has not done. The women he's slept with. The promises he's broken." Vicki's voice cracked. "M-men suck. Even the ones y-you think...you think you can c-count on."

Sierra bit her lip, looking indecisive as she glanced between brother and sister. "Maybe I should go and let the two of you talk?"

"I have nothing to say." Fresh tears spilled down Vicki's face. "I want to be alone."

"Okay." Sierra rose slowly. "Do you want any help getting back to your—"

"No. Just get out. Please." The word ended on a wail that knifed through Jarrett.

He was only distantly aware of Sierra's hand on his arm, tugging him into the living room.

"Don't worry," she whispered once they were around the corner. "I won't leave her alone for long before I check on her."

"Thanks." It would take time, but he believed Sierra would be able to help Vicki through this. In the week she'd been here—had it been only a week?—the physical therapist had earned Vicki's trust and respect. They didn't need him in the house, just another male who'd let his sister down. "I should get back to work."

"I can bring some sandwiches down to the barn later."

"Thanks, but I doubt I'll have much of an appetite."

"Jarrett." She waited for him to meet her gaze. Her green eyes shone with compassion he didn't deserve. "People in pain lash out at convenient targets. No one knows that better than physical therapists. You should hear some of the names I've been called." She squeezed his hand. "Vicki didn't mean it."

He flinched away from Sierra's touch, recalling all the lustful impulses he'd had down by the stables—the exact kinds of thoughts his sister would have expected of him. "She meant every word." He strode down the hall toward the front door. He needed to get outside, where he could breathe again. Out of this conversation, which made him feel as if he was suffocating on his own shame. "And she wasn't wrong."

Sierra followed after him, too close, crowding him. "I may not have known you very long, but—"

"Let it go. Forget about me, and focus on taking care of my sister," he said, opening the door. "That's what I pay you for."

She exhaled in an angry huff, but Sierra wasn't one to give up easily. "I'm more than just an employee. I'm your friend."

Friend? The word was so simple and benign, but it didn't begin to cover what he felt for her. "No." He stepped into bright autumn sunshine that did nothing to warm him. "You aren't."

THE LAST THING Sierra expected to see when she opened her eyes was Jarrett's face peering down at her in the dark. She jolted upright on the couch, nearly banging their skulls together.

He moved back just in time to dodge the head wound, and she saw he was holding a quilt. "I didn't mean to startle you," he whispered. "You looked so peaceful, I was going to cover you up and let you sleep down here."

"I must've drifted off while reading. What time is it?" she asked, smothering a yawn.

"A little after midnight." Moonlight through the window silvered his profile as he turned toward Vicki's closed door. "How is she?"

"Hard to tell. She barely said a word all night, but I curled up on the sofa with a book so I'd be close in case she needed me."

Vicki's earlier anger seemed to have drained away, leaving quiet despondency in its place. Figuring that someone who'd had her heart broken was entitled to one day of moping, she'd decided to give Vicki until morning before pressing her to talk or resume her therapy exercises. Sierra hadn't even bullied her patient into eating dinner. Although she'd cooked enough food for three people, she needn't have bothered. Shortly before seven, she'd seen Jarrett's truck drive off. He hadn't told them where he was going or when he would be back.

She arched her back, stretching. "You didn't go rough up Aaron, did you?"

"If I did, wouldn't I be pretty dumb to admit the crime to someone else?"

"Depends on how much you trust me. I could be very useful if you needed an alibi." She caught the brief gleam of his smile flash in the dimness. Earlier, she'd been reading by the light of a table lamp. He'd obviously turned it off when he'd decided to let her spend the night downstairs.

He sat in one of the armchairs, retreating into shadow. "Reckon I do trust you. Enough to tell you the truth."

"About where you were tonight?"

"Just shooting pool. I meant the truth about Vicki's accident."

Her breath stilled in her lungs, almost as if she were afraid the slightest movement would spook him and that'd change his mind. It wasn't that she wanted Jarrett to confide in her to appease some morbid curiosity; she wanted him to open up because she believed it would be good for him. Whatever misplaced guilt he felt over Vicki's accident, maybe talking about it would help him move past it. So she waited, motionless, hoping he took her silence as encouragement.

"That stuff she said this morning... About me and relationships?" His bark of laughter was full of self-deprecation. "Not that I ever experienced anything close to a real relationship. She was right about that. I liked women a lot, and I liked a lot of them."

"Not unheard of for an attractive man in his twenties," she said softly. Nonetheless, she didn't want to dwell on the thought of him with these faceless women.

"The night of Vicki's crash, she and I were supposed to go to dinner. I'd been on the rodeo circuit. She'd been away at college. We hadn't seen each other in months, and she caught a ride with a friend to come watch me compete. Then I blew her off."

She put the pieces together. "For a woman."

"I'm not even sure what her name is," he said raggedly. "I've narrowed it down to something starting with a *T.* That's how lousy a brother I am. I stood up my own sister. I sent her home in my truck so I could have a couple of naked and sweaty hours with a blonde stranger."

She tried to imagine how she'd feel if one of her brothers had done that, but she didn't have the kind of relationship with any of them that would have led to a one-on-one dinner anyway. They got together for group events as a family, but she wasn't friends with any of them. For the first time, that struck her as sad. Maybe she should take some initiative when she went home for Christmas to get to know her brothers better.

"My parents were devastated by the accident," he continued. "I'm not sure they've really recovered. Vicki was a sweet, enthusiastic kid with a bright future. You've only seen the angry Vicki who—"

"She still has a bright future," Sierra interrupted. "As you yourself pointed out today, she's not staying in the wheelchair. She's young and resilient. Her progress since I've been here has been tremendous. There's no reason she can't be back in college next semester."

"I hope she is. But I have no idea what the next few months will bring for my father. During Vicki's second surgery, he collapsed of a heart attack."

Sierra winced at the unfortunate overlap. "And you blame yourself for that, too?"

"The timing was no coincidence."

Probably not. But she suspected stress was only a trigger in conjunction with other causes. "A heart attack involves half a dozen factors, from genetics to eating habits. Shouldering sole blame for it is the height of self-absorption. The world doesn't revolve around you, cowboy." She said it lightly, but that didn't make the statement less true. "If you've made bad decisions in the past, start making better ones. But beating yourself up for other people's decisions—like the guy who chose to get behind the wheel after he'd been drinking—is a one-way ticket to crazytown."

For a moment, Jarrett didn't say anything. She hoped she hadn't sounded too cavalier about what his family had suffered, but he needed to accept that he couldn't change the past. What happened next, however, was entirely up to him. Vicki wasn't the only one who needed to move forward with her life.

"You don't think I'm a terrible person?"

"I think you're a person, period. We make mistakes." She could offer him forgiveness all day long, but it wouldn't solve the underlying problem. "Really, my opinion is irrelevant—this is between you and your sister. Have you apologized?"

"For a solid week after the accident, all I can remember saying to her is 'I'm sorry.' The words are damned inadequate, though."

"They're a start. Don't fall back on words alone. Be there for her."

"Even when she tells me to go the hell away?"

"Especially then. Obviously, there are moments she'll need her space, but too much space is just avoidance. Let her know you'll be there when she's ready to reach out." She yawned again. "Meanwhile, if *I'm* going to be there for her tomorrow, I should probably get some sleep."

"Sorry. This conversation probably should have waited until daylight hours. But honestly? It was easier to tell you in the dark."

She could understand that. But this midnight confessional had an air of intimacy that made her uneasy. On the day the Rosses had hired her, she'd told Vicki, *"I don't do 'bonding.'"* She'd said it to stem Vicki's argument that they weren't going to become friends, but, looking back, she realized the words had a lot of truth to them. She had plenty of acquaintances back in Dallas, but no one she missed enough that she'd called them during her time in Cupid's Bow. She loved her family from a distance. She was actively dodging her mom and couldn't recall an instance in her adult life when she'd sought out a brother's company just because she wanted to spend time with him. She'd slept with Paul for months, but she hadn't loved him. Was she emotionally stunted?

Nonsense. She blamed the uncharacteristic melancholy on the late hour. When she met someone worth falling in love with, she'd give it her all. Meanwhile, why settle?

She stood. "Are you coming upstairs, too?"

"Eventually." His tone was sheepish. "I thought I'd check the kitchen to see if there were any more brownies left. You're a hell of a baker."

"Nah, my family's housekeeper is a hell of a baker. I'm just an adept student. Good night, Jarrett."

"Night."

She'd made it to the bottom of the staircase when he softly called her name.

"Sierra? Just so you know, your opinion *is* relevant. What you think matters to me."

It was on the tip of her tongue to make a joke—to tell him she was glad, because she had plenty of opinions. But she couldn't do it. Instead, she climbed the steps, swallowing past a sudden lump in her throat. *You matter to me, too, cowboy.*

SIERRA WAS GROGGILY pouring her second cup of coffee when the doorbell rang on Saturday morning. Smoothing a hand over the hair she hadn't bothered to fix yet, she trudged to the front door. It wasn't until she opened it and saw Kate Sullivan standing there that she remembered they'd scheduled a breakfast meeting. They were supposed to go over all the booths and game areas with Vicki and figure out how best to use the ranch.

"Crap!"

Kate blinked. "Well, hello to you."

"I am so, so sorry." Sierra stepped out onto the porch and closed the door behind her. "It was a rough night here. Vicki's boyfriend broke up with her yesterday."

"Ouch."

"I completely forgot we were supposed to get together, and since she's still in bed, I'm assuming it slipped her mind, too."

"Understandably," Kate said, her expression sympathetic.

"I can go wake her up, but—"

"How about we reschedule? Although, it will need to be soon. The festival is almost upon us."

"Tomorrow?" Sierra said. "I swear we'll have our acts together by then. I'd volunteer for us to come to you so you don't have to make the drive again, but that kind of defeats the purpose of you getting the lay of the land here."

"Tomorrow, huh? We have a big family lunch planned after church, but my schedule is open once that's over. And don't worry about me making the trip twice. Gram's farm isn't far.

Besides, driving over here gave me a few minutes of peaceful solitude on a pretty day." She smiled. "When you're a parent, you appreciate those moments whenever you can get them."

"Thanks." She appreciated both Kate's understanding and her efforts to mitigate Sierra's chagrin. "After I have a chance to talk to Vicki, I'll text you about a time."

"Deal. But since I'm here, I wanted to ask you—are you busy tonight? Cole and I are going dancing. Want to come?"

"On your date with your fiancé? I appreciate the invitation, but I'd hate to be a third wheel."

"About that." Kate shifted her weight. "Cole's brother is planning to meet us there. Will Trent? You met him earlier in the week? When I told him you and I were working on the festival together, he mentioned he'd like to see you again."

"So this would be a double date?"

"Not at all. I just thought you might like a night out on the town before you leave Cupid's Bow. But, in the sense that I will be there with a handsome man and there will be another handsome man hoping to dance with you…" She widened her eyes, all innocence. "I can see where someone *might* think of it as a double date."

Sierra laughed. "If I ever decide I want to learn subtlety, I know who I'm coming to for lessons."

"I was once a straightforward person, but being the mother of a teenager is making me sneakier. Luke's a good kid, but he's got enough of a rebellious streak to resist the direct approach. I often have to disguise requests or make something seem like it was his idea in the first place. Not that I'm comparing you to a stubborn thirteen-year-old," she added hastily. "So, will you join us tonight?"

Sierra hesitated. On the one hand, she felt as if she should be here for Vicki. But if Vic was going to hole up in her room again, two nights in a row of couch vigil seemed lonely. *You can ask Jarrett to hang out with you.* They could play a board game or watch a movie. She thought about the two of them alone in the living room, recalling last night and the conflicted feelings that had kept her awake long after she'd crawled into bed.

"I'll go," she blurted.

"Yay! It's a date." Kate grinned. "Unofficially."

Sierra said that she wanted to take her own car, in case she was needed back at the ranch, and they agreed to meet at eight o'clock. By the time Sierra made it back to the kitchen, her coffee was cold.

Rinsing out her mug, she considered the night ahead. *I have a date with Will Trent.* Maybe not an official one—he hadn't even asked her himself—but she was spending the evening with an amusing, attractive man. So why didn't she feel more enthusiasm? Being out with him would probably be more fun than sitting around the Twisted R on a Saturday night.

It would definitely be less complicated.

Chapter Eleven

At nearly eleven, Sierra finally went in to check on Vicki, who mumbled "go away" and yanked the sheet over her face with her good hand.

"Sorry, kid." Sierra pulled the linens away. "All parties have to end eventually, and I'm declaring this pity party officially over. You'll feel better after a shower."

"I'll feel better when Aaron flunks out of history." Vicki glared. "Do you know he actually had me *edit his paper* before telling me he was seeing someone else?" She let out a shriek of fury.

"Bastard." Sierra wanted to take the anger as a good sign, but there'd been anger yesterday, too, before the despondency. "He's definitely not worth your lying in bed all day crying over him. He's a pig."

"That's an insult to pigs everywhere," Vicki said as they got her into her chair.

With the shower running, it took Sierra a moment to realize that the sound of someone knocking wasn't her imagination. "Okay," she said aloud, "there's no way I forgot *two* appointments today."

She answered the door, nearly bowled over by a trio of girls talking at once. It was hard to make out what each of them was saying, but she caught phrases here and there.

"Is Vicki okay?"

"...that rat Aaron..."

"...never be allowed to set foot in the Zeta Gamma Mu house again. Lifetime banishment!"

Sierra whistled to get their attention. "I take it you ladies are friends of Vicki's?" she asked once they were quiet. When they all opened their mouths to speak, she held up a hand. "One at a time, please."

"Not just friends," answered a curvy girl who'd cut the bottom of her sorority T-shirt into strips, creating a fringed crop top. "Sisters."

The three of them could almost pass for sisters. They were each about the same height with long, straight hair, although coloring and body shape varied.

The one in the middle wore glasses and was slender as a reed. "I'm Jemma. That's Bree and Matisse. Her mom's an art professor."

The girl in the altered T-shirt nodded. "I have brothers named Claude and Blue."

"We came as soon as we got Vicki's text," Bree said. "She sent Matisse a message last night—"

"But I'd accidentally left my phone in— Not important."

"Can we see Vicki?" Jemma asked.

"Absolutely." Sierra ushered them inside. Their company might be exactly what Vicki needed. While bad breakups sucked, venting to friends about guy troubles was such a reassuringly *normal* thing for a nineteen-year-old to do. Not like trying to reteach your legs how to support your weight or keep your pelvis perfectly aligned during standing exercises. "I'll just let her know you're here."

They trailed her down the hall, waiting as she went into Vicki's suite and knocked on the bathroom door. "Vicki? You have visitors."

The terse "who?" from the other side didn't sound very welcoming, and Sierra hoped she wasn't wrong about Vicki needing her friends right now. "Um, Jemma and—"

"My girls!" The door opened, and Vicki wheeled into the room.

High-pitched squeals and greetings ensued.

Sierra winced at the decibel. "I'll, uh, leave you guys to catch up."

Matisse beamed at her. "Don't worry. We've got it from here."

JARRETT GLANCED AT his watch. His stomach was growling and it would be nice if he had time to grab some lunch while he was in the house, but Mrs. Wilcox would be here in less than ten minutes for her boys' riding lessons. He was already pushing it by going inside to change; a morning of tractor repairs had left him covered in grease.

He banged open the door to the mudroom, already stripping off the soiled shirt to toss it in the washing machine.

The door to the kitchen opened, and Sierra hurried out to meet him. "We've been—" She stopped, her green eyes fixed on his torso with gleaming interest.

Her expression was damn good for his ego. As the moment stretched on, the urge to tease her became irresistible. "Hey," he said, "my eyes are up here."

Her face flushed with color. "I... Sorry."

Grinning, he let her off the hook. "No apology necessary. Trust me, darlin', if I ever walked in on *you* shirtless, I'd lose more than my train of thought."

The rosy hue in her cheeks deepened, and she looked away.

"What was it you were saying?" He should really find out what she needed and be on his way. Mrs. Wilcox was a stickler for punctuality. She'd once said the only way to keep five sons in line was to enroll them in so many activities that they had no time or energy left for mischief. As a result, she was always on her way to a lesson or a sporting match or to drop someone off for a part-time job.

"Oh, we've been invaded."

"Aliens? That would explain the crop circles in the pasture."

He didn't have the time to stand here making dumb jokes, but it was worth it when she laughed, her green eyes shining up at him.

"Three of Vicki's sorority sisters came to check on her," she said. "They're finishing a movie in the living room but already have plans to take over the kitchen and whip up appropriate comfort food. There was talk of something called 'armadillo eggs.' And lots of chocolate. In fact, I think I'm being sent to town with a sizable grocery list, if you need anything."

He shook his head, sidestepping her so that he could get into the house. "All I need is a clean shirt and more hours in the day." What he *wanted*, on the other hand, was to stay here with Sierra, making her laugh and enjoying the blatant interest in her gaze.

It was surprising how comfortable he was with her after what had happened yesterday. When Vicki had attacked him about his dating habits, he'd been ashamed that Sierra was there to hear it. Yet last night, when he'd told her about his carousing and Vicki's accident, she hadn't judged him at all—except to tell him to get over himself.

His mother had also told him to stop blaming himself, but she loved him, was predisposed to believe it wasn't his fault. Sierra was blunt with her opinions. If she'd thought his actions were unforgivable, she would have said so. Instead of condemnation, there'd been only matter-of-fact advice and a willingness to listen.

For a woman who routinely branded herself "difficult," Sierra Bailey was surprisingly easy to be with.

SIERRA HAD ALREADY made one trip inside with a bag of groceries when she heard footsteps behind her. She glanced over her shoulder and saw Jarrett—wearing a shirt, mercifully. She still felt foolish over how strongly she'd reacted to the sight of him earlier. She was a medical professional, for crying out loud! She'd seen plenty of unclothed bodies.

Then again, not every man had a body like his.

"Need any help?" he called from a few yards away.

"Nah." Sunset came just a little bit earlier every day, and she knew Jarrett's weekends were the busiest because of riding lessons and the boarders who came to visit their horses. "Jemma's coming out to grab the rest of it as soon as she finds her shoes."

At Jemma's name, he darted a glance toward the house that seemed almost nervous.

"Problem?" she asked.

"Of course not." He lowered his voice, leaning toward her. "But I went inside earlier to grab a quick bite and there was so much giggling. Are you sure there are only four girls total? It seemed like more. They're trying to cheer Vicki up by making plans for the spring, like concerts by bands I've never heard of. Sierra, they made me feel almost…old."

She grinned at his horrified expression. "I had that same sensation earlier. Like I was the den mother."

"Good to know it's not just me they've prematurely aged. Maybe tonight you and I should sit side by side in rockers on the porch and puzzle over whippersnappers these days with their instatwitter and facegrams."

Speaking of tonight… She needed to tell him she wouldn't be here.

"What?" He cocked his head. "You do realize I was kidding. I know it's not called facegram."

"Hey, I made plans with Kate tonight. Is that okay? I probably should have talked to you before—"

"Of course it's okay for you to take the night off. I hired you to be with Vicki so I can put in full-time days, but no one expects you to be at our beck and call around the clock." His mouth lifted in a sardonic half smile. "Especially not for what we pay you."

She lifted one shoulder as she reached into the trunk. "You'll make it up to me with glowing recommendations to any prospective employers."

"Right. Any hot leads?"

"Yeah. That clinic in Fort Worth wants me to come for an in-person interview, but not yet. Their human resource manager will be out on vacation this coming week, so we'll schedule it after she gets back."

"Well, that's…great." His tone didn't exactly match his words. When she shot a questioning look over her shoulder, he changed the subject. "So you and Kate have a girls' night planned?"

"Not exactly. I mean, yes. She invited me to the local dance hall, but it won't be just us. Cole and his brother will be there, too."

"You have a date with Will."

"More or less." Why did she suddenly feel guilty? "Is that a problem?"

"Why would it be?" His tight smile didn't reach his eyes. "Who you choose to spend your Saturday nights with is your business."

The front door opened, and Jemma came bounding down the porch stairs like a long-legged puppy, all youthful energy. "I promise I didn't forget about the groceries!"

I did. The last thing on Sierra's mind was the bag of food she held. She was far more concerned with trying to read Jarrett's expression, but he was already turning away.

"See you all at dinner," he said. "Assuming you'll still be here?"

She nodded. "I'm making a couple of pizzas. I'll head out after we eat."

He gave a crisp nod and headed back in the direction of the barn.

Was he angry? Disappointed that she hadn't heeded his warning about not going out with Will? The firefighter's aversion to commitment was hardly a deterrent. If Sierra's upcoming interview went well, she would be living in Fort Worth by October. The last thing she wanted was to fall for a man in Cupid's Bow.

"JARRETT? IF YOU don't grab a slice, there might not be any pizza left."

Vicki's words, which seemed to be coming from a lot farther than a few feet away, made Jarrett wonder how long he'd been standing at the counter, staring out the kitchen window. Truthfully, he wasn't very hungry. But at least his sister was voluntarily speaking to him after yesterday's blowup.

Good thing she was being civil since he'd probably alienated Sierra before she left the house. Having both the females he lived with ticked off at him seemed like a dangerous gamble.

When Sierra had come down the stairs for her date, Jarrett had been poleaxed by the sight of her in that figure-hugging black dress. He'd also noted the effort she'd put into styling her hair and fixing her makeup—trouble she'd gone to for Will Trent. He should have told her she looked beautiful. Or, better yet, said nothing at all. Instead, what he'd heard come out of his mouth was that she was overdressed for the local dance hall.

She'd narrowed her eyes. "Then maybe I'll set some new trends around here. Don't wait up for me."

Wasn't there a time when he'd been smooth with women, instinctively charming? He'd habitually doled out flattery to every female who'd crossed his path. So why, after a day of thinking how grateful he was to Sierra, had he insulted her instead of paying her a basic compliment?

Behind him, Vicki cleared her throat. "We're going to be using the TV. You didn't need the living room, right?"

In other words, could he please be somewhere else in the house instead of awkwardly lurking around like an unwanted chaperone? "Not at all. Maybe I'll go into town."

Last night, he'd shot game after game of pool with anyone who wanted to challenge him. Tonight he could catch a movie.

Or call a few of the rodeo buddies he hadn't seen much of lately and see if anyone wanted to go bowling.

But even as he had the thought, he dismissed it. Why bother lying to himself? He knew exactly where he was headed.

"YOU LOOK FANTASTIC," Kate said, raising her voice to be better heard over the live band. "I'm sure Will's already told you that."

He had, when she'd first arrived half an hour ago. Currently, Will and Cole were at the bar, getting them a round of drinks. When asked what she wanted, Sierra had said anything frozen. She normally preferred a glass of nice wine over cocktails that came with umbrellas or swizzle sticks of fruit, but two fast dances on a crowded floor had left her flushed with heat. Besides, while Cupid's Bow had a number of nice qualities, she doubted an upscale wine list was one of them.

"It's always nice to hear that you look good," Sierra said, "even if it's already been said." *Take that, Jarrett Ross.* Maybe she *was* overdressed, standing out among women who were mostly wearing jeans and red bandanna skirts, but none of her companions seemed to mind.

Lifting her hair off the nape of her neck and fanning herself with her free hand, she scanned the throng of people around her, hoping to see the Trent brothers returning with cold drinks. No such luck. "Cole seems great," she told her friend. The smiling man, who looked a lot like Will, radiated happiness every time he looked at his fiancée. "I've never met a town sheriff before. I think I expected someone more serious. All squinty-eyed and somber, ready to challenge bad guys in high-noon showdowns."

Kate's peal of laughter rang out over the band's fiddle solo. "You do know Cole's not a sheriff in the 1800s, right? Besides, it's Cupid's Bow. We're fortunate not to have too many bad guys. Mostly, our crime waves are limited to the Breelan brothers fighting among themselves and crafty old Mr. Wainwright, who has tried to sneak past the nursing-home administration to go streaking three times over the past year."

Sierra grinned. "Cupid's Bow has a senior-citizen streaker?"

"Well, he only successfully made it once. The other two times, he was spotted and cajoled back into the facility with butterscotch pudding."

"Butterscotch pudding? Y'all must be talking about Mr. Wainwright." Cole emerged from the crowd, carrying two beers. "The deputies are betting shifts of early-morning crosswalk duty on when he'll make his next attempt."

"I can't believe this," Will complained, handing Sierra a frozen margarita. "We leave you two ladies alone, presenting Kate a clear opportunity to talk me up to a beautiful redhead, and instead, my future sister-in-law decides to chat about an eighty-two-year-old." He shot a wounded expression at Kate. "Where's the love, I ask you?"

She grinned at him over the top of her beer. "Sorry. Go away again, and I'll try to do better."

"Oh, no. You've lost all credibility with me." Will dropped an arm around Sierra's shoulders. "Besides, if I keep leaving her alone, someone else is going to ask her to dance. Then where will I be? As it is, only Cole's stern cop glare is keeping other suitors at bay."

Sierra laughed out loud at that. "Stern cop glare?" She'd never met a man who looked more besotted and happy with his life than Cole Trent.

"Oh, I have one," Cole said. "But since I'm off duty tonight, I left it at home."

The four of them continued to joke around while they finished their drinks. Then Will asked if Sierra was ready to hit the dance floor again.

"Sure." She'd learned to dance years ago at her parents' country club, but she and Paul had rarely made time for it. She'd forgotten how much she enjoyed it.

They made it to the edge of the sawdust-sprinkled dance floor just in time for the last few power chords of the rollicking song. Then the music shifted into a slower ballad. Will pulled her against him—not indecently close, but definitely more snugly than he had for their previous dances.

Sierra stiffened, the contact making her feel an errant twinge of…guilt? That was ridiculous. There was no reason why she shouldn't be enjoying Will's company. They were both single adults, and he was a great dancer with a natural sense of rhythm. She took a deep breath, forcibly relaxing her muscles and leaning into him.

They matched each other's movements well enough, but there was none of the banter they'd been sharing up until now. Could Will tell she was wrestling a sense of discomfort? At the corner of the floor, he rotated their positions, and her feet collided with his.

"Sorry," he said, even though she was certain she'd been at fault. "Guess I'm not really feeling this song." After a moment, he admitted, "I got distracted."

She glanced up, surprised to see him staring intently across the room. Apparently, he wasn't just being gallant. Something—or someone—really had snagged his focus.

"Damn," he muttered under his breath.

She craned her head, trying to see what he was looking at, but her height put her at a disadvantage. "What's wrong? Bar fight? Ex?"

"I wish. At least I know how to deal with my ex." He met Sierra's gaze, his smile wry. "When you live in the same small town, you get a lot of practice running into each other—whether you want it or not. No, I spotted Amy Reynolds, this kid I've felt vaguely responsible for since her apartment caught fire. She used to date a real jerk—guy who makes the disreputable Breelans look like choirboys—but last time I talked to her, they'd broken up. Now he's with her in a dark corner. If he confronted her, I'm more than willing to ask him to back off. But if she came here with him tonight…"

She understood his dilemma. If the couple had reunited, he didn't really have the authority to make her stop seeing the guy. "Let's go find out. I'm new in town. You can tell Amy you wanted to introduce us, and we can check out the situation up close."

"Wonderful idea." He gave her a grateful smile. "My brother could use you for undercover work."

"I'd probably be terrible at it. I'm characteristically very blunt, which doesn't work well with deception. But Kate's been telling me about the merits of being sneaky."

He took her hand, but the contact felt more practical than romantic, as if he was just trying to keep from losing her in the crowd. Their progress was interrupted twice by women cooing flirtatious hellos to Will. If Sierra had been more invested in their date, she might have been jealous.

He's a great guy. There's just no spark. She'd suspected as much before she even arrived at the dance hall. She wasn't sorry she'd come—awkward slow dance aside, she was having a lot of fun—but if he asked her out again before she left town, she doubted she'd say yes. It would feel too disingenuous.

"Hey, Amy." Will's voice was deliberately cheerful, but Sierra could still see the tension he was trying to mask. Using his size, he muscled his way between her and her scowling blond companion to hug her. And, Sierra guessed, to discreetly check if she was okay.

"Will!" Amy brought one arm up to hug him, stumbling forward as she did so. "And who's this?" Even though she was holding a bottle of water and not a cocktail, her words were slurred.

"Sierra Bailey. Nice to meet you." Up close, the girl looked young, probably not even twenty-two yet. Judging by the lines on his face, the guy with her looked a few years older. Sierra definitely got a creepy vibe from him and could see why Will had been worried.

"So what are you two up to tonight?" Will said.

"We're on a date," the other man said, his tone clipped. "Which you're interrupting."

"Donavan." Amy frowned at him, blinking her glazed eyes a couple of times. "Will's my friend. Don't be rude."

"Didn't mean to be rude, baby." The man's voice turned syrupy sweet, but there was no true affection in the way he looked at her. "I guess I just like having you all to myself."

She tittered, smiling as if he'd said something romantic. "Will, you and I will have to catch up later. Nice to meet you, Sarah."

Between the volume of the music and Amy's less-than-alert state, Sierra didn't bother correcting her. Instead, she just gave the younger woman a friendly nod.

Donavan took her hand, dragging her toward the floor. "Let's dance, baby."

As they disappeared into the Saturday-night mob, Will clenched his jaw. "I hate that guy. There are rumors about him selling illegal prescription drugs. I swear he's given her something..." He stopped, shaking his head. "Sorry. I must win the worst-date-ever prize."

"No, that would go to the guy with the toe fetish who made obscene comments about my feet three minutes into our first—and last—dinner together." When he chuckled, she congratulated herself on making him smile again. He obviously had reason to worry about his friend. "Lots of people make questionable dating choices when they're young. I bet she'll wise up and kick him to the curb eventually."

Will nodded absently. "I could use another drink. You?"

"I wouldn't say no to an ice water." At the bar, they ran into a couple of the ladies she'd met at the festival-committee lunch. While she was talking with them, a fellow fireman challenged Will to a game of darts.

When Kate tapped her on the shoulder and asked, "Where's Will?" Sierra realized she hadn't seen him in a while.

"Darts, I think. We kind of split up."

Kate's mouth twisted, her eyes reflecting disappointment. "I thought you two hit it off."

"We did." Platonically, anyway. "He's a lot of fun. But…"

"But you probably aren't going to be his date to my wedding?"

"No."

"Too bad. He's been sort of aimless since his ex broke off their engagement, and you seemed perfect for him."

"I don't think he'll have trouble finding someone new," Sierra said wryly. She'd spotted him a few feet away, flanked by two brunettes.

Kate followed her gaze. "No, I suppose not. Although I can tell you for sure he's not interested in that one. She won him during a bachelor auction over the summer, and he said the resulting date was torture. She's very cloying."

That much was evident even from across the bar. Sierra watched as the woman on his left kept finding reasons to touch him. Will seemed as if he was trying to inch away, but his movements were hampered by the woman on his other side.

Sierra set her glass down. "If you'll excuse me, I'm going to rescue my date."

Will's eyes lit up when he saw her. "Sierra! Just the person I was looking for."

"You owe me a dance," she said, her tone chiding as she reached for his arm.

The brunette on his left glared but didn't try to stop them as they moved away.

"You are a very popular man," Sierra teased him.

"A mixed blessing. Why is it never the right women who try to plaster themselves all over me? If *you* wanted to make a move, for instance…" It was clear from the twinkle in his gaze that he was kidding. Mostly.

"I think Kate was hoping we would fall madly in love."

"Yeah, she has this notion that I'm still pining for the ex who broke my heart and keeps trying to help me find someone new."

"You're not pining?" Sierra asked as he led her into a fast waltz.

"No. Tasha and I met when we were both ten and dated all through high school. I loved her, and I would have married her. But when she backed out of the wedding, it occurred to me that I was single for, effectively, the first time in my life. Why not enjoy it?"

"Seems reasonable."

"What about you? Any close brushes with matrimony?"

"Not really. I was dating a doctor for a few months, until he moved out of the country. He's a great guy, but, like you, I'm not pining."

"And there's no one you have your eye on now?" he asked carefully. "The other night, at the ranch, I kind of thought..."

She abruptly stopped dancing. "Thought what?"

"Never mind. I'm probably way off base." He took her hand and twirled her, ending the conversation.

They danced through two more songs before the band slowed to another ballad. Sierra was considering excusing herself to the ladies' room when Will glanced over her head and laughed.

"Hmm," he said, "I think my competition has arrived."

"Competition?" She turned to see Jarrett hold his hand out toward her.

"Mind if I cut in?" he asked.

Unsure how to respond, she glanced back at Will.

He winked. "Maybe not so off base after all." He took a step back. "Catch up with you later?"

"All right," she agreed, suddenly a bit breathless. *From all those twirls and spins you've been doing.* Uh-huh. That was probably it.

Jarrett stepped closer, lacing his fingers with hers as his other hand slid to the small of her back.

Tiny electric sparks shot through her. It was nothing like when Will had held her. "Wh-what are you doing here?" she asked.

"Looking for you. There's something I forgot to tell you earlier."

They were swaying together, her feet moving in time with his, but the music faded into the background when he spoke to her. All her senses were focused on him—the way he smelled, the heat of his body against hers, the silvery gleam in his eyes. He bent close, his voice a murmur in her ear. "You look incredible tonight."

Her breath caught. *That* was what he'd wanted to say? "You drove all the way into town to tell me I look incredible?" Her brain was having a tough time catching up. "You said I was overdressed."

"That's because I'm an ass. A jealous one, apparently."

"Jealous over Will? He and I aren't even interested in each other romantically." Had everyone mentally paired them off as a couple?

"I still envied the time he was spending with you. You've been dancing with him. He got to hold you, laugh with you. *Be* with you. I only have a couple of weeks left with you, darlin', and I find myself irrationally resentful of the moments we don't spend together."

She felt faint. *That's what you get for not remembering to breathe.* She'd been too spellbound by his unexpected declaration for anything as mundane as inhaling and exhaling. "I think… I think I need some fresh air."

They abandoned the floor midsong, and she made a beeline toward the exit. Outside, the night was cool against her skin, but the second she looked into Jarrett's eyes, she was feverish again.

He spoke first. "I hope I didn't upset you with what I said."

"No." Agitated, maybe, with the way her heart was slamming against her ribs and her mind was racing, trying to find the right response to his words. But she wasn't upset. "I'm glad you showed up here. Glad I got to dance with you."

"We don't have to stop," he said, pulling her closer. The music was muffled but still audible from the parking lot.

"But maybe we should." Despite her sensible words, she leaned into him, indulging herself in the feel of their bodies tangled together. Her hands glided up his back. This was such a bad idea. "I work for you. Do you know why I left my last job? Accusations of fraternization with a male patient. My professionalism is very important to me." She was beginning to realize her job was all she had. "I would never compromise myself with a patient."

He brushed his thumb over the corner of her mouth, and she shivered. "Then I guess," he said as he lowered his head, "it's a good thing I'm not your patient."

Chapter Twelve

Jarrett hadn't known what to expect when he'd parked his truck outside the dance hall. He wasn't sure he'd be welcome, although he'd hoped Sierra would be happy to see him once he'd apologized. Never in his wildest imaginings could he have predicted that minutes after finding her, they'd be kissing in the moonlight.

Even as his lips captured hers, part of him couldn't believe it was happening. She was hot and sweet in his arms, lifting on tiptoe to meet him. He threaded his fingers through her hair, determined to make this stolen moment worth it. Instead of rushing, devouring her after wanting her for days on end, he traced the seam of her lips with his tongue, coaxing, seducing. He nipped at her full lower lip and drank in her soft moan as if it were exquisitely aged bourbon. It went straight to his head.

Their kiss grew hungrier, and his need for her sharpened. He desperately wanted to touch her, but Sierra deserved better than being groped in a parking lot.

He dropped his hands to his sides, breathing heavily.

She pressed her fingers to her lips, looking dazed.

"For the record," he said hoarsely, "that didn't lessen my opinion of your professionalism one iota. You're a fantastic physical therapist. Nothing that happens between us alters that."

Their kiss was about the chemistry between them and how the more he got to know Sierra, the more he wanted her. It had no bearing on the job she was doing with Vicki.

Vicki. His stomach knotted as he thought about the assurances he'd made that he'd stay away from Sierra, that he wasn't lusting after her. For now, he shoved away the recriminations. He couldn't bring himself to regret what had just happened.

And he prayed Sierra didn't regret it, either. She still hadn't said anything.

"You're quiet," he said, tucking a strand of hair behind her ear. "It's disconcerting."

"Good." Her mouth curved in an impish half smile. "I like to keep you on your toes."

If he were any more "on his toes" over her, some ballet company was going to draft him. "Do you want to go back inside?"

"I don't think so," she said slowly.

He nuzzled her neck, dotting a line of quick kisses toward the strap of her dress. "Any chance you want to make out in my truck?" he teased.

She huffed out a soft sound that was half sigh, half chuckle. "That's probably not a good idea."

Which didn't mean she didn't *want* to, he noted happily.

"I have a lot to mull over, and a raucous dance hall on a Saturday night doesn't seem conducive to deep thought."

"Do you want me to drive you back to the ranch? We can get your car tomorrow. Or I can follow you," he offered, trying to give her the space she needed.

"That sounds good. But I shouldn't leave without letting Kate and Will know." She pulled her cell phone from the pocket of her dress and sent a text. The response was almost instantaneous. "Okay."

He reached for her hand. Even though the walk to her car was only a minute or two, he wanted the contact between them. Once she'd unlocked her door and slid inside, he bent down to press a kiss to her forehead.

"Don't think too hard," he said lightly.

She cupped the nape of his neck and pulled him down for a proper kiss. "No chance of that," she said once she'd released him. "I don't think I've been in my right mind since I got here."

SIERRA WOKE UP to the blessed aroma of coffee wafting up the stairs and serious doubts about kissing her employer the night before.

When she and Jarrett had pulled up to the ranch, Vicki and her friends had been out on the front porch, enjoying the cool breeze as they chatted. Vicki had wanted to hear about her "date," although Sierra insisted she and Will were nothing more than friends. She'd evaded questions about the evening but let the girls talk her into having a late-night ice-cream sundae with them. There hadn't been any real privacy with Jarrett to discuss the kiss they'd shared.

Maybe that was for the best, since she still wasn't sure what to say.

You could say "kiss me again, cowboy." A great plan, except that the kisses would only make her crave more. *Too late.* She'd ached throughout the night thinking about his mouth on hers. For the first time since she'd come to the ranch, she'd been too hot to sleep. And she knew the air conditioner wasn't to blame.

Her jumbled sheets were a testament to the restless night she'd spent. Sitting up, she swung her feet to the floor. *Coffee.* At this point, it was her only hope of coherence.

She was accustomed to having the kitchen to herself in the mornings, since Vicki was often still in her room and Jarrett was usually outside working at an early hour. But today, everyone was piled into the sunny room. Vicki's sorority sisters were leaving sometime after breakfast, and all four girls were seated at the table, bemoaning their imminent separation. Meanwhile, Jarrett leaned against the counter, drinking his mug of coffee.

Sierra's hand flew to her tousled hair. In her polka-dot sleep-shirt and the cut-off sweatpants that served as pajama bottoms, she was a far cry from the carefully made up and accessorized woman who'd left the house yesterday evening. She wasn't indecent in her sleepwear, but she also wasn't polished. That only came after caffeine.

Yet as soon as Jarrett saw her, a slow, admiring smile spread across his face. His gaze swept over her from head to toe, the desire in his expression so evident that she almost blushed, glad none of the coeds happened to be looking his way. Despite the uncertainty plaguing her this morning, she had to grin back at him. There should be a special place in heaven for men who could make a woman feel this beautiful when she first rolled out of bed.

She went straight to him. "I'm surprised to find you here."

"I was waiting for you," he said. "I thought, since Vicki's going to want to spend a couple of hours with her friends before they leave, maybe you'd be free for your next horse-riding lesson."

Strategically, now might be the perfect time for her to get back in the saddle; she'd probably be too nervous about what was happening between her and Jarrett to remember to be scared of the horse.

He covered her hand with his. "Please?"

She melted inside, unable to resist the combination of his earnest tone and beguiling expression. He'd told her last night he wanted to spend as much time with her as possible during her remaining days in Cupid's Bow. *Admit it—he's not the only one who feels that way.*

"Okay," she agreed. "How about I meet you at the stable after I've had sufficient coffee and changed my clothes?"

"See you soon." He winked at her and headed for the door.

Oh, Sierra, what are you doing? Sighing into her coffee over a handsome cowboy didn't seem like the most professional way to spend her morning. Then again, as he'd pointed out, *he* wasn't her patient, so was there any real conflict?

"Hey, Vicki, do you need me for anything right now? I was,

um, planning to meet your brother at the stable. F-for my next riding lesson." She stammered through the explanation, but luckily, Vicki would attribute that to her fear of horses.

"Go for it!"

Well, that was one option.

After a very small breakfast, Sierra pulled on a pair of jeans and a short-sleeved silky top. The shirt wasn't standard-issue Western wear, but it was fitted enough not to flutter around and spook her horse without restricting any of Sierra's movements. Similarly, her cute fall boots hadn't been purchased for tromping around a barn, but the heel was appropriate for riding. She braided her hair and applied lip gloss as a quick concession to vanity. Meeting her own gaze in the mirror, she wondered if Jarrett would discover for himself that the gloss was chocolate-flavored. A rush of anticipation went through her.

Jarrett was waiting for her at the practice ring, his elbow propped on the fence behind him. With his black cowboy hat shading his handsome face, he was the Texas rewrite of Prince Charming.

"Sorry if I took longer than expected," she said.

He tipped back his hat with his index finger, smiling into her eyes. "You were worth the wait. Are you ready for this?"

No. But that didn't seem to be stopping her.

Shiloh was saddled and standing in the corral. Another horse was saddled and tethered to a hitching post on the far side of the paddock. As she had last time, Sierra approached the mare from the left, speaking softly.

Jarrett nodded approvingly. "I'm going to help you mount and lead you around the ring once just so you can get a feel for being on her. Then I'll turn the reins over to you and go through some basic skills—stops, starts, turns."

He stepped closer, only a breath between his body and hers, and her pulse kicked up a notch at his nearness. "Hold these like this," he said, sliding the leather reins into her hand. "I'll boost you up on three so you can put your foot in the stirrup. Swing your leg over and grab on to the pommel."

"Got it."

He hooked two fingers into the D ring on the saddle strap, his free hand moving down the back of Sierra's thigh until he'd reached behind her knee. "One, two, *three*."

Here goes nothing. Taking a deep breath, she did as he'd instructed. Between the two of them, she achieved enough momentum to land correctly in the saddle. Shiloh shifted beneath her, adjusting to the weight, and apprehension roiled in Sierra's stomach. The deal with Vicki had been that she'd get back in the saddle, right? *Achievement unlocked.* Maybe she could get down now.

Jarrett chuckled. "You should see your face."

"Sheet-white and terrified?"

"Equal parts reluctant and resolute. You look like you're at war with yourself. Also, you should probably never play poker. You'd be a complete failure at bluffing."

She arched an eyebrow. "I'm not a complete failure at *anything*," she said haughtily.

"Ah, there's the boldly self-assured Sierra I was looking for." He took the reins from her and patted Shiloh's neck, telling her what a good job she was doing. Sierra suspected the words were for her benefit as well as the horse's.

Jarrett started them off at a pace so slow it barely qualified as a walk, but steadily increased his speed every few feet. "How are you doing?"

"I feel very tall up here." Her undisciplined gaze dropped to the back of his jeans. "The view's nice."

When he cast a quick glance back at her, she lifted one hand from the pommel to indicate the pasture beyond and the horizon that seemed to stretch on forever.

He smirked. "Uh-huh. Well, if you're done enjoying the view, I think you're ready to proceed to the next step." He gave her a brief refresher on using the reins and directing the horse, and then she was on her own.

She felt like a kid riding a bike for the first time without training wheels—exhilarated and scared and triumphant. On her second pass across the corral, she leaned forward and tapped Shiloh with her heels, urging the mare to pick up her pace. They moved on to a trot, and Sierra regretted the years she'd let pass before getting on a horse again.

"You look like you're having fun," Jarrett observed. "Up for a short ride?"

"Definitely."

He grinned proudly. "I was hoping you'd say that." He untied the other horse, explaining that Major was the lead horse on trail rides. "Shiloh's used to following and won't give you any trouble."

His assurance proved true. The path was obviously a familiar one to Shiloh, and she stuck to it complacently, although she seemed to enjoy letting loose in the open section where Jarrett said it would be okay to try a canter. Racing across the meadow left Sierra's heart in her throat, but in a good way, like screaming down a roller coaster with a best friend. Still, she knew she wasn't up for a gallop yet and she doubted she'd ever try to jump a horse again, even with a helmet.

It was enough to know that she'd accomplished this and could enjoy riding with Jarrett from time to time. *You have no time. You'll be gone soon, remember?*

All the more reason to make the most of the moments they did share.

As they returned to the corral, she gloried in a giddy sense of freedom, knowing she was no longer constrained by old fears and wounds. She felt wonderful, although there was a slight tenderness along her inner thighs. The ride hadn't been long enough for her to get sore, but she was definitely more aware of parts of her body she didn't always notice. That awareness only heightened when Jarrett helped her down from the horse.

His hands settled on her hips, his gaze dropping to her face, and the twinges she'd felt between her legs escalated to a far more substantial ache. She met his eyes, not even trying to hide how much she wanted him.

He sucked in a breath. "Have I mentioned how grateful I am that you don't have a poker face?"

Leaving the horses temporarily secured in the paddock, he tugged Sierra into the stable. They'd barely made it through the wide entryway before he spun her against the wall and claimed her mouth in a ravenous kiss. His tongue dueled with hers, and he sucked hard at her bottom lip. Need shot through her. She gripped his shirt in both hands, never wanting to let him go.

She tilted her head back against the wooden beam as he kissed his way to the hollow of her throat. He caught the hem of her satiny shirt between his fingers. "Soft." Then his hand skimmed beneath the material over her skin. "Softer."

There was a fleeting ticklish sensation as his fingers grazed her ribs, but then he palmed a breast through her bra, and the would-be giggle she'd suppressed turned into a moan. When she tried to reach up on her toes to kiss him again, she almost lost her balance. No surprise, since she'd been unsteady since the second she'd slid down from the saddle and into his waiting arms.

"Blasted height difference," she muttered. "I'm too short."

"What you are is perfect." He scooped her up and carried her to the back of the stable, setting her on her feet long enough to pull a folded picnic blanket from a cabinet. He opened it with a flourish, dropping it on the ground and then pulling her down with him. He kissed with intent, every stroke of his tongue against hers making her a little bit crazier with desire.

Both his hands were beneath her shirt, and she was about to sit up and remove it completely when the horse in the nearest stall neighed, jolting her from her sensual reverie.

"Wait." She pressed a palm against Jarrett's chest, trying to focus on regaining her composure and not on the hard, unyielding muscles beneath her hand. "No, I—"

"No?" He scrambled back, looking crestfallen.

"Well, yes." Definitely yes. "But not now." She needed to get back to the house before Vicki's friends left, needed to make lunch and be ready for their meeting with Kate. No way would she flake out on her friend two days in a row. "And not here." Good Lord—was there hay in her hair? She really was living the cliché.

He nodded in immediate agreement, but he was clenching his jaw, betraying the effort it took to move away from her. "Later, then?"

Her heart beat triple time. "Later." The word had never sounded so sexy.

THE TIMING WORKED out perfectly—Sierra and Vicki had finished lunch and a set of PT exercises when the doorbell rang.

"Come on in," Sierra said, ushering her friend inside. "Sorry I didn't have the chance to tell you goodbye properly last night."

Kate waved off the apology. "It would have taken us fifteen minutes to find each other in the crowd to exchange a two-minute farewell. Texting was quicker. I'm just glad I had my phone out to show Anita pictures of the flower-girl dresses I found for the twins, or it would have taken me longer to notice." She laughed, patting the large binder in her hand. "Right now, I feel like my life revolves around two binders—wedding stuff and festival plans. Thank goodness the Harvest Day event is, as the name indicates, a single day. The Watermelon Festival back in July was four."

Sierra blinked. "How many festivals do you people have?"

"It's a small town," she said fondly. "We have to make our own entertainment."

They'd discovered last night that they had each lived in Houston. After her husband's death a couple of years ago, Kate had deliberately sought out the slower pace of small-town life. While she admitted that Cupid's Bow could be a little quirky, she embraced its eccentricities. Sierra was undecided. She missed the convenience of take-out Thai food, but she was growing accustomed to sleeping with only the sounds of nature outside her window and not city noise. And there was no question that she'd rather hang out with Kate and the Trent brothers and Anita Drake than the surgeons and attorneys she'd met at her parents' country club.

Cupid's Bow had its charms. Her gaze went to the huge bay window and the barn in the distance. She couldn't see Jarrett from here, but knowing he was out there somewhere made her smile.

Kate cleared her throat delicately. "Penny for your thoughts?" She glanced outside as if trying to find what Sierra was grinning at.

"I'm just having a good day."

They convened in the kitchen, where Kate spread out a bunch of papers on the table. The yellow sheets of paper had specifically scheduled events like games, performances and competitions. Typed on white pages were the names of different vendor sponsors who were helping pay for the festival and would each get a booth in return.

"We definitely have room for all of this," Vicki said, studying the list she'd compiled while Kate talked. "The biggest challenge will be parking. Can I make a suggestion?"

"Please." Kate nodded emphatically. "This is my first major volunteer project for the town. If I screw it up, my husband might not get reelected as sheriff."

Vicki laughed. "Sierra said that you originally volunteered your grandmother's farm, which is close by. It's not big enough for the festival, but do you think we can use it for the majority of guest parking? We can set up a rotation of volunteers to bring people from the farm down to our ranch via hayride."

"Sounds great," Kate said. "I'll run it by Gram, but I can't imagine her saying no."

"Good." Vicki propped her chin on her fist. "As long as we have places for people to park and a place for the portable potty trailers to set up, I think everything else will run smoothly."

They discussed the different areas of the ranch and how best to divide them. Sierra was impressed with Vicki's ideas, but the longer they talked, the more she worried that Vicki wasn't being very realistic about how much she could actually oversee on the day of the festival. The uneven outdoor terrain was not ideal for her wheelchair. She wouldn't be dashing from one tent to another.

When she tried to gently remind Vicki of that, the girl scowled. "I'm getting better at the standing exercises, and I took steps on Friday morning." With Sierra's assistance, she'd been practicing to show Aaron when he arrived. He'd left before a demonstration could take place. "The festival's not until next weekend. Maybe if I work hard, I can use a walker to—"

"Vicki, I applaud the ambition, but there's a huge difference between half a dozen steps in a controlled environment and being on your feet all day." The ground that was imperfect for the wheelchair would be downright dangerous with a walker. It might be months before Vicki was ready for hills, rocks and gopher holes. "I'm not saying you have to stay confined in the house—we'll get you set up at a volunteer table or the booth of your choosing—but you'll need to delegate some of the plans you've brainstormed."

"I have lots of willing bodies on the committee," Kate said quickly. "But we need you to point us in the right direction."

Vicki wavered, and Sierra could see her weigh the heady responsibility of being in charge against the frustration of her limited mobility. She smiled tightly. "Well, I suppose the festival *is* a team effort."

They worked for another half hour or so, with Kate and Vicki splitting up a number of phone calls that needed to be made this week.

"Give me the tough requests," Vicki said, "the ones people are most likely to refuse." She tilted her head, making her eyes huge and pitiful. "Who's going to say no to the kid in a wheelchair?"

Kate laughed. "Nice dealing with a kindred devious spirit." She packed all the loose sheets of paper back into her binder. "Now I'd better get home and figure out how I'm going to trick the twins into eating lima beans for dinner. Oh, speaking of food! Sierra, can you walk me out? Gram sent some of her famous jalapeño peach preserves, but I forgot to bring in the jars."

"Sure thing."

As the two women descended the porch steps, Sierra thanked Kate again for coming back and for including Vicki in the decision-making process.

"Hey, today benefited me as much as her. I wasn't expecting Becca to give me nearly so much power, but she's preoccupied with upgrading her house so that she can rent out a couple of rooms. I don't want to screw up the festival, and Vicki had some really great input." She opened her car door and leaned inside, grabbing an oblong box with three jars of preserves bearing homemade labels. "The whole Ross family is great, don't you think?"

"Well, I haven't met the elder Rosses, but Vicki and Jarrett—"

"I was sorry I didn't get a chance to say hi to him last night. Will said the two of you disappeared immediately after your slow dance." She nudged Sierra with her shoulder. "Guess that means the two of you were anxious to be alone?"

Too late, Sierra realized she'd been asked outside so that her friend could interrogate her about Jarrett. *Ambushed by the old peach-jam-in-the-car scam.* When was she going to remember that no matter how sweet Kate was, she was also sneaky?

She rolled her eyes, carefully not meeting the other woman's gaze. "Oh, for pity's sake. Last night, you were trying to play matchmaker between me and Will, and now, less than twenty-four hours later, you've imagined some grand affair between me and Jarrett? Have you ever considered that you're suffering from wedding brain? You and Cole are so deliriously happy, you're hallucinating potential romances all around you."

"Nice try. But Will doesn't have 'wedding brain' and he sees the chemistry between you and Jarrett, too. After Jarrett unexpectedly showed up last night, Will said that, with the sparks between you two, he never stood a chance. Not that he sounded upset, so don't let that make you feel guilty."

Part of Sierra was dying to tell someone about the kiss he'd shocked her with last night, if not the more intimate details of their make-out session in the barn. But it was still so new. She'd barely had a chance to process it herself, much less figure out how to explain it to someone else. What if Kate asked about the future? Right now, Sierra's future was no more than a couple of touchstones in the murky distance—her interview in Fort Worth next week, her brother's wedding in a couple of months. She hadn't planned for a sexy cowboy with silvery eyes and decadent kisses.

"Uh-oh." Kate misread the long silence. "I ticked you off with my prying, didn't I? I don't mean to meddle but— Well, I do, actually. It's the Cupid's Bow way. But I genuinely care about you."

Sierra impulsively hugged her. "Thank you. In a town this size, it would be easy to feel like the outsider, but you've made me feel like I belonged since the day I got here."

"So you'll forgive me for all the intrusive questions about your love life?"

"There's nothing to forgive. You're just being a friend."

"Exactly." Kate ducked into the driver's seat. "Are you *sure* there's nothing between you and Jarrett?"

"Kate!" If her friend didn't drive away soon, Sierra would end up spilling everything.

"All right, all right. I can take a hint." She closed the door, giving Sierra one last cheery wave through the window.

As she watched Kate drive away, Sierra gave in to the impulse to say the truth out loud, if only to herself. "There is definitely something between me and Jarrett." But only time would tell how deep it ran.

JARRETT STAYED AWAY from the house past sundown, stalling because he was half afraid he'd pounce on Sierra the second he saw her again. He'd been hard for her all afternoon, ever since she'd met his eyes with that sultry gaze and murmured, "Later." That promise had been taunting him for hours.

When he finally walked into the kitchen, he was met by the enticing smell of dinner, but he barely tasted the roast beef she served. Instead he kept remembering the night she'd brought him a roast beef sandwich and accused him of avoiding her. Maybe he had been, at first. But noble intentions and distance hadn't done him any good. She'd got under his skin all the same. Now, instead of taking sensible refuge in the stable, he was tracking her down in dance halls just to tell her she looked nice. It was almost hilarious.

There were only two things that kept him from appreciating the humor in the situation. First, she was moving away. Driving into town to find her was one thing; routinely driving to Fort Worth was out of the question—especially when he'd need to be here to make sure his father didn't try to take back too much of the workload. Second, as much as he wanted Sierra, as impatiently as he was awaiting bedtime tonight, he couldn't entirely escape the guilt over betraying his promise to Vicki.

Falling into bed with Sierra was exactly what his sister had predicted when he'd hired the beautiful redhead, exactly what he'd sworn wouldn't happen.

You haven't done it yet, his conscience pointed out. *There's still time to change your—*

Like hell. He was losing Sierra soon—he couldn't change that—but knowing that their desire was mutual, that he'd somehow won over this fiery woman, there was no way he would sacrifice this chance to be with her. He'd sworn to Vicki that attraction to Sierra had nothing to do with offering her the job, and that was still true. Making love to Sierra didn't retroactively taint his decision to hire her. She'd absolutely been the right person for the job, which she'd proved time and again.

"Jarrett?" Across the table, Sierra looked concerned, and he realized how withdrawn he'd been. Trying to keep his simmering lust under control had prevented him from interacting much with her. He hadn't said much to Vicki either, but she was quiet, too, probably missing her friends.

"Anything wrong with your food?" Sierra asked.

"Sorry. Guess my mind's…elsewhere." Specifically, upstairs. In a bed with her. But he took a couple of bites of dinner, not wanting her cooking to go to waste.

A few minutes later, Vicki gave up on her own meal and announced that she was going to bed early. After she left the room, Sierra stood.

"The good news is, we have plenty left over for lunch tomorrow." She carried her plate and Vicki's to the sink.

"I'll clean up the dishes," he volunteered.

"You sure? That would be great. I was thinking about taking a bubble bath. I could use the relaxation. I've been…strangely tense all day."

"Go take your bath," he said softly. "If that doesn't relieve your tension, we'll see if we can come up with something more effective."

She grinned, her eyes shimmering with banked heat. "Good to know I have options."

She went upstairs and he cleaned the kitchen, then watched some football. But it was all kind of a watercolor blur, pale and muted compared to the moments he spent with Sierra. Wanting to give her plenty of time, he considered calling his parents; he'd been giving them updates on the ranch and Vicki's progress every few days. But he opted against it, afraid his mom might take his distraction as a sign that something was wrong.

He headed up the stairs, struck by the novelty of how rare

it was to be with a woman under his own roof. There'd been a few furtive encounters at the ranch over the years, but a lot of his love life had taken place in motel rooms and the bench seats of trucks. When was the last time he'd woken up next to a woman he'd fallen asleep beside and started the day with her? He'd seen quite a few lovers naked, but he was woefully inexperienced when it came to actual intimacy. He liked that he knew exactly how Sierra fixed her morning coffee and how adorably disheveled she looked in her polka-dot pajamas.

He went into the bathroom for a quick shower, and the perfume of honeysuckle-scented bubble bath lingered in the air. He found the fragrance deeply arousing because now he knew what her skin would smell like when he slid into her. After his shower, he pulled on a pair of drawstring pajama pants but didn't bother with a shirt or boxer briefs. He wanted as little between him and Sierra as possible.

He brushed his teeth, getting ready for bed just like he did every night. But this wasn't any other night, and his fingers trembled as he replaced the cap on the toothpaste. The walk down the hallway was unnaturally long. He raised his fist to rap against the door with his knuckles, but it wasn't closed all the way and swung open as soon as he made contact.

She was sitting on the edge of the bed, wearing a button-down emerald sleepshirt with a satin collar and cuffs, a feminine play on a man's dress shirt.

"What, no polka dots?" he teased as he closed the door behind him.

Her smile was uncharacteristically shy. "This was the best I could do. I didn't exactly pack sexy negligees with me for this trip."

"You don't need fancy lingerie to be sexy." He walked to her and took her hands in his. "You already look like a fantasy come to life."

Her grin tipped up, more confident and sultry. "Had a lot of fantasies about me, have you?"

"Maybe one or two." Or a hundred.

"What's your favorite?" she asked.

He sat next to her, running his fingers through the damp silk of her hair. "The one where you say 'make love to me.' I'm not a complicated man."

She fell back on the mattress, pulling him with her. "Make love to me, cowboy."

"Yes, ma'am."

Chapter Thirteen

Sierra's life centered around physical responses and understanding the human body. But even with her vast knowledge, she was amazed by the overwhelming kaleidoscope of sensations she felt at Jarrett's touch. The weight of him over her, the stroke of his fingers along her upper thigh, the playful sting as he gently bit her earlobe—it was all jumbled together in a dizzying, addictive heat.

His mouth brushed over hers in teasing, minty kisses that made her desperate for more. Not a woman to be passive about what she wanted, she cupped his face and kissed him deeply. She felt his groan throughout her body, a rumble of approving thunder. By the time he unbuttoned her shirt, their kisses were becoming frantic.

He traced the slope of her breast with his lips. "I think you're my new favorite dessert," he said, glancing up with wicked eyes before his tongue flicked across her nipple.

She arched beneath him as he enthusiastically devoured her. Her hips rose to meet his in an unconscious rhythm that grew faster and more abandoned. Pleasure tightened inside her, and she trailed her fingers down his rock-hard abs until she slipped past the waistband of his pants and found something even harder.

He drew in a sharp breath, thrusting against her hand. "Damn, that feels good."

"You'll feel even better inside me," she said, barely recognizing the husky, passion-drugged voice as her own.

"I didn't want to rush you." He brushed his fingers over the excruciatingly sensitive skin of her inner thigh, closer and closer to where she needed him. "I wanted to make sure you—"

She grabbed his hand, shutting her eyes and breathing hard, not wanting to spiral any closer to the edge without him. "Trust me. I'm—" she parroted back his words from the ring earlier today "—'ready to proceed to the next step.'"

He grinned against her skin. "Smart-ass." Moving away from her just long enough to strip off his pants, he retrieved a condom from the pocket. She'd never been so happy to see a foil square in her entire life. He tore open the wrapper and she watched with unabashed eagerness as he unrolled the latex over the length of his erection.

He braced himself over her, and just as she was thinking the intensely possessive look in his eyes was the sexiest thing she'd ever experienced, he pushed inside her. After that, there was no thinking at all. He was big, but she was so ready for him that there was no discomfort, only tantalizing friction as she tightened around him.

Lacing his fingers through hers, he held her hands against the mattress as he moved inside her. He kissed her and the tight spirals of pleasure she'd experienced earlier were back, coiling and twisting and building on themselves until she shattered with an involuntary cry of release. Jarrett gripped her hips, thrusting into her more fervently, then following her over the edge. He buried his face in the crook of her neck and squeezed her to him. Squashed under his six-foot-plus frame, panting for breath and sweaty, she was utterly, blissfully content.

Would *wow* be a completely unsophisticated thing to say right now?

Eventually, he rolled off her, flopping onto his back but still holding her hand. Dazed, she watched the ceiling fan whir above them. It was set to a high speed, but hopelessly outmatched by the heat they'd just generated.

Thinking about the sky she couldn't see beyond the ceiling, she chuckled. "I've been meaning all week to go out one night and do some stargazing. I wasn't expecting to see stars in my own bedroom."

He propped himself up on his elbow, smiling down at her. "There were stars?"

"Shooting stars. Supernovas. A majestic orchestral score. It was like the best astronomy documentary ever."

He laughed. "For the sake of my fragile male ego, I'm going to pretend you didn't just compare me to a film in science class." After a moment, he said, "We'll go stargazing before you leave. You, me, a picnic blanket in a secluded corner of the pasture..."

Before she left. She swallowed, not wanting to think about that right now. "Do you know the names of a bunch of constellations?"

"Beyond the Big Dipper, no. But I'll learn them all if it impresses you."

She grinned at the idea of his still working to impress her even after he already had her naked.

For a few minutes, they lay there in companionable silence. Her eyes were starting to drift closed when he admitted, "I'm starving."

She wasn't surprised. Neither of them had eaten much at dinner. Had he, like her, been too keyed up with anticipation? "I wonder if we'd disturb Vicki if we went down to the kitchen for a late-night dessert run."

"Hey." He rubbed his thumb over her hand, his voice suddenly serious. "About Vicki... I think it would be best for her if she doesn't know there's anything between you and me."

"Huh." She bit her lip, considering. As he'd noted this afternoon, she had no real poker face. Being deceptive did not come easily to her. If she couldn't keep Will Trent and Kate from seeing her attraction to Jarrett, how long would she be able to hide it from someone who was living with them?

He sat up. "That's not a problem, is it?"

"Well, I wasn't planning on anything obvious like throwing you down on the breakfast table and having my way with you—"

"That's a shame."

"—but I've never excelled at keeping secrets."

"You work in the medical field. Doctor-patient confidentiality is standard, right? Can this be employer-therapist confidentiality?"

Actually, she preferred not to dwell on the fact that she was sleeping with the guy who signed her paychecks. In that context, it seemed unsavory.

"She's a kid who just got dumped," he continued. "Finding out about our getting together days after Aaron broke her heart would be cruel timing."

"I guess you're right." No point in rubbing salt in Vicki's emotional wounds.

"Thank you." His earnest gaze made it clear this was important to him. But after a moment, his expression turned playful. "I have some ideas about how I can demonstrate my gratitude." The seductive drawl in his voice brightened her mood considerably.

"Yeah?" She reached for him. "Like what, exactly?"

As he began whispering his very detailed plans, they both forgot all about dessert, their only hunger for each other.

As soon as the dinner dishes had been cleared away on Tuesday, Sierra declared, "Game night! Participation is mandatory." She delivered the announcement with a smile to make herself seem like less of a dictator, but no way was she letting Vicki disappear into her room for the remainder of the evening.

With the exception of two hours today at the weekly festival meeting, where Vicki had been as animated as any of the other women on the committee, she'd been fairly subdued since her friends left Sunday. Sierra was determined to keep the young woman engaged. Plus, structured evening activities for the three of them kept Sierra from counting the minutes until bedtime. Last night, Jarrett had appeared in her doorway to kiss her good-night. Which had taken three hours. So far, rain had made stargazing impossible. Luckily, the forecast for this weekend's festival was clear. She just hoped the ground had dried sufficiently by then so that the Rosses weren't hosting the first annual Harvest Day mud pit.

"Game night?" Vicki echoed disdainfully. "What is with you and the days-of-yore quality time? Last night, it was a jigsaw puzzle—"

"I'm still bitter we turned out to only have 1,499 pieces of a 1,500-piece puzzle," Sierra fumed.

"And now board games? Throw in some paper dolls and blue hair rinse, and you'd be the little old lady my parents used to hire to babysit me."

Undeterred, Sierra plopped the Monopoly box she'd pulled from the hall closet onto the table. "So, basically, what you're saying is you don't want to play because you know I'll win?"

Vicki narrowed her eyes. "Big talk for a woman who's about to get her ass kicked. I'll be the banker."

Jarrett unfolded the board, holding out the silver tokens in his palm so everyone could choose what they wanted to be.

"I'm the hat," Sierra said.

Jarrett set two pieces on Go. "And I've got dibs on the guy riding the horse, obviously. Vic?"

"I'll be the wheelbarrow. Closest thing to a wheelch— Wait, screw that. Give me the race car."

An hour later, Jarrett was smirking from behind a pile of money. Vicki didn't have quite as much cash, but, since she'd amassed far more property than her brother, she didn't have reason to worry yet. Meanwhile, luck had not favored Sierra, who'd landed in jail three times.

"These freaking dice are cursed," she muttered, preparing to roll them again.

"Sore loser," Vicki said.

"Hell yes," Sierra agreed, tossing the dice. She moved her token around the corner of the board, growling in frustration. There were only two spaces that already had hotels, but she had to land on one of them?

Jarrett didn't own much, but his strategy of investing everything he had was paying off. "Looks like someone can't afford the rent," he singsonged.

"Only because my employers don't pay me what I'm worth." Since she had no properties of her own, she couldn't even mortgage them to complete her turn.

Jarrett's teasing gaze dropped slowly over her, and her skin warmed at the memory of his touch. "Maybe we can work out some kind of trade for services."

Vicki whipped her head around. "Ew."

He raised an eyebrow. "I was going to ask her to bake more of those caramel brownies. Get your mind out of the gutter."

"I might as well make brownies. I'm done here." She tossed the top-hat token back into the box and pushed her chair away from the table.

"Guess it comes down to you and me," he challenged his sister. "To the victor go the brownies!"

She rolled her eyes. "You can't eat a whole pan by yourself."

"Shows what you know," he said, reaching for the dice. "I am a man of insatiable appetites."

Sierra poked her head into the pantry to hide her smile. Jarrett's insatiability was why their lovemaking had gone on for hours last night. He'd been teasing about going to his room for more condoms when she'd fallen asleep limp, exhausted and thoroughly sated in his arms. *But I'm wide-awake now.* She darted a glance at the clock.

All right, so she'd failed to avoid the bedtime countdown.

But she awarded herself points for temporarily delaying it. That qualified as willpower. Almost.

SETUP FOR THE Harvest Day Festival began on Friday after lunch. The entire festival committee showed up, many women accompanied by husbands and brothers to assist with the manual labor. Kate had both Will and teenage Luke with her.

"Cole said he'll stop by once he's off duty if we still need him," she told Sierra. She consulted the binder in her hand with a worried sigh. "We could be at this all night."

"I don't know." Sierra was less daunted by the workload. "Between Vicki and Becca, they have the troops whipped into shape and executing their orders with precision."

Vicki was stationed on the porch with half of a two-way radio set, signing in volunteers and surveying the landscape. Meanwhile, Becca Johnston, armed with the other radio receiver, was zipping around the ranch like a hummingbird that had just downed its first espresso. Sierra's theory was that the woman was moving too fast to be seen by the naked eye; the brain just filled in an image every time it detected the hot pink of her shirt flit by.

Jarrett was down by the stables, where pony rides would be offered in the small practice ring tomorrow. Goats and a friendly pig would make up a temporary petting zoo in the bigger ring. Sierra was relieved he wasn't anywhere in her vicinity, lest Kate see them together and somehow deduce their affair. The blonde's detecting skills were every bit as honed as her policeman fiancé's. At the committee lunch on Tuesday, Carrie Ann Rhodes, who was in her second trimester, said Kate had figured out she was pregnant before Carrie Ann had even taken the test.

"Kate?" A woman at the base of the hill cupped her mouth and yelled up to them. "Anita just got the sound system into the tent and says we're missing some cables. You happen to know where they are?"

"I'm on it." Kate headed in that direction at the same time a truck pulling a long trailer approached the house.

Sierra went to meet the driver to let him know Vicki had everyone's assignments. Three men climbed down from the mud-spattered cab.

The driver's eyes widened when he saw her. "And who might you be, little lady?" One of his companions ogled her outright, while the younger one ducked his gaze with a quick, deferential tip of his ball cap in greeting.

"Sierra Bailey, festival volunteer, physical therapist and ornery cuss who doesn't appreciate being called 'little.'"

The man laughed, nearly good-looking if it weren't for the tobacco-stained teeth. "Well, I'm Larry Breelan. This is my brother Daryl and my other brother, Grady. We've got the risers for the tent." He winked at her. "The Harvest Queen pageant is our favorite event of the whole festival."

She jerked a thumb over her shoulder. "You'll need to see Vicki about unloading the risers and anything else she needs your help with. Don't give her any crap, and there's fresh-squeezed lemonade and homemade brownies in your future."

"You can count on us."

Not only did she end up supplying snacks for the volunteers, the ranch was still bustling with volunteers by dinner.

"I took care of it," Vicki told her, rubbing the back of her neck. "The local pizza parlor is bringing us twenty pepperoni pies in exchange for special advertising at the festival tomorrow and preferential booth location."

Sierra leaned against the porch railing, regarding her with admiration. "I don't know what your major is, but you could have a future as some kind of events coordinator. You've done a fantastic job today." She hesitated, wondering if she should suggest the girl go inside and rest for a little while. She looked beat.

"What?" Vicki glared.

"I didn't say anything."

"You had that expression like you were about to ask me how

I'm doing. That's been the only thing I've hated about today, the constant questioning of how I'm doing. I'm *fine*."

Sierra held her hands up in front of her. "All right, no need to bite my head off. Just make sure you save some reserve energy for tomorrow. That's when the real work is."

"Nah. Tomorrow will be fun. Sunday is the part that will suck." Vicki screwed up her face, looking like a four-year-old who'd just been served a plate of broccoli. "Cleanup."

"Yikes. I hadn't thought that far ahead."

"Well, now that you've been warned, plan accordingly. Stay hydrated, take your vitamins, that kind of thing." She gave Sierra an assessing look. "You probably shouldn't stay up too late tonight."

Was there a hidden meaning in that? Sierra's stomach knotted. Did Vicki somehow know that Sierra's past few nights hadn't been all that restful? *Oh, hell, what if we've been making too much noise?* That was a mortifying thought. Then again, maybe the effort of keeping a secret was just making Sierra paranoid. She could be reading too much into Vicki's suggestion.

"I'll be sure to get plenty of sleep," she said, striving for a casual tone. "You do the same."

Before Vicki could answer, her walkie-talkie crackled.

"Victoria? Becca here. Holt Miller has a question for you."

Sierra took that as her cue to leave.

All of the people who were still present when the pizzas arrived expressed heartfelt gratitude and undying devotion to Vicki. Cole Trent teasingly asked her if she had ever thought about a future as an elected official.

"Mayor Victoria Ross," he said, reaching for the soda he'd set on the porch railing. "Something to consider a decade or two down the road."

Kate and Cole were the last ones to leave. By the time they drove away, Vicki was nodding off in her chair. Sierra helped with her pre-bedtime routine and didn't leave her alone until she was actually tucked in, sticking around longer than usual in case Vicki needed her for anything.

Now I just need someone to help me *to bed.* Stifling a yawn, Sierra tried to muster the oomph necessary to climb the spiral staircase. With slow, shuffling steps, she made her way to the top. Jarrett met her on the landing, toweling off his damp hair.

"You look as beat as I feel," he said sympathetically.

"Never tell a woman she looks tired."

"Okay. But when you catch sight of yourself in the mirror, don't say I didn't warn you." He wrapped his arms around her and kissed her on top of the head. "I'm assuming that we, by mutual agreement, are far too tired to fool around."

"I'd nod, but I don't have the energy."

He chuckled. "Don't worry. I'll leave you be tonight."

It was on the tip of her tongue to ask if he wanted to come join her in the giant bed anyway, just to sleep. Lord knew there was room enough for the both of them, and she liked waking up in his arms. But would his spending the night with sex removed from the equation be too much like a relationship? Was she attaching more significance to whatever was happening between them than actually existed?

Don't overcomplicate matters.

That was sound advice. Right up there with, don't pick a night when she had only half a brain cell awake to ponder whether the connection between her and Jarrett was a bona fide relationship...and whether she'd done something as crazy as fall in love.

THE MORNING OF the festival came way too early, but at least it was sunny and warm. After helping Vicki get out of bed and do a quick series of exercises, Sierra fortified herself with an extra-strong cup of coffee and prepared to enjoy her first Cupid's Bow festival.

Also, your last, she thought as she pulled on her boots.

Not necessarily. This town wasn't the mystical Brigadoon; Cupid's Bow wouldn't disappear for a hundred years once she crossed outside its borders. Texas might be a large state, but she could still come back for occasional visits. Kate had been hinting that she expected Sierra to be present for her wedding.

Jarrett, on the other hand, had never said a word about her returning. She supposed she should appreciate that he wasn't putting any pressure on her when her future was still undecided, but she wouldn't mind knowing that he wanted to see her again. She had fewer than ten days left here. When she was gone, would he simply forget about her?

Sierra didn't know if she'd see him again when her job on the ranch had ended. But she knew it would be a long damn time before she could ever forget him.

For now, however, she needed to push aside these questions. She and Jarrett were supposed to work together this morning, overseeing games of traditional cowboy skill. Becca had set up "horse" races, which would take place after the participating children decorated pool-noodle ponies with eyes, ears, manes and tails. There would also be rawhide braiding, lassoing and a station where each kid could design a brand and color it in marker onto a balloon cow.

But before she headed for her post, she needed to help set Vicki up at the tent where various events would take place throughout the day. After everyone had gone last night, Vicki had flatly reiterated that she had no intention of being "stuck on the porch all day while the rest of the town has a good time." Sierra went back to Vicki's room to make sure she was ready, and she gasped aloud at the sight of her patient taking a few stumbling steps away from her wheelchair.

"What are you *doing*?" Sierra demanded, rushing to her side just as she toppled. They'd discussed how important it was that her progress be done with Sierra's or Manuel's assistance. Without proper supervision, she could reinjure herself.

"Walking." Face pale, Vicki accepted her help back into the chair but her glower suggested she would bat away Sierra's hand if she could.

"Determination is good," Sierra said, "but only when paired with intelligent choices. You didn't even have a walker or crutch handy! Do you know how much a fall could set you back?"

"Maybe I only fell because you startled me," she said mulishly.

"You're smart enough to know that isn't true—momentary stupidity notwithstanding."

"I want to be able to go down the steps to my own house!" Vicki complained. "I want to participate in the cake walk. I want to be able to dance with a cute guy tonight." She huffed out a breath. "Did I tell you about my new positive visualization image?"

"No." But Sierra had figured it was no longer dancing with Aaron.

"It's me marching across campus, looking killer, finding Aaron and kicking him in the shin. Hard."

Well. It was a goal.

They got Vicki to the appropriate location, and Sierra mentally crossed her fingers that the surly girl would rediscover her people skills as the day wore on. She also hoped she regained her common sense. Should she ask someone like Kate to surreptitiously check in from time to time and make sure Vicki wasn't attempting to foolishly leave her wheelchair?

You already gave her the lecture. You can't be there for her twenty-four hours a day. The Rosses would be home in less than two weeks. Vicki wouldn't even be Sierra's patient anymore. In the meantime, if the teenager did take ill-advised risks, at least there was a first-aid booth nearby.

The festival hadn't officially started yet, so the first wave of visitors hadn't arrived on the flatbed trailer. But a lot of the volunteers getting set up had brought their families with them, so about half a dozen kids were gathered near the barn already. A teenager was distributing pellets to feed to the goats while Anita Drake and another woman were blowing up black-and-white Holstein-patterned balloons.

The children not playing with balloons or goats were watching Jarrett show off some roping tricks. He was spinning a lariat in a wide loop, jumping from side to side through it. The kids were laughing at his silly running commentary while the women working with balloons were sighing over his muscles and agility. Who could blame them for their sighs? It was difficult to imagine a man more appealing than a gorgeous cowboy who was good with children.

Especially one who moves like that, she thought appreciatively, her gaze following him. She wished she could walk straight up to him and kiss him good morning.

"Morning." He shoved his hat back on his head, giving her a wide smile. "Everyone say hi to Miss Sierra. She's exactly the person we need for our next demonstration."

A couple of the kids dutifully chorused, "Hi, Miss Sierra."

"Demonstration?" she asked. Their job was to guide kids through turns trying to rope posts. But Jarrett could have started that without her. Especially since she didn't know the first thing about lassoing. Her part was more crowd control, keeping an eye on kids in line to make sure no one started any fights. Or wandered off and ended up spooking the skittish mare in the stable.

He came over to where she stood. "You guys want to see a demonstration, right?" Taking her hand, he led Sierra to the center of the ring. Under his breath, he said, "Don't worry—your part is easy. And maybe much, much later, I can show you some of my favorite grown-up rope maneuvers."

She refused to encourage him by grinning. "Pervert," she whispered.

He winked at her. Then he backed away, holding the rope up and telling the kids about the different parts of the lasso and showing them how the honda knot was used to control the size of the loop. "When you throw, you aim with the tip. Bring your arm over your head and turn your wrist, keeping a good momentum and the loop open. Then when you're ready, you throw it like you would a baseball." He crooked his arm forward and the spinning loop came sailing toward her.

The kids cheered when it dropped over her, and Sierra laughed. A month ago, she couldn't have imagined willingly spending a day on a ranch. Now she was voluntarily riding horses and being used for lasso practice.

As more festival guests arrived, the number of children grew. Jarrett stopped demonstrating tricks and began handing them smaller lariats. Before long, Sierra was busy distributing small prizes for the kids who managed to rope a post and cheerfully consoling those who hadn't accomplished it yet. Spirits were high and no one seemed too discouraged by failure.

Behind her, Sierra heard a woman say, "Oh, no, honey, I think you're too little."

Sierra turned and saw a woman with wavy brown hair surrounded by the cutest little cowgirls on the ranch. Three identical toddlers stood with their mom in denim vests and matching pink dresses. They each wore a different colored hat, and the one in green was gesturing enthusiastically toward Jarrett.

"How about we go feed the animals instead?" her mom suggested.

"Not to undermine your authority," Sierra said, "but I think maybe our lasso expert could give her a hand if she wants a try."

The pretty brunette smiled. "Thanks. That would be sweet." Her other two cowgirls were hiding behind their mom's legs as she talked to Sierra. Obviously, the one in the green hat was the bold risk-taker of the group.

Sierra grinned inwardly. *My kind of kid.* "Hold on a sec." She informed Jarrett of the situation and he walked over to the triplets.

"Hi, I'm Jarrett." He shook the mom's hand.

"Megan Rivers. And these are my girls. Daisy was hoping to take a turn with the lasso, but—"

He dropped down to the little girl's level, and something inside Sierra melted. He tapped the brim of the toddler's cowgirl hat. "I like your hat. Is green your favorite color?"

She eyed him as if taking his measure, then shook her head. "Purple."

"Well, I don't have any purple lassos—only boring plain ones—but would you like to try one anyway?"

"Yes!"

"Mind if I pick you up?"

The girl immediately thrust her arms toward him, zero hint of shyness in her personality. Jarrett took her to the center of the ring. Keeping the girl balanced on his hip, he held the rope with a lot of slack, handing her only the looped end to whirl around. She hit herself in the face with it once. Sierra couldn't hear what Jarrett said to her, but whatever it was made the little girl giggle.

"Okay, on three we're going to toss it over the post," he said. "One, two...*three.*" As he said the last word, he charged forward, carrying the girl right up to the post, where she dropped the loop over the wood.

She responded with a joyful belly laugh, and several of the kids waiting in line applauded.

"Uh-oh," Megan said. "Now that he's set the example, he's going to have little ones asking to be picked up for the whole rest of the day."

Sierra suspected she was right. "Good thing he has strong arms."

Jarrett returned the little girl to her mother, who thanked him profusely before herding her girls toward another section. He watched the woman go with a bemused expression.

"What is it?" Sierra asked, battling a twinge of envy. The triplets' mom was extremely pretty. And *she* wasn't moving away in a week or so.

"She did say her name was Megan, right? Megan Rivers? That's Will's neighbor." He lowered his voice to a confiding tone. "He said she was a thoroughly disagreeable woman and that he's never seen her smile."

"Really?" Sierra craned her head, staring after the woman. "She seemed perfectly nice to me."

"Me, too. Either Will's crazy or she just plain doesn't like him."

"Weird. Will's a great guy. Total charmer."

"Careful, darlin'." Jarrett leaned close with a mock growl. "Last time I got jealous of you and Will, I dragged you out of a dance hall to kiss you senseless."

She laughed at his edited version of events. "That's the worst threat I've ever heard in my life. I've been wanting to kiss you for over an hour."

He groaned. "Becca scheduled breaks for us, right?"

"Becca is superhuman. I'm not sure she believes in breaks."

Behind them, another child was calling for Jarrett's help.

"Better get back to work, cowboy."

"How am I supposed to focus when you're standing here being distractingly beautiful?"

She grinned. "I suppose I could find Will Trent and see if he needs my help."

Jarrett gave her such a heated look that for a breathtaking moment, she thought he might actually stake his claim by kissing her right there and then. He settled for a drawled warning. "We are going to have words later, Miss Sierra."

She couldn't wait.

Chapter Fourteen

Jarrett smiled gratefully as Anita Drake handed him a glass of ice-cold lemonade. The day had got warm. "Thank you."

"Least I could do after you generously let us use the ranch for the festival. Will you get a chance to eat lunch?"

"Yeah." He checked his watch. "Deputy Thomas is supposed to take over for me in a few minutes, long enough for me to eat." He'd sent Sierra off to get some food for herself, though, and to check on Vicki. At the thought of his sister, guilt twisted inside him. He hated lying to her about Sierra. He'd never discussed his love life much with Vic—those weren't appropriate conversations to have with his little sister—but now he was surprised to find himself wishing he could share how happy Sierra made him. *A selfish wish.* The last thing Vicki would want to hear about in the wake of her breakup was that Jarrett was happier than he deserved to be.

Jarrett's stomach growled, adding physical discomfort to his conflicted mental state. Thankfully, being punctual was one of the deputy's trademark qualities. Deputy Thomas arrived and Jarrett decided to head for whatever food vendor had the shortest line. A large family over by the Smoky Pig booth got their food and stepped away, drastically reducing the crowd in front of the order window. Jarrett quickly jumped in the line.

"Hey, J-Ross." Larry Breelan walked up behind him. "We don't see much of you in town lately."

"I've been busy working the ranch."

"Yeah—must be pulling double duty since your dad's attack. With you secluded out here, we were afraid the legendary Jarrett Ross love life had finally slowed down. End of an era. Should have known you're too smart for that, eh? Figured out how to swing it."

"What are you talking about?"

The man elbowed him. "Settle a bet between me and Grady. You're sleeping with that pretty redhead, aren't you? As soon as we saw her yesterday, I realized we'd been all wrong about your dry spell, that you—"

"Ms. Bailey is one hell of a physical therapist, and my family owes her a great debt for how much she's helped my sister. I would take any disrespectful comments about her *very* badly."

Larry shrank back, wide-eyed. "Well, hell, man, I didn't mean any disrespect. But we all know your track record with the ladies, and she's one mighty fine filly."

An involuntary snarl came from behind Jarrett's teeth.

"Sorry. I realize now I had the situation all wrong."

"You make sure to tell your brother that, too." Who else was speculating about Sierra? Probably anyone who knew his reputation. He was Jarrett Ross, and she was a beautiful woman sleeping down the hall from him every night. People would assume they were having sex.

Which you are. That was the worst part. Anyone gossiping about it would be right.

"Is anyone else speaking ill of Ms. Bailey?" he demanded.

Larry looked confused by the question. "Thinking that she knocked boots with you isn't an insult. More like, it makes her part of a club. You've been with half the ladies in town."

"I have not!" It was a blatant exaggeration, but he only had himself to blame for how people saw him. "You know, I just realized I'm not in the mood for barbecue." With a terse nod to Larry, he gave up his place in line.

Jarrett hated that anyone might think he'd hired Sierra based on her looks or with plans to seduce her. *Just like Vicki first thought.* He'd assured his sister that he would keep his distance from the therapist, and now he'd broken his promise.

His feelings for Sierra were different than anything he'd experienced before—he'd believed they were making *him* different. Better. But Breelan's words had been a reality check. Even knowing how important Sierra's professionalism was to her, Jarrett had slow-danced with her in public, kissed her outside the dance hall where they could have been seen. And now he was sneaking around behind his sister's back!

Vicki deserved more from him. And even though he knew he was making Sierra happy in the short run, maybe she deserved a better man.

"HEY." SIERRA STROLLED into the stable, amused that there had been a time in the recent past when she'd had an aversion to being here. Now it was the source of some fond memories. She smiled at Jarrett, who was resting on a bale of hay with his long legs kicked out in front of him. "I was hoping to find you in here."

The sun had set an hour ago. The festival was still going strong, but most everyone was in the tent where the Harvest Queen had been crowned. There was live music and dancing. Although people seemed to be having fun, after the hectic frivolity of the day, Sierra was craving a little peace and quiet.

Be honest. Mostly, you're just craving him. They'd worked together all morning, but after lunch, it seemed as though every time she looked for Jarrett, he was suddenly needed elsewhere. Was it weird that, after only a few hours apart, she'd missed him? Not in some needy, codependent way. But every time something funny had happened, she'd automatically turned to joke with him about it—only to find that he wasn't there.

And there'd been a few heart-melting moments with cute kids that she wished she could have seen his reaction to. The sight of him with Megan's little girl that morning remained a high point of her day.

"How was your afternoon?" she asked him now.

"Fine," he said, sparing her the briefest of glances. "Tiring."

She nodded in commiseration, walking over and cupping his shoulders with her hands. Stroking her fingers toward his neck, she applied light pressure to his scalene muscles. "Did you know I am trained in therapeutic massage? If you're sore, I can—"

He stood, the motion effectively knocking her hands away. "Too bad I didn't know you when I was riding rodeo—talk about sore muscles. Today was a breeze compared to that."

She bit the inside of her lip, surprised at the rebuff. "All right." She wound her arms around his neck. "It was really just an excuse to touch you, anyway."

"Sierra." He backed away. "Someone might see."

Who, the horses? She resisted the urge to snap the question at him. She supposed it was possible that, in the event of a minor emergency, someone would come looking for the ranch owner. Regardless, Sierra had her pride—somewhat bruised for the rejection but still intact. She wasn't going to throw herself at an uninterested man.

But since when was Jarrett uninterested?

"Sorry," he said, his smile gentle. "But it would be really bad if Vicki heard about us from someone."

Then maybe we should tell her ourselves. But Vicki wasn't her sister, so she was deferring to his feelings on the matter. "Understood. I should go find her, anyway. Wish me luck persuading her she's had enough excitement for one day. See you back in the house?"

He nodded absently, but it was hours later before she heard him come up the stairs in the house. Pipes creaked, and she listened to the water run as he showered. If the situation were different, maybe she would have surprised him by joining him.

After his strange mood in the stable, though, she was leaving it to him to make the next move.

Only, he didn't.

Once his shower was over, she held her breath, waiting to see if he appeared in her doorway as he had on previous nights. Instead, he padded to his room and closed the door, leaving her alone and perplexed and wondering what had gone wrong.

ON SUNDAY, IT took hours to deconstruct booths and haul away trash from the festival. Once it was all finished and Jarrett had again accepted the committee's thanks for use of the ranch, he locked himself away in the study on the pretext of having work to do. *You do have work you should be doing. You just aren't accomplishing any of it.*

His biggest accomplishment today was driving himself crazy by staying away from Sierra. How long did he think he could successfully avoid her?

Too restless to sit, he paced behind the desk. Even now, he wanted to go to her, tell her how much he'd missed her for the past two nights. But every time he thought of Larry Breelan's lewd expression, the knowing chuckle in the man's voice when he'd basically congratulated Jarrett on scoring with her...

So he stayed in the office, knowing he would crack eventually and need to touch her again, yet postponing the inescapable moment of weakness. When his phone rang, he answered it gratefully, thrilled to have a legitimate distraction.

"Hello?"

"Jarrett! How are you?" his mother asked. The happiness in her voice made her sound like almost a different person than the one who'd stood in this very room and told him she and Gavin needed time away. The trip to Tahoe had done her a lot of good.

"I'm..." Conflicted. Miserable. Weak-willed. "...great. We got everything all cleaned up from the festival today, restoring order to the ranch. So, no worries, the Twisted R you come home to will be in the same condition as when you left." The ranch might be the same, but *he* felt irrevocably changed by the past few weeks.

"Oh. Good." His mother's voice took on a dull note whenever the ranch came up.

He sighed. "You really aren't looking forward to being back here, are you?"

"It's not that. Exactly. The Twisted R is my home, but— Of course I can't wait to see you and your sister again. She texted me a picture earlier today of her standing! That Sierra you hired must be a godsend. I'm sorry she'll be leaving so shortly after our return. I'd like to get to know her better, thank her properly for her help."

"Yeah, well." His throat burned, and he had trouble getting the words out. "She'll be moving on to other folks who need her." Her interview in Fort Worth was scheduled for Tuesday. She was driving up that morning and wouldn't be back until sometime on Wednesday. He felt confident that the people at the clinic would offer her the job. They'd be fools not to.

Just like you're a fool for letting her go. He scowled. What choice did he have? She'd never really been his to hold on to in the first place.

WHEN SIERRA CAME into the kitchen on Monday to fix lunch, there was a napkin sitting on the table. The words *Go riding with me?* had been written across it in bright marker. A gesture from Jarrett? Had she misinterpreted his aloof demeanor over the past two days?

Maybe being drained from all the festival-related activities had just left him cranky. Or maybe it was all the extra pairs of eyes on the ranch this weekend that had prompted him to keep his distance. She supposed she understood, but it stung, feeling like his sordid secret, unfit for acknowledging during daylight hours.

"Thought I heard you in here," he said from behind her as

she filled a pot with water for boiling pasta. "Did you get my invitation?"

She glanced toward the napkin on the counter, her mouth lifting in a half smile. "On the traditional Jarrett Ross stationery."

"I should really shop for matching envelopes." He looked thoughtful. "Maybe I could origami one out of a paper towel."

She laughed, feeling some of the strain that had plagued her since Saturday finally ease.

"So. Can you go riding with me this afternoon, or do you and Vicki have plans?"

"Just the opposite. I'm trying to get her to take it easy after an eventful weekend. She's doesn't appreciate my caution, though."

The girl seemed mad at her. She hadn't said much during the dinner they'd eaten in Jarrett's absence last night, but every once in a while, Sierra would catch Vicki looking at her with a displeased expression on her face. *Because she thinks I'm slowing down her progress?* Or was it something else?

Sierra sighed. "I guess I should remind her about her promise to be a model patient if I braved riding a horse." That gave her an idea of how to get back into the girl's good graces. She made a mental note to ask Manuel at Vicki's appointment Thursday about getting Vicki back into the saddle. Maybe that was something Sierra could help her accomplish before—

"You okay?" Jarrett asked. "I didn't realize she was giving you that much trouble."

"Oh, I can handle Vicki. I was just thinking how few days I have left here."

"Yeah." He looked away, his expression despondent.

Perhaps that explained his recent detachment. Was he just trying to prepare himself for their goodbye? It was nice to think he was so affected by the idea of her leaving, proving that he cared.

"I'd love to go riding with you," she said impulsively.

During lunch, she told Vicki about their plans and promised she'd ask Manuel this week what needed to be done for Vicki to ride again. The announcement didn't elicit quite the celebration she'd hoped for, but at least her patient wasn't actively glaring at her. After they ate, Vicki put in a DVD. Sierra promised she'd be back by the time the movie was over and that they'd work more on taking actual steps with the crutches. The new goal was for Vicki to walk up to her parents when they returned next week. It would be a lovely homecoming gift.

Down at the stables, Sierra helped with tacking up the horses, although Jarrett double-checked her work to make sure everything was secure.

"Nice job," he praised her. "If we had more time, I bet I could turn you into a first-rate horsewoman."

If we had more time... A pang went through her at all the ways that sentence could end. Not having more practice saddling horses wouldn't be what she regretted most when she left.

"We'll be going a bit off the usual trail today," he warned as they led the horses out of the stable. "I have something I want to show you."

Twenty minutes later, they passed through a copse of peach trees, where she mocked his constantly having to duck branches—"Finally, a bonus to being this short!"—and emerged in a small clearing. The house that sat in front of them was too oblong to be rightly called a cottage, but there was something charming about it nonetheless. Two untrimmed rosebushes flanked the front door, the flowers growing in fragrant profusion.

"What's this?" she asked as they dismounted.

Jarrett secured the horses to a hitching post. "The bunkhouse." He held the door open for her.

It was a little musty inside, the sunlight through the window illuminating the dust motes that danced in the air. The back wall was all stonework, full of rustic charm, but that was about all she could say for the decor. There was little furniture and even less style. A folding card table sat in the kitchen with two sturdy but mismatched chairs.

"Tell me the truth—you only brought me here so we could

fool around with no chance of Vicki catching on." It was supposed to have been a teasing comment, but there was an aggressive undertone to her words.

He blinked, obviously hearing it, too. "We agreed it was best if she didn't know about us."

More like, you *agreed.* "Maybe we should revisit that. I think she's suspicious that something's going on."

"She'd be suspicious anyway." Shoving a hand through his hair, he turned to gaze out a grimy window. "Even when I first hired you, she thought I had ulterior motives. Not only would telling her be hurtful timing, it would lower her opinion of me even more."

The recrimination in his tone reminded her of the night he'd told her about Vicki's accident, and she tried to lighten the mood. "Being drawn to me isn't a character flaw—it's just good taste."

He didn't respond, and she rested her cheek against his back. She still thought they should tell Vicki, but Sierra wasn't the one who would have to deal with any fallout from the conversation if it was the wrong decision.

He turned, wrapping her in his arms. Despite the momentary tension between them, it felt so good for him to be holding her again. "The real reason I brought you here was so you could see my future home. Obviously, it needs lots of TLC."

"But it has great potential," she said. All it took was some imagination to see what could be created. She admired his willingness to make the effort. Anyone in her family would probably take one look around and declare the place unfit for habitation. But a house didn't need thousand-dollar artwork and a three-car garage to be an inviting home.

"I want to completely remodel the bathroom," he told her, drawing her to the other end of the house for a quick tour. "I'm thinking whirlpool tub. The bedroom just needs some minor floor repair where the hardwood's warped and, obviously, furniture." He gave her a lopsided grin. "Maybe I'll ask my parents if I can take the king bed from the guest room. It's really too big for that room anyway, and I've developed a real fondness for that bed."

Desire rippled through her as she recalled the many delicious things he'd done to her there.

She couldn't imagine that the brick fireplace in the living room would be used often in the Texas heat, yet the image of snuggling in this high-ceilinged room in front of the flames was undeniably cozy. Her eyes prickled with sudden tears she refused to shed. She was touched that Jarrett had wanted to show her the future he was mapping out, yet knowing she wouldn't be part of that future hurt more than it should.

"...and a huge flat-screen TV," he was saying. "Seriously, huge. I mean, this is Texas, right? Go big or go home. And in here," he added, as they reached the kitchen, "I was thinking... Honestly, I have no idea. Most of my culinary skills center around coffeemakers and grills."

She laughed. "Well, coffee is the most important meal of the day."

He brushed his index finger over her lips. "I've missed your smile." A wave of anticipation went through her as he bent closer, cupping her face. "And I've missed doing this."

His mouth met hers in a kiss that started out as sweet reunion but ignited into something more arousing. Deepening their kiss, he dropped his hands to her butt and pulled her against him.

She unbuttoned the top of his shirt, kissing the exposed column of his throat. "I want you so much."

He walked them backward until he hit a chair, and she straddled his lap, their kisses frenzied. She had to get back to the house soon, and they didn't waste any time. Buttons and zippers were dealt with impatiently, and she almost laughed in wry frustration. It was a lot easier to remove pajamas than jeans and boots. But, between them, they managed. Jarrett was wearing only a condom when he tugged her forward, her unbuttoned shirt hanging loose at her sides. She slowly lowered herself over him, her breath hitching as he cupped her breasts, rubbing the tight peaks. She tightened her inner muscles around him, and he groaned her name.

It occurred to her that they didn't have to worry about being quiet, and when her climax rolled through her, she threw back her head with a cry of joy.

Afterward, she rested her head on his shoulder, her smile bittersweet. She'd finally got her wish—no longer only a guilty pleasure he saved for the wee hours of the night but his lover in the full light of day. She wished she could stay here, spend an idyllic afternoon in his arms, but she had to go. They were out of time.

ALL THROUGH SIERRA'S interview on Tuesday, she mentally chided herself for being too subdued. *They'll think you aren't excited about the opportunity.* But her worries turned out to be unfounded. Perhaps having a quieter demeanor was the key to seeming like a reserved professional, because by the time the clinic closed for the day, they'd offered her the job.

I should be happy about this, she told herself as she reached out to shake hands with the woman who'd led the interview. Fort Worth wasn't far from Dallas, which would make relocating easier. The pay was competitive for her field, and the people seemed nice enough—although, only time would tell whether they liked outspoken, headstrong Sierra once they got to know her. The Sierra in today's interview had been a well-behaved doppelgänger.

"Are you headed to a hotel?" the HR manager asked. "We'd be happy to take you to dinner and answer any other questions you might have."

"Thank you, but if you don't mind, I'll take a rain check," Sierra said. "I have a lot to mull over."

"Of course." The manager nodded approvingly. "You have a big decision to make."

After grabbing a salad from an upscale deli, Sierra checked

into a hotel room, ostensibly to think about her career. So why was she staring at the generic hotel wall art of a cowboy silhouetted on a horse and thinking only of the cowboy back in Cupid's Bow? She pulled out her phone and texted him that the job was hers if she wanted it, and they'd love for her to start next week.

Ten minutes later, she received the single-word response: Congratulations.

She checked the phone twice more to see if he'd added anything else, but, really, what was there to say? They'd both known from day one that she was looking for a new place to land, and now she'd found it. Congratulations, indeed.

A month ago, being by herself for the night would have seemed perfectly normal, but now loneliness gripped her. *Because it's too quiet in here.* She turned on the television, flipping past news and sports and stopping just long enough on a fashion reality show to watch the judges determine the week's winner. After that, she got bored and reached for her phone.

She could always call Jarrett. He might have more to say during an actual conversation than in a text. But she couldn't bring herself to dial his number. It felt too needy. If she couldn't survive one night without him, what was she going to do about the coming nights and weeks and months? That thought made her stomach churn, and she scrolled through her contact list in sudden desperation.

"Hello?"

"Hi, Mom." Sierra hoped the warble in her voice wasn't so pronounced through their connection.

"Sierra! How wonderful to hear from you, darling. I don't have long—your father and I are headed for a benefit tonight— but tell me everything. How's the job search?"

"I got an offer in Fort Worth today." She proceeded to tell her mom all about the clinic and the neighborhood it was in. Sierra planned to drive around a little bit and check into living arrangements before she returned to Cupid's Bow tomorrow. If she took this job, the clinic wanted her to start soon, so finding a place was top priority.

After chatting about that for a bit, conversation turned to her brother's wedding plans. Muriel was still obsessing over every detail. "Apparently, Kyle and Annabel didn't discuss much of this before he proposed, so there's a lot to hash out. But it's good that they're learning to argue respectfully and resolve differences. It takes compromise to make a marriage work. I know you probably think compromising is a sign of weakness—"

"No, I don't. I could make some compromises, for the right person." But how did you know when you'd found the right person—the one who would be worth the effort? *I love Jarrett.* She'd suspected it for days but had known it in her heart after he'd made love to her yesterday and she'd spent her entire walk back to the house trying not to cry.

She loved him, but she was uncertain what his feelings were. He'd admitted that, in the past, he'd had very shallow relationships. Was it arrogant to think that she was different, that she was special to him?

As she ended the call with her mother, Sierra knew that, if Jarrett asked, she would be willing to make some compromises in order to keep seeing him. But, so far, he hadn't cared enough to ask.

Chapter Fifteen

Passing the sign that said Welcome to Cupid's Bow gave Sierra an overwhelming sense of déjà vu. Had it been only a few weeks ago that she'd packed up her car and driven into this town with a sense of foreboding? She'd wondered if she could survive the isolation of the Twisted R for so long, but the time had flown.

Speaking of time. Battling back the emotion that had kept trying to well up, she glanced at her clock. She'd told Jarrett she wasn't sure when she'd be back. Given the approaching dinner hour, maybe she should call and see whether he was already cooking something or if he wanted her to pick up some food in town.

The phone rang so many times that she'd almost given up hope anyone would answer when she heard Vicki's voice.

"Hello?"

"Hey, it's Sierra. I'm back—just crossed the town line. I thought I'd see if your brother was already in the middle of making dinner."

"Ha! He's barricaded himself in the study. He is in a serious *mood*. I think it stresses him out to be left alone with me."

"Were you being difficult?"

"He hasn't spoken to me enough to give me the chance."

"Then it's probably something else. Worries about hay or

straw or grass seed or something." He'd once launched into a discussion of grass at dinner that had lasted a full half hour. Sierra had managed not to fall asleep, but only because she'd entertained herself by mentally replaying her favorite episode of an old sitcom.

"He could be grumpy because he misses you."

Sierra wanted to believe that, but she refused to cling to false hope. "You mean because he misses my cooking? I doubt my being gone had much impact. I was only away overnight."

"Then maybe he missed you last night. Tell me the truth—are you sleeping with my brother?"

She gripped the steering wheel, too startled to answer. Her natural impulse was to be candid, but that wasn't what Jarrett wanted. Honesty warred with loyalty. Meanwhile, the pause had stretched on so long, she feared it had become an answer all on its own.

She heard Vicki's intake of breath as she filled in the gap for herself.

Hell with it. If Sierra was going to get in trouble, she would do it by owning her actions, not letting a cowardly silence speak for her. "Yes. I am."

"I *knew* it. The two of you have been lying to me, and I knew it!" Judging from the pain in her voice, she'd been secretly hoping she was wrong.

Panic blossomed inside her. Oh, crap. She'd made the wrong choice, hadn't she? She'd betrayed Jarrett's wishes and, in the process, upset his sister. "Vicki, we—"

But the line was already dead.

JARRETT STARED AT the computer screen, but the jumble of numbers on the spreadsheet made no more sense to him now than they had the past twenty times he'd looked. He might as well be trying to read ancient hieroglyphics. The last thing he could remember clearly reading was Sierra's text yesterday saying that she'd been offered the job.

All was as it should be. She was an educated woman from a wealthy family. She should be building a successful career, not shacking up in some three-room bunkhouse with a cowboy whose reputation was a local joke. He thought of his mom, who tolerated life on the Twisted R for the sake of her family but didn't love the ranch, not the way Jarrett and his father did. Even if Sierra didn't have this opportunity in Fort Worth, how long could she have tolerated it here before realizing it wasn't where she belonged? *If you were a better man, you'd be happy for her.* But—

Something smashed against the office door, and he jumped in his chair. What the hell? He walked over to the door and opened it cautiously. One of his dad's Larry McMurtry novels lay on the floor. Vicki sat in her wheelchair a few feet away, her face red.

"Was that your version of knocking?" he asked, smoothing out the book's pages. When he realized how hard she was breathing, worry clutched at him. "Are you all right? Should I call a doctor, or—"

"I don't know which I hate more, that you slept with her or that you thought I was too stupid to notice! I'm crippled, not brain-dead."

The attack left him reeling. She'd found out about Sierra. His careful attempts to keep their relationship a secret had failed. "How do you know?"

"Because she told me! *She* had the balls to admit it, unlike you. What was it you said—that you didn't even see her as a woman? You are a liar, Jarrett. You still treat me like a dumb kid, like I don't have eyes in my head. You are so—"

"I know you're not a dumb kid. I've always wished I were as smart as you."

"Don't try to flatter or charm me! I'm not some rodeo groupie. In fact, don't speak to me at all." She turned for her room.

"Vic, we should talk about this."

"Yes, we *should* have. But you opted for lies and secrecy and patronizing your kid sister. So you'll just have to deal with the consequences."

ANY FAR-FETCHED HOPES that Vicki was indulging in the silent treatment and hadn't confronted her brother were dashed when Jarrett came storming out of the house the second Sierra parked her car.

His face was cold with fury, hardly recognizable. "How dare you! You went behind my back and—"

"I didn't set out to tell her." She sagged against the front of her car for support. "She asked me point-blank."

Should she remind him that, if he'd fostered a different kind of relationship with his sister, Vicki might have asked *him* instead? Never mind. Why poke the bear?

He rocked back on his heels, his scathing expression making it clear her explanation hadn't pacified him a bit. "How convenient. You've wanted to tell her from the very first night, and she handed you your chance. I wonder how many hints you had to drop to get that to happen."

"Are you insane?" Forget placating his temper. Now she was ticked. She marched up to him. The man might be built like a redwood, but she wasn't about to cower. "She caught me completely off guard, which is actually a little weird since I already *warned* you she was onto us. Just like I warned you that I don't keep secrets well! And I don't passive-aggressively 'hint.' I say what the hell I'm thinking. Maybe you could learn a lesson from me."

"About ignoring people's wishes?" he countered. "About crushing someone's feelings? You should have seen..." Some of the rage drained from him, leaving sadness in its wake. "It wasn't worth hurting her like that over some fling."

Some fling. The words landed like a blow. She pressed a hand to her stomach as if applying pressure could relieve the pain.

Ridiculous. The agonizing throb she felt wasn't in her abdomen. It was in her heart. "That's all this was—a fling?"

"You're leaving next week, Sierra. What else could it be?" He said it so matter-of-factly that she wanted to cry.

Not in front of him. "You're absolutely right. About us, anyway. You're wrong about my leaving next week, though. I'll be gone on Thursday, as soon as I've taken Vicki to her PT appointment with Manuel. Maybe once I'm out of the house, you and Vicki can..." As much as she wanted to be a mature person, she couldn't choke back tears long enough to wish him and his sister well. Instead, she simply fled into the house and up the stairs.

Jarrett didn't follow. She'd known he wouldn't. And she supposed that gave her all the answer she'd ever needed about whether he was the right person and whether he'd fight to make a relationship work.

Then again, why should he? In his eyes, they'd never had a relationship.

"I CAN'T BELIEVE you're leaving," Kate sniffed.

Despite everything, that made Sierra laugh. "Seriously? Because I've been telling you since the day we met that I wasn't sticking around."

"I think I'm too depressed to even order dessert."

Sierra had said her goodbyes to the Rosses this morning. Since Vicki was only speaking in monosyllables and Jarrett wouldn't look at her, it hadn't taken long. But she'd promised to meet Kate at the Smoky Pig on her way out of town for one last lunch.

"Maybe you could ask for a dessert to go," Sierra suggested, "and eat it later, when you're feeling more chipper."

Kate gave her a hollow, sad-eyed look that suggested her soul would never know joy again.

"That might be overdoing it a little," Sierra said. "Come on. You have friends here! Lots of them. And you're going to marry the gorgeous town sheriff and mother his adorable twins, who worship you. My sympathy for you is limited."

"Oh, all right." Kate flipped open the dessert menu, even though she probably had it memorized. "But it still sucks that you're leaving."

"Try to be happy for me." *Someone has to be.* "I'm on to bigger and better things."

Some people would say that there was nothing better than love. Sierra was less than impressed with it. She'd finally fallen in love with someone—and promptly had her heart broken. No wonder Vicki wanted to walk up to Aaron and kick him in the shin. Sierra had to admit that the idea of kicking a certain cowboy was tempting. But what would be the point? No matter where she kicked him, she couldn't hurt Jarrett as much as he'd hurt her.

WITH SIERRA GONE, the house was eerily silent all of Thursday night and into the next day. His parents wouldn't get in until Saturday, and as he cooked dinner Friday night, Jarrett wondered if Vicki planned to speak to him at all before then. What was she planning to tell them about her seething hatred for her brother?

Maybe they wouldn't even notice. After all, it wasn't much of a change from Vicki's attitude toward him before they'd left. In that moment, he realized how much progress had been made over the past couple of weeks. Siding with Vicki in their no-liver ban, teaming up with her to convince Sierra to give horseback riding another shot, laughing as Vicki won all his money in a board game. With Sierra in the house, he and his sister had begun to bond again.

And you destroyed that bond by sleeping with her therapist.

Well, she was allowed to be mad at him, but she wasn't allowed to starve herself. He turned off the stove and went to her room, knocking on the door. As expected, there was no answer, so he knocked more forcefully.

"Vicki, you have to eat. I'm not going away until you come

out of there." He had all night and no place to be. He could out-stubborn her if necessary.

Huh. Maybe Sierra had rubbed off on him. He recalled the day he'd hired her, how he'd meekly honored Vicki's wishes not to be disturbed, but Sierra had insisted otherwise.

She'd been right that day. Had she been right when she'd goaded him to tell Vicki about their affair? *The last thing my nineteen-year-old sister wants to hear about is my sex life.* But what he felt for Sierra went far beyond sex.

He knocked again. "I'm gearing up to sing 'a hundred bottles of sarsaparilla on the wall.'" She wasn't old enough for beer. "I'll make it a thousand if I have to."

"If I eat," she asked from the other side of the door, "will you leave me in peace?"

"Yes." Maybe.

Dinner was grim, and the chicken was rubbery, but he counted it as a victory that she had joined him at the kitchen table.

"No offense," she said, wincing at a bite of overcooked broccoli, "but your cooking sucks. I miss Sierra."

Just hearing her name was wrenching. He pushed his own plate away. "I'm sorry she's gone."

Vicki stared at him, her gaze penetrating. "Are you? I heard you yelling at her the other night."

"Only because she upset you." Even as he said that, he knew where the blame belonged. "All right, I know I'm the one who really upset you. I promised I wouldn't get involved with her, but I did."

"And you *lied* about it." Vicki's wounded tone suddenly made him question what she was more upset about—his involvement with Sierra or that he'd kept it secret?

Oh, Lord. Had Sierra been right all along? "I didn't want you to know," he admitted. "You and Aaron had just broken up. I figured the last thing you needed was to be trapped in the house with a happy couple, and—"

"Happy couple?" Her eyes widened. "Is that what you were? Or was she just another playmate?"

He flinched but supposed there were worse terms she could have used. "You know Sierra. She was never 'just' anything."

"Then what the hell, dude? Why did you let her go out with Will Trent? Why did you let her leave us?"

"I'm confused." He rubbed his temples. "You *want* me and Sierra together?"

"If the two of you make each other happy..." She spread her arms wide and gave him a *duh* look.

He sat back in his chair, too moved to respond. It said a lot about Vicki's strength of character that she wanted his happiness after he'd been such a crappy brother. "Frankly, I wouldn't blame you if you hated me." The admission came out low and gravelly, and he hoped she heard it because he wasn't sure he could say it again.

She sighed heavily. "After my accident, you hated yourself enough for both of us. I didn't start out mad at you, specifically. There was just so *much* anger. I was ticked that I couldn't go back to school, that I had to lie in a hospital bed for weeks, that I couldn't—" Her voice caught, and her eyes shimmered with tears. "But it wasn't all anger. I was scared, too. Even though every doctor said I'd be able to walk again, it's hard to believe that when you can't even sit up."

The familiar guilt stabbed at him again, but this wasn't about him. This was about his sister. He squeezed his hand. "Vicki, I'm so sorry for what you've been through. If I could have done *anything* to spare you that pain..."

"Well." She swallowed hard. "At least now I know how tough I am. I've survived the worst of it."

"You're a badass."

"I'm a Ross. Now the question is, how much of a badass are you? Are you man enough to admit when you're wrong? Sierra's forgiven me plenty of times for being a butthead. If you talk to her—"

"It's almost better that she left angry. It made saying good-bye easier."

"But why does it have to be goodbye? You care about her."

"Enough to want what's best for her. I don't think I'm it." When Vicki opened her mouth to argue, he added, "And Cupid's Bow was never what she wanted for the long term. She joked about it all the time when she first got here, how uncivilized we were and how the movie theater only shows films from before 2010."

"Yeah, but maybe her feelings changed. Maybe 'the town' came to mean a lot to her." She stared at him pointedly to make sure he knew she wasn't talking about Cupid's Bow. "But you'll never know unless you ask."

SIERRA SAT ACROSS the desk from the director of the Sports Medicine Rehabilitation Program, trying to be a full participant in the conversation. After all, they were trying to decide where she'd fit best at the clinic, so she had a vested interest in the outcome.

"You haven't done much work specifically in sports medicine," the director observed. "What interests you about the program?"

"Your work with high school athletes. I recently worked very closely with a nineteen-year-old, and it got me to thinking about adolescents. Teenagers, neither adults nor typical pediatric patients, are uniquely challenging. But also uniquely rewarding." Less tactfully, they were pains in the ass—which was right in her wheelhouse.

Suddenly, she heard Kate Sullivan's teasing voice in her head. *I know I'm being a pain, but meddling is the Cupid's Bow way.* The citizens of Cupid's Bow were opinionated and nosy and interfered in each other's lives. Sierra fit right in.

The thought gave her a pang, and she felt irrational annoyance at Daniel Baron for leading her to Cupid's Bow in the first place. Before his email, she'd never even heard of the speck on the map. From the start, Cupid's Bow had been a temporary gig. It had been a way station for her, not a home.

Then why do I feel so homesick?

A MONTH AGO, Jarrett had stood in this room waiting for his mother, afraid of what bad news she might bring. Now both his parents were cuddled together on the other side of the desk—Gavin in his leather chair, Anne perched on the arm of the chair as they went over facts and figures from the past few weeks.

"You two certainly look cozy," he couldn't help teasing. He was thrilled for them. He hadn't seen either of them this relaxed in a long time.

"Yes, well, Tahoe did us a world of good," Anne said.

"I've promised your mother we'll go back for two weeks out of every year," Gavin said. "Provided you don't mind being in charge while I'm gone."

"And *I* promised to quit bellyaching about everything around here." She looked around the room with a fond smile. "There are a lot of good memories in this house. I just need the break from time to time—and to know that your father loves me as much as he loves the ranch."

"More," Gavin said, suddenly serious. "So much more. Son, a word of advice from your old man? If you ever fall in love, make sure she knows it. Make sure you appreciate her and let her know every damn day how lucky you are."

The words resonated with him. He'd thought so often about what Sierra deserved in life...but didn't she deserve to know his feelings?

Maybe she didn't return them. Maybe she didn't belong in Cupid's Bow. Nonetheless, she was a strong advocate of the truth. And the truth was: he loved her. He wanted to tell her that face-to-face. As soon as possible.

His heart thudded wildly, like a stampede in his chest. "If you guys will excuse me, I have somewhere important I need to be." Fort Worth. He bolted from his chair, calling over his shoulder, "I may be gone a few days."

Not wanting to get their hopes up, he didn't add that, if luck was with him, they'd be meeting their future daughter-in-law soon.

JARRETT DRUMMED HIS fingers on the side of his truck as he watched the number of gallons climb on the gas pump and impatiently waited for the tank to fill. He was so antsy to hit the road that he hadn't even bothered packing—he had a wallet, his phone and the spare toothbrush he kept in the glove compartment of his truck. *I'll buy anything else I need.*

Except, the one thing he really needed—Sierra's forgiveness—couldn't be purchased.

Maybe he should call her. After all, showing up in Fort Worth was a grand romantic gesture, but he had no idea how to track her down once he got there. Plus, he really, really needed to hear her voice after so many days apart.

He dialed, mentally crossing his fingers that she answered. If she wouldn't take his calls, he supposed that gave him some indication of how upset she was.

But she answered on the second ring, her voice puzzled. "Jarrett? Is Vicki okay?"

"Everything's fine." Well, there was the matter of the gaping emptiness in his life ever since she'd left, but hopefully they would fix that. "I'm calling to let you know that I'm coming to see you. Please don't try to talk me out of it, because I'm already on the way."

"You're what?" she asked, her voice strangled.

Damn. She really didn't sound happy to see him. "Sierra, I know you're probably still angry with me—"

"That is true. But we have other problems. Where are you, specifically?"

"The gas station just outside Cupid's Bow."

She started laughing, and he couldn't tell if the sound was joy or some kind of hysteria. "The one close to the hospital?"

"Yes. I haven't made it very far, but—"

"Good thing. I'm across the street."

"You're *where*?"

"I just finished an interview at the hospital. Manuel helped me set it up. Meet me in the main lobby?"

He closed the gas tank, back in his truck before she even finished her sentence.

When the hospital's automatic doors parted five minutes later, he barreled inside, his gaze finding her familiar, beloved face immediately. After so many horrible hours spent here, waiting to hear how his sister was doing or for news on his father's condition, this was the first time he'd ever entered a hospital giddy with anticipation. She was here! That had to be a good sign, didn't it? Maybe it had nothing to do with her feelings for him—after all, she hadn't told him she was applying for a job—but at least now he knew she'd be willing to live in the area and would never have to worry that he'd badgered her into it.

Although, once he'd caught up to her in Fort Worth, he'd been planning to badger, beg or seduce as necessary.

She walked over to him, her expression disbelieving. "I can't believe you were coming to see me."

"I can't believe you're *here*." Unable to stop himself, he lifted her into an off-the-ground hug and swung her around. "God, I've missed you."

She bit her lip, hesitating for an agonizing moment before admitting, "I've missed you, too."

Encouraged by his success so far, he decided to go for broke. "I love you, Sierra Bailey."

Her green eyes were huge, her expression stunned. "Wh-what?"

"I love you." Saying it out loud was amazingly liberating. He felt as if a crushing weight had been lifted off his chest. He took a deep breath, joy radiating through him.

"But I thought we were just a fling," she said.

He smoothed her hair away from her face. "No, that's what I needed to tell myself in order to let you go. I wasn't sure you could be happy here, or that you could love a—"

"I can! I do." She stood up on her tiptoes and he ducked his head, and they met each other in the middle for a kiss so hot he momentarily forgot where he was.

In her ear, he murmured, "I suppose it would be wrong for me to rip off your clothes in a hospital lobby? They have beds around here somewhere, right?"

She laughed, tugging his hand as she strode toward the exit. "My hotel is close." Suddenly, she stopped dead in her tracks. "You're sure? That you love me?"

"Positive." And he'd tell her over and over until it sank in. He recalled a piece of advice she'd given him once, regarding being a better brother. *Don't fall back on words alone. Be there for her.* He vowed to do exactly that. There were lots of romantic napkin notes in her future. He'd fill her life with slow dances and trail rides and stargazing and as much happiness as he could give her.

Her eyes shone with tears, but she tried to keep her voice light. "I only ask because I can be…challenging. I'm stubborn and bossy and independent."

"You mean determined and confident and strong?" He grinned down at her, looking forward to overcoming all the challenges they would face. Together. "I don't love you in spite of those things, darlin'. I love you because of them."

* * * * *

Keep reading for an excerpt of
Cavanaugh In Plain Sight
by Marie Ferrarella.
Find it in the
Guarded Secrets: Anniversary Collection anthology,
out now!

Prologue

She felt tired as she walked out of the office building and into the large, deserted parking lot. It felt as if she hadn't gotten any sleep since the funeral.

Maybe that was the reason Krystyna Kowalski was having trouble shaking the feeling that someone was watching her. She hadn't actually seen anyone following her when she'd turned around, but it was a feeling gnawing away at the pit of her stomach.

Krys sighed, aware just how paranoid that would have sounded if she had said it aloud. She supposed that, examined in the light of day, it probably was.

The darkness made it more real, given the nature of the work she did. As a freelance investigative reporter, she delved into dark, hidden secrets while traveling down streets where most other people wouldn't even dream of venturing.

But her work required her to burrow into and expose secrets that were thought to be completely buried. It was her job to cast light on paths that the key figures of her investigations thought were safely out of sight.

During the course of her investigations, Krys had heard herself being cursed, threatened with bodily harm and told more than once that she would be made to pay for what she had so brazenly and callously done. That kind of thing had become part of her job. She accepted it as her due and even thought of it as her badge of courage. But her safety wasn't anything she haphazardly took for granted. Krys always made sure that she took the necessary precautions. As for the rest of it, she just shrugged it off and went on her way.

But this eerie feeling had haunted her nights for the last six weeks. That was definitely something new in her life.

Even as she had sat beside her mentor's hospital bedside, holding Ian Marshall's hand as he lay dying, that uneasy feeling that she was being watched kept eating away at her. So much so that each time someone entered Ian's room—usually a hospital staff member as well as an old friend coming by to pay their last respects—something inside of Krys would tighten and instantly go on the alert. She had to mentally talk herself down each time because a great many old acquaintances came by in those few weeks to see Ian—while he was still there to be seen.

But now Ian was no longer alive to distract her. He had passed away clutching her hand. She had no regrets about being there even though she had wound up missing her only sister's wedding. She refused to leave Ian's bedside, refused to take a chance that the man with no family would wind up dying alone while she was busy celebrating Nikola's big day.

Nik had understood why she couldn't come to her wedding. They were twins, and twins intuited things about one another that no one else could begin to comprehend.

But now Ian was gone and Nik was on her honeymoon with Finn Cavanaugh. Not wanting to think about how much Ian's passing affected her, not to mention how she felt about missing Nik's wedding, Krys threw herself back into her work with a vengeance.

In the last nine months, after doggedly following a trail that led from the middle of the country to the West Coast, she had written an intensely conclusive exposé about Alan Parker, a charming, dark-haired, rakishly handsome man who, for the purposes of her article—and the nature of his crimes—she had dubbed "Bluebeard." The man with soulfully seductive blue eyes and a smile that Cary Grant would have envied made it his business to romance wealthy, lonely women and marry them.

According to the research she had done, there had been at least six of these women over the course of the last few years, although she had a hunch that there were more who hadn't come to light yet. Parker separated them from their money and eventually, he separated them from the world of the living as well.

Krys had doggedly put together all the evidence until there was enough for the police to issue a warrant and arrest the man. Everything fell into place and the man the police thought of as "Bluebeard" faced certain conviction as well as prison.

But somehow, thanks to his connections, Parker managed to escape before he could be put on trial for the murders he committed.

Right now, he was out there, free to continue his spree unimpeded.

She remembered the way Parker had looked at her when he was being arrested and taken away. For one split second, the silver-tongued smooth-talker shot her a look of sheer hatred. In that moment, her blood had run absolutely cold.

By then, she was hot on the trail of her newest investigation. Weatherly Pharmaceuticals had sunk a great deal of their money into the research, development and test trials for a new wonder drug whose properties were believed to keep cancer from metastasizing and spreading to other organs. The researchers hoped to contain the disease if not drive it totally into remission.

Fifteen years in development, the drug was highly anticipated and promised to make Weatherly's investors richer beyond their wildest dreams. The drug was, in essence, too good to be true.

For Krys, that sent up bright red flags.

Unlike her twin sister, to Krys, if something was too good to be true, she believed that it usually wasn't—and it was her job to prove that. She was currently interviewing everyone associated with this new wonder drug, both the developers and the people who had been the drug's test subjects. She was determined to get to the truth of the matter. If her hunch turned out to be true, there would be an awful lot of unhappy people at Weatherly Pharmaceuticals. People who she felt would go a long way to make sure they *weren't* unhappy.

For her part, Krys would have never become involved in investigating something of such major proportions if she didn't feel she was able to prove that the emperor had no clothes.

Possibly that was why she was letting her imagination run away with her, why she felt there were threats to her safety lurking around almost every corner.

Maybe she just needed to take a break, wind down, be a person again instead of strictly a driven investigative reporter with tunnel vision who was focused on only one thing.

Making her way to her car in the almost completely deserted parking lot, Krys shifted the pages and copious notes that she had accumulated and brought with her to this latest meeting. As she opened the driver's side door, several of the pages slipped out of the pile and unceremoniously fluttered down to her feet.

"Damn," Krys muttered, ducking her head and bending down to retrieve the errant pages.

A jolting noise just above her head, sounding like a car backfiring, screamed through the night air and effectively pierced the silence. Krys had spent enough time at gun ranges to know what that sound actually was.

And even if she hadn't recognized it, the shattered glass raining down from just above her head onto the pavement would have cleared up the mystery for her.

Her mouth went dry.

Someone had just taken a shot at her.

Chapter One

Detective Jay Fredericks was the embodiment of a man on the cusp of middle age. Balding since the age of twenty-three and paunchy, Fredericks had the unfortunate habit of shuffling his feet when he walked, and he had long given up his battle with maintaining some sort of relatively decent posture. Consequently, walking or sitting, he gave the impression of being the personification of a perpetual parenthesis. Because of this, Detective Morgan Cavanaugh had given up trying to read his partner's body language as a way of gauging whether or not the news that the man was about to deliver was good, bad or of no consequence whatsoever.

"Hey, Cavanaugh," Fredericks called out as he walked into the Major Crimes squad room and crossed over to Morgan's desk.

Looking up from his computer monitor, Morgan waited for his partner to say something further.

There was a pregnant pause on Fredericks's part, either for effect or because he couldn't find the right words to explain what was on his mind. Since Morgan was currently catching up on his paperwork, something he viewed as just a shade better than having a root canal, he had no patience for whatever Fredericks was attempting to communicate.

"Are you just trying out my name because you've forgotten

how it sounds, or do you actually want to say something?" Morgan asked.

By now Fredericks had reached the two desks that butted up against one another in the squad room. Fredericks eyed his desk, obviously tempted to take a load off, but there was apparently something stopping him.

"Umm, didn't you tell me that one of your cousins just got married?" he asked, stumbling his way into the reason he had come looking for Morgan in the first place.

The latest Cavanaugh wedding had just recently taken place. The entire police department had been invited and most of them had attended. Fredericks was one of the few who had not because his wife had insisted on picking that exact week for their annual vacation.

"You know I did," Morgan told his partner, doing his best to hold on to his patience. "Finn and Nikki. I showed you their wedding pictures," he reminded Fredericks. "Why? Where are you going with this?"

Fredericks bit his almost nonexistent lower lip. "I'm not sure," he confessed.

Morgan temporarily abandoned his paperwork and pinned the man hovering over his desk with an impatient look, waiting. Sometimes Fredericks could become exceedingly tongue-tied. That was a direct result of his wife of eighteen years never allowing him to get in a word edgewise.

"C'mon, Fredericks. Spit it out. What is it you're trying to say?" Morgan pressed.

"Would you happen to know if the newlyweds were due back early from their honeymoon?" Fredericks asked awkwardly.

"They weren't," Morgan answered without any hesitation. "Why? And for heavens' sakes, sit down and stop hovering like a seagull that's circling a garbage heap, looking for lunch," he said, exasperated.

Shifting and obviously undecided, Fredericks remained on his feet. "You think I could see that picture again?" he asked. When Morgan looked at him quizzically, his partner elaborated. "You know, the one from their wedding?"

Morgan had brought the photograph in to show one of the people he worked with who wasn't able to attend the ceremony. After he did, he shoved the photograph into a drawer and then promptly forgot about it. That was the only reason the photograph was still in the squad room rather than back at his place.

Morgan thought Fredericks's request was rather odd, but he shrugged. "All right." Opening the wrong drawer at first, he located the photograph and took it out. He passed the photograph to his partner. "Okay, again I ask, what is this all about? Or do you just have a thing for wedding pictures?"

Fredericks frowned as he studied the photograph Morgan had handed to him. "Yup, it's her all right," he murmured under his breath.

"'Her?'" Morgan questioned uncertainly. Just what was Fredericks getting at? His partner was known to be quirky on occasion, but this was downright weird.

"Your cousin's wife," Frederick answered, handing the photograph back to Morgan. "You'd better brace yourself," he warned. "I think something's wrong."

Definitely weird, Morgan decided. "You know, for a detective with the Aurora Police Force, sometimes you can be as clear as mud. What the hell are you talking about, Fredericks?" he demanded.

Fredericks pressed his lips together, making them almost disappear altogether. "She just came in asking for you."

"*Who* came in asking for me?" He was barely able to keep from shouting the question.

And then, before Fredericks could make another attempt to explain himself, Morgan suddenly had his answer. Finn's wife had just come walking into the squad room and now appeared to be heading straight for him.

He had only met Nik a handful of times, one of which was at the actual wedding. He had no idea why she would be back from her honeymoon so soon but by the expression on her face, something was definitely wrong. Not only that, but out of all the Cavanaughs who were available in this building, why would she be coming to see him? If there was some sort of a problem going on, he would have thought that Uncle Andrew, the former police chief of Aurora and the real family patriarch, would be the one the newlywed would be more inclined to turn to, especially since she had been instrumental in helping to bring Andrew's father, Seamus, around after a mugging had thrown the older man into a depressed tailspin.

Morgan rose from his chair just as his new cousin-in-law reached his desk. A dozen questions went through his head, none of which he felt were his place to ask. But still, maybe he could. After all, she had sought him out, he reasoned. He wasn't the one who had come to her.

"I take it you're Morgan Cavanaugh," the woman said to him just as she reached his desk.

Morgan gave her a bemused look. Granted, she had met a great many Cavanaughs on her wedding day, even more than she had initially met at Uncle Andrew's party on that first occasion. He knew that kind of thing could be very confusing for some people, what with trying to keep all those names straight, not to mention remembering who was married to whom. There was a time when he had gotten confused himself and he was family, although, at the time, that had been a huge revelation, finding himself related to such a huge family.

He smiled at the shapely blonde. "We met at Uncle Andrew's party," he reminded her.

She surprised him by firmly shaking her head and denying his assumption. "No, we didn't," she told him.

Morgan opened his mouth, about to tell her that she was the one who was making the mistake, but then he closed it again. He wasn't about to argue with her and get off on the wrong foot with this newest family member, so he just let her statement go.

Instead, he decided to try another approach. "Where's Finn?"

"Still with my sister would be my guess," Krys answered.

"Your sister," Morgan repeated, feeling as if he had suddenly, without any warning, somehow slipped into an alternate universe.

As far as he knew, from what Finn had told him, his new Mrs. had no family. Certainly none had come to the wedding. Having a family was part of the appeal of marrying into the Cavanaughs. They had family members to spare coming out of the woodwork in all directions, he thought with a smile.

"Yes," Krys said slowly, wondering if she had ultimately made a mistake by coming here. "My sister," she repeated.

But someone had taken a shot at her and that was a police matter, although, after that one attempt, there hadn't been any further ones made on her life.

Maybe she was overreacting, Krys thought. She usually had nerves of steel, but this had really rattled her rather badly. But rattled or not, she was used to doing things on her own. Maybe she could trace this back to the source instead of asking for help. Still, if she were being honest, she had to admit that this attempt on her life had made her feel rather vulnerable.

What had prompted her to come here, seeking Morgan's help, was that Nik had mentioned Morgan to her by name during one of their lengthy phone conversations just before the wedding. The fact that he was a detective assigned to the Major Crimes Division *was* a plus, and it was what had made her think that Morgan might be the right one to get a handle on this.

"ARE YOU SAYING that my cousin is cheating on you?" Morgan asked her, stunned. In his opinion, Finn was as straight an arrow as had ever walked the earth. His cousin was totally incapable of cheating. Morgan would have bet his life on that.

"On me?" Krys questioned, confused. "Why would he be cheating on me?" And then it suddenly hit her. She realized what Morgan had to be thinking. She had gotten so caught up in this thing that was happening to her, she had completely forgotten that other than an inch difference in height—she being the shorter one—she and Nik were totally identical.

"Oh, wait," Krys cried. "I need to explain something to you first."

Morgan could see Fredericks out of the corner of his eye. His partner was totally hanging on every single word that was being said, clearly fascinated with his cousin's wife.

"Go ahead," Morgan urged, crossing his arms before his hard, rather well-sculpted chest and waiting to hear what this extremely attractive, squirrelly woman had come here to tell him—especially since she was insisting that she and he hadn't met yet—which they definitely had.

"I'm Nik's twin sister," she told Morgan, hoping that would settle the matter.

It didn't.

He stared at her. "You're her twin sister."

This was the first he had heard of a sister, much less a *twin* sister, and he was willing to bet that he wasn't the only one in the family who had never heard about Nik's so-called twin.

Morgan found himself feeling sorry for his cousin. Finn had obviously married a beautiful but slightly delusional woman—or worse. He recalled that Finn had said something about his wife being an insurance investigator. Maybe she fancied herself a CIA agent or something along those lines.

Well, whatever the case, Morgan was willing to step up and help his cousin get help for his new wife any way he could.

"Yes," Krys confirmed patiently. She could see that he wasn't convinced. She reached into her back pocket and took out her wallet. Flipping it open to her driver's license, she held it up in front of the detective for his perusal. "Her twin sister. Krystyna Kowalski," she introduced herself. "We were born five minutes apart. I'm older," she added, anticipating his next question.

"Why weren't you at your sister's wedding?" he asked. "Or can't the two of you be in the same place at the same time?"

Very funny, she thought sarcastically.

Instead of answering Morgan's question, she opened her wallet again and looked through the different compartments. Finding what she was searching for, Krys took it out and held the photograph up to him now.

It was a picture of the two of them, Nik and herself, taken almost twenty years ago.

"See, we *can* be in the same place at the same time," she told him with a deliberately cheerful expression. "The problem is that we haven't had the occasion to be in the same place at the same time these last few years. Nik works for an insurance company while I do freelance work as an investigative journalist. My work takes me out of the state on a regular basis." Her point made, she did smile at him this time. "Different but the same," she told him. Krys's eyes met his. "So, do you need any further proof?"

"No, this'll do it for me," he told her. Morgan paused for a second, thinking, then went on to say, "I do have one more question for you."

Krys braced herself. This was for Nik, she told herself. That was also the reason she had sought Morgan out, looking for help. Because of Nik. Because what had happened to her made her afraid that whoever had done this might go after Nik by mistake.

"Go ahead," she told him patiently. "What is it you want to ask?"

"Why weren't you at your sister's wedding?" After a beat, Morgan added, "I'm just curious since according to you, the two of you are so close."

"It's not according to me," Krys corrected, taking offense at his implication. "It's a fact. And although it isn't really any of your business, I wasn't at the wedding because I was sitting at a sick friend's bedside."

Morgan raised an eyebrow. "Your significant other?"

"No," she told him almost grudgingly. "My mentor." Before Morgan could ask, she volunteered the information. "He had no family of his own and I didn't want him to have to die alone."

Morgan found himself slightly embarrassed and applauding her sentiment. "Oh."

Krys eyed him, waiting for the other shoe to drop. "Any more questions?"

"No, not right now," he replied in a voice that was totally free of any emotion. The truth of it was, he felt like an idiot for having barged into where he had no place being.

Taking in a deep breath, Morgan decided to start over. "So tell me, what brings you here—specifically to Major Crimes as well as to me?"

"I came to you," she told him, "because I thought you might be able to help me."

He felt as if he was inching his way across a thin layer of quicksand, about to sink in and go under at any second. "Help you do what?"

"Help me find whoever it is who's trying to kill me and why," she told him without any fanfare.

Morgan stared at her. It took a second for her words to sink in. There was nothing run-of-the-mill about this woman, he couldn't help thinking. "Maybe you better start from the beginning," he suggested.

"Maybe I should," Krys agreed. Aware that the man who had brought her in here was still hovering around, straining to overhear what she was saying to Morgan, she tactfully asked the detective, "Is there someplace where we can go to talk?"

Subscribe and fall in love with a Mills & Boon series today!

You'll be among the first to read stories delivered to your door monthly and enjoy great savings.

MILLS & BOON